WITH LOVE, WHEREVER YOU ARE

A NOVEL

With Love,

WHEREVER YOU ARE

DANDI DALEY MACKALL

Tyndale House Publishers, Inc., Carol Stream, Illinois

Visit Tyndale online at www.tyndale.com.

Visit Dandi Daley Mackall's website at www.dandibooks.com.

TYNDALE and Tyndale's quill logo are registered trademarks of Tyndale House Publishers, Inc.

With Love, Wherever You Are

Cover designed by Gearbox

Interior designed by Dean H. Renninger

Edited by Sarah Mason Rische

Unless otherwise indicated, all Scripture quotations are taken from the *Holy Bible*, King James Version.

Epigraph taken from the *Holy Bible*, New Living Translation, copyright © 1996, 2004, 2015 by Tyndale House Foundation. Used by permission of Tyndale House Publishers, Inc., Carol Stream, Illinois 60188. All rights reserved.

For information about special discounts for bulk purchases, please contact Tyndale House Publishers, Inc. at csresponse@tyndale.com, or call 800-323-9400.

Library of Congress Cataloging-in-Publication Data
Names: Mackall, Dandi Daley, author.
Title: With love, wherever you are / Dandi Daley Mackall.
Description: Carol Stream, Illinois : Tyndale House Publishers, Inc., [2017]
Identifiers: LCCN 2016040796| ISBN 9781496421210 (hc) | ISBN 9781496421227 (sc)
Subjects: LCSH: World War, 1939-1945—Fiction. | GSAFD: Love stories. |
  Christian fiction. | Historical fiction.
Classification: LCC PS3613.A27257 W58 2017 | DDC 813/.6—dc23 LC record available
  at https://urldefense.proofpoint.com/v2/url?u=https-3A__lccn.loc.gov_2016040796&d
  =DQIFAg&c=6BNjZEuL_DAs869UxGis0g&r=ZlF6A1J_SMm9xAyjgyDor34CB
  -fqQRaraBLNVSdnrVo&m=_um7EZC4G5GD3MzJo6HdDVZvxQb33kvvj
  _fk7sfEz6Y&s=fYZYb52YT85dV5i3H70EDscu-QgmVPiCL9LhDSOHVkI&e=

Printed in the United States of America

23   22   21   20   19   18   17
 7   6   5   4   3   2   1

For Mom and Dad, two of God's best gifts

"My grace is all you need. My power works best in weakness."

So now I am glad to boast about my weaknesses, so that the power

of Christ can work through me. That's why I take pleasure in my

weaknesses, and in the insults, hardships, persecutions, and troubles

that I suffer for Christ. For when I am weak, then I am strong.

2 CORINTHIANS 12:9-10

Helen

What now? Helen Eberhart elbowed her way through the mass of student nurses crowding the hospital bulletin board. If *she* were in charge, she would come up with a better system for assigning duties and shifts. Couldn't this top-notch hospital afford more than one bulletin board, at the very least? Student nurses had to check several times a day, and heaven help the would-be nurse who missed one duty, one time change, one announcement.

She scanned the list until she got to her name. "Swell," she muttered. Extra duties *and* extra hours. When was she supposed to study for her anatomy test?

She turned and stood on tiptoes to relay the bad news to her roommate. At five feet eight, half a foot taller than Helen, Lucille was easy to spot. "Lucille! Get coffee! We've both pulled extra—"

"Shhh! Shush, everybody!"

Helen wasn't sure who'd said it, but the whole group quieted to a murmur. The PA system crackled and screeched—another thing she'd see to if she ever got to run things. Two white-jacketed interns strutting up the hall stopped and stared at the metal loudspeaker as if waiting for God—or the chief of staff—to issue at least ten commandments.

True, they didn't get many announcements, but Helen didn't have time to gawk at a disembodied voice. "Coming through!"

"Quiet!" Nurse Benchley frowned at her.

Helen didn't appreciate being shut down. If Benchley weren't one of her instructors, she wouldn't get away with it either.

"*. . . Hawaii from the air.*"

She'd missed the announcement, but she caught enough to know this wasn't a page from the chief of staff. The hospital was relaying a radio broadcast.

"*Just a moment. . . . I'll repeat that.*"

The hallway froze, interns transformed into wax statues with identical stunned expressions. Old Dr. Laban, his glasses crooked as always, dropped his arms to his sides like broken twigs snapping from a tree trunk. His clipboard dangled from one hand. Everybody seemed to move farther away from Helen, although nobody had budged. Sound froze too, leaving an eerie silence decibels below hospital-zone quiet.

Only the voice from the loudspeaker filled the hall, filled the hospital, filled the world:

"*President Roosevelt says the Japanese have attacked Pearl Harbor in Hawaii from the air. . . .*"

Helen couldn't hear any more because suddenly the silence became a buzz. She thought the buzz must be in her head, growing louder and louder, like locusts in Cissna Park on a summer's night.

Then the space around her exploded in cries and questions fired at random, aimed at nobody. The chaos was so rampant that Helen would have believed it if someone told her a bomb had struck the hospital.

"Did they say bombs? Actual bombs dropped on us?"

"I can't believe it!"

"Dear God in Heaven!"

"Where's Pearl Harbor?"

"They'll come here next. You'll see. What do we do now?"

"Chicago will be a target for sure."

"I want to go home!"

"Jimmy's in the July draft. What if they send him over there?"

"So we're at war? I mean officially at war?"

"I always thought it would be the Germans. Why Japan?"

The questions bounced off Helen. She wouldn't let them in. Not yet. Not when she was so close to becoming a real nurse. War would ruin everything. Besides, as long as she could remember, there had been wars somewhere, or people talking about them.

Her war had been to make a tin of corn bread stretch for a family of thirteen during the worst days of the Depression. Her battles had been standing up to big brothers who weren't so sure she belonged in their family and to a father who said her place was on the farm, not learning how to take care of sick strangers in Chicago.

"Helen? Did you hear me?" Lucille shouted above the cacophony of voices that echoed in the halls. She elbowed her way to Helen's side. "Come on. They're showing us where the bomb shelters are."

The crowd of nurses and doctors and patients flowed like floodwaters down the hall toward the stairwell. Lucille got pulled in with them, but not Helen. She shoved in the opposite direction, a lone fish swimming upstream.

"Hey! Where are you going, Eberhart?" Lucille shouted after her.

"Where do you think?" Helen called back. "I've got extra duty. I'll be in room 301 if you need me!"

"Helen!"

"Nurse? This way." An intern grabbed her arm and tried to spin her around and take her with him.

She jerked her arm away. Nothing was going to stop her. Not him. Not the Japanese. Not Roosevelt. Not the Germans.

She was going to graduate from nurse's training. She had come here to live in a city where people danced to the big bands and wore furs like women on the covers of magazines. But most of all, she'd come to be a nurse, the best nurse Chicago had ever seen.

Helen Eberhart had known since she was nine years old what she'd do with her life. It had been a drizzly fall day when she'd hurried home after school, as usual, to do her chores.

"Look out, Gypsy!" Her brother Eugene rammed her from behind, nearly knocking her off her feet. They were both small for their age, but he was two years older, wiry and tough.

"*You* look out!" She didn't mind being called Gypsy, not anymore. She'd never really believed her brothers when they told her gypsies left her on their doorstep when she was a baby.

"Race you home!" Eugene shouted, passing her on the left.

Helen hiked up her skirt and ran, following Eugene through the Weinigers' lawn, over the flower beds, and up the street to home. But her brother the athlete pulled farther and farther ahead.

She was breathing hard by the time she reached home and spotted Eugene in the garden, standing by the roses. "Guess I win!" she shouted, heading for the back door, the official end of every race.

Eugene didn't move. Helen thought he was shivering, but that was dumb. It was stove-hot outside. She called to him, but he didn't answer.

"What's the matter with you?" She plodded back to the garden, braced for one of his tricks. "Eugene? Why are you standing—?"

And that's when she saw her mother. Ma was lying on the ground, one leg twisted under her, her hand still wrapped around cut roses. A dark pool spread around her, a growing red puddle shaping the dirt beneath her legs. From one leg, bright-red blood spurted like a fountain being shut off and on.

"Ma!" Helen dropped to her knees and held her mother's head in her lap. Mom's lips moved, but nothing came out. Her mother's kind brown eyes twitched. There was too much white in them.

Helen shouted, "Call Dr. Roberts!" Eugene didn't move. His cheeks were wet from crying. "Eugene, go call the doctor!"

He dropped to his knees.

Helen set down her mother's head and barked orders at her brother. "You wait with her, hear?" She didn't stick around for an answer but tore into the house, up half a flight of stairs to the kitchen. She cranked the phone on the wall and screamed into it, "Get me Dr. Roberts! Fast!"

"'Lo?" came Doc's slow, deep voice. "Dr. Roberts here."

"Dr. Roberts, this is Helen Eberhart. You have to come. Quick!"

"Which one is it? What's the matter?"

"It's Ma, Doc! She's bleeding. Her leg. She's in the garden and—"

"You listen to me now, Helen. I'm coming right over. Can you see the wound still bleeding?"

"It's spurting up. There's so much blood." She wouldn't cry. She couldn't cry.

"It's her veins. And we need to stop that bleeding before I get there. Is Ed home? Or the twins?"

"There's just me." She couldn't count on Eugene.

"All right then," he said, like he'd just then decided something. "You'll have to do. I want you to get a dime and take it to where that blood's spurting."

Helen knew he wanted her to say something. But her heart was pounding too hard in her ears.

"Helen, can you do this? I know you won't like the blood, honey."

"It's not that. Where am I going to find a dime?"

"You find it. That's all. I need you to press a dime to your mother's leg where it's bleeding. A penny won't do. Too thick. You get a dime, and you press it hard. Now go!"

She heard the phone click and dropped the receiver. It slapped against the wall.

A dime. A dime? You didn't find change in this house. Not under cushions. Not sitting on tables. *Dear Gott im Himmel, where on earth am I going to—?*

Then she remembered. The jingle in her dad's coat pocket, his Sunday coat. She could almost hear it, like the angels in heaven ringing their bells.

Helen tore into her parents' room, where she was only allowed when it was her turn to dust. There was the coat hanging over the back of the door. She had to stand on tiptoes to reach the pocket. *Please, God!*

She felt something. "Got it!" She drew out three pennies and a dime. Clutching the dime in her scrawny fingers, she raced back to the garden. "I'm coming, Ma!" She slid to the ground, tearing her stockings on the rosebush. The blood. How could there be so much blood in one leg? The red fountain continued to spurt. Helen took the dime and forced it through the blood onto her mother's leg. The coin slid against the red-drenched skin, but she pushed it hard, thumb on top of thumb. Blood oozed around the sides of the coin. Then it stopped.

"Ma, you're going to be okay," she whispered. "You're not bleeding now. Dr. Roberts is on his way."

Her mother twitched. Her dress was blood-soaked. Ma only had two dresses: this one and the one for Sundays. Her eyes rolled back, and her lips fluttered like moth wings. Helen imagined prayers coming from those lips, secret pleas and exchanges with God that her mother would never reveal.

Helen's fingers pushed hard against the dime. Blood and sweat made the coin slippery, but she kept it over the hole. She pressed so hard that her fingers began to ache. Her mother's red hair had come unpinned, and strands, redder still from the blood, clung to her cheek. Helen wanted to cradle Ma's head in her lap, to smooth the hair off her face, the way Ma had done for her when she had the fever.

But she couldn't let go of the dime.

"Eugene, help me hold this on her leg. I can't do it any longer."

Eugene didn't move. He stayed kneeling in the dirt, his fists rammed to his mouth.

Furious, Helen started to scream at him. Then she saw his eyes, wide with a terror that made his whole body shake. She took a deep breath, filled with the scent of roses, peonies, mums . . . and blood. "She'll be okay, Eugene. I promise, Genie. She will."

Her brother crept closer, then stopped. "I can't do it," he whispered.

And he couldn't. She knew that the same way she'd known that dime would be in Dad's coat pocket. The same way she knew she *could* keep the pressure on as long as she had to. "It's okay. Go out to the road and flag down Doc Roberts."

He took off at a run. Helen pressed on the dime, not letting it slip a hair to either side. The hole wasn't bleeding anymore, but she wasn't about to stop. Helen loved her mother, and Ma loved her. She knew that without it ever being said. She also knew that every one of the kids believed their mother loved him or her best.

What kind of talent, or love, was it that made everybody think you loved them best?

Helen's thumbs went numb. Her nose itched. Her hands and arms ached. How long could it take for Doc to drive a mile and a half?

Finally, she heard the old Ford crawl up and Eugene scream, "He's here, Helen! Doc! This way! She's in the garden." Doc and Eugene both came running.

Dr. Roberts squatted next to Helen, and still she was afraid to stop pressing down on the dime. "It's okay," he said. "You can let go now."

She looked up at him. His hat was crooked. Sweat stained his shirt under his arms. "Are you sure?"

He placed his big, rough hands over hers, then tugged her fingers away from the wound. "See there? You stopped that bleeding all on your own, girl."

It was true. Nothing came out of the pinprick hole in the large purple vein of the leg. Helen pulled down her mother's dress and straightened her apron. "Will she be all right?"

Ma groaned and said something Helen couldn't make out.

"I'm here, Mary." Doc lifted Ma's head and fingered one eyelid open, then the other. "You lie still now. Let me bandage that leg. We're going to have to do something about those varicose veins of yours. I warned you this could happen. One prick, one bump, and that vein could open again." He unbuckled his bag, took out a roll of bandages, and began wrapping the leg with the skill of Ma sewing school clothes.

By the time Doc had the leg wrapped, Ma was struggling to get up. "Thank you, Dr. Roberts. I'm fine now." Her voice sounded pinched, words squeezed through a hole. "Who found me?"

Helen felt the doctor's hand on her head. "Your Helen found you, and it's a good thing she did. You'd have bled to death if it hadn't been for little Helen here."

"Eugene and I both found you." Helen tossed her brother a grin.

"Well, I hope I didn't give you a scare," Ma said.

"I'll tell you this, Mary. You've got a nurse here. I couldn't have stopped that bleeding any better myself." He squatted down to Helen's level. "Miss Helen, I'm going to make you a promise. I'll do everything I can to get you into nurse's training after high school."

Helen felt heat rise to her face. Except for Dr. Roberts and their teachers, of course, she didn't know anybody who'd gone to school past high school. She frowned up at him, unwilling to be teased. "Really, Dr. Roberts?"

"Really."

It was all the good Helen would ever need, hearing that. But there was more.

"Helen Marie Eberhart," Dr. Roberts said, helping her to her feet, "someday you'll go off to the best nurse's training in the country. Then you can come back here and be my nurse. How's that sound?"

Helen smiled. "It sounds good." Half of Doc's prophecy sounded better than good. She would become a nurse, the best nurse she could possibly be. But she wasn't coming back to Cissna Park,

Illinois. There was a whole world out there, and she was going to be part of it.

Now, as Helen stood outside hospital room 301 and straightened her uniform, repinning her nurse's cap, she doubled the promise she'd made herself almost a dozen years ago. She was going to be a nurse. And she was going to see whatever there was to see in the world.

Maybe Eugene was right. Maybe she was a gypsy after all.

~⌣~

John Roberts, MD
Cissna Park, Illinois
20 December 1941

Dear Helen . . . or shall I say "Nurse Eberhart"?
    I received your letter of 10 December and thank you kindly for taking the time to write it. I understand better than most, I believe, the arduous schedule and the dearth of free time imposed upon a young woman in pursuit of her nursing degree, which I have no doubt you will achieve with honors.
    Allow me to express my heartfelt agreement with your decision to complete your training. Do not permit that heinous Japanese emperor the victory of thwarting your plans to become a nurse. Did you hear that Harold Messner was killed in that terrible act of aggression in the Harbor? They say his ship was sunk with hundreds of boys drowned or burned. You probably knew Harold, Clive's oldest. He dropped out of school and enlisted in the Navy last spring. I delivered that boy on the Messners' kitchen table. His mother suffers heart palpitations, and I fear the depth of that poor woman's grief.
    I spoke with your own dear mother on Sunday following church. Your father was there, though not very talkative and

rather eager to be off home. Mary's worry over her boys shows in her countenance. Your brother Ed signed up the minute those bombs dropped in the Pacific. Left his tractor in the field and walked into town to enlist. Mrs. Messner said she saw him storming past their place on his way to the recruiting office, fist raised like he was looking for a fight. It's a wonder they took him with those eyes of his, but he says he's going to be an MP. I know your father would have preferred to keep his eldest down on the farm. But I can see Ed as military police, with his strong farm arms, can't you?

As for the twins, your mother reports that Wilbur enlisted, but Walter was turned down for his epilepsy. Your mother says it has hit him hard, but something tells me that brother of yours will find a way to serve his country. I've always liked the twins, even though they gave me a time at delivery.

Eugene is pressing to sign up, but your father will soon be in a wheelchair, and someone needs to farm. Eugene isn't Louis's first choice, but he has ruled that Eugene will farm, though sons no longer listen to fathers as they did in my day.

Take care, my little Nurse Helen.

Respectfully,
Dr. John Roberts, MD

❦

30 December 1941
Helen Eberhart
Evanston, IL

Dear Eugene,
Don't you dare! Do you hear me? Don't you dare enlist, you knucklehead! Do I have to come down there myself and shake some sense into that thick head of yours?

Believe me, I get it. Dad can be . . . well, so Dad. He's a hard man, and I'm sure he's taking his frustration out on you. But you can't leave Mom. And you can't sign up to shoot people, Genie. Besides, with Clarence and Bud gone to the Pacific, Dad can't get along without you, although he'd never admit it under torture.

Which reminds me . . . has Dad honestly been telling people that the Eberharts are not German, but German-Swiss? Is there really an "uneasiness" in Cissna Park about being German? That's goofy! One glance through our small phone book from the Ackermans and Baumgartners, to the Kaufmans and Kruegers, all the way to the Weinigers and Zieglers, should assure everyone that we're all in the same boat when it comes to proving whose side we're on. What does Dad think will happen? Is he afraid they'll round up American citizens just because their ancestors lived in Germany or Japan? That may be Hitler's game, but surely it's not ours.

Nurse Benchley said she's thinking about enlisting in the Army as a nurse. Can you imagine that? If she does, she says she'll try to get me on as head nurse to take her place on the floor, if I've gotten my degree by then. I don't know if she really means it, but it's a nice thing to say. And she doesn't say that many nice things.

Eugene, think about Mom. Promise? She has enough to worry about with four sons in the war. If you leave, it will kill her. She needs you home. We all do. In some way I can't explain, I need you home in Cissna.

Love,
Nurse Eberhart

2

FRANK

St. Louis, Missouri
Dec. 7, 1941

Frank Daley checked the chart at the foot of the old man's hospital
bed. Admiral Ralph Jacobs was the unlucky age of Frank's dad, old
enough to have caught action in the Great War, but young enough
to still be in service for this whatever-it-was in Europe. That's where
the good admiral had picked up the nasty infection that had landed
him here, in the disease ward of the Washington University hospital. Frank liked the fellow well enough, but it was hard to look the
old codger in the face without laughing. The French were the ones
people called "frogs," but if any man ever deserved the name, it was
this one, with his big, wrinkly eyes and sagging jowls that got lost in
his bulbous neck.

Admiral Jacobs cleared his throat and struggled to sit up in bed. "Are you sure you're a doctor? I've got boots older than you."

"I noticed that when they brought you in, Admiral. Can't the Navy afford new boots for its admirals? What do lowly sailors do? Go barefoot?"

The admiral sputtered. Then his frog eyes lit up, and he almost chuckled.

Frank whipped out a wooden tongue depressor and told the admiral to open wide. "I'm a lowly intern, sir. If it makes you feel any better, *my* shoes are older than *you*." He removed the tongue depressor and made a mental note of the swollen tonsils.

"Intern?" Admiral Jacobs scoffed. "Don't know why they can't get a real doctor in here instead of some kind of want-to-be doctor."

"More like a *going-to-be* doctor." Frank had three firm offers for residency, all from great hospitals, and three more from hospitals with great locations, like Miami. He loved the beach and thought that one day he might set up private practice in a city with gorgeous beaches.

"Hmmpf. What's your name, son?"

Frank had given the man his name at least eight times in three days. He wondered if the old chap forgot locations and battle plans that quickly. "Frank R. Daley, soon to be known as Dr. Daley or F. R. Daley, MD."

"The armed services can always use an almost-doctor. You ever picture yourself enlisting?"

"Only in my nightmares, sir."

"You've got some lip on you."

"So they say." Frank took out the pen his sister, Dotty, had given him before he started med school and scribbled notes on Admiral Jacobs's chart: *Swollen tonsils. High blood pressure. Persistent fever. Forgetfulness.* The man wouldn't be leaving anytime soon.

"Pencils not good enough for you?" Jacobs snapped, pointing to the chart with the pencil dangling from a string.

"I like pens."

"What if you make a mistake?"

"I don't make mistakes."

The admiral laughed, a croaking that ended in a cough.

Frank waited for the cough to ease. "You okay, sir?" He slipped the stethoscope from his neck to his ears and held the silver plate to the old man's back. There was enough fluid in his lungs to launch a small ship.

"Fool question," the man muttered. "Of course I'm not okay. Not with my ship dry-docked in Boston and my crew on leave. You boys in white better get me out of here and back—"

He was interrupted by the hospital's loudspeaker. It crackled like it was on fire, then howled as if burned. Frank almost welcomed the interruption, which was usually a page for a surgeon or a general call for duty nurses to report to OR or ER.

"Attention, please. Could I have your attention?"

That was a new one. Frank recognized the voice of the chief of hospital staff, Dr. Macy. Old Mace never *asked* for attention; he demanded it.

"There's . . . there has been an enemy attack on our forces. President Roosevelt reported that the Japanese have attacked Pearl Harbor. They're saying it was a surprise air attack. There were multiple explosions . . . and fatalities."

Voices clashed in the background, coming through the speaker system like thunder rumbling and lightning striking. Then Dr. Macy came back on.

"I guess . . . I mean, we're hearing that our forces in the Pacific are under bombardment even now, as we speak. We don't know what else is happening. Please carry on with your duties. We will keep you advised. And . . . and God bless America."

Admiral Jacobs threw off his blanket before Frank could stop him. "Those sneaking, motherless . . . I have to get out of here! I need to get to my ship."

"Admiral, get back in bed." Frank had to forcibly hold the man down until he quit fighting. "Sir, you're not going to help anybody until we get you well." The admiral was a lot stronger than he looked. Or maybe Frank was as weak all over as he was in his knees. He had to steady himself against the bed rail. His mind wouldn't stop spinning. It made him dizzy, and all he wanted to do was run out of the room and call home.

"They don't know who they're messing with." The admiral coughed, then wiped his mouth with the back of his hand. "They're in for a surprise themselves. We've got fleets in the Pacific, just waiting for those Japs to do something like this. They're going to be sorry they ever—"

"Sir?" Frank couldn't wait another second. "My sister's in the Philippines."

"What's she doing there?" Jacobs demanded.

"She's a nurse. Dotty joined the Army Nurse Corps in '38. Last June she took an assignment to the Philippines." Frank stared at the admiral, barely seeing him. "She loves it there, taking care of malaria patients, going to after-duty dances. She met a guy a couple of months ago, a lieutenant." His throat felt tight. Dotty, his *big* sister, was barely five feet tall, too small to be in the thick of . . . whatever this was. "What's going to happen to her?"

"Now, son, don't you worry. The Philippines aren't in Hawaii." He pronounced it *Ha-why-ya*. "Not even close to Pearl Harbor."

Frank could feel his heart slow down. The sounds around him came into focus—shouts from the hall, the clatter of a meal tray, a scratching from somebody's radio. Ordinary sounds. Normal sounds.

Jacobs smiled, and the frog lines disappeared. He looked like somebody's kindly grandfather, the one everybody would get to dress up like Santa Claus at Christmas. "Don't you worry. This whole mess will all be over in a couple of weeks. Three weeks at the most. That's how long it should take our Navy to get to Japan and kick them across their own country and all the way to kingdom come. We'll show 'em not to mess with our boys. You'll see."

Frank wanted to believe him. And why not? He was an admiral in the United States Navy.

"Son, trust me. Three weeks, and this show will be over. Now, get me out of here."

———❧———

18 December 1941
To: Lt. Dorothea Daley APO Philippines
From: Frank Daley

Dear Dotty,

Sis, what have you gotten yourself into now? I know you wanted to travel, but this is ridiculous. A week ago, all we heard in the papers was how we'd beat back the Japanese and the whole thing would be over in nothing flat.

Dad said you couldn't get newspapers on the island, but I'm sure you've heard we've declared war on Germany and Italy, too. That Miss Rankin from Montana was the only dissenting vote in Congress when FDR got the declaration of war against Japan. What is wrong with that woman?

With the draft like it is, every intern and resident I know has signed up for deferment, which means I'll get to complete my residency as long as I agree to show up for basic the day after I finish. Fine with me. I can't imagine the world will keep fighting that long. Even Jack and I can't keep fighting that long.

You remember my buddy Anderson? I brought him home for Thanksgiving right before you set out for the Philippines. He gets the New York Times, and they're saying we've checked the Japanese on land and have sunk three of their ships. I guess we're chasing Japanese warships all over the Pacific while our fighter pilots are doing what we pay them for. So that sounds pretty good, if you ask me. (Nobody is asking me, strangely enough.)

Talked to Jack this morning. He was very mysterious about where he was calling from, but it sounded far away. I'm telling you, our brother is a spy, or my name's not Frank the Great. His sources tell him the Japs dropped bombs on Clark Field, where your "Boots" is. Hopefully you've seen Boots or heard from him by now. Let us know, will you? We're awfully worried about this guy we've never met.

You know how I told you I didn't pray much? I'm rethinking that one.

Stay safe, Dotty,
Frank

⌒⌒

23 December 1941
Not that far from Manila
From: Lt. Dorothea Daley

Dear Frank,

I don't know if you'll ever get this letter. No post offices in the jungle. Sometimes I give a letter to a soldier, or leave one with a patient.

Merry Christmas. Things aren't good here, but could be worse. Two of our nurses at Camp Hat were captured, and five in Guam.

I can't describe how surprised we were when we heard the bombs fall here at Fort Stotsenburg. The night before, we'd all been dancing. I got to the hospital early and was there when the first wave of bombs hit. It felt like an earthquake. I had no idea bombs could feel like that—not just a big boom, but a violent shaking of everything.

I stayed on duty with a few other nurses for 48 hours—no sleep and no food. I never did get back to the dorm. Our little

200-bed hospital got 500 patients from Clark Field almost instantly. When the first casualties arrived, I kept asking about Boots. I lifted every sheet, unzipped every body bag. He wasn't there, thank God.

When we ran out of space in the hospital, the tropical disease patients, all on their own, walked out to go fight. Bernie and I were the last two to leave our post. I only left because I fell asleep standing over an open wound and nearly put my head in some soldier's chest. I guess it's time to go when that happens. We couldn't return to the barracks, and we didn't want to get far from the hospital, so we crawled into a space in the airway under the hospital and took turns catching a little shut-eye. We barely fit, one lying down, one sitting up. I always knew being this small would come in handy.

I pray Boots is all right. Haven't heard from him in 11 days. I love him, little brother. I should have told him when I had the chance. I'm going to marry that guy the next chance I get. Maybe we'll meet up in Bataan. MacArthur ordered us to leave Manila for the peninsula so we can man the emergency hospitals. Unfortunately, Mac wasn't exactly specific on how we're supposed to get there.

Be good,
Dotty

~⚬~

29 April 1942
From: Lt. Dorothea Daley Engel

Dear Frank,
This whole island has been under attack since Jan. The commander of the Philippine forces, Wainwright, rode through on his horse and ordered us nurses to evacuate or be Japanese prisoners. Then he and the soldiers left by boat.

*We did what we could for our patients, carrying and
dragging them on stretchers made of branches. None of us is
strong anymore, but we hauled as many as we could deep into
the jungle with us. The ambulatory patients helped. We've
been hiding out here for weeks, with nothing but rice and an
occasional drop of meat "of undetermined origin." We told
Franny, who does most of the cooking, not to tell us where our
cute pet monkeys have gone.*

*Boots showed up, thank God (and I mean that!). He made
it through the first three attacks by the skin of his teeth—powder
burns on his uniform to prove it. He comes and goes (mostly
goes, fights, comes back). He asked me if I'd gotten to meet
General Wainwright. I told him, "No, but we ate his horse."
True story.*

*I am now Mrs. Emanuel Engel, wife of "Boots." On Feb.
19, 1942, Father Cummings pronounced us husband and
wife. We started the ceremony in our makeshift hospital and
ended the service in a foxhole, when somebody over-celebrated,
I guess, and dropped bombs so close the dirt in the foxhole
covered my bridal khakis. Good thing I wasn't wearing a
wedding dress.*

*After a wonderful six-hour honeymoon (which you're too
young to hear about), the groom returned to duty at the beach
defenses in Mariveles. I hardly ever saw him until he showed
up in the hospital with malaria. Then we saw each other for a
week straight. What kind of a war is this when your husband
getting malaria is good news?*

*I'll bet Daddy expected MacArthur to rescue us, and I admit
we did too. But "Dugout Doug" left a month ago. Guess he
figured that captain-going-down-with-his-ship scenario doesn't
play well in the jungle.*

*April has been the worst. I haven't seen Boots for weeks. And
now they're saying he must have been with the 75,000 Filipino*

and American soldiers captured at Mariveles on April 9. The Japs haven't got a prison large enough here, so they're making the soldiers march the length of the Bataan peninsula to prison camps. A boy who escaped by playing dead is full of stories about Japanese soldiers making ours march day and night without sleep or food or water. He said prisoners who collapsed were run over by jeeps. He claims he saw stabbings, beheadings, throats cut, soldiers shot as a game.

I think he's making it up. I pray he is. My Boots is tough. He'll be okay.

I'm glad you're praying. I've been ordered, along with eight other nurses, to stand ready for evacuation. After dark, a PT boat is supposed to take us out into the ocean. It's eerily quiet today, a Japanese holiday. We're to catch a PBY aircraft, even though we know the last PBY out caught the reefs, and the nurses barely made it back to land, where they were captured by Japanese forces and put in prisons.

That's not what worries me. That's not why I don't want to go. My husband is officially listed as missing in action. But I know better. Boots is still here.

Wish you were here. Not really. Stay in med school.

Love,
Dot

Helen

Helen Eberhart juggled the stack of patient files as she quick-stepped to keep up with the small group of interns. Like them, she strained to hear Dr. Knight's muttered instructions for the new mothers on her floor. Interns might be tested on what the doctor was telling them, but as head nurse on four, the only tests Helen had to pass were real-life.

They were clustered inside Mrs. Vande's private hospital room, a suite so large they could have held conventions in it without disturbing the patient. Helen wondered how rich you had to be to get a swell room like this.

"Take Mrs. Lehman in 423 off IVs. And show Mrs. Friedman how to take the iron with her vitamins. I'm planning to send her home tomorrow, if she has no objections." At six foot three and 220 pounds, the silver-haired Dr. Knight, chief of ob-gyn, made an impressive figure. But he mumbled.

Helen edged in closer so she wouldn't miss any instructions. She scribbled notes on the chart, knowing she'd be the one to remove the intravenous. She'd be the one to give flighty Friedman her lesson in vitamins and iron and to prepare her for going home and taking care of her baby. More likely, watching a live-in servant take care of her baby.

"Nurse, get me a glass of water!" Mrs. Vande commanded from her hospital bed. She was surrounded by the extra pillows she'd ordered the morning she'd arrived, three full weeks before she went into labor.

Helen glanced back at the bedside table, where a pitcher of water stood beside two clean glasses. Couldn't she see that Helen's hands were full? "I'll be right there," Helen said, her voice sounding a hundred times sweeter than she felt. "Give me just a minute."

"No." Mrs. Vande made no attempt to match Helen's sweet tone. "I want it now."

Helen should have been used to women like this one. The only downside to nursing in the wealthy Evanston Hospital were the wealthy, spoiled women who came here. When Helen became rich, *she'd* never act spoiled. Or maybe just a little. And she *would* be rich, no matter how hard she had to work to get there.

"I understand, Mrs. Vande," she said, her tone not quite as sweet as before. "I'll get a ward boy in here soon as we step into the hall."

"No you will not. *You* get me a glass of water *now!*"

Helen risked a glance at the interns, none of whom lifted a finger to help. *They* weren't carrying trays and charts. Would it kill them to get the water? To hold the files for two seconds so she could get it?

"Do you hear me?" Mrs. Vande shrieked. They could have heard her in Berlin and Tokyo.

"There, there," Dr. Knight offered.

There, there? Helen swallowed the anger that rose like bile in her throat. "I'm sorry, Mrs. Vande. We won't be five minutes. I promise."

Dr. Knight had apparently lost interest in the war of wills and was already mumbling dosages for the next patient. The pack of interns trailed out of the room after him, their lab coats forming the train of his royal robe.

"Nurse!" Mrs. Vande shouted. "Don't you dare leave this room! I want that water. And I need to sit on the side of the bed. I haven't dangled my legs all afternoon."

"Soon as I can," Helen called, ducking out as if the woman's insults were arrows she could dodge. She was missing Knight's orders. He wouldn't repeat them, either.

One of the ward boys rushed by, pushing a metal tray in front of him.

"Benny!" Helen called. "Mrs. Vande in 401 wants a glass of water. Please? And I wouldn't wait if I were you. Tell her I'll be in later to help her dangle her legs."

Helen liked Benny. He reminded her of Eugene, who had joined the Army against everyone's wishes but his own. "And Ben?" she called, catching him before he entered the lioness's den. "Try to get out before she throws a fit." *Or the water glass.*

"Nurse Eberhart!" Dr. Knight hollered all the way up the hall.

She trotted to catch up before they disappeared into the next room.

Two hours later they finished rounds, caring for twenty-eight new or expectant mothers. Helen had managed to update every chart, recording orders for the floor nurses. Some of the "patients," like Mrs. Cox in 424, had been in the hospital nearly four weeks, and still, nurses had to help them dangle their legs. Helen's mother had birthed her children on the kitchen table, "then rose to serve a hot breakfast afterward," Helen's brother Walter liked to say.

Helen got an ice-cold glass of water from the nurses' station and headed for Mrs. Vande's room. She'd offer the ice water as a truce, even though she had no doubt that Benny would have taken good care of Mrs. Vande already.

"Nurse?" Benny caught her before she reached 401. His facial contortions warned her this wasn't good. "McCafferty wants to see you in her office."

"Tell me you're kidding." Already she'd be an hour late getting out of here. And a visit to the chief of nursing was never a good thing. So far, Helen's record as a registered nurse was outstanding, although this wasn't her first trip to the "principal's office." Never for being late or shirking duty. Even her rivals couldn't fault her work habits *or* her work. It was just that it was taking a while to master the art of swallowing her words along with her pride. But everybody knew skilled nurses could have their pick of assignments, and Helen intended to see the world in its highest-paying hospitals. She didn't need bad references.

Benny shook his head. "I think she said 'stat' and 'immediately' in the same sentence."

Helen sighed, chugged the water herself, and handed him the empty glass. "Boy oh boy. Wish me luck, Benny."

She was admitted to the chief's office, a corner room with two glass walls and a great view of Lake Michigan. Nurse McCafferty was facing the window, studying the skyline, when Helen entered. From the back, McCafferty's shoulders were a match for most men's. And when she swung her chair around, her front barely disappointed the notion. Her square-toed shoes clomped the floor with the force of combat boots. "Nurse Eberhart, what's this I hear about you being rude to one of our patients?"

Helen knew herself well enough to start counting to ten before she answered. She only made it to two. "*Me?* That's just swell! I wasn't the one being rude."

McCafferty lowered her bushy eyebrows, making it look like a woolly worm was creeping across the woman's nose. "Nurse, watch your tone."

That's all Helen did. Every day, all day, she watched her tone. She bit off words before they had a chance to break out. She hadn't let a cross word escape her lips—at least not to her patients—for six months. It had been nine months since she'd been summoned to McCafferty's office. Helen didn't trust herself to speak. When on earth was *she* going to be the one people had to bite their tongues around?

McCafferty continued, "Mrs. Vande says she had to beg for a glass of water."

"I have twenty-eight patients on my ward. Have I *ever* refused to do anything for a patient out of laziness?"

McCafferty picked up a pencil and fingered it. "No."

"Yet *I'm* the one getting chewed out?" She struggled to keep her voice down. Helen knew she should stop right there. She didn't have to justify herself.

She didn't *have* to . . . but she couldn't help it. "That woman is a pill! She kept demanding her glass of water, even though she could see I had my arms full of charts. I had a doctor and six interns expecting me to record every word of instruction. And—"

"And, Nurse Eberhart, you had the wife of one of our chief bene-factors in need of your assistance."

It was a good thing Helen had her nursing degree and knew hearts couldn't actually pound out of chests, or she would have sworn hers was doing just that. "I sent a ward boy the second I left the room. And I was on my way back to her room—with another glass of water, I might add—when you called me in."

"That's fine then. Go back and apologize, and I think—"

"Apologize? Me?"

McCafferty's tiny bird eyes flashed.

"You're not serious," Helen tried. But of course, she *was* serious.

Helen strode purposefully out of the office and took the stairs up to four, muttering gypsy curses with every step. She exploded into the hallway and stormed past the nurses congregating at the nurses' station. Then she turned on her heels, dashed into the patient kitchen for a tall glass of water, and headed up the hall. She'd handled seven wise-guy brothers and three lazy sisters, dozens of married doctors and keen-to-go interns. What was one spoiled woman, right? Besides, maybe by this time, Mrs. Vande had cooled off and come to her senses.

Helen halted in front of room 401, shot up a quick prayer for peace, straightened her cap, and whisked into the room, the ol' Eberhart smile casting light before her.

"There you are," Helen chirped. "Thanks for your patience, Mrs. Vande. Did I tell you that's my favorite dressing gown? Talk about the cat's pajamas." The fur-trimmed pink silk nightgown probably cost more than Helen's entire wardrobe.

Mrs. Vande didn't acknowledge the compliment. "My water?"

"Ah. The water."

Helen started to hand her the glass when Mrs. Vande snapped her fingers. The woman couldn't dangle her own feet off a bed after lying in it for weeks. She couldn't pour herself a lousy glass of water, but she could snap her fingers?

Helen kept her smile frozen as she handed over the now-sweating glass. "There you go."

"I hope Mrs. McCafferty gave you a good talking-to, Nurse. Your behavior was inexcusable. That's simply not the way my husband's hospital treats its most important patients." She barely sipped the infernal water and held it out for Helen to take.

"They taught us in nurse's training that *all* of our patients are our most important patients," Helen said sweetly.

"Don't be insolent with me, Nurse." She made a show of leaning up from her pillows. "Well?"

Helen set down the full glass of water and started pulling out pillows from Mrs. Vande's back. She had to press her lips together to trap the names that wanted to come flying out: *Dumb Dora. Pickle puss.*

Loose lips sink ships, Helen told herself. You couldn't go anywhere without seeing that wartime poster. Well, this was *her* ship. Without a word, she tried to pull Mrs. Vande to a sitting position, but Helen weighed 105 with her shoes on, and Mrs. Vande was twice that, with little of it owing to the birth of her daughter. The woman did not budge.

"Careful, you foolish girl!" Mrs. Vande jerked her arm away, making Helen stumble backward.

"Let's try that again," Helen said, amazed at the softness of her voice. She should get a Purple Heart for this.

After a few minutes of shuffling, nudging, and cajoling, Helen finally had Mrs. Vande sitting on the side of the bed. "Now, can you move your legs a little?" Helen couldn't bring herself to use "we" the way most of the nurses did, although the word actually fit with this woman, who never did anything on her own.

"Of course I can't move my legs. That's what you're here for."

Helen wanted to ask who moved her legs for her in the Vande mansion, but there probably was some poor gal whose sole job was to move the woman's tree-trunk gams. Helen took an ankle in each hand, no easy task. "Here we go." She lifted one foot a few inches, then the next.

"Careful!" Mrs. Vande kicked, barely missing Helen's nose. "You have no idea of the terrible ordeal I've been through. You obviously have never given birth."

"I'm not married," Helen said. Not that she hadn't been asked. Ray Scott had asked her to marry him a dozen times since Valentine's Day. But she had no intention of getting married for a long, long time. Maybe never. She wasn't sure she knew any happily married couples. None of the women on this floor got visits from adoring husbands. They were lucky if they got flowers sent by secretaries. Besides, there was too much of the world to see.

"Like not being married ever stopped a nurse from having a baby," Mrs. Vande muttered.

Helen pretended not to hear.

"Ow!" The woman batted at Helen's hands, like a child protesting bedtime. "Stop it. That's enough." Her thick calves became dead weight, and Helen released the ankles.

"I'm waiting for your apology, Nurse." For the first time, Mrs. Vande actually focused on Helen. She had the art of looking down her nose at the same time she stuck it in the air. "Well?"

Loose lips sink ships. Loose lips sink ships. "I apologize for upsetting you earlier, Mrs. Vande. If I did or said anything you interpreted as rudeness, I'm very sorry." There. That wasn't so bad really.

"Hmmpf." Mrs. Vande tried to scoot back, without success.

Helen jumped to the rescue, easing her onto the pillows. "But you must have known that reporting me to the head of nursing was overkill. You saw that my hands were full. I had to write down the doctor's orders." She wanted Mrs. Vande to understand, and she knew her voice was reasonable, her words filled with logic and respect. She plumped the last pillow and placed it behind Mrs. Vande's head. All she wanted was a peaceful end to this conflict. After all, wasn't peace what they all wanted, especially with the whole world going nuts?

"I'll tell you what I think," Mrs. Vande began. "This hospital should pay me for educating you nurses in the common decencies of the civilized world."

"Excuse me?"

"Ah, there you are." Mrs. Vande stared past Helen.

Nurse McCafferty entered the room and beamed at the patient. "Is everything all right? Satisfactory?"

Helen waited for Mrs. Vande to answer. She wasn't worried. She'd done exactly what her boss had demanded, and more.

"No. Everything is *not* satisfactory."

"What?" Helen felt betrayed. She'd given everything to this woman—water, pillows, apologies—and what did she get?

McCafferty turned to Helen. "Nurse Eberhart, didn't you apologize for your behavior earlier?"

"Yes! I apologized!"

"See? See what I mean?" Mrs. Vande demanded, sounding—for the first time—satisfied. "Now you've seen it for yourself. Her attitude is despicable. I simply will not tolerate it."

Helen studied her boss and thought she caught the hint of a struggle in her eyes. Margery McCafferty was no dupe. She had to know the score. For a brief instant, Helen watched her boss battle with herself . . .

And lose. "Nurse Eberhart, it appears you need to apologize again, perhaps with a better attitude?"

"Exactly! She needs to know her place." Triumphant, Mrs. Vande lifted her chin at Helen. "Well?"

My place? My place! Because I come from podunk Cissna Park, Illinois? Because my entire wardrobe cost less than your nightgown? Because you spend more on cigarettes in a day than I make in a week?

A calm, or maybe it was a kind of peace, swept through Helen like a Lake Michigan breeze. Helen Marie Eberhart knew her place, all right. And it wasn't here.

"I quit."

Helen

EVANSTON, ILLINOIS

It felt grand strolling out into the brisk chill of early March. Helen's only regret was that she didn't have a photograph of Mrs. Vande's face when Helen made her dramatic exit. One day Helen Eberhart would have that fur coat and walk right up to Mrs. Vande—preferably when the woman's hands were full—and ask for a glass of champagne. Life was too short to play nursemaid to spoiled rich women. There was a world out there to be seen and experienced. She stuffed her hands into her jacket pockets and twirled on the sidewalk.

"Whoo-hoo!"

The wolf whistle didn't faze Helen. She was used to them and usually paid no attention. She had to cross some rough neighborhoods to get to the nurses' dorm, but there was nothing to be afraid of as long as she was wearing her uniform. She still had her cap on, and

33

she hadn't buttoned her coat, so they'd see she was a nurse. Nobody ever threatened a nurse.

"Hey, babe! I'm talking to *you*!"

Surprised, Helen turned to see two men who were definitely not together. A withered character straight out of a Dickens novel sprawled on the steps of a dilapidated warehouse. His black hair fell in greasy strands over deep eye sockets with no more than black dots to fill them. He clutched a brown bag, and she could see the dark-green neck of the wine bottle. Next to the old man stood a young sailor, his white uniform starched to the nines. He looked keen when he flashed his smile. She wondered how long it would take him to dress down the old man for disrespecting a nurse.

She shook her head at the wino and hoped the sailor could read her smile. Then she started off again, grateful for the added protection of the US Navy.

"Say, doll, how about you and me getting us some bubble juice? I know a real cozy place."

Helen wheeled around in time to catch the sailor's wink. *He* was the whistler? He stuck out his arm as if he expected her to take it and throw herself at him.

"What's the matter with you, sonny?" The old man came to life and was on his feet in a split second. He grasped the sailor's arm and twisted it behind his back before the boy knew what hit him. The wino must have been stronger than his emaciated body looked because the sailor struggled but couldn't get away. "I believe you owe this fine nurse an apology."

"What? I was just—" The sailor flinched and dipped his shoulder in a way that made Helen think the older man knew a bit about pressure points. "Okay, okay!" he wailed. "I'm sorry."

"Like you mean it, young sailor," the old man urged. "And don't forget you're talking to a lady."

The boy bowed his head. When he glanced up, Helen saw that he couldn't have been as old as Eugene. "I'm real sorry, ma'am."

"I know," she said. "Thanks. Thanks to both of you." She felt lousy for thinking the whistle had come from the older man. That would teach her to judge books by their covers. "And good luck . . . to you both."

It wasn't until she reached the corner that she realized an amazing thing. She had just been given the apology, the respect she'd been denied at the hospital today. It couldn't have been a coincidence. Her mother would have said it had come straight from *Gott im Himmel.* God in Heaven.

Instead of turning up Sherman Avenue, she walked the extra blocks to Lake Shore Drive. Helen could hear waves crashing seconds before the blue waters of Lake Michigan came into view. An icy wind made her shiver, and she buttoned her jacket, then stuck her hands back into her pockets. Choppy whitecaps smoothed out toward the horizon . . . and beyond.

She slowed as she passed the stone mansions with their wrought-iron gates. Ray knew the owner of the biggest house, the one with three turrets. He promised he'd get them invited to a party there. What would it be like to live in a mansion like that? Ray said she'd know soon enough if she'd say yes to one of his marriage proposals.

Footsteps sounded behind her. "Helen! Hold up!" Her roommate, Lucille Green, trotted up beside her. "What happened? You never leave early. McCafferty was breathing fire. Did you two have a run-in?"

"Did we have a run-in?" Helen repeated. "More like a run out."

"How's that again?"

"I quit."

"You dope. You did not." Lucille laughed, but her smile faded when Helen didn't join the laughter. "Eberhart, say it isn't so!"

Helen shrugged and started walking again. "It's so."

"Wait!" Lucille ran after her. "You're telling me you actually quit? And you meant it?"

"I meant it all right. Say, maybe they'll make *you* head nurse! You deserve it." Lucille was such a good gal. When Helen had been picked head nurse over gals with years' more experience, Lucille hadn't let anybody say a word against her. And Lucille cared like crazy about patients, even the spoiled ones.

They walked in silence up Nurses' Row to their dorm. Then Lucille used her long stride to get ahead of Helen and peer back into her face. "I can't believe you really and truly quit. Holy cannoli. So what are you going to do now?"

Helen stopped short in front of the door to their dorm. She could see her reflection in the window, dark-blonde hair in a windblown pageboy, blue eyes stunned wide open. What *was* she going to do? Was it possible the thought hadn't occurred to her until now?

"Helen? You okay, Eberhart?" Lucille slipped past her and jerked open the door. "It's freezing out here, in case you hadn't noticed."

Dazed, Helen followed her friend inside, where they were hit with a blast of hot air. She'd been flying high, filled with the euphoria of leaving those spoiled women behind. But what lay ahead? Where would she work? Where could she live? She'd have to leave the dorm. You couldn't stay there unless you were a student nurse or you worked as a registered nurse for the hospital, like she did. Like she used to do. She'd never find a room this cheap.

"I'll bet you haven't even talked to Ray about this, have you?" Lucille said, shrugging out of her wool jacket.

"Ray? Why would I? He's a great dancing partner; that's all." Helen knew her friends thought she and Ray were an item. Ray did too. But she'd never pretended to want anything but dancing from the guy. And she'd turned down every proposal the second he made it.

Lucille elbowed her. "Incoming at ten o'clock. Make a run for it?"

Mae Rogers, the old Red Cross woman who haunted the dorm, was heading straight for them. That tireless vulture in her starched blue uniform trolled the lobby day and night, waiting to pounce on nurses with a fresh load of war guilt.

Rogers touched the tip of her cap, which never budged from the precise apex of her wiry, gray-black hair. She had a bird face, right down to the pointy beak and BB eyes that were trained on Helen. "Evening, ladies. I suppose you've heard the rumors about the upcoming all-out invasion on the Jerries."

"We try not to listen to rumors, even war rumors," Lucille quipped. "Helen and I keep our radio tuned to Guy Lombardo and Glenn Miller and Kay Kyser. We don't allow the *Trib* in our dorm room. Too darned depressing. Just the same, we hear enough war gossip to bring us down, thank you very much."

"Helen?" The Red Cross woman leaned in so close Helen could smell her chicken-noodle breath. "Have you thought about your brothers today? How many are in harm's way tonight? Four? Five? What if they're wounded in battle, bleeding and moaning on the muddy field far away on foreign soil? And what if there is no nurse who can tend their wounds? One might find the fortitude to crawl to a nearby hospital, only to find it empty."

The spiel wasn't much different from the barrage of words fired on nurses night after night as they tried to get to their rooms. But Helen could picture the scene.

"Come on, Helen," Lucille urged.

Usually, at this point in the harangue, Helen ducked out, dodging the "Red Cross–fire" as if her words were bullets.

Not this time. She stayed where she was.

"Helen," the volunteer persisted, "have you given thought to your brothers' plight *over there*?"

There wasn't a day that went by that Helen hadn't thought of her brothers and wondered where they were and what they were going through. She'd prayed for them. She'd tried to believe that was enough. "Yes, I've thought about my brothers. Golly, yes."

Poor Mae Rogers looked shocked, as if her bullet words had ricocheted and struck her head-on. She'd probably expected the usual jokes at her expense, or a strong defense against her melodrama. Her bird face drew taut, dubious. "Well . . . yes. Of course you have. That's good."

Helen wasn't kidding herself. She wasn't being swept up in some false sense of guilt that she was putting her brothers in danger by staying in America. In fact, Wilbur, for one, would have tied her to the bedpost to keep her from going if he hadn't been off fighting in Europe. Clarence and Bud would laugh themselves off the decks of their ships at the thought of their sister in the Army. Ed, already an MP in England, would lock her up and swallow the key. And Eugene would call her Gypsy and accuse her of wanting to roam the world like her ancestors.

Helen glanced around the lobby at the war posters she walked by every day: the one with the sad, strange man in a wheelchair; the one with the young nurse receiving her white cap under the slogan *Become a Nurse, Your Country Needs You.* Another poster had a woman in an Army uniform smiling, the light making her look angelic: *Enlist in a Proud Profession: Join the US Cadet Nurse Corps.* A dozen gals had told Helen she was the spitting image of the poster girl.

Helen knew that Nurse Benchley and others had joined up in a wave of patriotic fervor after Pearl Harbor. If she hadn't been in nurse's training, she might have been swept up along with them. But she couldn't quit training. And when she got out, there was a position at the hospital, an opportunity that might never come around again. The war, on the other hand, felt like it would go on for the rest of her life.

Now she didn't have that job. She didn't even have a place to live. She sure as heck wasn't going back to Cissna Park. She still wanted to be rich, but she also wanted to do big, important things with her life. To see the world.

A group of nurses rushed in, chattering and giggling, and the Red Cross volunteer, apparently sensing fresh prey, started off toward them.

"Wait!" Helen cried.

Mae Rogers frowned back at Helen, no doubt expecting a wisecrack. It wouldn't have been the first. "What is it this time?"

"Where do I sign up? I'm going *over there.*"

FRANK

Frank stood in the hospital payroll line and tried not to imagine what the Army would do to him when he showed up late for basic training. He'd written letters and made phone calls, trying to get them to understand that there was no way he could get to El Paso, Texas, the day after graduating in St. Louis, Missouri. Nobody listened.

He and Anderson and almost every other resident he knew had enlisted with deferments so they could finish their residencies. Deferment had been a good deal, ensuring they'd enter the Army as lieutenants. Griffin and Diaz, who had interned with him in Miami, hadn't enlisted, and they'd been drafted as privates, pulled out of residency, and sent overseas. Nobody knew where they were now.

Frank was not his old man. Dr. Pete Daley, as much soldier as doctor, had been the first Missouri physician to sign on to help train medics. Frank, on the other hand, still couldn't believe he'd let himself be dragged into this mess. He'd been counting on the war being over by now.

"So, *Dr.* Daley, how does it feel to finally get those *MD* initials on your name tag?" Nurse Margaret Stemmons scooted in front of him and fingered the letters: *F. R. Daley, MD*. Maggie was the biggest dish on the nursing staff, voted so by secret ballots from the male medical staff. Nobody wore the whites like Nurse Stemmons. With her long blonde hair, she could have doubled for Veronica Lake, and she knew it. "Ready to conquer the world, Doctor?"

"I don't know, Maggie. Do *you* think I'm ready?"

"Don't tell me Frank Daley, MD, is finally doubting himself . . . just a bit?" She put a hand on his arm, showing off bright-red nail polish. "Is there a unit you *haven't* worked in at this hospital? Let's see . . . burn unit, disease ward, cardiac, ob-gyn, ER, orthopedic—"

Frank interrupted. "That one was punishment imposed by the chief after that little prank backfired in the ER."

He joined in Maggie's banter, but his heart wasn't in it. His medical training readied him for a top-notch, high-paying hospital, not some medical tent on the other side of nowhere, which was where the Army would send him *if* he survived Camp Barkeley and six weeks of drills, marches, and obstacle courses. Frank's buddy Lartz had already reported there for duty, and his letters made Frank consider going AWOL before he was even *present* without leave.

"Are you sure you can't celebrate with the nurses tonight?" Maggie asked.

"Tempting." He grinned down at her. He was already going to be late for training. What could it hurt to show up later than late? What would the Army do? Shoot him twice? Probably.

Maggie turned to Anderson, next in line behind Frank. "How about you, Dr. Anderson?"

"Delighted to oblige the nurses, as always." Anderson knew how to work the system. Somehow he'd gotten himself forty-eight hours before he had to report. The guy had a Clark Gable confidence most people couldn't resist.

The line moved up, making Frank next in line after Bell, who had to report for basic in North Carolina.

Frank glanced at his watch, the one his folks had given him for graduation. His dad had worked hard his whole life, delivering babies in exchange for lettuce and tomatoes or meat from the butcher, bread from the baker. The watch must have chipped into their savings. Frank wasn't sure what Dotty and Jack had received for their graduations, aside from lavish parental praise for being valedictorians. To Frank, the not-valedictorian, the watch was a reminder of what must have been approval from the old man, even though he hadn't said so.

It was almost five. Even if the bus got in on time, he'd never make it to Texas by roll call the next day. Buses were crammed with soldiers, and they stopped at every town.

Maggie interrupted his thoughts. "Say, that's you, big boy." She pointed to the hall speaker.

"Dr. Daley. Paging Dr. Frank R. Daley."

Frank's body stiffened like it did every time they paged him, which had only been five or six times in two years. He always expected bad news. His dad's heart. Dotty.

"Dr. Daley, report to the nurses' station by administration immediately."

He was already at administration. Frank reached in front of Bell, grabbed his own paycheck, and moved toward the nurses' station up the hall.

"Dr. Daley, come to the hospital phone at the nurses' station! General Maxwell is calling Dr. Frank Daley."

"Hey, Frank!" Anderson called after him. "What's going on?"

"Beats me!"

He was out of breath when he reached the nurses' station. Fine soldier he was going to make. Anderson, Bell, Maggie, and half a dozen others were right behind him. Frank turned to them. "This is a mistake, right?"

Anderson shrugged. "You better take it anyway."

"Is one of you Dr. Daley?" The nurse behind the counter held the phone away from her, as if she were afraid of the thing.

"I'm Frank . . . Dr. Daley, but I think there's been a mistake."

"Huh-uh." She swallowed so hard it looked like she had an Adam's apple. "It's General Maxwell, and he wants to speak to *you*." She lowered her voice and added, "He doesn't like being kept waiting."

"What's a general want with *him*?" Anderson asked.

"Are you sure he wants Daley?" Frank couldn't think of a single reason why a United States general would want to talk to him. "Not Bailey? Or Paley?"

The frightened nurse shook her head and stuck the phone in Frank's face.

Maggie moved in closer. "Wasn't there a general in here with a ruptured appendix last April? Didn't you assist on that?"

"Must have done a crack job," Bell said, slapping him on the back. "Well done."

"I guess." Frank had assisted in loads of surgeries with lots of doctors. And generals looked the same as civilians on an operating table.

"There was a general on the malaria ward last year," Anderson said. "Or was he a colonel? Maybe he's a general by now."

Dr. Reed, the senior staff on duty, dropped a chart on the desk and leaned in. "Take the call, Doctor."

"Right." Frank took the phone and instinctively turned his back on the little crowd. "Frank Daley here. Dr. Daley."

"Finally! It's about time." The voice was gruff, muffled . . . but there was something familiar about it.

"Uh . . . I'm sorry I kept you waiting. Is there something wrong? Or something I can do for you, General?"

The crowd around him had grown to a dozen, their whispers hissing like steam from a leaky radiator. Frank frowned at them. "Shhhh!"

"You tellin' me to shush?" demanded the voice on the other end.

"No, sir. General."

"All right then!" The gruff voice transformed. "Because you should never shush your big brother."

"Jack?"

"Jack?" Anderson's brow wrinkled and he tried to get closer to the phone.

"General Maxwell's first name is John, I think," one of the residents whispered. "John . . . Jack. Probably a nickname."

Frank remembered his audience. "Sorry, General. Tell me what you need."

"This is so exciting," Maggie whispered.

Frank moved away as far as he could, keeping his back to them so they couldn't see him smile. It was just like his brother to impersonate a general. In college when Frank's freshman English prof was a no-show on the first day of class, Jack, a junior business major, had shown up out of nowhere and pretended he was the professor. He'd taught the class for a week before the real prof showed up.

"What exactly can I do for you, *General*?" he asked, risking a glance at his captive audience.

"Get your gear and be out in front of the hospital in fifteen minutes. That's an order!"

"Will do!"

The phone clicked off, so Frank handed the receiver to the nurse. "Thanks." He turned to Anderson and the others. "I have to go."

Frank took off for his locker, shouting good-byes to his baffled buddies. He was outside in time to see a jeep pull into the hospital drive. The horn honked their old code—four longs, two shorts—and the jeep screeched to a halt inches from his feet.

"Hey, little brother!" Jack, in Army dress greens and a military lid, left the motor running and vaulted out of the jeep. He grabbed Frank's duffel bag and flung it into the back. Then he gave him a bear hug that lifted him off the ground. "Come on!"

Frank threw in his backpack, then climbed in just before Jack hit the gas. "Good to see you, Jack!" he shouted over the roar of the engine. "We were worried."

Jack flashed him that toothy grin of his. "Told you not to."

"Listen, you better take me straight to the bus station. I have to be in training camp tomorrow."

"Why do you think I'm here?" Jack bellowed. "Did you really think I'd let you go to El Paso without me?"

"But how did you know?"

"I have my ways," Jack said in a terrible German accent.

He had his ways, all right. Further evidence that he was a spy. Jack had signed up in 1939, when the government had appealed to accountants to help organize the armed forces from the inside out. The select group of pencil pushers were called Thirty Day Wonders because that's how long they committed to service in the US Army. Only the "wonder" had come months later, when thirty days stretched to ninety, then a year. None of them had gotten out of the Army as far as Frank knew. And he was sure they were all part of some secret service, maybe the new OSS. It was no use asking Jack about it. He never said or did anything he didn't want to, and he always did exactly what he set out to do. Frank thought his brother was a true hero, even though people might never know it.

So was his sister. After being stateside almost two years, she still wasn't back to her fighting weight. She was convinced Boots was alive, and since the Army refused to let her return to the Philippines to look for him, she spent most days on the phone or at the typewriter, trying to get the Army involved.

Dot had received a Royal Blue Emblem for bravery and other honors from the president, but she never talked about it. She didn't even tell them about the ceremony until it was too late for any of the family to get to Washington. All she cared about was finding Boots.

"Dotty finally sent me a photo of her with President Roosevelt and Eleanor at the White House. That ceremony must have been something."

"You're right about that," Jack said. "She and those other five nurses were the first women to be decorated for bravery in this war—did you know that? You should have seen her face when Eleanor pinned those medals on her."

"You were there? She wrote me that nobody from the family was there."

Jack twisted his grin. "She didn't know."

"But . . ." Frank let it drop.

"So, little brother, are you ready for war?"

There was that question again. Frank had tried to imagine himself in his big brother's spy shoes, risking his life every day. And Dotty? She'd sacrificed so much. But Frank had no heroic illusions about himself. Two heroes in the family were plenty. "Guess I'm about to find out."

<hr />

Frank R. Daley, MD
Battle Creek, Michigan
8 April 1944

Dear Dotty,

Why didn't you warn me about boot camp? Was that really live ammo they were shooting over our heads while we crawled in the mud under barbed wire? Anderson and I kept reminding our crazed sergeant that we were doctors, not Marines, but he didn't get it. I think that sick, sick man enjoyed doing calisthenics before dawn and believed we would as well. Tell me they never made you climb walls with dangling ropes.

My last week at "camp," I came in first on the obstacle course, which ended in a 20-mile run. I ran fastest because a 2nd lieutenant swore the ammo was real. Anyway, I got bragging rights over Anderson and Lartz for a while . . . until Sarge pointed out coming in ahead of a pile of doctors was nothing to brag about.

I think the only reason I got out of there in one piece is that some general issued orders for me to report to Battle Creek, Michigan, two weeks early because Percy Jones Hospital is under the mistaken impression that I'm a disease expert. Apparently we're woefully short of those fellows. I tried to tell them I'd interned a few weeks in Krueger's disease lab, but he was the expert, not me. Ever notice how the Army doesn't listen?

As head of the rare disease ward, I try to solve mysteries and come up with cures for the few patients on my ward. I guess I'm not that bad at it—it's like figuring out whodunit in an Agatha Christie mystery. I only have 12 patients right now, but they keep saying I should expect my 150 beds to fill. Hope they're wrong. I need my rest and playtime. Anderson says there's a new crop of nurses coming in tomorrow.

Battle Creek is loads better than El Paso. I know, I know. It's not like I had to eat pet monkeys. On second thought, have you tasted C-rations? I could swear they've got a primate-y flavor. But you're the expert.

Dotty, don't listen to the Army. You're not a widow just because they list you as one. I think you'd know in your heart if you'd lost Boots.

Yours truly,
Frank

P.S. You'd be proud of me. Tomorrow is Easter, and I've talked Anderson and Lartz into going to church with me.

Lt. Helen Eberhart, Army Nurse
Somewhere between Chicago and Battle Creek, Michigan
April 8, 1944

Dear Eugene,

No, you cannot call me Lieutenant Gypsy.

I'm on a train bound for my holding assignment in Battle
Creek, Michigan. Ever hear of it? It used to be Battle Creek
Sanitarium, run by Dr. Kellogg, the guy who invented flaked
cereal and radiation therapy for cancer patients.

The Army bought the place a couple of years ago and set up
the hospital to treat wounded soldiers. They named it Percy Jones,
after an Army surgeon who drove ambulances in the last war.

After basic, they asked each of us what our overseas
preference would be. I thought of a million places I'd like to go,
but the only choices were Europe or the Pacific. You know I hate
the heat. So I asked the guy, "Which place will be hotter?" He
looked at me like I had a milk mustache and answered, "The
Pacific." "I pick Europe, then," said I.

I'm so excited I can almost understand why you ran off
to join the Army. Life feels new. Not at all like Cissna. Since
tomorrow is Easter, I should have a chance to look around, eat
some cereal, and write you again. I sure wish I could do more
than write to you. Do you hate being a soldier? Do you still hear
bombs all the time? I can't imagine you shooting anything except
a basketball, Genie.

Don't worry about me. How much trouble can one gal get
into in the Cereal Capital of the World?

Love,

Lt. Gypsy

6

Helen

Helen tried not to gawk like the country girl who still stumbled inside her, but she'd never seen anything like Percy Jones Hospital. Fourteen stories in magnificent stone stretched high above the surrounding land. The base of the hospital complex looked like the entrance to a Grecian palace, with columns supporting the entire face of the building. Those columns, lit up like a fairy-tale castle, had been the first thing she'd seen when she finally caught a car to Battle Creek from the station.

"Keep up, Nurse," Captain Walker called over her shoulder. "This isn't a tour of the countryside."

"Sorry." Helen trotted to catch up with the long-legged Captain Walker. Helen figured the stately nurse was in her forties, single by choice, Army by career. She strutted like a soldier—shoulders back,

49

chin up—and she dressed like a soldier: plain khakis, but a skirt instead of pants. Helen liked the brown-striped seersucker they'd been given at training. It was the only thing she did like about boot camp.

"I'm sure you're aware," Walker was saying, "that the hospital specializes in neurosurgery, plastic surgery for the burn victims of war, and artificial limbs."

"At Evanston Hospital, we—"

"I'm not interested in where you worked or went to school. An Army nurse receives her training from the Army. We were a fifteen-hundred-bed hospital when the war began, but we're ramping up to receive five times that many patients."

"That's amazing." Helen felt the sting of rebuke. She hadn't been trying to show off her education or her experience. In fact, she wanted to warn Captain Walker how little experience she had in their specialties.

They walked in silence for so long Helen thought she should say something so Walker wouldn't think she was upset. "Don't you think the whole place still smells a little like cereal? Or is that my imagination?"

Walker didn't bother responding, and Helen wondered if the woman was following an Army script with no room for comment.

"You'll have to get into town to buy your uniforms," Walker said as they passed a group of gals with outfits like hers, minus the bars.

"I have this uniform already, and it's pretty swell for most climates." Helen had a grand total of twenty-six dollars in her savings, and she sure didn't want to blow it on uniforms, especially if they looked like Captain Walker's. "Do I really have to buy another one? Not the shoes, surely." Walker's shoes were hideous brown things that must have weighed five pounds each. Was that what she'd have to wear? And—insult to injury—pay for herself?

Without comment, Walker halted at the column entrance to the L-shaped complex. Etched in stone above the columns were the words *Percy Jones Army Hospital.* Helen got chills reading it. She knew this was just a stopping point for her, a step in her new adventure. During basic, she'd had plenty of regrets about signing up. She'd even wished herself back in Evanston moving rich women's legs on the side of the bed, instead of moving her own legs up a muddy hill. Still, the realization that she was now part of this hospital knocked her socks off.

"This, of course, is where you'll work. Your ward is the fourth floor." Captain Walker turned toward a much younger gal who was jogging toward them. She sported the same drab uniform as Walker, and her hair, like Walker's, barely poked out from under the cap. "What is it, Lieutenant?" Walker demanded.

The lieutenant muttered something too low for Helen to overhear.

"Tell them I'll be right there." Walker turned back to Helen, and the lieutenant jogged off without so much as an eyelash flicker her way. "I'm afraid you'll have to go on without me, Nurse Eberhart." She glanced around, then hollered to a man in soldier khakis, "You! Ward boy!"

The man came running. "Captain?" Up close, Helen could see his medical arm patch. Tall and lean, he towered over the captain.

"Show this new nurse to her ward," Walker commanded. "Fourth, starting today."

"Today?" Helen couldn't keep the panic out of her voice. She hadn't met her head nurse or duty nurse. She wasn't sure which wards were on fourth. She hadn't even unpacked. "It's Easter," she said weakly. "I thought . . . I mean, we passed a chapel."

Captain Walker frowned. "Do you think the enemy stops fighting because it's a holiday?"

"Of course not. But—"

Walker cut her off. "You're allowed a thirty-minute break. If you choose to take it at chapel, that's your choice. But tell the ward boy so he can cover for you. Now, I have to go." She rushed off before Helen had a chance to ask her any more questions.

Hopefully the head nurse on four would be more understanding, or at least human.

"This way, Nurse." The ward boy led her inside the hospital lobby.

She stopped at the bottom of the wide staircase and stuck out her hand. A few soldiers and nurses strode around them without paying attention. "I'm Helen Eberhart."

He shook her hand. "Bill Chitwood. We better get. I think the nurse you're replacing took off for Fort Custer."

Helen tried to keep up with him as his long legs took the first flight of stairs two at a time. "They must be shorthanded on four, huh?" Maybe that explained why she had to start working on Easter Sunday. In Evanston, it got awfully wild when they worked the floor a nurse short.

"We're shorthanded, all right."

By the third flight, she'd fallen twenty steps behind. She plodded the rest of the way to the landing, where Chitwood waited, leaning against giant wooden doors.

Helen struggled to catch her breath. "Say, do you know the duty officer and head nurse on my ward?" She flashed him a smile and whispered, "Are they good eggs?"

Chitwood broke into a laugh that echoed in the stairwell. "You'd know that one better than me, I reckon. Today, you're duty officer *and* head nurse on four." He swept an arm toward the double doors. "It's all yours." Grinning, he took off down the steps.

All mine? Helen didn't know whether to laugh at the guy or not. She wished she hadn't been so mousy around him. He was probably teasing. They wouldn't make *her* duty officer, not on her first day. And not head nurse ever, not here.

Taking a deep breath tinged with ammonia, a familiar hospital smell, and something unfamiliar and rancid, she took hold of the long, metal door handles. With a quick prayer and one swift motion, she yanked open the doors and stepped in.

It was a long room filled with rows and rows of white-sheeted beds shoved side by side. At first glance, she saw that most of the boys were in traction, an arm or leg bandaged, suspended from planks and ropes, like puppets with nobody to pull the strings.

Only that wasn't the worst. Every single patient had parts missing—an arm, a leg, two legs. The nearest bed had a boy who couldn't have been as old as her youngest brother. Both of his legs were missing, leaving two white stumps rounded at the knees. In the next bed, an armless mummy lay on his pillow, his face wrapped tight, except for one eye peeking out of the darkness.

It was a room of incomplete bodies, unnatural losses made common by war.

Helen realized she was still holding the doors open, her arms stiff against the heavy wood. Her head felt light, and her eyes blurred, making the beds spiral like sheets waving from the line on a Cissna Park washday. Without thinking, she backed up, letting the doors slam shut in her face, blocking out the images of those poor, poor boys.

She turned and ran down the hall with no idea where she was going. When she saw a door marked *Men's*, she dashed in. The tiny tiled room—two urinals and a sink—was deserted. Her head swam, and she thought she might faint, although she'd never fainted and wasn't sure what a faint felt like. She braced herself, stiff-armed above the sink, her body shaking.

Then came the tears. They pushed up from her chest, burned through her throat, and came out in sobs that racked her body. She gasped for breath, for balance, for anything that would help.

The door opened. She didn't care. She kept crying and heard the door close again. Then she looked up at the mirror. She almost didn't recognize herself, tear-drenched, helpless, and pitiful. When was the last time she'd cried? She hadn't shed a tear when her mother lay in the garden, bleeding from a ruptured vein. She hadn't cried when she broke her arm playing basketball with Eugene the summer after eighth grade. Not even when her first true love broke her heart in high school. And she hadn't cried when her brothers went off to war.

Tears weren't going to help now. They certainly wouldn't do those amputees back there any good. "Helen Marie Eberhart, registered nurse, lieutenant in the United States Army, Gypsy, pull yourself together!"

She splashed cold water on her face, straightened her uniform, and inspected herself in the mirror. "That'll have to do."

She turned and pulled open the door, just as a tall, dark soldier pushed in.

"Sorry," he said, checking the door. He grinned, then tapped the *Men's* sign.

"That's quite all right," she managed, as if she were only too glad to share the facilities. "Be my guest." She strode away fast, hoping he hadn't gotten a good look at her because if she hadn't been mistaken, there was a doctor's insignia on that broad shoulder. All she needed was to have a run-in with a doctor already.

At the end of the hall, she took a breath, then pulled open the wooden doors.

"Hey! She's back!" somebody called. "We didn't dream her!"

Helen glanced around the ward and saw three ward boys but no other nurse. Summoning her best and broadest smile, she said, "Well, of course I'm back." The ward grew quiet, the laughs and murmurs settling to the bottom. She raised her voice, wanting the whole ward to hear her. "I'm Nurse Eberhart, and I'm awfully pleased to meet you!"

"Well, *we're* pleased to meet *you*!" shouted one patient.

The ward exploded in wolf whistles, and she laughed. If wolf-whistling from a hospital bed helped these boys feel better, she was all for it. She gazed at them, one by one, not looking away. Their faces were beautiful when they smiled like this, and an inexplicable love took root inside of her, as if they were all her little brothers.

The whistles were so loud that she didn't hear the ward doors until they slammed shut. Helen turned to see Captain Walker storm in like a fire-breathing dragon. "Stop that noise this instant!"

Patients stopped as suddenly as if they'd run out of air at the same time.

"There will be no more of that behavior in this hospital!" Walker turned her fury on Helen. "What do you think you're doing, Nurse? Is this what they taught you in that fancy hospital in Evanston? It's a wonder you ever graduated from Northwestern."

So Nurse Walker knew where she'd done her training after all. "No, Captain," Helen said sweetly. "They didn't teach us about whistles."

A gurgle of laughter flowed through the ward, then stopped when the captain gave them her evil glare. "You are still soldiers, and our goal is to make you useful again in the service of your country. You will behave like soldiers." She raised her finger and shook it, as if scolding children. "And that means no, no, *no* wolf whistles!"

Helen raised her hand. "Excuse me, Captain?"

Walker frowned at her. "Nurse?"

"If these men are to behave as soldiers, my experience with soldiers is that they do employ wolf whistles."

"What?"

"Sailors, too."

"That has been your experience, has it?"

Helen nodded.

Captain Walker's face reddened. "Well, then, you are on your own, Nurse. Don't come running to me for help." She sputtered, as if trying to jump-start another tirade but unable to get it going. Then she stormed out the way she'd come in.

The second the doors closed, an odd shuffling noise broke out across the ward, a dulled slap from some corners, a thumping from others.

Helen realized it was the sound of amputees clapping.

7

FRANK

Battle Creek, Michigan

"Daley! Where've you been?" Anderson stormed up the walkway like he was escaping enemy fire. "This Easter church thing was your idea, in case you forgot."

Behind Andy, Lartz and two doctors from Iowa strolled up. Over the loudspeakers came a scratchy recording of some hymn Frank knew but couldn't name. He glanced at his watch. He'd lost track of time waiting on the hospital steps for that nurse to come off fourth. He had to see her again.

He trotted down the steps to the little pack of lieutenants, fell in with fellow stragglers, and tried not to let on he'd been struck by lightning. He hadn't gotten a great look at that nurse as she burst out of the men's room, her face blotched with tears, but what he had seen was pretty incredible. "Anderson, you owe me."

"Are you still talking about that ten bucks of yours I lost in five-card on the train?" Andy gambled—and lost—entirely too much. Frank would use his friend as a cautionary tale and make sure that when *he* became a rich young doctor, he wouldn't gamble away his money.

"Glad that hasn't slipped your mind completely," Frank said. "But I was referring to the debt you owe me since, for the first time in our colorful history together, you're not the one keeping everybody waiting." He got the seconding laughs he so richly deserved.

"You're complaining about me showing up late on occasion?" Anderson joked. "How very Army of you, old man. I think we all know why we joined 'this man's Army'—good-looking nurses."

"Does Alice know that's why you joined?" Frank asked.

Andy ignored him. "A fresh crop of the gals in white have been trickling in since yesterday, men. Dozens of gorgeous possibilities. Before the day is out, I intend—"

"Do you guys want to shut up?" Lartz broke in. They were at the door of the chapel, which was packed with soldiers.

Anderson turned on Lartz. "What's it to you? Aren't you Jewish or something?"

"Something," Lartz muttered. "Which is more than I can say for you."

Frank thought Lartz's mother was Jewish and his father Catholic, but they never talked about religion. Almost overnight, he and Lartz had become friends in residency, although they had little in common. Frank grew up in a small town, and Lartz had only lived in cities. Frank was half a foot taller than Lartz. Lartz claimed he'd been going bald since high school, while Frank had enough hair on his head for a dozen soldiers. Lartz weighed fifty pounds less than Frank, but in a fight, Frank would have picked the wiry New Yorker over any guy in the unit, including Anderson.

Inside the chapel every folding chair had a soldier in it. Every inch of floor space had someone sitting on it. Soldiers leaned against the wall all the way around the room and out the door.

"Standing room only," whispered Larabee, one of the Iowa doctors. "Must be a war on."

His buddy chuckled. "Take no chances. Hey—is it a bigger sin not to go to church on Easter or to show up late?"

"Will you guys pipe down?" Lartz whispered. "I want to hear what's left of the sermon."

They weren't the only latecomers. A pack of soldiers and a few nurses clustered behind them. Frank heard the sermon in stereo, from inside and from speakers overhead. He thought about the little church back in Hamilton, where he and his siblings had never missed a Sunday. Then he hit college, where, if he didn't sleep in on Sunday, he had more enticing options than church available. Dotty kept telling him he needed to make God a bigger part of his life, especially now. Judging by the crowd this morning, the thought wasn't unique.

"Incoming at eight o'clock." Anderson nudged Frank and nodded behind them, where three nurses were weaving through the crowd, edging in closer.

Frank stopped breathing. That wavy blonde hair, that adorable figure. And those eyes. He had never seen eyes that blue. There had never been eyes that blue. It was his girl from the men's room.

"Hubba hubba." When Anderson didn't get a response, he frowned. "Daley, are you all right, sport?"

Frank stared at her, willing her to turn his way. "That's her."

"Who?"

Her gorgeous eyes were trained on the preacher, as intent as if he were speaking directly to her.

Anderson wouldn't leave him alone. "Hey, do you know that nurse?"

"Not yet," Frank said. "But I will."

The minute the service ended, Frank shoved his way to the mystery nurse. Anderson and the others followed, laughing. When Frank stopped in front of the nurse, the others flanked him, effectively blocking her path.

She raised her eyebrows at them, and her eyes twinkled. That's the word that sprang to Frank's mind, even though he'd never said or thought such a worn-out expression. Yet what other word conveyed the sparkles of silver in the blue ocean of her iris, against the pure white of her sclera?

"Um . . . excuse me, boys." Her voice sparkled too, soft, musical, and sweet.

Frank felt somebody shove him forward. "We . . . I . . ." He couldn't remember the last time he'd had trouble with words. Words were his ace in the hole, his best weapon. He tried again. "I wanted to welcome you to Battle Creek."

"Did you?" Her eyes did all the smiling anybody would ever need.

"And," he added, "to offer my services to ensure you have a delightful time while you're here."

Anderson horned in. "We could start with a tour of the grounds? The dining hall? The men's quarters?"

Frank watched the twinkle extinguish from her eyes. But a second later, she smiled at them, so maybe he'd imagined it.

"Awfully kind of you boys." She checked her watch. "But I'm on duty, and I have to get back."

"You pulled duty on Easter, and you just got here?" Lartz commented. "Sounds like something Captain Walker would do to one of her new nurses."

The group still encircled her. She took a step forward, but it was as far as she could go. "Excuse me?"

The crowd thinned around them, but Anderson and the Iowa doctors closed in on the nurse. "Not until you tell us who you are," Anderson said. At six foot two, he towered over her by a foot. Frank felt like slugging him. The letch. He'd already dated half the nurses here, and he had sweet Alice, his wife, at home in Massachusetts.

She gave Anderson a look a teacher might give a wayward child. "All right." She paused, as if the name were new to her and she had to get it right. "Lieutenant Eberhart."

"And I am Lieutenant John Anderson." He clicked his heels and bowed curtly.

"That's swell. *Now* may I get back to the ward so the Army won't fire me on my first day?"

Frank couldn't let her go, not with Anderson the last thing on her mind. He stepped between them.

She sighed and cocked her head to the side, making her hair bounce on her shoulders. "I suppose *you* want an introduction too?"

Frank grinned. "No. We've already met."

Her eyes narrowed as she looked him over. "I don't think so."

"You've forgotten already?" He feigned a hurt look. "Fourth floor, main hospital. We were both in a rush—me to get in, you to get out. I was reading signs; you weren't."

He watched her gorgeous face redden as the realization sank in. "Don't tell me—"

Frank couldn't help laughing. "Listen, I'll share anything with you at any time."

She started pushing her way through the line of soldier doctors. "I really do have to go." Flustered, glancing back at Frank, she added, "Go to the ward, I mean."

He laughed. "Need an escort? In case you get the wrong door?"

She kept running toward the hospital, passing soldiers who turned their heads for a better look. Frank couldn't blame them, although he did. He wanted to yell for them to back off. She was taken. He watched until he couldn't see her any longer.

"What was that about?" Lartz asked.

Without taking his gaze from the last spot he'd seen Lieutenant Eberhart, Frank confided, "I've just met the gal of my dreams."

Helen

8

Battle Creek, Michigan

Helen hoped she'd never see that doctor again. How had he recognized her? Of all the places to meet!

She raced up the hospital steps, glancing back to make sure nobody had followed her. Her cheeks still stung with mortification. She couldn't deny that he was as cute as they came—tall, big brown eyes, and thick, curly black hair that even the Army ought to have sense enough not to cut. Still, she would die if she ever ran into him again. If you asked her, they were all pretty full of themselves, those doctor soldiers. She had enough on her plate at Percy Jones without *that*.

Helen pushed through the doors of the fourth ward and was met by *heys* and *howdys*, along with a few whistles. The ward already felt like home in a way.

"Next time, I want all of you to go to church with me!" She

63

unpinned her cap and set it on the rack. She hated hats. They were regulation, and Captain Walker would probably have her head, hatless or not, if she caught her without that cap, but that was just too bad.

Helen conferred with her three ward boys. Bill Chitwood made an appearance and assured her that there would be more nurses on the floor tomorrow. They went through charts, checked IVs, and administered medications. The biggest job would be changing bandages every day and dressing the wounds.

She walked around the ward and introduced herself to each patient. She tried to remember their names. When she worked her way back to the front, she stopped at the bed of the man, or boy, whose head was wrapped, except for a slit at his mouth and another allowing one black eye to peer out. "Hey, soldier." She picked up his chart, studied it, then took his vital signs. "I'm Lieutenant Eberhart, but you can call me Nurse." She waited for him to introduce himself, the way the others had.

He didn't respond, so she double-checked his name on the chart. "You must be Hudy. Sounds like a good Texas name, right? Hudy Bolin. I don't think I've had the pleasure of meeting a Hudy before." She kept up the chatter while she recorded his vitals and increased the IV rate. "Bet you celebrated Easter with kinfolk in Texas. In Cissna Park, Illinois, where I'm from, we'd all go to church in the morning. Then in the afternoon, we had a giant egg hunt, which was funny now that I think about it, because most of us hunted eggs in the chicken coop every day."

His left arm was bandaged up to his neck. His right arm was gone.

"I'll bet you're thirsty, Private. This IV is supposed to take care of that, but it's not the same as feeling the water pass over your tongue and down your throat, is it?"

He didn't nod or shake his head or give any sign that he'd heard her. She wondered if he'd lost his hearing in whatever explosion must have caught him. There was something about his eye, too—the black dot that stared out from the cocoon of bandages. The pupil lay like an embedded marble in his skull. She peered into it, and he didn't flinch. She waved her hand in front of his face. He didn't blink. There was nothing on the chart, but she thought he was blind.

"Hudy, promise you won't rat me out to my boss," she said, as if conspiring with him, "but I'm going to sneak you a sip of water. Be right back." She dashed to the nurse's desk, poured a glass of lukewarm water from a clear pitcher, then searched drawers until she found a straw.

"Okay, Hudy. I'm going to stick the straw through this slit." His lips were swollen and disfigured. "Just one tiny sip until we see if it goes down all right."

Hudy took a sip, then leaned back against his pillow. "Thank you, ma'am. That there's about the best drink I ever had."

So he could talk, and hear. And she'd been right about Texas, or at least close. Even hoarse, he sounded like a cowboy. "There's more where that came from, but we better wait a little while, okay?"

Helen moved to the next bed, where a boy she guessed to be about eighteen struggled to sit up. His wide grin showed straight, white teeth. With his boyish looks, he'd probably had his share of high school sweethearts. From the waist up, he looked normal, handsome. An Army blanket covered him from the waist down, resting smooth and flat where it should have been raised by legs. "You're Danny, right?"

Danny gave her a huge smile. "Say, that was all right, what you did for Hudy." He lowered his voice. "He hasn't talked to nobody except Jimmy and me since we got here."

She took his wrist and read his pulse. "Were you in the same unit?"

"Jimmy, Hudy, and me, we were with a fleet headed to the Russell Islands, north of Guadalcanal. The Japs had retreated, and we were just supposed to shore up defenses. Jimmy and me knew each other from base, and we got to know Hudy on board. None of us had seen action—had to wait until we turned eighteen to sign up. Anyways, we got excited when we saw the beach ahead. We were first in line to disembark. Hudy started up with this whooping and hollering, and Jimmy and me, we laughed so hard we almost fell off the plank."

Danny stared down at his hands. "I don't know which one of us set foot on land first. The next thing I knew, there was a boom, and I was flying through the air, with blood spraying around me. I landed hard on my back. I remember smelling smoke and seeing sand and flames. Hudy was on fire. All three of us took that first step on the beach and that was it. The Japs had planted mines before they took off."

Helen didn't know what to say. "I'm sorry, Danny."

"Yeah. Guess I had about the shortest military career in history." He glanced over at Hudy, who hadn't moved since she'd left his bedside. "Things could be worse."

"Not here they can't," she said. "Not if I can help it."

Helen worked through dinner and well into the night, even after another nurse came on for the night shift. Finally she trudged down the four flights and into the cool darkness outside. She breathed in fresh air. No cereal smell this time.

"Hi there, Lieutenant Eberhart."

Startled, Helen turned to see a soldier stand up from the bottom step.

"I was beginning to wonder if you'd fallen asleep in there."

It took a second to recognize him—the doctor from the men's room. "You! What are you doing here?"

"Waiting to walk you home, since you didn't come down for dinner." He was even more handsome than she'd thought, or maybe it was the dark. In the starlight, though, she clearly made out two dimples and a boyish grin that made her grin back, until she caught herself.

She was too tired for this. "Tell me you haven't been waiting here all night." She glanced around for the others from chapel. But he was alone.

"I haven't been waiting *all* night." He squinted at his watch. "We have forty-five minutes until midnight. Plenty of time for a stroll."

"Not for me, thanks." She started toward the nurses' quarters. He fell in beside her. "I'm dead on my feet," she said, wondering if her legs had ever ached this much. "I'll be lucky to make it back to my quarters without collapsing."

"Then I better accompany you. Can't have a new nurse collapsing on the old sanitarium grounds. What would people think?"

She laughed. She couldn't help herself. "Fine. But don't expect witty conversation because I'm too beat to talk."

"Understood." He walked, not saying another word, his hands clasped behind his back, until they reached her quarters. Then he took off his hat and made a bow.

She managed a smile and turned to go, when she realized she still didn't know who he was. She turned back and found him standing there, watching her. "Say, I don't even know your name, Dr. Soldier."

"Frank. Frank Daley, at your service. Good night, Lieutenant Eberhart."

9

FRANK

For the next five days, Frank was waiting outside the nurses' quarters each morning when Helen walked out, and on the hospital steps every night. Frank had never shirked hospital duties as Anderson did, but he'd managed to glide through with as little work as possible. All this nurse did was work, and yet she fascinated him more than any girl he'd ever met.

On Day Six A. H., "After Helen," Frank's alarm went off and he rolled out of his bunk. Most of the forty-eight men in their barracks had fought over bottom bunks, but he liked the top. At least nobody would come crashing down on him in the middle of the night. He tried to be quiet climbing down, but Anderson's bunk below him creaked when he stepped on it.

Anderson groaned. "Give it up, Daley. Take a hint, sport. If she hasn't come around by now, she's not going to."

"Ah, but you don't understand true love, Anderson."

Andy groaned again and rolled over.

Frank raced through the crisp, cool morning, still black as night. The stars, brighter than flashlights, lit his path while the Milky Way swathed the sky in starlight.

The steps were too wet with dew for him to sit on, but he didn't mind standing. He never minded waiting for Helen. It gave him time to think. He wondered if this was how Dotty and Boots had felt when they met under these same stars thousands of miles away.

Fifteen minutes later, he heard soft, pattering footsteps, followed by the click of a door opening. He knew it would be Helen, always the first nurse out.

"Morning!" He strolled up the steps to meet her. She looked incredible in moonlight, like an angel. There was a touch of adorable sleepiness in her eyes, but the rest of her looked as if she'd spent hours making herself gorgeous just for him.

"Lieutenant Daley, good morning."

"Frank, remember?"

"I remember." She glanced up at him, and her eyes narrowed. "You look very serious this morning. Penny for your thoughts."

"That's about all they're worth. I was thinking about marriage."

Helen's eyebrows shot up. "Who's the lucky woman?"

He laughed. "My sister, Dotty. And she does consider herself lucky, even though her husband is probably in a Japanese prison." As they began walking, he filled Helen in on Dotty and Boots.

"Your sister sounds like a remarkable woman." Helen said this in a way that let Frank know she really meant it. "It's certainly not your run-of-the-mill war marriage."

"And we all know where those end up—one more casualty of war."

"I like that," Helen said. "'Relationship casualties of war.' Marriage and war being fraught with equal danger."

They walked without talking for a minute. Frank didn't care. It was being with her that made him wake up ready to take on the world.

"Do you always get up this early?" she asked.

"Never before."

She gave him a tiny laugh. "No early hours on your ward, then?"

"By some elaborate Army design that only makes sense in Washington, I'm the duty officer on the disease ward. I choose my hours."

"Diseases? Was that your specialty in med school?"

"Nope. I did work in the lab of a disease expert. I guess charting test tubes qualifies me as an expert in the eyes of the Army. How about you? How did you end up at Percy Jones?"

They were at the hospital, and she stopped and turned toward him. For a second, he considered grabbing her and kissing her.

"Sorry," she said. "I better go in. Maybe another time?"

Another time? Kiss her another time? Then he realized she was talking about answering his question. "Right. Another time. Don't suppose you're taking a dinner break today."

"Cheese and bread." She patted her bag. "I'll eat on the ward." She trotted up the steps, waving back at him. "Bye!"

He waited for her to turn around—just one more look—but she didn't.

"I'm telling you, Daley, she's giving you the cold shoulder. Nobody in the Army works that hard. She's probably seeing somebody else." Anderson made a face at the beans on his fork, but he stuck them in his mouth all the same.

They were dining in the big mess hall, where long tables covered the floor. Framed pictures of the Kellogg family sneered down at them from cherrywood walls. Frank knew Helen wouldn't show, but he couldn't help watching for her. "You're nuts, Andy. *She* works long hours because she's the real deal, a dedicated nurse. Not what *you* look for in a nurse, but—"

"Right. Like you're any better. What about Nurse Jean? Or those lovely student nurses we lusted after and—?"

"Ancient history. I admit her physical beauty attracted my attention at first. But now I admire her dedication."

"Did you ever ask yourself what she's actually doing on that ward all those long hours? And with whom?"

The clink of dishes made it hard to hear. "What are you saying?"

"I'm saying, don't be a chump. I hate seeing you waiting night and day like a puppy, chasing a nurse you'll never catch."

"What do you know about it?"

"I know there's more going on behind those closed doors than you think. Isn't that New York doctor, Reynolds, on four?"

"So?"

Anderson glanced over at Larabee. "Let's just say that Reynolds considers himself a ladies' man, and the ladies don't disagree. Tell him, Larabee."

Larabee lit a cigarette, then snapped his lighter shut. "I went to school with Reynolds. He dated and kept score. He liked to show us his scorecard."

Frank didn't want to hear this. "You're both crazy. That nurse doesn't leave the ward."

"That's just it, ol' boy," Anderson said in that patronizing way of his. "She's on the ward all that time . . . with Reynolds."

Frank stood up without a word and headed to the mess line, where he dipped his dishes in soapy water, then hot rinse water. Anderson had a complex. The jerk actually believed he knew everything, especially when it came to women.

But once outside, Frank couldn't shake Andy's words. What did go on behind those doors? He'd been so interested in getting Helen to talk about herself that he hadn't asked about her ward. He wanted to know her, not her patients. And certainly not the doctors.

Instead of walking back to his quarters, he decided to stroll over to the hospital, even though Helen wouldn't be coming out for hours. Nodding to a group of giggling nurses, he tried to think what Nurse Eberhart had that they didn't. Soon, his logic melted into dreamy visions of her eyes, her smile, her hair, the way she sprang off each foot when she walked, like her whole cute little body was wound and knew exactly where it needed to go next.

When he got to the hospital, the moon was beginning to rise. Normally, he didn't mind waiting for Helen any more than he'd minded waiting for Christmas morning. His mother used to say, "Anticipation is greater than realization," one of many quotes she used to get her own meaning across. But it didn't apply to Nurse Eberhart; her presence topped his anticipation every time.

Yet tonight, thanks to Andy, Frank couldn't enjoy the wait. Minutes dragged with the viscosity of mud, the speed of quicksand. After thirty minutes on the hospital steps, he couldn't take it. Maybe he'd go inside and wait for her on the landing. Nothing wrong with that.

He took the steps two at a time. The door to Nurse Eberhart's ward hadn't shut all the way, and a crack of light seeped out. Against his better judgment, Frank eased in closer. He heard voices, and when he peeked inside, he saw Helen standing by a bed a few feet away. He slipped back behind the door and flattened himself to the outside wall. He was pretty sure she hadn't seen him.

"Hey ya, gorgeous!"

Frank could hear the soldier-patient clearly enough, although he couldn't see him. He felt guilty eavesdropping, but he wasn't really doing that. He was simply waiting to walk Nurse Eberhart home.

"Hey yourself, good-looking." Frank didn't need to see Helen to recognize her voice. He pictured her smile, the spark in those blue eyes.

"Nurse, have I told you that you have the most beautiful hair I've ever seen?"

"Hmm . . . let me think, Danny. Yes, I believe you have."

Frank fought down his aggravation. *He* should be the one complimenting her beautiful hair. Why hadn't he? He'd thought it often enough.

"You sure are pretty, and that's a fact."

"Thanks, Danny. No prettier than you. Bet you had all the girls banging on your door back home."

"Back off, Danny boy!" somebody else shouted. "I saw her first."

"Heck you did!"

"Play nice, gentlemen," Helen warned.

Frank couldn't blame the patients. Helen Eberhart was probably the most beautiful woman they'd seen in a long time. Maybe ever. He couldn't blame her either. Only, did she have to enjoy their compliments so much?

He heard a soldier call, "Nurse, could I ask y'all a favor?" Frank resumed his stance behind the door, where he could hear what this favor was.

"You bet, Hudy." Helen's steps grew closer, sounding inches from him. "As long as it's not a back rub, like Danny and Jimmy are always asking for. Could I sit here?"

Frank was dying to know where "here" was, but he couldn't risk being seen.

"Okay, Hudy. You know you can ask me anything."

Something changed in her voice, the joking or flirting replaced by a womanly warmth and tenderness. Frank couldn't explain why, but this sudden intimacy pricked a jealousy deep inside of him. He wanted her to speak to him that way.

Hudy took a minute to answer. "See, I got me a letter a couple days ago."

"Well, that's great."

"Only I can't exactly read it myself."

"Here, let me scoot closer."

Come on. This was the oldest trick in the book—Frank had used it, or versions of it, himself.

"I haven't wanted anybody else to read it, but maybe you could read it to me? Danny says it's from my gal back home."

"Mmmm—the envelope smells good. She must be something, that gal of yours."

"Lila's something, all right. She smells like a Texas rose."

In the quiet, Frank heard papers shuffled. "I'd love to read it to you, Hudy. It'll give me a chance to size up my competition."

Frank felt lost, confused. Anderson's thoughts mixed with his own. He felt guilty for listening in on Helen, and on Hudy. He didn't spy on people. If he wanted to talk to Helen, he should go in and talk to her. He stood up straight and yanked the door.

The first bed he saw held a boy with two stumps for legs. Helen perched on the side of the next bed, where a patient lay wrapped in bandages. This was the amputee ward. He should have known that. It wasn't like he'd never been on this floor, though never the ward. He just hadn't paid attention. He stepped out again. Helen couldn't have seen him, although some of the patients might have. Frank lurked outside the door, feeling the weight of the war in a way he hadn't before. He couldn't shake the vision of those boys, kids the age Jack and he had been when they used to box each other for fun or go skinny-dipping in the reservoir. No one in that room would ever be a boy again.

He leaned against the door and heard Helen's clear voice through the crack. "Let's see here. 'Dear Hudy.' I guess that's a good start. 'Dear Hudy, First, I got to say how truly sorry we all were to hear about your injury. Your mama shared her news with the whole church, and everybody prayed you'd get your sight back, and we was real, real sorry. Some women was crying like it was their own sons.'"

Frank had to see. He squatted down where the crack was biggest and at the right angle. Patients on both sides of Hudy seemed to be eavesdropping too.

Helen glanced at her patient, then stared down at the letter, quiet for a minute.

"What is it?" Hudy asked.

"What? Nothing." She cleared her throat. "To tell you the truth, though, this perfume is a little gagging. Definitely not something I'd wear."

"Go on. Please?"

Helen squeezed the bridge of her nose as if adjusting invisible glasses. "Where was I? Oh yes. 'Hudy, I have always considered myself the luckiest girl in the world that you would want to marry me. Every girl in town would trade places with me in a heartbeat. I've been thinking a lot about our plans.'" She coughed, then set the letter on her lap and covered her mouth. Without picking up the letter, she continued: "'The problem is, I don't know if I can handle being married to a real live war hero. That's what you are. And who am I? Nobody. So if you don't hear from me for a while, don't worry. I'm here thinking about you. I guess we'll all have to do some thinking after this war is over. I better go now. You have more important things to do than to hear from the likes of me. You're my hero, and you're too good for me—everybody says so. But I will never forget you. Lila.'"

Frank watched it all. Helen's eyes hadn't moved as she read . . . because she hadn't read. When she lifted her head, tears streamed down her cheeks. Her voice never once betrayed her sadness or her tears. In a cheerful, sweet voice, she said, "Sounds like your whole town will give you a parade when you get home."

"Could I have the letter, please?" Hudy's voice betrayed no emotion either.

Helen placed the letter on his chest, and Hudy put his one bandaged arm on top of it. "I thank you kindly for taking the time."

"My pleasure, Hudy." She swiped her tears with the back of her hand.

"Hey, Nurse!" shouted the patient in the next bed, a good-looking kid in a wheelchair. Frank could tell there were no legs under the Army blanket that covered his lap. "Could you come here a minute, please?"

"Sure, Danny." She pulled Hudy's sheet higher, covering the letter. Then she strode to Danny's bed. He said something to her, and she pushed his wheelchair toward the door. Frank prepared to hide, but they stopped just out of sight, though close enough to hear the wheels squeak.

Danny lowered his voice. "Nurse Eberhart, what you read to Hudy—that wasn't the letter *I* read."

Helen was quiet for several seconds. Then she said, "Maybe it should have been."

When Helen came off the ward, later than usual, Frank was waiting for her. She gave him a sad smile, then turned away. He followed her lead and didn't say a word as he fell in with her. Together, they descended the four flights, crossed the lobby, and went outside. Silently, he walked beside her to the nurses' quarters, thinking that if what he'd felt for Helen Eberhart before tonight was lust, this must be love.

~❦~

From: Eugene Eberhart,
Somewhere "over there" in Europe
May 10, 1944

Dear Gypsy Nurse,
    When is this thing going to end? Don't tell Dad, but I'd give anything to hear him yell at me, instead of listening to my sergeant take his frustrations out on me every day.
    War is loud. Even when guns and bombers take time out to reload, they're still exploding in my head. If by some accident I fall asleep at night, I dream loud and wake myself up. Not just myself.
    I have a lot of buddies. Dan and George are from Illinois— Dan from Danville, George from Rantoul. Good guys. And they're brave. I don't know how they do it, Gypsy. George's brother was killed in battle last year, and Dan's been wounded

twice. But they're the first ones to run onto a muddy, bloody field. They don't shake the way I do when things are over. I've started smoking. If you end up here, bring cigarettes!

I want to tell you not to worry about me, but somebody should.

I have to go. But I'll mail this anyways.

Eugene

Helen

Battle Creek, Michigan

"Gott im Himmel," Helen muttered as she stepped outside the barracks and started down the steps.

As usual, Frank Daley was waiting for her. Her days started and ended with him, and she found herself anticipating his dimpled grin. But the grin dissolved quickly. "Did I just hear you speaking German? Not a great idea these days."

"You heard that?" Embarrassed, she thought about denying it, then changed her mind. "*'Gott im Himmel.'* That's what my parents have always said. Pretty sure Dad uses it as a swearword. But with my mother, it's always a prayer to a God she needs and believes in."

"And what about you? Swearing or praying?"

"Praying. I believe in my mother's God, all right." She sighed.

He swung in front of her and walked backward to peer into her face. "Are you okay, Nurse?"

"Why? Don't I look okay?" She forced a weak laugh.

"You always look okay. More than okay. I just thought . . . maybe you'd gotten some bad news. Are your brothers all right?" Frank moved back beside her and slid her arm though the crook of his.

She told herself it was his companionship she enjoyed, but she couldn't deny the rush of schoolgirl jitters when his hand brushed hers or she bumped against him. She knew he was waiting for an answer. "It's Eugene," she said at last.

He stopped walking. "Did something happen—?"

"No." She tugged him back into a walk. "Although how would I know? I hate thinking of him on a battlefield or in a trench in the middle of nowhere. He's never made friends that easily. I keep picturing him so frightened he can't move, can't shoot, can't do anything except get shot at. And I can't do a thing about it!" There. She'd said it. *Why* had she said it? Eugene would be hurt if he knew she'd confided her fears, *his* fears, to this almost-stranger. Eberharts were private people. What was wrong with her? In the space of a few minutes, she'd dumped her thoughts about God and her fears about her brother right into this man's lap. Helen wanted to run back to the barracks and hide. She couldn't look at Frank. She withdrew her arm, pretending she needed it to shove her hair behind her ears. "Sorry about that. Guess I need more sleep, huh? Forget I said anything."

"I don't know how you do it," Frank said, his voice soft as velvet.

"Do what?" She risked a glance up at him and saw pain in the lines of his face.

"I have one brother and one sister, and I do worry about them. But they're both tougher and braver than I'll ever be. You have five brothers in active duty. You'd have to be crazy *not* to worry." He scratched his head. "You know, I think I'd like Eugene best. He and I have the most in common." They'd arrived at Helen's ward. Frank touched her shoulder and smiled at her. "See you tonight, Helen."

Helen watched him walk away. She could still feel his gentle hand on her shoulder.

That night, they took the long route to Helen's barracks. She'd been afraid things would be different between them, awkward. But Frank greeted her with the same broad grin. "Clear sky tonight. The stars are waiting for us." He was relentless in his pursuit to point out constellations she'd never noticed before.

"Says you," she teased. So far, she'd made out the Big Dipper, kind of. Probably. He took her hand. Or maybe she took his. "All I can say is it's a good thing I went into nursing rather than astronomy."

Frank's arm shot up. "There! See it? The Dog Star, Sirius."

Helen stared through thousands of stars lining the Milky Way, but she couldn't see anything that remotely resembled a dog. "Sorry. I still can't make it out."

He took her face in his hands, tilted her head up. "See it now?"

Helen's heart sped up, making her shiver. His hands were rough—in a good, honest, and earthy way—but his touch was gentle. She was having trouble seeing anything except the silhouette of his face against the moon. "It's no use."

His fingers, firm at her jawline, guided her head. "Look for the brightest star in the sky. That's the Dog Star. Those two stars above it are the shoulder and the eye of the Big Dog constellation."

Helen could barely breathe, much less see what he wanted her to see. She wondered if his fingers, searing her skin, might leave marks people would ask about.

Still, his grip stayed gentle on her face. "Over there's the nose. Below, you can make out two front paws." He removed his hand from her face to point to the sky, and she felt the loss of his touch like a splash of cold to her cheek. The night smelled like wet leaves and fire. "Back there," he said, pointing, "that's a back leg, and two stars for the tail. Pretty soon, we'll get the Little Dog too . . . if we're still here." He grew still as the night, the only sound the whip of a flag battling the wind. He slid his arm around her shoulders.

She liked the way his arm felt, secure and comforting, without force or demands. "What do you mean, if we're still here?"

"First thing I do every morning is check the assignment boards. We all do—even Anderson, who claims he doesn't care when he goes."

"We do it too." Helen leaned into him as they strayed off the path. She felt the chill of the night. "Nurses crowd around that board like they did in Evanston. The stakes are a lot higher now. Did you put in for the Pacific or the European theater? Or is that top secret?"

He laughed, a lovely, genuine laugh. "The Pacific. I love the heat. When I get out of this, I'm thinking about starting a practice in Miami, or maybe California, somewhere I can play tennis every day without shoveling snow off the courts." He looked down at her. "How about you? Pacific or European?"

"I can't stand the heat, so I asked for Europe."

"Ah." He sounded disappointed. Was he? Was *she*?

"When do you think they'll send your unit over?" She wasn't making conversation. She cared about this answer—more than she wanted to. The last thing she needed was to get caught up with a carefree doctor who only wanted to practice medicine so he could play tennis and lie on beaches.

"Your guess is as good as mine. The whole Army thing is hurry up and wait. They don't really need me here, now that the disease unit's up and running. Those patients are going to be there a long time, but most of them are ambulatory and noncrisis." They'd reached her quarters, but neither of them made a move to leave. "Before you got here, Helen, I felt like I was ready to go overseas and get on with it. Get it over with and come back for my real life."

The words *before you got here* played in her head. "And now?"

He moved in front of her and put his hands on her shoulders. She felt caught up in his dark, bottomless eyes. She was sinking, drowning. Panic gripped her, stealing her breath. She did not want to feel like this—not now, not here. Not ever.

She backed away and glanced down at the sidewalk, where tufts of grass between cracks looked like fingers trying to get out of the concrete. "Thanks for the walk. And the stars. The constellations. Tomorrow's visiting day. I have to get there early. I better go in." She was talking too fast, but she couldn't help it. She bolted for the barracks and stumbled over his boot. He caught her elbow, preventing her from crashing. "Thanks," she muttered. "'Night."

The next morning, in spite of herself, Helen felt an excitement as she brushed her hair and pulled on her cap. She hadn't slept much, so she should have been dragging.

"What's with you?" asked Peggy O'Hare, one of the nurses from New York who'd arrived the same day as Helen. None of the nurses had much time to get to know one another, but Peggy seemed like a good gal. She had curly red hair, and Helen would bet she had the temper to go with it.

"What do you mean?" Helen tugged her uniform straight.

Peggy stared at Helen's reflection in her tiny mirror propped against her bedroll. "You're ready an hour early, and you've been humming for the last thirty minutes."

"I have? Gee, I'm sorry. I didn't realize—"

"Exactly. You're humming without realizing it. And you're . . . okay, don't tell anyone I used the word . . . glowing."

Helen felt her cheeks flush. "I am not! It's just hot in here."

"Right. And this has nothing to do with that extremely handsome lieutenant who walks you home every night." Peggy yanked out a curler from her chin-short bob and yawned. "Kiddo, if I had *that* waiting for me, I'd be up hours early too."

"He is pretty swell, isn't he?"

Frank was waiting when she stepped into the surprisingly muggy morning. His back was turned, and for a second she stopped and took in the sight of him, his broad shoulders and lean build, his slightly crooked hat. When he turned around, his smile pierced her heart. Corny, but that's how it felt.

"Helen!" He waved as if they hadn't seen each other in years, rather than hours.

"You're up early." She fell in beside him and looped her arm through his. "You could have slept in, I'll bet."

"Everybody else in my barracks is snoring so loud, I don't think I could have slept if I'd wanted to." He grinned down at her. "And I didn't want to." They walked a few paces. "Saturdays are the worst on the disease ward. Patients know the other wards get visitors. Do you have families coming in?"

Helen nodded. "Quite a few. We'll need to get the boys all spiffied up. For some of them, this will be the first time they've seen their families since they left for the war."

"And the first time their families have seen them," Frank added. "That can't be easy on anybody."

"I think it will really help some of the patients. Once they get their prostheses and get going on rehab, they can pick it up at home. So their families are important to recovery."

"Any chance you can get off at noon?" He glanced at the murky sky. "Lartz says it's supposed to clear. I thought we could go on a picnic."

Helen smiled. "You and Lartz?"

He laughed. "Right. Lartz was my first choice. But since he's already got a picnic date, I thought of you. What do you say?"

She sighed. "I'd love a picnic, even if I am your second choice. I just don't know if I can get off. Or if the visitors will be gone by then. You should probably go ahead without me."

"Are you kidding? There's no picnic for me without you, Nurse. And with you, it's always a picnic."

"You, sir, don't know me very well."

"I'm working on it."

He walked her up the four flights, and they said good-bye at the door to her ward.

The second she walked in, Helen saw chaos. Half a dozen ward boys struggled to get patients dressed or bathed or into wheelchairs. Bill Chitwood shouted orders.

Ramona, the night nurse, came shuffling up. "Thank heavens you're here!"

"Rough night?"

Ramona was already putting on her sweater. "I've got to get out of here. You mind? I don't know which patients are worse—the ones getting visitors or the ones not getting visitors." She grabbed her pack. "Good luck. You're going to need it."

"She's here! Nurse! Lieutenant Eberhart! Over here!" Jimmy motioned with his head, the best he could do with no arms. He occupied one of the older wheelchairs. Its seat needed re-caning, and the wooden arms tilted out as if ready to applaud.

"Hi, Jimmy!" she called. "You're looking good, guy." His uniform was too big. She wanted to pin up the sleeves so they wouldn't flap like deflated wings. But somebody had slicked back his hair and tucked in his shirt.

Danny sat on the edge of his bed, using his forearms to balance his stump legs. "Can you get them to hurry up with my wheelchair?"

"I'll see what I can do." She took off toward the nurses' station.

"And Hudy wants one too!" Danny called.

Helen glanced back at Hudy, still wrapped like a mummy. She'd figured out how to position the bandages so he could move in bed. Yesterday he'd sat up for a half hour, although she knew it must have been painful. She couldn't imagine getting his burned body into a wheelchair, but she wasn't about to hold him back. "Hudy? Is Danny right? You want to get up in the chair?"

"I reckon," Hudy answered.

"You got it." She flagged down Bill Chitwood. It hadn't taken her long to learn that he was her go-to guy. She didn't ask where he got the things she needed, and he didn't offer. "Bill, Hudy needs a wheelchair, and so does Danny. Can you round up two more?"

Bill didn't blink. "Comin' right up." He took off for parts unknown.

Helen dashed to the nurses' station and checked charts, making sure the meds had been given. She'd see that Hudy got his morphine right before visiting hours, although she wasn't sure if he'd be getting any visitors.

Four extra duty nurses floated on the floor now, but they could have used twice that many. The stench of sweat, rubbing alcohol, and uneaten hot cereal permeated every aisle in the ward. Helen kept trying to work her way back to Danny and Hudy, but she got roped into changing bandages on a sergeant who wouldn't let anyone else dress his wounds. After that, two patients needed help with their prostheses, which they wanted to be in perfect working order for showing off to their wives, who were traveling in together from Minnesota.

By the time she got back to Danny, he was doing wheelies in his wheelchair, making Jimmy laugh so hard that one of the nurses kept shushing him. Hudy's chair was parked beside the bed, but Hudy was exactly where she'd left him, lying in bed. How on earth would she manage getting him into a chair?

She grabbed the clipboard on her way over and glanced down the list of visitors. Danny's parents were near the top of the list, which meant they'd registered the first chance they got. Everybody had to go through proper channels or they weren't even allowed in the building. She scanned the visitor list twice but didn't see sign-ups for Jimmy or Hudy. Poor Hudy didn't need to put himself through the agony of getting into that chair when he didn't even have a visitor.

Helen returned the clipboard and strode over to the boys.

"That's her, ain't it?" Hudy said. "I can tell those footsteps anywheres."

"You're something, Hudy," Danny said, wheeling his chair next to Jimmy's.

Jimmy had one of his bandaged feet draped over Hudy's chair, as if somebody might steal it. "You better get a couple of them boys to help you haul Hudy into his chair, ma'am."

Helen studied Hudy and tried to read his thoughts in that one glassy eye. "Hudy, are you sure you want to go through with this?"

"I'm sure."

"He's sure," Danny seconded.

"Yep. We're all sure," Jimmy said.

"I see." Helen hoped Danny and Jimmy weren't making Hudy do something he'd regret. "You know, this is starting to sound like a conspiracy."

"See? I told you she was smart." Hudy shifted slightly against the pillows. "Go on, Danny. Tell her," he urged.

Helen glanced from one to the other. "Tell me what?"

Danny looked at Jimmy and got the go-ahead. "Okay. Me and Hudy and Jimmy, we made this pact, see?"

"What kind of pact?" She rolled the wheelchair to the other side of the bed, where there'd be more room to maneuver.

"Kind of an all-for-one, one-for-all pact," Jimmy explained.

"Uh-huh." Helen was only half listening. If she could get two ward boys—no, three—maybe they could lift Hudy and not have to scoot him at all. Scooting would hurt his charred skin beyond the toleration point. She needed to give him his morphine shot.

Danny continued, "We promised we'd stick together on visitor days. If one goes somewheres, we all go. Right, guys?"

They mumbled agreement.

"That's really nice, Danny. Sharing your families. I'm sure your parents would love to meet your buddies." She smiled at him, thinking he must have great parents to have raised such a sweet, kind boy. She supposed most of the boys would be so excited about seeing their families they'd forget about anyone else.

"Not just meet 'em," Danny said. "I want Jimmy and Hudy with me. The whole time."

"Your parents may want time alone with you, though, don't you think?" she reasoned. "They haven't seen you for so—"

"No!" Danny's face hardened to stone, and his eyes narrowed to black slits. He looked older, like a soldier instead of a boy. The transformation took her by surprise. "We made a pact, Nurse Eberhart, and I aim to keep it. We all do."

"Okay, Danny."

"So we're sticking together, Jimmy and Hudy and me. That's the way it's going to be. That's the deal." He glanced desperately at his two buddies and seemed to get what he needed from them. "We worked it out, ma'am. And we mean it."

"I'm sorry, Danny. I didn't mean to argue with you. That's fine. Whatever you guys want to do is okay by me." She'd never seen him so wound up. She wasn't even sure what had set him off.

"Only that's where you come in," Danny said.

"Me?"

"We need you to make the pact with us."

"I don't understand."

"You can't just, like, let my ma come in and push me away. You tell her, tell my folks, that Jimmy and Hudy need to come too. Swear you're in the pact with us, okay?"

Helen knew she was missing something, but she didn't have time to figure out what. Visiting hours started in less than an hour. "Okay. You're the boss."

11

Helen

BATTLE CREEK, MICHIGAN

It took four ward boys and another nurse to get Hudy into the wheel-chair. He was so brave, but Helen ached with him at every move. She cringed each time they had to touch his brittle body. When they finished, finally, and Hudy sat in the wheelchair, stuck like a cigar in a coffee mug, she wondered at the stuff these boys were made of. They were the same sort of boys who'd teased her in grammar school, shoved her on the playground, joined her brothers in calling her Gypsy. Yet the war had stripped them of everything except . . . what? Guts?

"Nurses! It's time!" Captain Walker shouted from across the room. Helen had to admit the old gal had come through. Without her, they never would have gotten the ward and the boys ready for their families.

Helen jogged over to the other nurses.

"Your cap, Nurse?" Captain Walker frowned her disapproval.

Helen stuck on her cap and straightened her uniform. She'd do anything to help the boys and their families, and it might help them to know the care at Percy Jones was top-notch professional. She'd even salute if it came to that.

"Here's the list." Walker gave the clipboard to Nurse Becker, teacher's pet—not that Helen cared.

"Yes, Captain!" Becker took the clipboard as if it were a secret dossier only she was worthy to touch. "I'll see that no one gets in unless they're on this list."

"Because we'd hate to have a patient visited by an unlisted visitor," Helen muttered.

Bill chuckled, then hurried off before someone yelled at him for it. After today, he ranked as Helen's all-time favorite ward boy. He reminded her of a rubber band being shot from one place to another. Only the shooter was usually Bill himself.

"Everyone!" Walker shouted.

The noisy ward quieted, but it only made the rumble of visitors on the other side of the doors louder and more ominous. It struck Helen as a strange sound—not laughter, not tears, nothing like a crowd gathering before a college game or a sale at Marshall Field's. In some way she couldn't explain, it was a war noise, the stirrings of combat readiness, civilian soldiers, not knowing what lay ahead yet ready to burst through the doors with invisible weapons.

Captain Walker nodded to Becker, who barked orders to the ward boys. "Open the doors and don't let anyone through until I check their names!"

The doors opened to a wide-eyed group. Some hung back; others shoved forward.

"Ladies and gentlemen, please!" Nurse Becker shouted. "Form a single line right there. One at a time, please."

Why? Why couldn't they run to their sons, their husbands, their fathers? Helen's gaze was drawn to the children in line, holding their mothers' hands as tightly as their hands were being held.

Suddenly a short, dark-haired woman burst across the line. "I'll not be waiting another moment, and you can tell it to the Führer if you've a problem with it!" Nobody tried to stop her as she plunged into the ward. "Danny! Danny boy, where are you, Son?"

Helen smothered a grin. She should have known. "Mrs. McCarthy?"

The woman wheeled on her. "Aye. That's me."

"I'm so glad to meet you." Helen shook her hand and held on to it. "Danny's been looking forward to your visit. Is your husband with you?"

As if she'd forgotten about her husband, she turned toward the crowd. "Michael, get yourself over here!"

A tall, thin man with hair as black and thick as Danny's stepped out of line and tiptoed in as if dodging land mines. Helen introduced herself and led them to Danny, who sat ramrod straight in his wheelchair, a giant grin plastered to his face.

Mrs. McCarthy threw her arms around her son, crying his name over and over. Her shoulders shook with the force of her tears. Then all of a sudden, she stopped crying and stood back from him. "I'm sorry for that. I'm just that happy to see you."

Helen had to give the woman credit. She didn't know how she would have handled seeing her legless son for the first time.

"Well, Michael," his wife scolded. "Are you going to stand there all day, or will you come give your hero son a proper hello?"

Her husband squeezed his hat, which he held in both hands in front of him. His head nodded, and his eyes looked everywhere except at his son. "Danny."

Helen couldn't stand the tension. "Danny is one of my favorite patients." She looped her arm through his father's and drew him with her. "This is Hudy, and this rascal is Jimmy. They're fast friends, these three, and I have to keep my eye on them."

"I'll bet that's so," said Mrs. McCarthy. Helen loved the woman already. She was trying so hard that sweat beaded on her brow, but she kept her eyes soft and her voice cheery. They could have used a hundred Mrs. McCarthys on this ward. Helen had the feeling the woman wouldn't have flinched changing bandages. She might even have sung an Irish lullaby as she did.

Helen glanced around at other groups of visitors and patients. Some were crying, and others stood so awkwardly apart that it made *her* want to cry. She swallowed that thought and turned to Mr. McCarthy. His head was bowed, as if he were praying, but his sides heaved. She had to do something. "Say, has that foggy sky lifted yet?"

"It has indeed," Mrs. McCarthy answered.

"What would you say to a stroll around the building? We could take the elevator down, Danny. Would you like that?"

Danny's mother grabbed the back of his wheelchair like she'd won it in a contest. "That's a grand idea!"

Danny shot Helen a look filled with accusation . . . and fear.

"Of course, we'll have to take all the boys out," Helen said. She watched the tension drain from Danny's face. "I can't play favorites. You can push Danny, Mrs. McCarthy. Mr. McCarthy, will you take—?"

Mr. McCarthy, without a word, shuffled, then ran toward the exit.

"Michael!" his wife called after him. A shadow passed over her face. Then she sent it away as fast as it had come and turned to her son. "That man," she said, a lilt in her voice. "He has the bladder of a two-year-old, he does."

Helen knew that wasn't why he'd taken off. She'd seen the look before. Hadn't she had the same reaction the first time she'd walked onto the amputee ward? She couldn't blame him. He couldn't help it. Only now what was she going to do?

"Nurse Eberhart!" Nurse Becker sounded eerily like Captain Walker. "We need you here!"

"You can't go," Jimmy whispered.

Mrs. McCarthy was already getting a feel for Danny's wheelchair, pushing it away from Hudy's bed. "Let me see here. I think I can manage well enough."

"Wait!" Danny's panic was palpable. "We can't go yet."

"Nurse!" Becker yelled again.

Helen felt torn. She couldn't push Jimmy *and* Hudy. But she'd promised not to leave any of them alone. Mrs. McCarthy was halfway to the ward doors already, with Danny turning back, panic-stricken. Betrayed.

And then Frank appeared, strolling onto the ward as if he'd been watching the whole thing and reading everybody's mind. He took Danny's wheelchair out of Mrs. McCarthy's hands as smoothly as if she'd given it to him. "Hey, Danny. Bet this is your beautiful mother you told us so much about."

Danny looked baffled, but he came through. "Sure is . . . Lieutenant."

"Lieutenant Daley, ma'am." Frank shook her hand as he turned the wheelchair and headed back to Hudy and Jimmy. "Would you rather push Danny or one of the other boys? We always go out in threes. Company rules. You know the Army."

"I didn't know," Mrs. McCarthy said, put off balance for a minute.

"Nurse, if you take Jimmy, and I get Hudy, I'll bet Danny's mother can keep up."

"Nurse Eberhart!" shouted Becker. "I need—"

"Thank you, Nurse!" Frank called to her. "We have things under control. Carry on!"

Helen grabbed Jimmy's wheelchair and made for the door before Becker could stop her. "This way!" She led them to the service elevator.

"Yeehaw!" shouted Hudy.

They crowded into the tiny elevator, which barely held the three wheelchairs. Helen and Frank and Mrs. McCarthy stood in the back, squished together like Spam in a can. Risking a glance up at Frank, Helen mouthed, "How did you know?"

He wiggled his eyebrows. The elevator door opened, and he and Hudy were the first ones out. "Last one to the flagpole is a nasty Nazi!" Frank shouted.

It was late when Helen finished her shift and she and Frank left the hospital. Her feet ached, and she realized the only thing she'd eaten all day was a stale cookie. Frank had stuck it out through the whole wild visiting day. She'd barely said two words to him, but she'd glimpsed him across the room, visiting with parents, wheeling patients to the bathroom, getting cookies for kids.

Lightning bugs flashed as they crossed the grounds to her barracks. The twang of crickets faded in and out, like somebody playing with the radio volume. Helen looped her arm through Frank's. "Danny and Jimmy and Hudy are amazing, aren't they?"

"They are," he agreed. "They better get those medals pretty soon—they earned them all over again today."

It was funny—in a way, it felt like they were talking about their kids. The thought shocked her, and she hoped Frank had finished reading minds. "It's pretty swell the way they stick together." She laughed, remembering how serious they were about it. "The boys made a pact and made me part of it. I had to promise I wouldn't leave any of them out today. I suppose Danny didn't want the others to feel bad because his parents showed up and theirs didn't."

"That's not it."

"What?"

Frank smiled down at her, but even in the dark she could see how sad the smile was. "Danny was the one they made the pact for."

"I don't understand."

"Hudy and Jimmy weren't worried about *not* having family there. They made that pact so Danny wouldn't have to be alone with *his* family. I'm guessing he wanted somebody with him who really understood."

Of course. She should have seen that's what was going on. Danny had been terrified he'd end up alone with his parents. Hudy and Jimmy made sure he didn't. But how had Frank understood?

Helen glanced up at this man and wondered what else he understood.

Sunday morning, Helen slept past eight o'clock. She couldn't remember the last time she'd slept in. Frank had probably been waiting outside for an hour. Chapel started in fifteen minutes. She hadn't mentioned church to him, but he'd been there on Easter, her first Sunday, and he'd gone with her every Sunday since.

Pulling out the only clean uniform she had, she dressed, washed, did the best she could with her hair, and tore outside. "Sorry I'm—"

Helen stopped. The door slammed behind her.

Frank wasn't there.

She glanced both ways, then jogged to the side of the barracks and peered across the quad. Soldiers moved in groups of three and four, but she didn't see Frank towering over them.

Maybe he'd slept in too. Or maybe he didn't feel like getting up for church. He'd spent himself on her ward yesterday, even though he could have taken the day off. The guy deserved a rest. Besides, it wasn't like they'd made plans to meet. But a heaviness settled over her, and no matter how she tried to reason it away, she recognized it for what it was—disappointment. And not just a little, too-bad variety of disappointment. Not finding Frank waiting for her cut into her heart and scraped her soul, leaving an emptiness.

Don't be such a dumb Dora, she told herself, setting off for the chapel. But as she walked faster and faster, she couldn't deny that even her feet were in on the hope of finding Frank already in church.

He wasn't there.

Helen tried to focus on the sermon, but the words swirled around her, just out of reach. She sang the hymns, but two minutes after closing the hymnal, she couldn't have said what the songs were.

When the service ended, she stayed where she was as nurses and soldiers streamed out of the chapel. She scanned the little crowd, half as big as it had been on Easter, but she didn't see any of Frank's buddies.

An uneasiness was working its way deeper into her heart and mind.

He couldn't be gone. Not yet. Not like this.

~⌣~

Dorothea Daley Engel
Hamilton, Missouri
June 21, 1944

Dear Frank,

Sounds as if the war in Europe may be over before you get there. I sure hope and pray so. I try to picture you with a gun, and I can't. Boxing gloves, a baseball bat, an ice pick (like the one Daddy had to pull out of your hand after you and Jack played catch with it in the garage) . . . but not a gun. I never got a gun in the Philippines, so why should you? Which reminds me, have you heard from brother Jack lately? I wouldn't be surprised to learn that those meetings of the Big Three (although I still can't believe we're supposed to befriend Stalin) are really meetings of the Big Four, counting Jack.

The US State Department still isn't taking me seriously. I have friends who feed me information about the "Bataan Death March," as some refer to it. There were survivors. We think there may be hundreds in prisons, where they can't get word out. I know that's where Boots is. I want to go there and find him myself, but the Army won't let me.

Take care, little brother.

Love,
Dotty

12

FRANK

CAMP ELLIS, ILLINOIS

Frank lifted his Colt 45 and squeezed the trigger: *bang, bang, bang, bang, bang, bang.*

"Not bad for a medical man," Anderson conceded.

Frank squinted at the target some forty yards away. His ears were ringing, and his hand still felt the jolt of the gun. Sweat trickled down his arm, making his grip slippery. He'd never even shot a gun before the war. "No bull's-eyes, but at least they're all on the target." And Dotty couldn't picture him with a gun? He should have brought his camera to war. "How'd you do, Andy?"

"I think I hit Lartz's target once by accident. Otherwise, I've no idea where the bullets landed. Hope I didn't hit anybody. Are these real bullets?" He turned his pistol around and peered into the barrel.

"Anderson, are you nuts?" Frank jerked Andy's arm down. "Don't point that thing at your head, you idiot!"

Anderson shrugged. "Don't worry. I never hit anything I aim at. You, on the other hand, better watch yourself. If you're not careful, they'll send you into combat armed with guns instead of bandages."

"If it would get me out of here, I'd go." Camp Ellis had been constructed in six months, turning seventeen thousand acres of Illinois corn and beans into an Army Service Unit Training Camp, with over two thousand buildings, if you could call them that. Standing on the firing range, Frank could hear rifles to his left, machine guns farther out, and hand grenades exploding too close for comfort. To top it off, in addition to GIs being trained for the medical corps, signal corps, engineer units, and quartermaster troops, Camp Ellis was home to a couple thousand German POWs, all of whom received better treatment than the Americans. Thanks to the rules of the Geneva Convention, prisoners received pay for their labor—eighty cents an hour. So it paid, literally, to be a prisoner. And prisoner work shifts couldn't go over twelve hours. Frank's hospital shift was twelve hours, and field training, hiking, marching, and obstacle runs took up the rest of the day. It was inhuman. The artillery hill, where they were standing now, marked the halfway point of their thirteen-mile hike in full gear, and it had to be a muggy one hundred degrees.

Still, Frank would have gladly put up with anything if he could have had five minutes with Helen. His unit had been called up and carted out of Battle Creek like thieves in the night. And now they were incommunicado with the rest of the world. No calls or letters in or out. What if Helen thought he hadn't cared enough to say good-bye?

"*Her* again?" Anderson reloaded his pistol with the resolve of a man threading twine through a needle.

"What?"

"The fair Nurse Helen? You get that look in your eyes when you're thinking about her."

"Then I must have that look all the time. If I don't talk to her soon, I'm going AWOL."

"Relax. Have you not noticed that what our ugly Camp Ellis lacks in natural beauty, it makes up for in beautiful nurses and secretaries?"

Frank *hadn't* noticed. "I can't get her out of my head, Andy. I can't sleep because I keep seeing that face, those eyes. I miss her voice. Her laugh. I'll bet she has a swell singing voice." When he closed his eyes, he could see her walking beside him, her arm through his. She was probably a great dancer, the way she floated along effortlessly. The thought of her dancing with some other guy made Frank a prime candidate for a duodenal ulcer. "What do you suppose she thinks about me? I just left. I didn't say good-bye. I didn't tell her how I feel about her."

"Patience," Andy said. "In time, you won't even remember—"

"Reload, gentlemen!" Sergeant Miller peered into Anderson's face, a feat he could only achieve by positioning himself higher on the hill than Andy. Miller was a fireplug, short, with arms that made Frank think of Popeye the Sailor Man. Doctors entered the Army as lieutenants, an unfairness that had to gall career soldiers like Sarge. "And this time, *Lieu-ten-ant*," he barked, "see if you can hit the target!"

"Don't suppose you could keep it down, sport?" Anderson quipped. "I've a bit of a hangover."

"Now!" Sergeant Miller screamed.

Frank was already aiming his next shot. He fired. Miraculously, he hit the center circle—not the bull's-eye, but darn close. He grinned at the sergeant and got a snarl in return.

Anderson shot. Missed by a mile. Shot again.

Frank couldn't watch. Sarge must have smelled liquor on Andy's breath. Their first night at Ellis, Frank had gone with Andy to the on-site tavern. He'd nursed a beer while Anderson drank the way he did everything, with reckless abandon. Frank left after Andy's fourth whiskey.

Every night they could hear Andy whistling or singing as he

stumbled up the rows of barracks, identical clapboard shacks thrown together in a couple of days and filled with double-decker bunks that were little more than pillowless cots. It was a miracle he staggered into the right barracks.

Frank fired off the rest of his rounds, including the seventh in the chamber. He missed every shot. At least the sergeant wasn't watching.

On the run back to the encampment, they had to trek through rough, wooded terrain, where they'd be practicing maneuvers, although Frank didn't know why. It wasn't like they'd be on the battle-field dodging bullets. Doctors would be in hospitals sewing up lads who *failed* to dodge battlefield bullets.

The unit looped around the small landing field, past the con-struction area, where engineering units practiced building barracks and bridges, and demolition units practiced blowing them up. Frank imagined walking this same route with Helen, talking about how crazy war made people, training them to build with one hand and destroy with the other.

He was second from the lead, only a few feet behind Sergeant Miller, when they reached the concrete posts and barbed wire that separated the POWs from the rest of the camp. A few prisoners were digging post holes or laying brick, while a dozen leaned against a barracks and smoked Lucky Strikes.

Frank was glad he'd never picked up smoking in med school because of his occasional bouts with asthma. Most of his colleagues smoked. Half of Andy's paycheck went for cigarettes or drinks, and the other half to paying off his poker debts or incurring new ones. Did Helen smoke? He'd never seen her smoke. But most of the nurses did, calling it one of the few pleasures the Army allowed.

What about poker? He imagined teaching Helen to play seven-card stud, draw, high-low, buy-in baseball . . .

It was no use. He could try thinking of other things—the pris-oners, Anderson, the war, even this never-ending run—but every thought led him back to Helen. He'd never felt like this about anybody. He'd had his share of dates—had even taken a nurse home for Christmas when he was a resident, but only because he knew his mother would like her.

Christmas. He pictured Helen decorating a tree, reaching for the top branch, needing his help—

Stop it.

"Lieutenant Daley!" Sarge was screaming his name.

Frank stopped running, suddenly realizing nobody was ahead of him.

"We're through with the run, Lieutenant," Sarge said. "Unless you feel like going again?"

"No, sir!"

Sergeant Miller shook his head. "Supper in five, and you losers better be smelling like roses!"

In five minutes, maybe seven, Frank was in line at the mess hall. About forty soldiers stood between him and what would pass for food. He was hungry enough to eat whatever they plopped onto his tray. He glanced back, gratified to see more soldiers behind him than in front, all dangling the same metal mess kit, which made food taste like tin.

Lartz let two soldiers in front of him so he'd be next to Frank. "You okay?"

"I can't stop thinking about Helen."

"Now there's a news bulletin for the *Stars and Stripes*."

"Tell me the truth, Lartz. Do you think Helen's thinking about me? I mean, do you think she feels about me like I feel about her?"

Lartz grinned. "Yeah. I've seen the way she looks at you. Reminded me of the way you look at her."

"Really?"

"Really." They were up to the food now. Lartz stuck out his plate a second before the private ladled some goulash concoction onto it. Lartz stared at the brown pile oozing on his silvery plate. "Ever wonder why they bother dividing plates into three parts when the food ends in a glob anyway?"

Frank received his mound of food and followed Lartz to the coffee. They had a long night ahead of them, and he'd need all the caffeine he could get. "Lartz, nobody knows when this war will be over, and you can't put life on hold. Right now, this moment, that's all we have, right?" He didn't wait for a response. "If we weren't headed into a war zone, I'd write Helen dozens of letters that would convince her I'm the only guy for her. We'd go to picture shows and get ice cream and meet each other's folks and get to know the same friends. Then we'd both know we wanted to spend the rest of our lives together."

Lartz stared at Frank. "Are you saying what I think you're saying?"

Was he? Yeah, he was. He really and truly was. He'd known Helen only a few weeks. His mother would have told him he had brain fever. His father wouldn't have said a word—just dropped his head with a disapproving shake. But the truth was, Frank hadn't pleased his parents in a long time, not like Jack and Dotty did. He couldn't name the moment when he'd given up trying to get his parents' approval, but he had. Besides, they didn't know Helen. Wonderful, beautiful Helen. "Lartz, I want to marry that gal!"

A grin spread across Lartz's face. "Good for you! Couldn't happen to a nicer guy . . . or a nicer gal."

"And I'm not waiting on the Army for an all clear." Frank's heart pounded as hard as if Helen were there waiting to be asked. "Tonight, I'm going to ask Lieutenant Helen Eberhart to marry me!"

13

FRANK

CAMP ELLIS, ILLINOIS

Frank was the first one to climb into bed that night. He tried to read the Mary Roberts Rinehart mystery Dotty had sent him, but even his favorite author couldn't hold his attention.

Lartz was next to settle in. "'Night, Daley," he shouted up at Frank from the next bunk over. "Think I'll check in early."

"'Night, Lartz," Frank said, not looking up from his novel. He turned the page in case anyone was watching.

Anderson, of course, was nowhere to be found. He'd disappeared before Frank's hospital shift ended. When they moved to Camp Ellis, Frank had been switched from working with disease patients and put on "minor surgery" detail—if you could call setting broken legs and removing gallbladders and appendixes "minor." This evening, he'd removed a bullet lodged so deep into a soldier's femur that nobody had realized it was there until the patient ran a fever. Maybe the fact that three other bullets had been removed in a field hospital had something to do with the oversight.

Now, lying in his bunk, the minutes dragged. No danger of falling asleep and missing his chance to call Helen. He wouldn't sleep until she said yes.

The Army, in its infinite wisdom, had removed telephones from the hospital at Camp Ellis. Doctors were on duty around the clock, so why would anyone need to make a phone call at the Army's expense? But there was a phone outside headquarters. . . .

After what seemed like hours, snores erupted around the barracks. It sounded like gruel boiling—a bubble here, a bubble there, and finally mad, constant snoring. How had he ever gotten a minute's sleep in this place?

The last light went out, and seconds later he heard Anderson in the distance, singing: "'Daisy, Daisy, give me your answer, do. I'm half crazy all for the love of you!'"

The guy wasn't half crazy. He was 100 percent certifiable. The next line in the song went, "It won't be a stylish marriage." Why not just broadcast Frank's marriage proposal over the loudspeaker?

Anderson stumbled in. He thumped each bed, counting bunks as he moved down the row, immune to the curses and groans.

Great. Now the whole barracks would be awake, and Frank would never get to a phone.

Andy shuffled to Frank's bunk, where Frank was trying to play possum. "Frank?" he whispered at the level of a normal person's conversation. "Isn't marriage a bit drastic, ol' man?"

"You're married," Frank whispered, trying to shield himself from Anderson's whiskey breath.

"Ah, but not like you'll be."

"I'll take that as a compliment."

Anderson plopped onto his bunk. "My wife is the happiest woman I know. Alice doesn't enter into any of my dalliances."

"Lucky for you she doesn't," Lartz muttered.

Andy just laughed, which gave him the hiccups. *Thunk, thunk,* went the sound of his shoes being kicked off. Two seconds later he was snoring louder than anybody.

Frank knew he shouldn't go yet, so he conjured up images of Helen. He relived the first time he saw her coming out of the men's room. Had he fallen in love with her then? Or was it at the Easter service, when she'd hung on every word of the sermon? He could picture each walk they'd taken, the touch of her hand on his arm. She had to feel the same way about him, didn't she? He couldn't feel this much unless she did.

Getting her on the phone wouldn't be easy if she didn't have night duty. The only number he had was the hospital's. He rehearsed what he'd say. First, he'd apologize for leaving without saying good-bye. She must know by now that the whole unit had been reassigned. Then he'd let her know how much he missed her. And loved her. And wanted to marry her.

He couldn't stand it. If he waited one more minute, he'd explode.

Frank pulled on the shoes he'd hidden under his blanket. He'd gone to bed in pants and a T-shirt. As quietly as he could, he climbed down from his bunk.

Lartz got up, his bunk creaking as he did. "Shouldn't you wait another hour, Frank?" he whispered.

"I can't."

"Here." Lartz pulled the blanket from his bed, rolled it up, and handed it to Frank. "Stuff it under your blanket."

Frank shoved the roll under his blanket. It looked like a small animal was in his bed. "This isn't working, Lartz."

Lartz reached into his duffel bag and came out with his helmet. He had to stand on tiptoes to place it under Frank's blanket. "What do you think?"

"I think we better hope Sarge drank as much as Anderson tonight."

"Good luck, Frank." Lartz held out his hand.

Frank shook it. "Thanks, Lartz. Here goes everything."

Frank stepped out into a muggy night and flattened himself to the barracks wall to get his bearings. A mosquito landed on his arm and bit before he could swat it. Inside, there had been the stench of too many bodies too close together. Outside wasn't much better. At one time, the fields around Ellis must have been heavy with the scent of new grain and grass and wildflowers. Now those smells had been replaced with a blend of rancid garbage and pure latrine.

That was it. If somebody stopped him, he'd say he was looking for the latrine. If he got too far away, though, maybe he could claim he was sleepwalking. Anyway, now wasn't the time to think about getting caught. He didn't even care if he got caught, so long as he got to talk to Helen first. The thought of her voice on the other end of the line gave him a rush of energy and resolve.

Glancing both ways, he jogged up the row of barracks, keeping to softer ground so his footsteps wouldn't echo. Crouching as he traversed the open space, he passed the victory garden that, ironically, German prisoners had planted.

When he reached the barbed-wire prisoner section, he spotted two guards in towers, but their backs were to him. He swung south, giving a wide berth to the guardhouse. The farther he got, the better he felt. He had to be close to headquarters, and so far nobody had seen him. He felt invisible. Invincible. He was a man in love, a soldier to be reckoned with.

When he spotted the flagpole, he almost ran for it. The pole stretched up one hundred feet, where the flag flew night and day. A spotlight shone on the red-white-and-blue batting against the night's breeze. He could clearly see the phone, which was good. But it meant he could be seen once on the phone, which was not so good.

Too bad. Frank made a dash for it as if he were under machine-gun fire. Without looking back, he grabbed the receiver. When the operator came on the line, Frank gave her the number of Percy Jones Hospital.

"One moment, please."

He waited while the phone rang. Once, twice, three times. His heart beat twelve times per ring.

"Hello? Percy Jones. Nurse Rider speaking."

Frank racked his brain to remember Nurse Rider.

"Hello?"

"Sorry. Um. This is Dr. Frank Daley. I was in Battle Creek—"

"Dr. Daley? How are you? You just up and disappeared without a word. You're not overseas, are you?"

He still couldn't place her. "I can't really say where I am. You understand."

"Army business, huh? We sure do miss you and Andy. Things haven't been the same around here since you boys left."

"Listen. I'm kind of in a rush." He glanced over his shoulder and didn't see anybody, but he felt like a sitting duck. "Is Nurse Eberhart on duty?"

The lilt disappeared from her voice. "Don't think so. Nah. I'm sure she's not." She yawned. "Listen, it's nice chatting with you, but I better go."

"No, wait!" He couldn't let her hang up. "Is Peggy O around?"

"Sure. I'll get her." The line went silent.

Frank clutched the phone and prayed that Nurse Rider hadn't hung up on him. Finally, Peggy's brash voice came through the line. "How the heck are you, good-lookin'?"

"Peggy, am I glad to hear you!"

"You sound like you're hiding out. Those Japs got you in prison already?"

"Not exactly. Listen, Peggy. I have a big favor to ask."

"This wouldn't have something to do with a gal named Eberhart, would it?"

"How did you—?"

"I'm not blind, sweetheart. But you're out of luck. Ebby isn't on duty tonight. Guess you'll have to call back."

Frank knew he was asking the moon, but . . . "Peggy, I need you to go get her."

"You're joshing me, right?"

"Nope. I have to talk to her."

"Frank, I'd have to wake every nurse in the barracks to find her."

"Do what you gotta do. Please! I'm begging you."

A rush of air came through the phone, followed by Peggy's hoarse laugh. "Okay, fella. But you owe me for life."

"Yes! I love you, Peggy!"

"Something tells me I'm not the one you love. Hang on. This could take a while."

"Thanks a million!" Frank realized he was talking to dead air. Peggy was gone.

Now all he had to do was wait.

He waited and waited. His fingers ached from gripping the receiver. His mind played tricks on him. He thought he heard something in the distance. A whistle? It *was* a whistle. Someone was definitely whistling, and it was getting louder. He heard footsteps coming his way.

There was nothing to do but drop the phone and hope nobody noticed the dangling receiver. He dashed between headquarters and the review stand and dropped to his stomach. Still in view, he'd be harder to see than if he stood by the phone.

An armed MP, still whistling, strolled onto the quad. His short legs traversed the grounds, passing only a couple of yards from the phone.

Keep going! Hurry up! Frank wanted to shove the soldier on his way. What if Helen and Peggy were back? He pictured Helen picking up the phone. What if she thought it was a practical joke? She'd hang up. She'd never let him speak to her again.

The second the MP faded out of sight, Frank scrambled to the phone, which still swung like a pendulum. "Hello? Are you there?"

Nobody answered. He strained to hear voices, noises, anything that would tell him he was still connected, that Helen hadn't come and gone. How long had it been? Long enough for her to have gotten there and left again?

Then he heard, "Peggy, if this is a prank, you're going to be sorry."

Helen. He'd know that voice anywhere.

"Pick up the phone, gal," he heard Peggy say. "And don't take this out on me. I'm only following orders like a good Army chap."

Helen laughed. The phone crackled. Then she said, "Hello?"

"Helen!"

"Frank? Is it really you? Peggy said . . . but I didn't . . . Where did you go? Why didn't you at least leave me a note?"

"I couldn't. Listen, I'm not supposed to be talking to you now."

"But where are you?"

"I can't tell you."

"Ooooh, sometimes I hate the Army. They're so . . . *Army!*"

"Helen, I miss you."

"I miss you too."

He wanted her to say it again. "I mean I *really* miss you. I can't stop thinking about you. I didn't know it would be like this."

She laughed, that beautiful, lilting laugh he would have risked everything for. "I know what you mean, Frankie."

Frankie. She'd never called him that before. He liked it. He loved it. He loved her. And he had to tell her so. Fast. "Helen?"

"Still here."

Footsteps! He heard footsteps. No. Not yet. "Helen, someone's coming."

"Is that bad? Are you in danger?"

He heard the whistle now. The MP was coming back. "I can't talk. But I have to tell you that I love you, Helen. I do. I love you more than anything."

"I—"

"This war. It's crazy. But the one thing I'm sure of is I love you. And . . ." He couldn't stop now. "I want to marry you, Helen Eberhart. Will you marry me?"

A silence draped over the other end of the line. A cold silence.

Behind him, the footsteps of the MP grew deafening, beating in his head against the emptiness of the telephone line.

"Helen?" He was afraid they'd been disconnected. Yet he could hear her breathing. He gripped the phone. They'd have to pry his fingers away if they wanted to arrest him. He didn't care. All he wanted, all he lived for, was to hear Helen's voice again.

And then it came. "Are you out of your mind?"

~⌒~

6 July 1944
From: Lt. Helen Eberhart, RN
Battle Creek, MI

Dearest Frankie,

That phone call was so very difficult, and I have been having a hard time trying to write you ever since. Your call was so surprising. I hadn't any idea that you wanted to marry me. I guess, to be trite, "this is all so sudden."

I know that you will feel hateful toward me now. You are the finest, most decent boy I have ever known. If I wanted to marry at all, I would marry you. I want you to know that. But I don't know if I'll ever get married.

Frankie, do you remember on one of our walks together at B.C., when we talked about marriage and war? We agreed that war marriages are dangerous. (We were, of course, talking about others—"relationship casualties of war.") When I joined the Army, I made up my mind not to marry anyone. I want my marriage—if I have one—to stick always. You and I haven't known each other long enough to give us that certainty.

My mother and father have been unhappily married for the past 20 years, perhaps longer. I can only swear to the years

I've observed them. I never have confessed this to anyone before, but it hangs over me. I believe I sensed it all along: my mother's unhappiness, my father's tyranny. That kind of marriage, even when it sticks, is no fun, especially when the child watching can do nothing about it.

I am sorry if I've made you unhappy. You are too sweet to be hurt by anyone. I don't know what else to write, but perhaps you can find a way to understand? Please forgive me.

I would give anything to talk to you in person. Can't we arrange it? Are you so far off? Can you get a leave? I have the whole day off this Sunday and would come wherever you are if you can't come to Battle Creek. But we would have more time to talk if you can make it here. Say you can, please?

Love,
Helen

14

Helen

BATTLE CREEK, MICHIGAN

Helen walked—alone—to the hospital in the early morning darkness. Only the *click, click* of her footsteps cut the silence of dawn. By this time, Frank would have received her letter. She hoped, prayed, that he'd understand and find a way to come to Battle Creek. She'd done a little investigating and discovered that most medical units leaving Battle Creek went to a place called Camp Ellis in Illinois. That couldn't be too far by train, could it?

Maybe Helen's unit would get sent to Camp Ellis while Frank was still there. That would be wonderful. They'd have more time to get to know each other. Rumor had it that Helen's unit, the 199th, could be assigned any day now. Captain Walker claimed there would be a whole turnover of nurses by Christmas.

If only Frank could come back for a day, they could talk through everything. She could make him understand that she did feel about him the way he felt about her. He loved her. He'd said it more than once in that crazy phone call. *Her.* Helen Marie Eberhart. Out of all the nurses who would have given anything to marry the handsome Dr. Daley, he'd asked her.

And she'd told him he was out of his mind.

Why had she said that? He'd risked sneaking to a phone in the middle of the night, and in so many words, she'd told him to commit himself to a mental institution.

What she hadn't told him, though she knew it was true, was that she loved him. She couldn't even write it in the letter . . . except to sign her name with love. *Coward.* She hoped he'd see that closing, how she'd signed "Love, Helen." But he'd never know what it had cost her to pen that word.

At least she'd made it clear that she wanted to talk. She'd practically begged him to come to Battle Creek on Sunday, when she'd have the day off. So it was up to him now, wasn't it? He had to come. He just had to.

Helen stopped in front of the post office. She was too early for mail call, but she spotted a light inside. She tried the door, and it opened. Bulletin boards plastered with typed messages covered both walls. A musty smell made her want to prop open the door. She stood at the counter and peered into the back room. "Hello? Is anybody here?"

The old soldier who ran the post office shuffled out, toting a box of letters. The way his back bent, like her dad's, she suspected he had severe osteoporosis. "I'm closed." He used his forearm to push his wire-rimmed glasses to the bridge of his nose. Then he squinted at her, and a wave of recognition passed over his face. "Ah, it's you, the charming nurse from Illinois."

Helen returned the smile. "Sorry to bother you. I saw the light and thought I'd see if I had anything. I probably don't."

"Eberhart, right?"

"I can't believe you remembered. I'm sorry. I don't think I know your name."

"Jones. Jonesy, they call me. I think I saw something for you." He riffled through the box. His fingers made her think of dry branches scraping the cellar window in Cissna Park. "There it is." He shuffled to the counter.

Helen took the letter. "Thanks so much. I really appreciate it."

"You have a good day now, hear?"

"Same to you, Jonesy."

She didn't look at the letter until she was outside, but she knew it was from Frank. She walked briskly toward what should have been sunrise, waiting until she reached the benches outside the hospital. Settling under the streetlight, hands shaking, she opened the envelope.

6 July 1944
From: Frank R. Daley, MD

Dear Helen,

I have asked you to marry me and you have turned me down. My first impulse was to pound the telephone receiver against the wall, but thankfully, sense prevailed and I ran for cover seconds before two MPs patrolled the ground I'd been standing on.

In the hours since our call, however, I've realized that every woman has the right to say no. Rest assured, dear Helen, this will be the last you hear from me.

First, I am wondering why you thought I asked you to marry me . . . . aside from the fact that you question the state of my mental health. Possibly you thought I was lonely, lacking in female companionship. I won't deny that I feel lonely, but not for female companionship. I've never had a lack of that.

I've been lonely for you. And that in itself led me to consider how I feel, how I felt, about you.

I'm aware that there are those who want to marry quickly in order to get a larger paycheck while overseas. But if you check with your adjutant, you'll discover that a nurse is not considered a dependent, and my paycheck would not increase.

If you've wondered why I asked you to marry me, I suppose I've wondered why you said no. Anderson says there must be another guy in the picture, and I suppose he may well be right. You couldn't have a better reason than to have a better guy in the wings. Or perhaps you just can't see me as the guy—and that's okay. Nobody can fault you for how you feel . . . or how you don't.

But before I sign off, will you allow me to leave you with the real reasons why—not why I wanted to marry, but why I wanted to marry you? I have a feeling that some of these may seem too little for you to have noted, but they counted a lot with me. I must have loved you, then, because:

1. You have spirit.

2. You have ideas of your own, even if some are wrong in my book. I loved that you had opinions on everything, and they were truly and deeply your own.

3. You didn't go out with everyone who asked you.

4. You realized the value of money, but I think—perhaps in spite of yourself—you are beginning to see its limitations.

5. You respect and even emulate your mother's faith in "Gott im Himmel."

6. You seemed to know what you want, and what you don't—my misfortune.

7. You made yourself appear 100% always, yet never acted as if you had any idea how beautiful you are.

8. You were okay to look at any time of the day or night.

I wasn't out of my mind when I told you I loved you. That's one thing I'm more sure of than ever (not that it changes a thing). I believe that love is when you can see the two of you trudging through 30 or 40 years of life together, and I can see that even now, although it will never be. Love is when sexual relations are secondary to understanding, companionship, and sense of humor. It's when you care more for someone than for yourself and are willing to trade your inconvenience for someone else's happiness.

That's why this will be my last communication. I want you to be happy.

Strangely enough, your decision, instead of making me angry and hurt, only served to increase my respect for you and causes me to wish that I had proved more deserving. As it is, best wishes, Helen, for all time.

Love,
Frank

P.S. Andy says that any gal who turns me down must have good sense and I shouldn't give up, but selfishly, it's easier on me if I do.

Helen had to wipe away tears. Nobody had ever said things like that to her, and her heart warmed with every word. He wrote eloquently about love, about marriage, and about her, even though she'd accused him of having lost his mind.

But it was clear that for Frank, it was marriage or good-bye, all or nothing. He was hurt. She had hurt him. And he didn't want to be hurt again. That's what would happen if they kept seeing each other. She couldn't get married. She couldn't live like that—her in Europe, him in the Pacific. Even in the best of circumstances, marriage was a gamble. She didn't want to end up like her mother—lonely, struggling, unhappy.

Frank had made it clear that their relationship was over. He had chosen to move on, and she couldn't blame him.

Suddenly she remembered the letter she'd sent him. Why hadn't she left the man alone? Hadn't she hurt him enough? She'd even invited him to come for a visit. How insensitive could she be? He had asked her to spend the rest of her life with him, and she'd responded by urging him to come for a picnic? Or go on a hike?

Think. Frank would get her letter. He'd probably wad it up and throw it into the garbage without reading it. Or if he did read it, he wouldn't take the invitation seriously.

Still . . . what if he did? She would love to see him again, to walk with him, to— But what about Frank? She couldn't be that selfish. She couldn't put him through everything all over again. Even if they had a perfect day, it would end horribly.

She had to uninvite him.

Clutching the letter, she ran back to the post office. "Jonesy! I have to send a telegram right away!"

8 July 6:22 AM
To Lt Frank Daley MD at 11th General Dispensary
Camp Ellis

Received your good letter STOP Ignore mine STOP We
had a gay time but I can't change my mind STOP Best
not to come again STOP Always Helen

"You sure about this, Miss Eberhart?" Jonesy asked. He pulled a neatly folded white handkerchief from his back pocket and handed it to her.

Helen took the hankie. "I'm sorry. I'll launder it and give it back." She couldn't stop crying. What was the matter with her? She never cried. Eugene used to tease her that gypsies had forgotten how.

"I'm not worried about that kerchief." Jonesy stared at her a long minute. "You want to think about this telegram before I send it? He'll still get it today, even if you send it later this afternoon, after you've had time to think on it."

Helen shook her head. "I need to send it now." She paid him and ran outside.

Sunday morning Helen was dressed and ready before her seven o'clock shift. Unable to face a day off and nobody to share it with, she'd signed up to work on Sunday and cover for Peggy, who had a twenty-four-hour leave to see her sister.

Since she had a half hour to kill, Helen strolled to the chapel and took a seat in the empty building. The wood walls smelled damp and earthy, like Dad's barn in Cissna Park after a rain. Outside, geese honked out of sync.

My Gott im Himmel, she prayed. *God in Heaven, but here, too. Thank goodness You're here, too. And with Frank. I hate that I hurt him. Hurt myself, didn't I? Hurt us? But it frightens me to care about him so much. Did I do the right thing? It doesn't feel that way. But it's too late to undo.*

Laughter coming from outside the chapel startled her. She glanced at her watch. Almost seven. If she didn't run, she'd be late for the second time in her career.

She was out of breath when she burst onto the ward. "Made it!" Unpinning her cap, she glanced around to see who else was on duty.

"Nurse Eberhart?" Hudy called.

"They said you weren't coming in today," Danny said.

"Hope you're not too disappointed," she teased.

"Yeah, right," Jimmy said. "But weren't you—?"

Captain Walker strolled up, frowning. "Nurse Eberhart?"

Great. Walker was working the ward? Helen repinned her cap. "Morning, Captain Walker."

"I thought I gave you the day off."

"You did. But I didn't have anything to do, and Peggy won't be back until tonight."

Walker shrugged and walked away.

This was going to be a long day. But at least here she wouldn't be alone, even if she was lonely. Painting on her smile, she gathered gauze and bandages, tape and scissors, and headed for Hudy's bed-side. "How are you feeling, Hudy?"

"A heap better now that you're here, ma'am."

"That's nice to hear." She started with his right foot, where the bandages had worked loose. "Have you been going out dancing when my back was turned, Private Bolin?"

"She's onto us," Jimmy said. Using his stocking feet, he maneu-vered his wheelchair to the other side of Hudy's bed.

Danny wasn't about to be left out. He arm-walked himself out of his sheets to face Hudy.

"We'd have told you about the dancing," Hudy teased, "but we didn't want you to get jealous."

"Well, I *am* jealous. So you better take me with you next time."

Hudy's leg jerked, and he let out a groan.

"Sorry, Hudy. Almost done." His skin around the ankle had a bit of color, but he was a long way from being able to tolerate grafts.

"Well, I'll be."

Helen glanced at Jimmy, who was grinning at the doorway.

"Guess we won't be the ones going dancing today," Danny said, his smile even bigger than Jimmy's.

"What are you guys talking about?" Helen tied off the last bit of tape. They didn't answer. She turned around to see what had their attention.

And there he was.

"Frank? Wh-what are *you* doing here?"

15

Helen

BATTLE CREEK, MICHIGAN

Frank's smile dissolved on his handsome face. He produced her letter and waved it at her. "I thought you invited me."

Helen stood up so fast she nearly knocked Hudy over. "I did. I wrote that letter. That was me." A wave of gratitude washed over her as she realized he must not have gotten the telegram. Maybe Western Union hadn't delivered it. Maybe Jonesy hadn't sent it. Maybe God had torn it up. Helen didn't care.

"Say something that makes sense," Hudy whispered.

"I—I . . . you're here. Really here. I'm glad you're here."

Frank's smile returned, an even better one than she remembered. "I'm glad you're glad." He nodded to the guys. "Hi, Hudy. Danny. Jimmy."

"Hey, Doc," Hudy called. The others greeted him. "You sure took off in a hurry. Where'd you get yourself off to?"

"Camp Ellis, a place you want to stay out of, Hudy."

"Must have taken you a good while to get here," Jimmy said.

"On a train that stops every two miles," Frank said.

Danny grinned. "Must have had an awful good reason to go through that."

Frank returned Danny's grin. Helen felt like a spectator until Frank walked over to her. She'd forgotten how tall he was. "When you weren't at your barracks, or chapel, I thought you might be here. You said you had the day off."

"Oh no! I did."

"Did? As in, you don't now?"

Helen couldn't believe it. He'd come all this way, and she'd volunteered to work.

Captain Walker strutted over, probably to tell her to get back to work. What a nightmare! And there was no way Frank had tomorrow off too, even if she could get someone to work for her.

"Is there a problem here?" asked Walker.

"Hello, Captain." Frank offered his disarming smile.

"Doctor." Walker nodded, then turned to Helen. "Nurse?"

"I—I didn't think he was . . . I mean, I wasn't sure Frank, Lieutenant Daley, could make it here today."

"I see. Well, then you'd better be on your way. This *is* your day off."

"What?"

Walker leaned in and whispered to Helen, "If I had a man like that come to see me, I wouldn't even ask. I'd just go. Now get out of here before I change my mind."

Helen felt like hugging the woman, but she knew better. "Thanks, Captain. That's really swell of you!" She turned to the boys. "You guys be okay without me for a day?"

"Sure!" Jimmy answered.

"We're going dancing anyways," Hudy said.

"You kids have fun," Jimmy added.

"Guess we might as well be off." Frank held out his arm.

She slid her arm through his and felt a rush at the sensation of their arms interlocked. *Thank You, Gott im Himmel.*

They took the stairway down, exchanging grins but not words. Helen wanted to explain why she'd said no to him. She wanted him to understand that she did love him. If there had been any doubt before, there wasn't now. But she didn't want to spoil this moment with him, when she felt herself dissolve into him, electrified and joyful.

As soon as they were out in the bright sunshine, she asked, "Where to, Doctor?" She hadn't had time to think about what they could do with a whole day. They'd always had to scrape for minutes, or an hour here or there. All they'd ever done was go on walks. Today felt like their first date, or maybe a date to the prom. Her mother had refused to let her go to the prom, even though Helen had been invited by half the boys in her class, even though she'd been elected prom queen. She'd told her friends there was no money for a prom dress. That was true. But even if she'd wrangled a dress, her mother wouldn't have let her go. She hadn't wanted the attention to go to Helen's head.

"How about Gull Lake?" Frank's pace quickened, and he gently tugged her along.

"Good idea. *Swell* idea, in fact!" She and Frank had strolled all the way to the lake once. It had taken an awfully long time.

"I've got my suit and a picnic lunch." He swiveled so she could see the pack on his back. She'd been so captivated by his big brown eyes that she hadn't even noticed it. "We can swing by your barracks so you can get your suit."

"That'll be swell." If she said *swell* one more time, she was going to throw up. "I'll bring lotion. The sun's pretty hot." She wasn't one for lying out in the sun, but they had umbrellas on the beach, and maybe beach chairs. Battle Creek had turned the lake into quite a recreational haven. And sitting on the beach would give them time to talk.

Helen dashed into her barracks and slipped on her swimsuit, checking herself in her tiny mirror before putting her summer khaki uniform back on. Her swimsuit was the only civilian clothing the Army allowed, and she wasn't even sure it was officially allowed. Most of the girls had one, though.

She stood on tiptoes to get one more look at herself before going back out. Even though she knew Frank would be there waiting, her heart rushed as she left the nurses' quarters, and the pounding of blood in her ears didn't stop until she spotted him. This time he held her hand as they walked to the lake, and she felt every movement of his fingers wrapped around hers.

Helen waited for Frank to bring up the awful way she'd treated his proposal on the phone. She hadn't done much better in her letter. But she sure wasn't going to be the one to bring it up now or to mention the telegram that would be waiting for him when he got back. It was hard to fight off the notion that this would be their last day together. If it was, then she wanted it to last as long as possible.

"Can you ride a bicycle?" he asked.

"Sure." She hoped she could anyway. One of her friends back in Cissna Park, Anna Schlesinger, had owned a bike and taught Helen how to ride it. She'd picked it up fast and loved riding that bike, although she'd known better than to ask for one. Didn't people use the expression "It's like riding a bike" to say that a thing like that came back to you?

Like a magician, Frank darted behind his old barracks, which they happened to be passing, and brought out a bike.

"How did you—?"

He disappeared again and returned with a second bike. "They're ours for the day."

Both bikes were drab olive green, like everything the Army issued. Hers felt clunky, heavier than she remembered Anna's bike being. She put her leg over and sat on the seat, balancing with one foot firmly planted on the ground. Frank was already moving ahead on his bike.

She stepped on the pedal and took off. The bike wobbled, snaking from side to side on the walkway. Thank heavens it was Sunday and almost nobody was around to see this.

"You okay?" Frank circled back for her. "Been a while?"

"You could say that. I'm getting the feel of it, though." Maybe if she rode faster, she wouldn't wobble so much.

Frank pedaled onto the grass to stay next to her. "You got it."

"You go first." Helen didn't look at him. It took all of her concentration to keep the bicycle going.

Frank led them onto a path Helen recognized from one of their moonlit strolls. Slowly, her bicycle confidence returned, freeing her to glance up from the handlebars. By the time the lake came into view, Helen's thighs ached. But the sight of the water, rippled by the wind and bluer than the sky above it, renewed her energy. Families picnicked under umbrellas on the beach. Two little boys splashed each other in shallow water, while their mother—Helen supposed the woman was their mother—watched a few feet away. The smells changed as abruptly as if they'd entered a different universe where fresh air and wildflowers reigned.

She wanted to tell Frank how happy she felt, how happy *he* made her feel, but he was too far away. And besides, she didn't know how to say such a thing. Fellas she'd dated said things like that, and it had always made her uncomfortable. Better at speaking her mind than speaking her heart, she'd turned their words into teasing, to joke them out of serious talk.

Lagging farther behind, Helen stomped the pedals, trailing Frank up a low, but long, hill.

Frank glanced over his shoulder, then circled back. Now that she'd stopped zigzagging over the whole pathway, he could pedal next to her. "What do you hear from Eugene and Wilbur and Clarence? Any word from Bud? Or from Ed since he left Italy?"

"Clarence stays under the radar. He likes the Navy better than farming, though. We haven't heard from Bud or Ed in ages, but they're not big writers. I think Ed is in France now. Let's see . . ." It wasn't easy to talk while doing the stand-up pedal uphill. Frank kept to her pace, and she appreciated it. "Wilbur is Wilbur. He just got demoted, again, to sergeant."

Frank laughed. "He didn't punch another officer, did he?"

She'd told Frank about her brother's first demotion, which happened a year earlier when he'd slugged his lieutenant to keep him from pilfering private shops in a village they'd liberated. "This time he punched a captain. Wilbur said he warned the guy twice not to go inside an old Italian woman's house to 'liberate' the silver candlesticks in her window. So in my brother's mind, he was fully justified in knocking the captain out cold."

"I think I like this brother of yours."

"Me too. But he'll never get above the rank of sergeant, no matter how long he stays in the Army. The only reason he's not court-martialed is that the captain would have to admit his own crime."

"Walter's his twin, right? Must be hard on the boys to be separated."

"Walt does more good for the Army by staying in Chicago and running his wartime factory than he would on a battlefield, but I know he still wishes he could have gone in."

"And Eugene? How's he doing overseas?"

Thankfully, they'd reached the top of the hill and could coast down. She kept her feet on the pedals, working the brakes to keep from going too fast. "Genie hates everything." In his letters, he ranted about the littlest things—C-rations, mud, the smell of other soldiers. But Helen could read between the lines. "I think he's terrified."

Frank grew quiet for a minute, and Helen wondered if she'd betrayed her brother again by confiding his fear. Then he said, "Anybody with an ounce of sense should be scared of war."

"I think he's as scared about shooting someone as he is about getting shot." Helen felt a lump rise in her throat and coughed to clear it. "How's Dotty? Has she heard from her husband?"

"No. And she resents the Army for officially listing her as a widow."

"That must be terrible!"

Frank grinned. "Dotty said it's a bunch of gobbledygook from dog-faced donkeys who don't have the sense they were born with. She says she'll find Boots on her own, in spite of those knuckleheads. I think those were her exact words."

Helen laughed. "Well, that sister of yours is one tough cookie. She's definitely no quitter."

Frank smiled at her, meaningfully. "A trait that I've been told runs in the family."

16

Helen

BATTLE CREEK, MICHIGAN

Frank had managed to get six Army towels, which equaled about one beach towel. He and Helen arranged four of the towels on the sand, close to the water.

Helen turned her back while she shed her uniform. Her swimsuit had been a gift from a nurse at Evanston who left to have a baby and figured she wouldn't fit into it for a while. The black string-tie top wasn't fashionable, but Helen knew she looked okay in it. When she faced Frank, she could tell he thought so too. He grinned, then looked out at the water, his cheeks adorably flushed.

Funny. Growing up, Helen had never known if she was pretty or not, not even in high school, when boys kept asking her out. Nobody got compliments in the Eberhart household. Mom had been too afraid she'd create vain children. Not until Helen got to college did she realize most guys and gals thought she was pretty great-looking. By then, it didn't seem to matter. What had mattered was making it to nurse's training. Yet she couldn't pretend Frank's opinion on her looks didn't matter to her now.

She settled onto the towels while Frank stuck a sun umbrella into the sand. It was still morning, but the sun shone like high noon.

He sat on a corner of the towels that left him outside of the umbrella's shade. "I love the hot sun." Helen remembered that his love of hot weather had made him request the Pacific theater. Since she'd asked for Europe, this might be the last time they'd see each other. Her heart felt as if someone were squeezing it.

He reached into his backpack and pulled out peanut butter sandwiches. "I don't know about you, but I'm starving."

Helen bit into hers. "Mmmm. Perfect."

"I agree." Frank grinned at her.

"So, how long do you think you'll be at Camp Ellis? Captain Walker told us we'll be shipped to Ellis ourselves before long. Wouldn't it be swell if we were there together?" She risked a sideways glance at Frank.

Frank shook his head. "I get the feeling we won't be there much longer. They've been working us hard on obstacle courses and firearms."

"Really? Will doctors carry guns?"

"The field hospitals aren't far from the front. I guess they figure the Japs, or the Germans, will be shooting at us, so we better know how to shoot back. Battalion aid stations are right on the battlefield, but I don't think we'll go there—those are for medics. Anyway, there's already talk about being sent to the staging area on the coast. Boston or New York, but could be San Francisco. We won't know until we get there."

It scared her to think she might lose contact with him, this time for years instead of days. Maybe forever. She swiveled toward him. "Say, we should come up with a secret code so we can stay in touch and get past the censors."

"I'm in! Did I tell you I love mysteries and puzzles?"

"Swell!" Helen said. "Have you seen mail after the censors get to it? One letter from Wilbur had half the lines cut out."

"At Ellis, we had a session on what we can and can't put into a letter. They said we'd hear more about it while we're waiting for transport overseas. I guess locations grab attention, even if they have nothing to do with war."

Helen thought about it. Locations were what she'd *want* to put into a letter. "Morse code?"

"I have a feeling the Army's onto that system," Frank said.

"True. And I'm not."

Frank got the cutest little thinking wrinkles in his forehead. "How about this? Say that I want to let you know I'm in Manila."

Helen felt warm inside. She hoped he really would want to let her know. "Go on."

"Okay. We spell out *Manila*, but use the first letter of each sentence. Like 'Many are here.' And the next sentence: 'And I miss you.' Then: 'Now I'm done.' You get the idea."

"Clever! You should be a spy like your brother. Only let's skip every other sentence to make it harder. And we shouldn't start with the first sentence—too obvious."

"You're the one who should get a spy degree. So how will we know where the code starts? We could read a letter and miss the code."

They batted ideas back and forth—an ink spot, indenting, quotation marks. But those would draw attention, when the whole point was *not* to draw attention.

Still thinking out loud, Helen said, "What if we did this, Frankie? The sentence before we start spelling the city's name, we write something that's totally out of place, something you and I would see as ridiculous, but the censors would skim over."

"Like I could tell you that I picked up my pink blouse from the cleaner's."

Helen laughed. "And I could say that I got my tooth pulled at the veterinarian's."

"Deal." Frank stuck out his hand. She shook it, holding on longer than necessary.

They ate their picnic and talked about all sorts of things, without mentioning the phone call or Frank's proposal. The nearest he came to it was when he told her about sneaking out of the barracks to use the phone. "I had to run past the POW encampment. I even waved to a German prisoner out for a smoke." That made her laugh so hard her eyes watered.

A welcome breeze kicked up. Helen gazed at the lake, rippling in sunlight that made diamonds dance on the water. "It's so beautiful, isn't it?"

"Wait till you see it from the middle."

"What?"

"I rented a boat." Frank stuffed the remains of lunch into his pack and got to his feet. He reached down and helped her up. "Come on!"

"Wait a minute. You rented what?"

"A canoe! We've got it for the whole day." Still holding her hand, he started across the hot sand at a jog. They raced along the shore until they reached a long dock with sailboats and fishing vessels tied up.

"I don't really know how to . . . to work a boat."

"Nothing to it." He untied the smallest, skimpiest, worst-looking boat there. "I can do all the paddling from the back. Ever been in a canoe?"

Helen couldn't speak, so she shook her head.

"Then you're in for a treat. Much better than a rowboat. You're closer to the water."

Closer to the water? That's all she needed. The canoe was a tiny bit of nothing between her and the water. It was her guilty secret that water terrified her. She couldn't swim.

The only time she'd come close to swimming was when Ed and Clarence had thrown her into the cistern in the basement of the Cissna Park house on her seventh birthday. They hadn't meant to hurt her, or even scare her. She'd been wearing her only fancy dress, and the boys thought it would be funny to get it wet. They'd learned to swim before they learned to walk, and they just hadn't noticed that she never swam with them. If Walter hadn't reached in and pulled her out, she'd have gone straight to the bottom of that murky pool. She'd never gone near a swimming pool since. A couple of times in college she'd gone to the beach, but she'd always talked her way out of swimming.

But this wasn't swimming, right? Boats were safe. Frank knew what he was doing. She'd be fine.

"All aboard!" Frank said.

She clung to her towel as if it were a life preserver. "Say, don't they have life preservers in these things?"

"Guess they figure we're headed for a war zone, so why bother. Ladies first!" He hunched over the boat, holding the sides and waiting for her to step in.

Helen focused on the yellow paint peeling from the splintery wooden canoe. Her legs felt wooden too, as she forced herself to edge closer. Her heart flickered as she stepped in and sat down, the boat bucking like a bronco beneath her.

"Unless you want to be the one to paddle, you need to scoot to the front." He flipped the rope into the boat.

"Oh, right." She gripped the sides and slid forward. Splinters embedded themselves in her palms, but she couldn't loosen her grip. Facing the triangular front, she felt Frank plop into the boat behind her. Water sloshed in. "Are you sure the boat isn't leaking?"

"Nah." He shoved off from the dock.

Helen gasped.

"Why don't you turn around so we're facing each other?" Frank suggested. She sensed him squirming, making the boat tilt.

"Right." Her fingers uncurled, and she forced herself to let go with one hand. Then she turned, regripped, stepped around, and sat.

Meanwhile, Frank dipped the paddle, pulled it back and around, making a J in the water. The canoe slipped through the shallows toward the center of the lake. His arms moved steadily, and she could see the outline of his deltoids, pectorals, triceps, abdominals.

Plop! Splash!

Helen screamed as water doused her arm and leg. He'd splashed her.

"Sorry." But his laugh said he wasn't sorry at all. Frank went back to paddling, and the boat fell into a rhythm, gliding smoothly. He hummed to the beat, and she recognized "It Had to Be You."

Her toe tapped, and she couldn't help singing along while Frank whistled. The words fit Frank, and they fit her. She wondered if he was thinking about the lyrics too. Then came the last line, or at least the last one she knew: "'For nobody else gave me a thrill. With all your faults, I love you still. It had to be you, wonderful you. It had to be you.'"

For what seemed like minutes, neither of them spoke. They simply stared into each other's eyes—into their souls, Helen thought. Frank was such a good man. She wanted him to talk about his proposal. She knew she should explain her refusal and apologize for the way she'd turned him down.

But she couldn't. He'd proposed, and she'd said no. Now he wasn't pressing her or asking again, and that's the way she wanted it, wasn't it?

He pulled in the paddle and reached into his pack, producing her favorite candy bar, Hershey's with nuts. "Probably a little melted."

"I can't believe you." She took the chocolate. She hadn't had one in so long.

He handed her a second bar. "I'm not really hungry. Save this one for later."

"Not on your life." She handed it back, then opened hers. "Now this is what it's all about." She took her first bite, savoring the rich chocolate.

He watched her with an expression she couldn't name. Pleasure? Delight? . . . Love?

"Eat your candy bar, soldier!" she commanded.

He grinned. "What was the line in that song about trying to be boss?"

She reached over the side of the boat and splashed him. For the last few minutes, she'd nearly forgotten she was in the middle of a lake. She stretched out her legs and leaned back a little. An insect buzzed around her, and she swatted at it. "So, what was life like growing up in Hamilton, Missouri?"

Frank answered her questions with anecdotes about his older brother, Jack, who taught him to box and let him win, who quit his job waiting tables at a great restaurant when they were in college so Frank could be hired there.

He talked a little about his parents, but Helen could read between the lines. Peter and Sina Mae Daley hadn't approved of their son's zest for a life outside their little Missouri community. They didn't understand why he refused to return home and take over his dad's practice. She got the feeling Frank's mother hadn't been any freer with compliments than her own had been.

Helen had to work hard to keep Frank talking about himself. Before she realized it, he'd guide the conversation back to her life. She found herself talking more openly to him than she did to Peggy.

"I know you're a churchgoer," he said. "First day at Battle Creek and you showed up in chapel."

"Ma saw to it that we never missed a Sunday. She marched us all there like ducklings." She remembered the small white building, the brown pews, sticky with heat.

"Didn't you want to go?"

"I never thought about it. Not going wasn't an option."

"Me too. I don't think I doubted the Bible stories, but I never gave them much thought. I admit I didn't hear much of the sermons, thanks to Jack making me laugh and getting me in trouble." He was quiet for a minute. "I wish I *had* paid more attention."

"I know what you mean."

"Maybe that's the one good thing the war's doing," he said. "It makes us think. Since Dotty's been home, she talks about Boots and about God like she knows them inside and out, like they're all war buddies."

"I think that's how my mother feels about her *Gott im Himmel*. We Eberharts aren't big on showing our feelings, much less talking about them. Besides, Ma prayed in German, so I didn't always know what she was saying. But I had no doubt that God was listening." Helen gazed at the sinking sun. They had spent the entire day on the lake—and miracle of miracles, she'd enjoyed every minute.

"I'm awfully hot," Frank said. "How about you?"

Helen inspected her reddish arms. "I'd say I'm burning hot."

He stood up in the canoe.

The boat rocked, and she grabbed the sides. "What are you doing?"

"Time for a swim!" Frank said, a devilish twinkle in his eyes.

"No thanks." She tightened her grip on the splintery edges of the boat. "You go ahead."

"Ah, you gals never want to get your hair wet, right? I'll bet you look great with wet hair. How about we see?" He straddled the canoe, rocking it harder.

"D-don't!" Helen cried.

"Didn't you ever hear that expression, 'Tip a canoe . . . and Helen too'?" He jumped to one side, and the canoe tipped.

Helen screamed as the boat flopped all the way over, flinging her into the lake. She opened her mouth to cry out, but water rushed in.

"Come on!" Frank shouted when she surfaced. "The canoe won't sink. Race you to that buoy and back!"

Helen thrashed, trying to keep her head above water. It felt like something was pulling her down, dragging her to the bottom of the lake. "Help! Help me!" Water rushed into her mouth again.

"Helen?" Frank was calling her from somewhere. He sounded far away.

She stopped kicking and felt herself sinking, down, down, down. *No!* She struggled, arms flailing until—after what seemed like forever—she burst through the dark, heavy water and into the air. She gasped, filling her lungs with a mixture of air and water.

"Helen! I'm coming!"

She heard splashing. Then she felt something grab her around the waist. She kicked at it, slapped it. She struck with all her might.

"Helen! Stop! It's me. I've got you."

But she couldn't see who or what had her. She couldn't think. All she could do was scream and yell and scream some more. With her eyes shut, she felt the dank waters of the Cissna Park cistern close around her. She kicked and cried, "Somebody help me!"

A motor sounded so close that she had the sensation of being run over.

"Ma'am? We're here. Let the lady go!"

Helen sensed more arms around her. She felt herself being lifted out of the water and onto a boat. A bigger boat. Three men in uniform surrounded her. A second boat came at them from the other side. She watched as that boat sped so close to Frank it might have cut him in two. Two MPs towered above the water, standing in the boat, rifles pointed down at Frank.

"Stay where you are!" the burly MP shouted.

Frank's eyes were huge. He tried to hold up his hands, but it made his head bob underwater. "Wait—I didn't know she couldn't—"

"Shut up!" shouted the other MP. The guy hollered over Frank's head at the men in Helen's boat. "We got him! We'll bring him in, ma'am. You'll need to press charges so we can—"

"What?" Helen's head was splitting. Her teeth chattered so hard her eyes ached. "No—I—"

One of her rescuers put his hand on her shoulder. "Don't feel bad, ma'am. It's not your fault. You think you know a fellow—"

"But I do know this one!" She could see Frank's feet as they hauled him into the MPs' boat, slamming him against the side. The engine roared, ready to take off.

Helen stood up in the boat. "Stop! You can't take him away. That's my fiancé! We're going to be married."

17

FRANK

Battle Creek, Michigan

Frank kept his arm around Helen, his fiancée—he loved the sound of that—and waited until the last minute to board his train. They'd barely had time to dry off and change clothes before catching a ride to the station. The whistle blew and soldiers scurried, but Frank stayed rooted to the platform. He didn't want to let go of Helen, and the astounding thing was that she didn't want to let go of him.

Helen nuzzled against his neck. "When can you come back, Frankie?"

"I'll work something out."

Steam from under the train sent a billowing white puff around their feet, completing the image—they were floating on a cloud.

"All aboard!" the engineer shouted at Frank. The train jerked. Frank leaped onto the metal step.

From the platform, Helen kept pace with him, her tiny hand still in his. He leaned down and kissed her one more time, their lips barely brushing. "I love you, Helen Eberhart!" Their grip gave way, and her fingers slid from his.

"I love you too!" Waving wildly, she jogged alongside the train. Other spectators moved out of her way—it was that or get run over. "Listen! When you get back, you'll have a telegram waiting. Tear it up, Frankie! I didn't mean—"

"A telegram?" Frank grinned. "Something about how I shouldn't come for a visit?"

Helen stopped short, then ran faster to catch up. "You got my telegram?"

"Sure. I knew you didn't mean it."

Helen laughed, that tinkling laugh he thought he could call up wherever the war took him. She shouted something, but the words were drowned by the clank of the tracks as the train chugged through the yards and picked up steam.

Frank grasped the side bar and leaned out, waving until he couldn't see her anymore.

Inside, the passenger car was already smoke-filled, not a good thing for his asthma. He knew he shouldn't complain since he didn't have a ticket or a legitimate pass. Miller, the staff sergeant for the newly formed 11th General Dispensary, turned out to be an okay joe, in spite of his sadistic nature during obstacle training. When he learned this would be Frank's last chance to win over Helen, he'd cut false papers, declaring an "emergency assignment" for one Frank Daley. The papers wouldn't hold up to close scrutiny, but so far there hadn't been any scrutiny at all.

Miller hadn't been the only one to come through. Andy volunteered to answer for Frank in roll call, an offense that would have gotten them both in trouble if discovered. Lartz was covering for him at the hospital.

But man, had it been worth the effort! Helen Eberhart was going to become Helen Daley. He was the luckiest man on the planet.

Twenty-four hours later, when Frank sneaked back into Camp Ellis, he expected to be greeted by attack dogs or a firing squad. Instead, someone was singing "Sweet Adeline."

"Andy!" Frank caught up with him.

"Glad you're back, sport! I'm tired of being you . . . and me. How did it go with the lovely Helen of Troy?"

"She's going to marry me."

Anderson sobered fast. "Congratulations, old boy! This calls for a drink!"

"Not now, Andy." He hustled Anderson to their barracks as taps sounded over the speaker. They didn't always play taps, and Frank wasn't sure why, although Lartz claimed there weren't enough buglers to go around. They ducked into their barracks as the last note faded.

Lartz was reading in bed with a flashlight. "Frank! How did it go?"

"We're getting married, Lartz!" Anderson shouted before Frank could.

Quickly, Frank said, "*Helen* and I!"

"Yeah?" Robbie, a medic assigned to the 11th General until they found a battalion for him to return to, gave a thumbs-up. "Congratulations! I married my sweetheart right before I got shipped out. Keeps me going, I tell you."

"Yeah, right," somebody said.

"Hey, I've seen pictures of Helen," Sergeant Miller said. Frank could make out the sergeant's unshaven face by the red glow of his cigarette. "Lieutenant Daley deserves hearty congratulations."

"So when's the big day?" Lartz asked. "Where are you having the wedding?"

Frank shrugged. He hadn't even thought of that.

Little by little, the whole barracks woke to the news. Frank was glad he didn't have to hold it in any longer. He wanted to shout from the rooftops. He climbed to his bunk and stood as much as possible without banging his head. "I'm getting married to the most wonderful gal in the world!"

Laughter rippled across the room in tiny waves. "Better marry her fast," Robbie said. "We're shipping out soon."

The room grew quiet for a second, but Lartz ended it by shouting, "Three cheers for Helen and Frank!"

The cheers were so loud that Frank suspected the entire camp heard them. An MP was probably on the way. He soaked it all in, wishing Helen could hear them too. These guys made up his outfit now, the 11th General Dispensary. He felt something for them—not just camaraderie, like he'd had with college chums or fellow slaves in residency. He felt protective, like he wanted to keep every one of them safe, no matter what he had to do. For the first time in his life, Frank felt like a soldier.

How ironic that on the very night he realized he was going to be a husband, he also realized he was going to be a soldier—not just a doctor, but a soldier, too. He only hoped he had what it would take to be all of the above.

~~~~~~

From: Helen Eberhart
10 July 1944
Battle Creek, MI

My dearest Frankie,

I am the happiest girl on earth because you want me. And because I want you, too. I can hardly believe that I've found the man of my dreams, and that we're going to be married. I know exactly the style of wedding dress I want and the bridesmaids I'll pick, along with my sisters, of course. Will Cissna Park seem so very far for your parents to come for a wedding? We were both

so much in shock (you nearly in leg irons!) that we didn't talk
about that big question: when.

   To tell you the truth—something I vow always to do with
you, even if it means admitting a thing like that I can't swim—
last night I woke up in a cold sweat. My first thought was,
"Gott im Himmel, what did I do?" But then I closed my eyes
and pictured my handsome husband, and I smiled myself to
sleep. I shall burst if I don't tell someone my news. I must tell
Peggy why I'm the happiest she's ever seen me.

Later:

   Frankie darling, BIG NEWS: We are shipping out, going
overseas soon. That's the rumor. You remember Victoria, who
flirted shamelessly with you? Tall and thin, long coal-black
hair? Peggy claims she'd make a better Mata Hari than a
nurse. Victoria says she heard there's a big push in Europe to
end this war, and they need nurses NOW. She thinks we might
skip Camp Ellis and head straight to Europe. How I wish
I hadn't requested Europe, and all because I didn't want to
be hot.

   What are we going to do? Peggy says not to pay attention to
anything Victoria says because that gal is too stuck on herself to
know what's going on with the rest of the world. On the other
hand, Victoria is skilled in the art of flirting with high-up
officers.

   Peggy and I have talked and talked, and I think if you and
I don't marry very soon, it will be too late. I will be gone. Cissna
Park will take too long. I'm out of July days, but I could fight
Captain Walker for two August days and marry you in Chicago!

                                                        Love,
       Helen, soon to be H. E. D., Helen Eberhart Daley. Helen
                   Daley. Mrs. Frank Daley. All very good!

From: Frank Daley
10 July 1944
Camp Ellis

My dearest Helen,

I wrote you on the train, but I was standing up and hadn't slept in two days, so even I couldn't make out my handwriting. I shall make a fine doctor one day, with this penmanship.

I wish you could have heard the heartfelt congratulations of the 11th General. Even Andy celebrated our happy news, though he had been out celebrating already.

Let's set a date—soon! Nobody knows when our unit will ship out. I'd marry you tonight if we could pull it off. I don't want you to give up your dream wedding, though. As for me, all I need is you.

Sun is coming up. Must run. Literally—18-mile hike starting now!

Love always,
Your Frankie

P.S. I'll call my parents to give them the good news.

15 July 1944
From: Sina Mae Daley
Hamilton, Missouri

Dear Frank,

I have had ample time to reflect upon our phone conversation, and I remain more convinced than ever that you *are heading into a folly filled with lingering regret. As William Congreve put it, "Marry in haste, repent in leisure." Please know, however, that Daddy's and my disapproval is in no way the explanation for our refusal to attend your wedding ceremony (such as it is). He cannot be spared from the Army's training base, and I have my own commitments with the Red Cross.*

Yesterday I had occasion to work side-by-side with your former liaison, Jean Gurley, at the Red Cross blood donation in town. She asked that I send you her kind regards, though I doubt she would have extended such courtesy had she known your present intentions.

As I can see that your mind is closed on the matter of matrimony, there remains little for me to say in this epistle.

Yours truly,
Mother

~❦~

17 July 1944
From: Mrs. Louis Eberhart
Cissna Park, Illinois

Dear Helen,

Are you out of your mind?

Marriage? To a stranger your mother has never seen? And this from my sensible child? From Vin or Eugene, I might expect, or at least understand, such a thing, but not from my down-to-earth Helen.

Gott im Himmel, preserve us!

Your mother

18

Helen

EN ROUTE TO CHICAGO, ILLINOIS

Helen gazed out the window as branches smacked the windshield, while wisps of clouds swallowed the pale moon, then let it go again. "Thanks for driving me to the station at this ungodly hour, Dr. Reynolds."

"You know you're making a big mistake, don't you, Helen?"

"So you've said many times." Helen knew Dr. Reynolds flattered and flirted with half the nurses at Percy Jones, but he'd tried extra hard with her, probably because she'd refused his advances. If there had been anyone else to drive her, she never would have let him do it. His motives were blatantly ulterior, but what choice did she have? Bill had planned to drive her but got called away by Captain Walker at the last minute.

"War marriages never last." Dr. Reynolds turned his boyish grin on her. "Seriously, Helen, sneaking off in the night to marry someone you barely know?"

"You sound like my mother." Helen didn't want to think about the last letter from Ma. This wasn't the way either of them had envisioned her wedding day.

"A wise woman, your mother."

"She usually is. But she doesn't know Frank." Helen had already received letters from three of her brothers warning her to change her mind before it was too late. Only Eugene offered congratulations. And even his letter was so short and distant that it made her sadder than all of her other brothers' letters put together.

"It's not too late to admit you made a mistake, you know," Dr. Reynolds said. "I can turn this car around and—"

"Don't you dare!" But the thought was there. What if they did turn around? The rumors had died down about getting shipped overseas without training at Camp Ellis. She and Frank didn't have to rush like this, did they? Part of her couldn't believe she was going through with marrying a man she'd known only a few weeks, only to be sent to opposite ends of the earth until the war ended.

One lone light illuminated the train depot. Helen hadn't expected so many people gathered on the platform. Dr. Reynolds got her duffel bag from the backseat. "You're breaking a lot of hearts, Nurse Eberhart, mine foremost."

"Something tells me you'll get over it before the sun rises, Doctor." She walked with him to the train. Next to them, a soldier and his gal were lost in a tearful embrace. Helen shook Reynolds's hand. "Thanks again for the lift."

He kissed her cheek. "I'll be sitting in the car in case you change your mind."

"You're incorrigible!"

"And don't you forget it." He pointed to his sedan. "Right here until the train pulls out. Plenty of time to come to your senses."

Helen joined the last few passengers crowding onto the train.

She found a seat at the back, by a window. She just hoped she wouldn't get anything on her uniform before walking down the aisle in it. No wedding dress. Balancing her duffel on her knees, she unzipped the side pocket and pulled out a sack tied with twine, a wedding gift from "her boys." Danny, Hudy, and Jimmy had made her promise not to open it until she got to Chicago. But she'd never been good about waiting to open gifts. Besides, she was on her way to Chicago.

Inside the bag were four small packages, each wrapped in twisted white toilet paper that one of the boys must have stolen from the officers' club, though she couldn't imagine how. A homemade card said *CONGRATULATIONS* on the front. Inside, it read: *This is from all three of us and my mom, who helped us get what we needed. Ma says you can't have a wedding without something old, new, borrowed, and blue. Wish we could be there. Love to our favorite nurse (and our favorite doctor, who better be mighty good to you), Jimmy, Hudy, and Danny.*

She unwound the tissue from the first gift. It was a mirror with a note stuck to the back, written in the same hand as the card—the only hand among the three that could still write, Danny's: *This OLD mirror went to the Pacific with me and back without getting a crack. Guess that means I get 7 years without a lick of bad luck, huh? I give them to you. Hudy.*

Helen put down the mirror and opened the next gift, a beautiful braided-leather necklace. The note said, *I made this before I knew you, Nurse, back when I had fingers and could braid leather goods for merchants back home. It's brand NEW and never been worn. Jimmy.*

She had to swallow the lump congealing in her throat. A note was stuck to the next gift, a delicately laced handkerchief: *This one is BORROWED on account of my ma says she'll skin me alive if she don't get it back. We all felt bad that you don't have a fine wedding dress, but here's something my ma carried when she got hitched. Ma says she'd be real proud if you carried it down the aisle. Danny and Ma.*

One gift left, and one note: *BLUE almost did us in! Everything in this hospital is white. You have Danny's Aunt Millie to thank for this gift. Wait till you see what she sent her legless nephew for his birthday.*

Helen opened the package and found a pair of blue non-Army-issued wool socks that Danny couldn't have worn even if he still had feet. She laughed until her laughter changed into crying. Her own brothers may not have wished her well, but her boys did. She fought the tears, but it was a losing battle. What would happen to the boys once she went overseas? What would happen to all of her amputees? She felt guilty for her happiness when she thought about what lay ahead for those soldiers.

Oh, Gott im Himmel, how can I leave these boys? Helen prayed.

Through the train's smudged window, she spotted Dr. Reynolds's car, with the good doctor behind the wheel, waiting as promised.

Helen felt her heart skip—not the dime novel–romance heart skip, but the atrial fibrillation she'd inherited from her mother. In fourteen hours, she'd be Mrs. Frank Daley. Nothing to worry about . . . unless her mother was right and she really was out of her mind.

19

FRANK

En route to Chicago, Illinois

Lartz floored the jeep they'd "borrowed" to get to the station. "Do you have the ring?"

"*Now* you ask me?" Frank patted his pockets until he felt the tiny box. "I wish it were bigger. Do you think she'll like it, Lartz?"

"*Now* you ask me?"

Humor—just what Frank needed. He relaxed a little, as much as a guy could on the most important day of his life.

"Hard to believe next time I see you, you'll be an old married man," Lartz mused.

An old married man. For a second, Frank shuddered. If he'd thought of marriage at all, he'd pictured it way down the line, after he'd sown a few more wild oats.

"So what's in the bags?" Lartz nodded toward the backseat, where

Frank had a duffel bag, a backpack, and a shopping bag. "Nobody in the Army has that much gear."

"Presents."

"From your family?"

Frank shook his head. He'd written Jack but hadn't heard back from him. His brother was probably deep into Germany, unreachable. Dotty's letter, though, exploded with congratulations and joy and how great it was being married. If she could be so happy married to a guy she hadn't seen in two years, surely he and Helen could make a go of it. "The gifts are from me. Except for the Little Red Riding Hood cookie jar you guys gave us. I wanted Helen to see it." He'd never enjoyed shopping until he shopped for Helen. Good thing Helen's brother Walt insisted on paying for their honeymoon, along with making the wedding arrangements.

"Sure wish I could have gotten a leave to go to your wedding."

"Me too. Then I'd know somebody there besides Helen. Her brother's my best man, and I haven't even met the guy. At least the service will be short and sweet. We could only get the chapel, and there are about fifty weddings scheduled today."

"Be glad it's not a Jewish wedding."

"I'll bite. Why should I be glad it's not a Jewish wedding?"

"Because there's no such thing as a short Jewish wedding."

Frank lucked out and found a seat on the train, although his bags weren't so lucky. He ended up holding them, stacked on his lap like wedding cake tiers.

Wedding cake! Was the groom supposed to provide the cake? How many other details had he missed?

By the time the train pulled into Chicago's Central Station, Frank was starving. It was a good thing he didn't have the wedding cake because he would have shown up with nothing but crumbs. He counted his money and decided he had enough for half a sandwich, which he downed in two seconds. Then he settled onto one of the benches facing the northbound tracks. If all went according to plan, Helen would be there in two hours, and they'd be married in three.

The Chicago heat was making him sweat through his uniform, the only wedding suit he had. Every so often, he left his bags to check the boards.

Finally, the board posted track 8 for the train from Battle Creek, *on time*. In one hour he and Helen would be promising to be husband and wife for the rest of their lives. He thought about her first reaction to his harebrained proposal. *"Are you out of your mind?"*

Maybe. A fellow had to be out of his mind to think someone like Helen Eberhart would want to spend the rest of her life with him. He wondered if she ever thought *she* was out of her mind for accepting his proposal. Would she regret it someday?

Today?

The last thing Andy had said to him was "I hope that gal of yours doesn't wise up. Nothing worse than a guy who gets jilted at the altar, unless it's a guy who gets jilted in the train station and never makes it to the altar."

The train was late. Frank checked the board: *On time.*

Liars. Ten minutes late already. Fifteen. Twenty.

In the distance, a train snaked in from the yards. Tracks crisscrossed. He held his breath as the train pulled into track 8. "Helen!" he shouted, jogging backward, peering in at the crowded shapes. He waved wildly, even though he couldn't see her.

The train hissed to a stop and began coughing out passengers. He tried to stand his ground in the middle of the platform, where he could see all exits. A man in a suit came off first, and Frank wondered how he'd gotten out of military service. Two soldiers stepped down and were grabbed by a couple of women waiting for them. An older woman, a child at either side clinging to her, stepped off the train and squinted left, then right.

Where was Helen? She should have gotten off the train by now.

A minute passed, and nobody else got off. Nobody.

Please don't back out on me. Grabbing his packages, Frank pushed up the steps, past the conductor.

"Hey, soldier! Last stop. Everybody out." The burly conductor nodded to the track.

"I'll be right back." He ran down the corridor and through the next car and the next. They were empty. Helen wasn't there.

He should have known. It was too good to be true. *She* was too good to be true. Maybe if he hadn't pressed so hard . . . if they'd had more time together . . .

His knees felt weak as he stepped back down to the platform.

"Frankie!"

He looked up and saw her, his Helen, running toward him.

Frank dropped the packages and swept her off her feet. He twirled her in his arms and kissed her. "You came!"

"You goose, of course I came!" She kissed him back. "I fell asleep. Can you believe it? Well, I was up all night. Then I got off the train, and you weren't there. And I thought—"

He kissed her again. She was here in his arms.

And that was all that mattered.

20

Helen

CHICAGO, ILLINOIS

"Walter! Over here!" Helen waved as the black sedan pulled to the station loading zone.

Sarah, sophisticated and lovely as always, waved back. Years ago, Sarah had been a hosiery model for a nylon stockings company down South. Her legs had been pictured in magazines all across the country. Helen's mother thought it was scandalous, but Helen considered it pure glamour. This morning Helen had used her eyebrow pencil to draw a stocking seam up the backs of her bare calves. She hadn't seen silks in months.

The car stopped close to the curb, and the window rolled down. Sarah held one gloved hand over her hat, a furry pillbox with a tiny net. "Why, sugar!" she exclaimed in her Tennessee drawl. "Will you just look at y'all? You're beautiful! I'd say being a fiancée agrees with you. Come give me a kiss."

Helen leaned in and kissed her on the cheek. The scent of French cologne brought back memories from nurse's training, when Sarah would breeze into the dorm and kidnap her sister-in-law to take her shopping, always Sarah's treat.

"Wait till you meet Frank, Sarah!" Helen turned to make the introductions, but Frank was loading their luggage into the trunk. He and Walter were already laughing and shaking hands. She'd known they would like each other. Dashing back to them, she laughed too, then looped her arm through Frank's and stood on tiptoes to kiss her brother. "Thank you, Walter! Thanks for everything."

"Sarah loves this stuff," Walter said. "She'd fix up a wedding for her worst enemy."

Walter drove too fast, turning the Chicago haze into a blur through Helen's window. Minutes later, they were walking around the giant stone cathedral to the chapel in back. Helen had gone to church with Walter and Sarah a number of times, but she'd never been in the chapel. Tiny red flowers lined the sidewalk, and thick-trunked trees bowed over a steepled annex.

"Three minutes!" Walt took the lead, and Sarah fell back with Helen.

"It's a shame your mama and daddy couldn't be here. They must feel just awful."

"It was pretty short notice." Helen didn't add that her mother hadn't sounded filled with regret when she'd given her regrets. She still hadn't heard from Dad.

"That's the war for you." Sarah turned to Frank. "And your mama and daddy couldn't make it either? Helen said your father's still in the Army?"

Frank gave Sarah his warm smile, but Helen thought there might be a hint of sadness behind it. "Reserves. He trains medics, and Mother volunteers for the Red Cross. They couldn't get away."

"I understand, sugar," Sarah said, clearly not understanding.

"Time!" Walter pointed to his watch and held the chapel door open. Music flowed out, a lone piano playing the wedding march.

As it turned out, the wedding assembly line was running late. They watched a private in uniform stroll down the aisle with a girl in white who looked younger than Vin, Helen's little sister. Helen thought how swell it would have been to have her sisters here, but she shoved the thought away.

The next wedding was Navy all the way, with the groom and four best men decked in Navy duds. The bride, however, wore a real wedding gown, high-necked, with old-fashioned lace.

Then Helen remembered. "I have to go to the car!"

"What?" Frank looked worried.

"Walter, give me the keys!"

"It can wait, can't it?" Sarah begged. "Y'all are up next."

"Keys!" she demanded, holding out her hand.

Walter ran to the parking lot with her. "Is this your way of getting out of marrying him? There's still hope with Ray, you know."

"Walter Eberhart! Open that trunk." She didn't know if he was kidding or not. Walt had really liked Ray and the fact that his little sister would have had a great house and all the money she'd ever need. He didn't know Frank from Adam.

Do I?

The thought struck her as if slapped to her forehead. Her feet kept moving, but the world stopped spinning. How well did she know Frank? What would married life be like after the war? Did he really want to live somewhere hot like Miami? They hadn't talked about that.

Are you out of your mind? Helen had always considered herself sensible. Was this sensible? Marriages were crumbling all around her, and war marriages were the worst.

"Helen?" Walter stared at her, the trunk of the car wide open.

She could get into this car right now. Tell Walt to drive her anywhere she wanted . . .

She wanted Frank. She loved him more than anything. And so what if they hadn't known each other very long? She knew all she needed to know about the love of her life. Didn't she?

"Right!" Helen dove into her duffel bag and came out with the treasures from her boys. The tiny mirror fit in her pocket with the hankie. Walt fastened her braided necklace around her neck. But those blue socks . . .

"Don't tell me you're wearing those." Walt frowned at the socks dangling from her hand. "Sarah will have heart failure."

"I don't think they'd fit under my shoes. Come on! I'll think of something."

The crooked grin on Frank's face when she came back into the chapel made her laugh out loud. She kissed him. "You didn't think I'd run out on you, did you?" she teased.

"Couldn't blame you if you had, I suppose. But I'm glad you thought better of making your getaway." He took her hand.

The pastor waved them up as the pianist began banging out the wedding march for the umpteenth time, debunking the myth that practice makes perfect. Frank laced Helen's arm through his and whispered, "Ready?"

The socks! "Almost!" She stuck the woolly blue socks into his pocket. "Don't ask."

They walked the short aisle together, with Sarah and Walt behind them. Helen wondered how many couples had walked this very aisle today, this week, this month. Were they all insane to be marrying with a war going on, knowing they'd be starting their lives together apart? Maybe so. But at this moment, right now, she didn't care how many insane couples had walked this aisle. She was glad to be one of them, proud to be part of this testament that life would go on after the war. *They* would go on.

Sarah threw rice as Helen and Frank made a dash for the car.

"Are you going to let your sister-in-law do that to your wife?"

Helen challenged, picking grains of rice out of her hair as they settled into the backseat of Walt's big Ford.

"You don't like rice, Mrs. Daley? *I* do." Frank grinned. "I do. Those are two pretty great words. I like the way you said them in there."

"Do you?" They kissed, husband and wife.

In the front seat, Sarah snuggled closer to her husband. "Walter, honey, we're late for the reception. Off to the Blackhawk!"

The Blackhawk's private dining room was the height of elegance, with a gorgeous chandelier and a waterfall in one corner. Helen and Frank slid into a curved booth at the edge of the little dance floor, and the waiter appeared with a bottle of champagne.

"We ordered prime rib and potatoes," Sarah said, "because, of course, the order had to be placed ahead of time."

"Prime rib?" Frank glanced at Helen, as if checking to see if Sarah was serious. Helen shrugged.

"Y'all only get married once, you know," Sarah said.

"You better only get married once," Walt added, narrowing his eyes at Frank.

Frank put his arm around Helen's shoulders. "Once will do."

A waiter appeared with a giant bowl of lettuce greens, nestled on top of crushed ice. With a flair, he waved salad tongs as a girl in a black vest set down individual bowls. "To your greens," the waiter began, his French accent thick, "I add fresh romaine and a hint of sweet onion, finely minced." He kept the bowl spinning as he narrated his every move, slicing in tomatoes, cucumbers, mushrooms, and cheese, twirling knives and tongs with a magician's flair.

While they ate their salads and waited for dinner, Frank thanked Walt and Sarah a dozen times. They talked about everything—Percy Jones, Helen's "boys" there, Frank's disease ward. Sarah quizzed him about his family, and Frank asked them for Eberhart news.

"Our brothers don't say much in their letters," Walt complained. "Except for Wilbur, who says too much. His letters come with half the words cut out and the others marked out in black. Clarence sends Mom postcards from the Pacific like he's on vacation. He was laid up with some disease for a couple of weeks, but he's okay now. Bud sent me one of those little voice recordings. Have you seen those?"

Helen shook her head.

"It's like a record, but small and a horrible sound, although you can tell it's Bud."

"Has anyone heard from Eugene?" Helen asked. "He sent me a sweet letter and congratulated me, but it was so short. Nothing at all about him."

"No!" Sarah said. "And I know your poor mother worries about him."

So she wasn't the only one, then. Helen said a silent prayer for Eugene and tried not to worry, not tonight.

Sarah changed the subject so smoothly, while keeping the conversation flowing and making sure everyone had what they needed. Helen hoped she'd be half the hostess—and half the wife—Sarah was.

Walt took Sarah's hand. "M'lady, may I have this dance?"

Frank followed suit, and he and Helen took to the dance floor.

"Sorry," he said, when they bumped feet. "I know you love to dance. I will too, now that I have you to hold."

"We'll have lots of time for me to show you some fancy steps." She nestled her head on his chest. "But for now, this is swell."

The meal was a celebration, filled with insider Eberhart stories that Frank graciously laughed at. Helen was only half listening to her brother's version of the day "little Helen" saved their mother from bleeding to death in the garden when the waiter came out carrying a three-layered wedding cake, topped with an Army groom and bride and a tiny American flag. The music switched abruptly to "It Had to Be You."

"Oh, Sarah. How on earth did you manage this?" Helen asked.

Sarah clapped her hands. "Isn't that topper just too much! I found it at Marshall Field's. I'll hang on to it until y'all get back from this dreadful war."

This dreadful war.

Helen laughed along with Sarah and cut the cake with Frank's hands covering hers and making a mess of the job. But she couldn't get the words out of her head. The whole day had been an enchanted dream. What would happen when the dream ended, when she and her new husband went to opposite ends of the world? What would happen to them in *this dreadful war*?

FRANK

Chicago, Illinois

Frank knew he'd never be able to repay Walter and Sarah. They were fantastic. But he wanted Helen to himself. He whispered in her ear, "We should get going, sweetheart."

"We can't be rude, Frankie."

Frank would do anything for Helen, but every last drop of patience had drained from him. "It's okay to be rude on your wedding night. Only not to each other," he added quickly. "Walter, Sarah, we'll never be able to thank you enough. Everything was perfect. But . . . well—"

"How about a nightcap, Frank?" Walter asked. "We only live thirty minutes away, and we have a pool table. Do you play pool?"

"Well . . ."

"Then it's settled," Walter said. "What do you think, Frank? Best two out of three?"

"That's . . . uh . . . nice of you, Walt. It's just . . ." He stared at Helen, willing her to jump in.

"Walter Eberhart!" Sarah scolded, elbowing her husband. "You quit teasing this dear boy right this minute!" She turned her gracious smile on Frank. "Now, we'll get y'all to the Palmer House. Express, no stops."

Frank felt like a dupe. It wasn't often that he was the one who got had. "I'll take a rain check on that pool game."

"I'll hold you to it," Walter said.

Frank shifted his weight from one foot to the other as they waited for their turn to check in at the Palmer House. The hotel lobby was even more glamorous than the Blackhawk. Velvet and satin couches stretched over thick rugs, with crystal chandeliers everywhere. Half of the people in the lobby wore uniforms, most of them Army. The other half, in black tuxedos and sequined gowns, looked like they inhabited another world, *this* world.

Finally, he and Helen moved up to the counter. As he struggled with all the bags, Frank didn't miss the fish-eye the well-dressed hotel clerk gave Helen. "May I help you?"

"Lieutenant and Mrs. Frank Daley. We have a reservation for three nights. The honeymoon suite." He felt his cheeks flush and didn't risk a glance at Helen.

The clerk raised his eyebrows.

Frank wasn't sure if the guy didn't believe him, didn't approve of Army marriages, or couldn't find the reservation. "Is there a problem?"

"Not exactly. You're checked into the honeymoon suite for one night."

"But we booked three nights!" Helen protested.

"This is true. But our new policy is to provide each couple with one night so that we may better serve the members of our armed forces."

"What are we supposed to do tomorrow?" Frank demanded.

"You are booked into the Drake or the Edgewater tomorrow night, depending on availability. You'll be quite well taken care of, I assure you. Mr. Eberhart has seen to everything." He handed over a brass key with a metal plaque that said *501* and pointed to the winding staircase. "Next?"

Frank balanced his bags under his arms, with a duffel bag in each hand, and headed for the staircase.

"Let me take some of that," Helen offered, reaching for her bag.

"Not on your life." He tried not to let on how heavy the load was, but by the time they reached their suite, he couldn't hide the fact that he was out of breath. He dropped the bags and fumbled with the key. "There." He pushed the door open.

"Golly!" Helen peeked in at the palatial room that looked like a mini lobby, with its own couch and table by a window covered in lace and silk striped curtains. Helen started to go in, but he stopped her.

"I believe this is how it's done." Frank swooped his bride into his arms and carried her across the threshold. She was lighter than the bags and much softer. They kissed before he put her down and brought in the bags.

"What a room!" Helen twirled, then dashed over to her duffel bag. "And I thought women were the ones who brought too much stuff. What could you have in all those bags?"

Frank grinned. "You'll find out."

The room had its own bathroom, and Helen took her duffel in with her, while Frank unpacked his bags. His plan had been to give Helen a gift each night, but he couldn't wait. He set out the cookie jar from the guys. Then he opened the package from Walt—a bottle of schnapps. Frank had never tasted schnapps, and he had no desire to do so. But he set the bottle on the bedside table in case Helen had a secret love for the stuff. There must be a million things he didn't know about his wife. For a second, he stopped unpacking and let that thought race through his brain. Did his wife drink? Did she smoke? Did she like animals? Children? Baseball?

He shook it off. They'd have a lifetime to get to know each other, wouldn't they? He pulled out the gift he'd spotted in a shop window in Galesburg. The minute he saw it, he'd known he had to get it for Helen. It hadn't even been for sale, just a stuffed dog decoration in a furniture display. He'd talked the store's owner into selling him the shaggy black dog, which might have been a Scotty.

He set their "pet" on the bed and got out his last gift, yellow silk pajamas. Not real silk, but they looked like the ones Betty Grable and Lana Turner wore in the picture shows. He'd had to borrow money from Dotty to pay for them, although his sister said not to worry about paying him back, that it would be her wedding gift. Frank had no idea what size Helen was, so he'd sized up the shopgirl and asked for two sizes smaller.

Frank sat on the foot of the bed and stared at the door to the bathroom. "I'm still out here, in case you wondered!"

"Ready?"

"Yeah. I want you to see—"

Helen came out in—well, he wasn't sure what it was—a slip? Or the skimpiest nightgown he'd ever seen.

"Do you like it?" She bit her bottom lip.

She looked more beautiful than he'd imagined. And he had imagined. "I like it."

"Peggy and the gals went in on it. I think it cost an awful lot."

"Worth every penny."

She darted to the bed as if the ground were cold, which it wasn't. Then she pulled back the covers and shimmied under them. They sat for a minute, Frank at her feet, neither of them speaking. They were medical professionals and could explain to a roomful of people the mechanics and biology of what they were about to do together. But suddenly Frank wondered if he knew anything at all about wedding nights. And Helen looked every bit as nervous as he felt.

Her gaze darted around the room. "Say, what's this?"

"Schnapps," Frank answered, without looking.

Helen picked up the stuffed dog. "Well, how do you do, Schnapps? You're as cute as you can be."

Frank realized his mistake. "No, I meant—" He stopped. *Schnapps.* Somehow it felt like the perfect name for the little dog. "Do you like it?"

"I love our first dog!" She pretended to whisper in the dog's pointy ear. "You and I will be great friends. You can keep me company when Daddy is away."

Daddy? Frank hadn't given that concept much thought. In theory, he kind of liked the idea of a son. Or a daughter. But for now, he'd probably have to work too hard at being the daddy of a stuffed dog. "Schnapps, ol' boy," he said, taking the dog from Helen and setting him on the floor, "we grown-ups have some grown-up business to take care of." He shut off the lamp, grateful that enough light shone through the window to let him see every inch of his new wife.

Frank was pretty sure he hadn't slept all night. His neck and shoulder ached. He hadn't wanted to move Helen's beautiful head off his shoulder, so he'd been trapped for the last couple of hours in an uncomfortable position. He didn't mind at all. He'd choose this over any other spot on earth. He'd thought he was the happiest man in the world when Helen said, "I do."

Now he knew it.

22

Helen

BATTLE CREEK, MICHIGAN

Two letters. Helen grabbed them from Bill and hurried back to her bunk. She ripped open the letter from Frank. He'd finally gotten a three-day leave so he could come back to Battle Creek this weekend. They'd been married over a month, but she hadn't seen her husband since their honeymoon. Twice, she and Frank had made plans to rendezvous, only to have leaves canceled at the last minute. She held her breath as she unfolded the thin sheets of paper—only two pages—and read the first sentence: *My darling, they did it again.*

Helen burst into tears.

Peggy was there in an instant. "Helen? What's happened? It's not Frank, is it?"

Helen nodded.

"Aw, honey." Peggy sat next to her and put an arm around her.

"He's . . . not . . . coming," Helen said between sniffles.

Peggy looked relieved. "I thought . . . well, I thought it was worse news. I've never seen you cry before."

"I will never understand the Army! They do everything to keep married couples apart, but cut their paychecks because they're married."

"I thought you two were trying to keep your marriage on the down-low as long as possible so you'd each get your own paycheck," Peggy said.

"We did try, but you can't fool the US Army. Peggy, I miss Frank like crazy. It's not fair."

Peggy tapped the crumpled letter in Helen's lap. "His letters help, don't they?"

She nodded. Writing Frank three times a day helped ease the pain of separation, especially since he wrote just as often.

Peggy got up. "Then I'll leave you to it. Wish I could smuggle you out in my duffel bag. When you write that husband of yours, tell him Peggy says he needs to go AWOL."

Helen couldn't quite muster a smile, but she stopped crying. She hated to cry, especially in front of someone. "Thanks, Peggy. I'm just being a baby."

When she was alone again, Helen smoothed out the crumpled letter and read, skipping that awful first sentence. The rest of page one, as always, was filled with love and longing. She wondered what that felt like for a man. None of her brothers, with the exception of Eugene, ever talked about the girls they fell for. Was Frank's longing for her as deep as hers for him? When he signed a letter *With love,* was his love as strong as hers?

The second page turned out to be for Schnapps, even though Frank knew full well that she'd shipped the stuffed dog to Cissna Park for safekeeping. She smiled, remembering the night Frank gave her their "first dog."

Dear Schnapps,

There's something I need to get off my chest. Lately, I've had a lot of time to think about your wonderful mother/my wonderful wife. Our honeymoon was perfect. Yet there is one thing that's perturbed me. It was something your mother said in a recent letter, something about "kowtowing" to me and doing everything I wanted her to. Does she feel that I don't try to do everything I think she wants me to? Does she really think I would take advantage of her because she is so obliging and considerate? I only hope to be more obliging and considerate of her.

Be good and take care of your mother, for I love her more than anything.

With love,
Daddy Frank

Helen felt tears threatening to return. She'd wanted to go dancing on their honeymoon, but Frank wanted to go on a walk. She'd given in. But later, in one of her letters, she'd written about that decision, saying she didn't mind kowtowing to him. *That's what my mother always did,* she'd added. Helen had written it without much thought. She hadn't really meant it, had she? But maybe she had, at least enough to hurt Frank and make him bring it up after all this time.

She replaced the letter in its envelope and set it aside. Then she opened her other letter. It was from Dotty—this woman she'd never met, who was now her sister-in-law.

Dotty Daley Engel
12 Aug 1944

Dear Helen and Frank,
I had a card from Boots (my husband) last week! It must be from him because they wouldn't know to call him Boots.

I'm enclosing it with this note, but please hang on to it for me. (Remembering Frank's penchant for losing things, like my yearbook and his house key, I'm sending this to Helen.)

1. I am interned at Philippine Military Prison Camp No. 1.
2. My health is excellent.
3. Message:
    Will not lose much time in words being limited. Am looking forward to the day when I hear from you as no word has been received. Hope everybody is well and time short when we will be together again. Best to all, love, Bootsy, Emanuel Engel, Jr.

Tears came again, a quieter cry, filled with shame and guilt. Dotty and her husband had been apart for two years, rather than one month. Yet her letters weren't pouts and poor-poor-me rants. What would Helen do if Frank ended up captured and imprisoned? Or worse?

There it was again. Nausea swept over her at the speed of light, wiping out every other thought. She barely had time to bolt from her bunk and make it to the latrine.

"Not again, Helen!" Victoria scurried out of the way. "That's disgusting."

Lydia, one of the new nurses, came to stand in the doorway. Tall and slender, she would have looked more at home behind the perfume counter at Marshall Field's than behind a scalpel with the 199th. The other gals had already passed a thumbs-down on her, but Helen liked her. What they saw as arrogance, Helen believed to be a combination of sophistication and shyness. "Honestly," Lydia said, "if the Nazis don't get us, the mess hall will."

Helen thought she might have caught one of the diseases floating around Percy Jones Hospital.

A week later, she knew she was wrong.

Lt. Helen Daley
Battle Creek, MI
15 September 1944

My dear, dear Frankie,

I have some news to tell you, and I hope you can be happy about it. Or at least not too upset. You and I haven't even had the time we need to be husband and wife. How I wish we had more time together!

I'm delaying, aren't I? Is your wife a coward?

What I'm trying to say is that Schnapps is going to have a little brother or sister. There. I said it. Are you sitting down? I suppose I should have asked that first.

Darling, I have so much to say, but I want to hear from you first. Please tell me it's all right? Tell me you're happy. I am. But I can't truly be happy unless you are.

With love,
Helen

Midnight, 17 September 1944

Dear Frankie,

You're lucky you don't have to watch your wife vomit. Not a pretty sight. Everybody here thinks I have the flu, so they're keeping their distance. I wasn't even allowed to take my shift this morning.

Hey, you. I thought I'd have a phone call by now. I know you have to sneak out for that. Hopefully, by the time you get this we will have talked, and we'll both see what a dumb Dora I've been to worry about what you're thinking of our big news. It's understandable if you're not excited yet, what with all we have ahead of us, but I know you will be. We are so blessed. This baby will have the happiest life! Schnapps agrees. In fact, Schnapps and I have been tossing around names. What do you think of Maureen? (Only if Schnapps is having a sister, of course.)

We're waiting for that phone call. But a letter will be all right, too.

Still your loving wife,
Helen

✦

18 September 1944

Dearest Frankie,

Still no word from you. I don't really know what to do. Nobody suspects that Schnapps is expecting a sibling, and I want to keep it that way until I can talk to you. When should we tell our families? Maybe I could stay here at Percy, although I'm not certain the Army will keep me on once they know about the addition to our family.

20 September 1944

You will never guess where I am as I write this letter. Do you remember where we met? I'd run away from the amputee patients and ended up in the men's restroom, where I met my husband, the dashing Frank Daley. Well, here I am again, standing over the sink and wondering what on earth I've gotten myself into. I couldn't quite make it to the latrine for ladies, so I dashed in here to rack my body with dry heaves, as if my insides were being scraped. When I splashed water on my face and caught my reflection in the mirror, I had to agree with Lydia.

I look like death curdled. She also said that it's a good thing my handsome husband isn't around to see me. On that note, I disagree.

22 September 1944

Frankie, if you're in shock, or denial, you can still call or write me, can't you? We never talked about children, and it's understandable that husbands and wives—fathers and mothers—feel differently about babies. Sweetheart, everybody is getting mail except me. This total silence from the father of my child is driving me insane. Maybe you need time. Well, I don't have time, Frankie. Any day now, my unit will be called up.

Still with love,
Your Helen

~~∘~~

23 September 1944

Dear Frank,

This is the longest I've gone without hearing from you. I've tried to call you twice, but nobody would put me through. In my rational moments, which are few and far between, I believe that you are not at fault. I imagine you as frustrated as I am because you want to tell me you're pleased about Baby.

I won't even tell you what I picture in my irrational moments.

24 September 1944

Dear Frank,

As I feel this pregnancy has altered our relationship as well as our plans, I realize I must make some decisions for me and for my baby. You don't need to worry about us. Dad always said, "God helps those who help themselves." And that's what I'll do. When it's time, I'll talk to the colonel about getting reassigned to stateside duty, perhaps staying on at Percy Jones for as long as possible. I have no doubt that I could get my former job back at Evanston Hospital, but I'll need help with the baby for a while. I'll write my mother in a few weeks and arrange to have the birth in Cissna Park. I could even work for Dr. Roberts there for a time.

You and I need to talk. And you need to write.

Be safe,
Helen

23

FRANK

Camp Ellis, Illinois

Frank had never been angrier at the Army. No mail in. No mail out. No word from Helen in weeks.

"Attention!" Sergeant Miller burst into the barracks, barking like the career sergeant he was. The 11th General Dispensary fell into straight rows in front of bunks.

"This must be big," Lartz whispered.

Frank had to agree when Colonel Croane marched in, followed by General Blaine. The guy didn't pop over for routine inspections. Blaine saluted. "Soldiers, our time has come. We need you and your skills overseas, now more than ever. Tomorrow at this time you'll be on your way to an undisclosed staging area on the East Coast, where your unit will await transport to the European theater."

"Europe?" Anderson echoed.

Murmurings passed up and down the line like electrical currents. Every man in the unit had put in for the Pacific.

"You heard correctly," General Blaine said, his tone stern, with no hint of apology. "This is the Army, soldiers, not a travel agency. You go where you're needed. We are launching final attacks in Europe, and the enemy is pushing back hard, sending us more casualties than anticipated. That's where you come in."

Anderson groaned, and he wasn't the only one.

Not Frank. He punched Anderson's shoulder. "Europe, Andy!"

Anderson rubbed his arm. "I heard."

"Way to go, Daley," Lartz said.

Europe! He and Helen would be on the same continent! He could find her, be with her.

The colonel took over and rattled instructions. "Pack wools, gents. We bug out in twenty-four hours."

Frank had to get word to Helen. Somebody asked a question, but Frank missed it.

"No," Colonel Croane answered. "That's all I can tell you about locations, and it's a good deal more than you can tell anyone outside the 11th General. None of this leaves the barracks, understood?"

General Blaine stepped forward, and Frank could see hints of why a man like this, who looked more like somebody's unmarried and annoying uncle than a four-star general, had risen in the ranks. He eyed the men one by one, as if mowing them down with machine-gun fire. Nobody moved. "I understand your disappointment," he began. "But we are not playing at war, gentlemen. This is the real thing. One leak, one slip of the tongue, and you could put your entire unit in peril."

Once they were gone, the whole unit descended on Sergeant Miller as if he were the enemy.

"Hang on, will you?" Sarge shouted. "We have our orders. Nobody uses the telephone. They're releasing mail this afternoon, so

I'll get that for you. Those letters will be the last until we're on the other side."

"Are you serious?" Frank demanded. "The Army can trust us to patch up its fighting men, but it can't trust us to get mail?"

Sarge shrugged.

Frank wouldn't give up that easily. "If I write my wife, could somebody here mail the letters after we leave?"

"It would take a whole battalion to mail *your* letters," Anderson said.

"And an ant could mail yours, Andy."

Sarge ran his fingers over his head, as if forgetting that he no longer had hair. "Write your letters. I'll make sure someone mails them soon as they're censored. Which reminds me: film on censorship tonight at seventeen hundred hours."

Frank raced to his bunk to write Helen. He hoped he remembered the code. *First letter, every other sentence after the cue.*

Lt. F. R. Daley, MD
25 September 1944

Dearest Helen,
  How I've missed hearing from you! I hope you've been
receiving my letters. Big news, my darling! I wish I could tell
you where we're going, but the censors would cut this letter into
pieces. So I'll have to drown my sorrows in a big bowl of banana
pudding.
  Everywhere I go, I think of you. I had hoped we'd meet at
Camp Ellis before I left for the staging theater. Until Sarge
returns with mail, I feel lost. I have no idea when you'll leave
Percy. Really, the only thing that keeps me going is your love.
  I now enjoy saving from my measly paycheck each month,
for our family.

Oh, my base pay is $166.67, with a 10% increase for overseas: $16.67. And they take out $21.00 food ration.

Please know I buy war bonds for $37.50 and insurance for $6.80 each month too. I hope to put into our savings account $90.00. Each month, that leaves $28.04 to be paid to me directly overseas.

Helen, we shall meet soon!

Love,
Frankie

That evening when Sergeant Miller delivered mail to the barracks, he was mobbed. Frank only had two letters, both from Helen, dated a week apart. "Sarge, are you sure this is all you've got for me?"

"Not Helen's usual dozens?" Anderson said. "Guess the bloom is off the rose, as they say."

Frank ignored him. "There have to be more. Could you look again, Sarge? I'm begging you."

Sarge sighed. "Yeah. Okay."

Frank went back to his bunk and carefully opened the first letter. Everything else disappeared as he read Helen's words. By the end of the letter, he was so worried about her nausea that he was considering going AWOL to take care of her. The date on her second letter was a week after the first. The Army's mail delivery was a mystery, and Helen probably had written letters that would show up later. But what if she was really sick, so sick she couldn't even write?

He tore into Helen's second letter and skimmed it. Then he reread the sentence that would change his life forever: *What I'm trying to say is that Schnapps is going to have a little brother or sister.*

He read it again. *I'm going to be a dad. A daddy.* He surprised himself, the way he felt. He knew he should be worried about bringing a child into the world. But this would be Helen's child, Helen's and his. He let out a whoop that could be heard all the way to Missouri.

Lartz, lying in his bunk reading a book, looked up. "Sounds like good news."

"You said it!" He would love to tell Lartz. But it didn't feel right. The person he needed to talk to was Helen. He couldn't wait another minute. He needed to write her now!

My darling Helen,

You have made me the happiest man on earth. I'm going to be a daddy! I intend to shout it for the rest of my life (except when Junior is sleeping). Me, a daddy! Do you suppose I'll be any good at it? You would make a better father than I, I'm afraid. But you can't be both mother and father, so I'll just promise to do my best.

Darling, this means that you should get to stay in the US now. How I wish we could sit together and work out the details, but I'm confident my capable wife will do what's best for her and for Junior. I'm sorrier than you'll ever know that I can't be there with you.

Tell Schnapps to give you the hug I can't.

With all my love,
Your Frankie, husband and father

Frank had just finished addressing his letter to Helen when Sarge came barreling in.

"Attention, soldiers! We're bugging out! One stop at the staging area, then on to you-know-where!"

"When?" Andy asked.

"Now! Transit trucks are outside! Move it!"

Pandemonium broke out in the barracks. They'd been on twenty-four-hour notice so long, they'd grown lax. Now, men shoved gear into duffel bags and packs.

Frank didn't know whether he felt relieved to finally be on the way or panicked that he wouldn't see Helen before he left for Europe.

Thirty minutes later Frank and his unit were squashed in a transit truck that couldn't have been designed to transport humans, or at least not this many humans. He tried to tamp down his overstimulation of the vestibular apparatus, which was how he preferred to think about nausea. He told himself that Helen's nausea put his to shame.

The truck jerked, sending men sliding like dominoes, nearly pushing Lartz and Frank out the open back. But all Frank could do was laugh.

"You sure you're all right, Frank?" Lartz asked.

"I'm swell, Lartz!"

"*You* like being reassigned," Anderson grumbled. "This isn't fair."

Frank smelled a storm brewing. He could barely see in the dark, tarp-covered transport. Headlights were swallowed by fog clouds that swirled around the truck. He closed his eyes and pictured Helen—the way her smile took over her whole face, like a wave rolling first to her eyes, then moving to her tiny nose, and finally reaching her mouth. He called up the mental picture of Helen talking to Hudy as she changed his bandages. He loved her strength, wrapped in gentle kindness. Helen was the best person he'd ever met, the best wife in the world. And now they were going to have the best son . . . or daughter.

"Knock it off, Daley," Mort said. "I'm sick of that smile." Mort was the kind of guy who'd complain if he got sent to Florida for the winter. He griped about the food at every meal and about his "buddies" in between. But he'd lent Frank his flashlight so Frank could write Helen once his stomach settled a bit. And right now, Frank loved everybody, even Mort.

Sarge maneuvered his way over to Frank. "I posted your letter myself, Lieutenant, and the PO gave me these." He pulled a handful of letters from his pocket. "Enjoy them. They may be the last you'll get for some time."

Frank thanked Sarge, then dug into his pack until he found the Bible the Army gave to every soldier. He could use it as a desk to write Helen again after he read her letters. Carefully, he opened the first of seven letters from his wife. As he read, his chest began to burn, from his esophagus to his abdomen. Helen sounded more distant with every letter. She believed he didn't want their baby. She actually thought he wasn't writing her because he was too upset about her pregnancy!

Frank wanted to jump out of the truck and go to Helen, wherever she was now. Instead, he pulled out his stationery, not knowing when, or if, she'd ever get his letter.

Lt. F. R. Daley
In transit to Staging Area on coast

Dearest precious Helen,
How I wish I could be with you now so that you would see for yourself how happy I am! Helen, why would you think I'm not writing you? Why would you assume I'm angry? Surely you know me better than that.

A wave of nausea washed over him and forced him to stop writing. He focused on the road behind them until the nausea passed. He knew he'd better wait to write, but he felt like he'd be okay to read Helen's last letter. He just hoped she'd come to her senses in this one.

Dear Frank,
You no longer need to worry about a child. I have suffered a miscarriage. I feel it's my duty to write. Even that urge has drained from me. So much has happened since I've heard from you that you barely feel real. Nothing seems real, not even war.
When I was in fifth grade, our teacher, Miss Huntsinger, arranged for each student to write to a pen pal. My "pal" lived on her grandfather's plantation in South Africa. We exchanged dozens of letters, and I remember thinking that this girl would always be my best friend. But one or the other of us stopped

writing. And by then, it didn't matter. The girl in the far-off country had ceased being real to me.

You don't need to hear this, and I'm sorry. Perhaps it's best if I stop writing too.

Love,
HED

Frank put down the letter and stared at the Bible on his lap, wondering if he'd ever felt this sad, this empty. They had lost their baby. It didn't seem to matter that he'd only known about the baby a few hours. His grief spread through every vein and artery in his body.

Heart pounding, Frank tore up the letter he'd begun writing to Helen. Then he found another piece of stationery.

My dearest, most precious Helen,

I have only this minute read your sad, sad news that you are no longer carrying our child. How I wish I'd been by your side, sharing this roller coaster of emotions. I can hardly find words adequate to convey how I feel. Like you, I was ecstatic at the notion of a child. My total joy surprised even me. And like you, I am now devastated at our loss.

It's important for you to know that in no way was the miscarriage your fault. You are an incredible woman, capable of taking charge and doing what most of us can only watch in amazement. But this is out of our control. I love you so much, Helen. When the time is right, we will have our family. And our children will be the luckiest kids on the planet because they will have you as their mother.

With all my love,
Frank

P.S. Helen, my only regret is that you believed the worst of me when my letters were held up. It saddens me that you don't

know me well enough to trust in my steadfast love. We are
distant in miles and hours, but not in my heart.

Frank turned off the flashlight. There was more he wanted to say, like how hurt he was by her lack of faith in him. Had she really decided to stop writing him? That wasn't the Helen he knew, and it wasn't the Frank she should have known.

24

Helen

CAMP ELLIS, ILLINOIS

Helen's unit had received no more advance warning about their move to Camp Ellis than Frank's unit had. She'd struggled to keep down the fierce hope that Frank might still be there. But of course, he wasn't. He hadn't even left her so much as a note.

Over the next few days at Camp Ellis, Helen kept busy with marching drills, arms training, and regular nursing of soldiers on base. At the end of the day, she curled up on her bunk and played solitaire. She wrote no letters, and she received none.

Lydia eyed her from the next bunk, where she, Peggy, and Naomi were locked in a game of gin rummy. "So your husband hasn't written lately, Helen," Lydia said. "Is that any reason to be so morose?"

"Yes," Helen answered.

Naomi tossed in her cards, then joined Helen. Naomi reminded her of her own mother—quiet and gentle, but a force to be reckoned with. She was big-boned and older than most of the nurses, and she had a husband back in Ohio, though she rarely talked about him. Peggy said the guy had gotten himself a deferment but encouraged Naomi to join. "Helen, what if Frank is on a boat to the Pacific right now? How would that make you feel, knowing you haven't written him?"

It made her feel rotten, but she wasn't about to let Naomi see it.

"Fine," Naomi said. "I'm heading to the post office. Want me to check for you?"

"Don't bother." Helen lay back and curled into a ball.

She sat up again when Naomi returned with a handful of letters. "One for me. And six for you. All from Frank."

Helen hugged her. "I'm a lousy friend. Sorry, Naomi."

Naomi pointed to the stack of letters. "Tell *him*."

Even as she opened the first letter, Helen told herself not to care what Frank had to say. He hadn't wanted their child. She'd gotten through everything just fine on her own.

The first line she read changed everything: *My darling Helen, You have made me the happiest man on earth.*

She kept reading, ignoring the tears that fell like raindrops on the letter. Her husband had been every bit as thrilled about becoming a father as she had about being a mother. He'd been devastated when he learned of the miscarriage.

She loved Frank. She should have known how he'd really feel about being a father, instead of assuming the worst. *Gott im Himmel, why am I always so quick to pull inside my turtle shell and go it alone?*

She fell asleep rereading Frank's letters.

In the middle of the night, Helen bolted upright in bed. *The letters.* She'd missed something. She'd been so overcome with her husband's sweet understanding that she'd paid attention to little else. Flashlight in hand, she began scanning the letters again.

Then she found it. "Whoopee!"

"Helen, will you shut up and go back to sleep?" Victoria shouted.

But there would be no sleep for Helen, not tonight. Frank claimed he planned to drown his sorrows in banana pudding, a dish he abhorred. And there was the code.

He wasn't on a ship in the Pacific. He was on his way to Europe! Now all they had to do was get there and find each other.

25

FRANK

US East Coast

Frank piled off the train behind Anderson and plunged into a darkness that might have been outer space, except for the smell of salty brine. Blackouts and silences were strictly enforced on the US coastal regions, and not a single light from the city showed. Even the sky obeyed orders and hid moon and stars. The train ride from their staging area hadn't taken long, but they'd had to stand up the whole way. Crammed into club cars, soldiers fell asleep without falling down, propped up by other soldiers. Frank had felt carsick, but he'd kept swallowing, forbidding his nausea to erupt because if he got sick, a whole battalion would feel it.

"Smell that sea?" Lartz said behind him. "Can you make out anything? Your eyes are better than mine."

As his eyes adjusted, Frank made out the form of a gray hull, then ship after ship lining the dock like overgrown, mismatched blocks. "Ships, Lartz. Dozens of them." Some vessels were large as ocean liners, others small as tugboats.

"Men of the 11th General!" Major Meredith called. His voice, which resembled a squeaky hinge, cut through murmurs around them. Meredith had joined the unit in Ellis, but kept to himself, abstaining from football and poker. He was older than most of the doctors, and his most distinguishing feature was a large mole the shape of Texas, positioned where a beard might have grown if permitted. Frank had spent a couple of late nights with Lartz and Andy speculating how the major could shave without slicing the panhandle.

Meredith waved his arms. "This way! Follow me!"

Frank and Lartz shuffled toward the major, falling in with others from the 11th. They filed onto a narrow bridge that made Frank think of metal catwalks, only wider. He shivered, but he didn't know whether to blame the icy winds off the Atlantic or the thought that he was actually boarding one of those hunks of metal. He followed the others across the gangplank, where midway they were met by smiling Red Cross workers.

"Here you go, soldier." An attractive young girl with perfect white teeth shoved a paper cup of something hot into his hands.

Frank took it gratefully and let it warm his fingers. "Thanks." He traded smiles with the girl as he downed the bitter coffee in two gulps. "Are you coming along for the ride?"

"Me?" She laughed. "No, I—"

Anderson shoved between them. "Mustn't talk to that fellow," he told the girl. "He's an old married man."

"Hey!" Frank began. Then he thought better of it and laughed along. Yet inside, he wasn't laughing. Anderson was an older married man than he was. And besides, did being married mean you couldn't talk to another gal?

The gangplank jerked, then dropped, as if to lower them to the tanker below. Frank grabbed the railing. Somebody slammed into him from behind, jamming his barracks bag into his shoulder and making him clobber the poor fellow in front of him. He could see the end of the gangplank. It fed onto a tiny deck of what really did look like an oil tanker. "We can't cross the ocean in that."

"Of course not," Anderson said. "That one's probably a supply tank. Right, Lartz?"

"Doubt it," Lartz said. "The Army's using everything they can to get forces overseas."

"Not this," Andy said.

"I read about these. They call them cement boats." Lartz sounded almost gleeful to see one in person. "DuPont couldn't keep up, so the Army uses an oil tanker mold from Kaiser."

Anderson cursed DuPont, Kaiser, and the Army.

Names were already being called out for the 11th General as they moved along the plank toward the cement monster that waited to swallow them whole. Frank heard his name and shouted back, "Here!" He was here all right—marching like a lemming over the abyss. He held the railing as he stepped onto the rough and narrow tanker deck. His mind flashed back to the patio his dad had built behind their house, the house that also served as his dad's office. Frank and his brother had seen the wet cement as an unprecedented opportunity to leave their mark for all mankind. Not settling for simple handprints or names etched with sticks, they'd ridden their bikes through the thick cement, then tossed finely ground chat into the mix and added a few leaves. Jack had taken all the blame, as usual, but they'd both been punished—sentenced to yard work by day, confined to their room by night. As rough as that patio deck remained for the rest of their years, this tanker deck was rougher.

Major Meredith led them down into the hold, where the stench of oil was strong enough to confirm Lartz's theory about tankers. The major sounded like a tour guide. "This is the hold, or the hole, where you men will take turns at watch duty. We'll guard against ships and submarines and anything else the enemy might throw at us. It will be up to you men to keep us safe."

They marched down a cement corridor that went on and on. The oil smell grew stronger with each step. Frank scanned the round windows, looking for exits, in case he couldn't keep his coffee down where it belonged. Already, the tanker sloshed and rocked, forcing them to steady themselves with outstretched arms.

"Where do we sleep?" Anderson shouted. Nervous laughter rippled through the throngs of soldiers.

"Almost there, soldier," Sergeant Miller answered.

Still, they trailed up a flight, through a barren room, down endless steps, winding left, then right, until a door was flung open to reveal metal bunks, stacked four high to the ceiling. The narrow bunks were wedged in so tight Frank wondered how anybody could reach the ones in the back. Men shoved past him, claiming bottom bunks by tossing their equipment onto the not-quite-cots. Mort and Anderson staked out bunks close to the door.

Frank and Lartz had to settle for upper bunks in the next-to-last row. If the boat were attacked, they'd be stuck.

"Attention, men!" Major Meredith stood in the doorway and eyed his men. Up until now, Frank hadn't been able to see past the mole on Meredith's chin. It struck him that the man's eyes were unnaturally large, showing too much white. His face had the sunken look of someone constantly chewing on the insides of both cheeks. "On this ship, the 'eyes' have it. We will be in a constant state of vigilance. Therefore, when you are in this barracks, you can sleep, knowing there are men in the hole guarding you. We'll work in shifts as battle-ready teams. Sergeant Miller will give you the call, and it will be your duty to respond immediately."

Sarge read a list of names for the first shift. Frank thanked his lucky stars that his name wasn't among them.

Those whose names hadn't been called wandered back to the deck. Frank followed Lartz, who had a keen sense of direction, something that eluded all Daley men. It was a wonder Jack could succeed as a spy. Only Dotty could find her way out of a paper bag, in the middle of a sea filled with paper bags.

The stench of oil, still overbearing, thinned on deck, assaulted by the salt spray as waves spanked the sides of the tanker. It felt like they were in the depths of the sea already.

"Mess hall must be down there." Lartz pointed to a stairway blocked with soldiers.

Frank didn't even want to think about food. The boat rocked, and his stomach lurched.

For a second, clouds parted, and the moon sent a jagged stripe of light onto the deck. Caught in the moonbeam was a line of soldiers on the gangplank, still pouring onto the ship. "Lartz, tell me we're not still anchored to the dock!"

"You thought we'd set sail already, Daley?" Taggerty, one of seven lieutenants in the unit, laughed heartily. Tough and able as an Irish gangster, Taggerty was someone you'd only want by your side in a fight. "You'll know when we're on the sea, you landlubber."

Hours later, Frank understood what Taggerty meant. He'd gone back to the barracks to write Helen, but that had made him so nauseated that he'd inaugurated their latrine with the remnants of breakfast. He told himself that even if the Army had come up with the seasick medicine he needed, he would have thrown it up already.

Two violent bouts of nausea later, he made his way back to the deck by asking half a dozen enlisted men for directions. Once on deck, he found Lartz, and the two men hung on to the railing as the tanker groaned and chugged. It was a miracle no one went flying overboard. Taggerty informed them that they were in the middle of a convoy of seven ships, though Frank could only see the two behind them, and one of those was already passing their tanker. That vessel, twice as big as theirs and several stories high, looked brand-new and oil-free as it sped past them.

"On the move now, we are," Taggerty said, frost clouds billowing from his mouth. He wasn't a bad guy, but Frank doubted they'd have been friends out of the Army. The fellow had a chip on his shoulder. Frank thought Taggerty might have been teased in school for the trace of a harelip that would have made him lisp as a boy. "I can tell you where we're likely headed," Taggerty said, leaning on the railing next to Frank.

"Where?" If Frank knew, he could get the location to Helen, in case her ship followed before his company moved on. Lartz pressed in closer too.

"We had orders to dock at Brest." Taggerty shielded his words with a hand to his mouth. "But those orders were remanded."

Anderson, who had appeared out of nowhere, swore. "Doesn't the Army know Brest is among my favorite locations?"

Taggerty ignored him. "Instead, we'll dock in the British Isles and make our way to Camp Pinkney. It's a stopover for troops leaving for a combat zone through one of the channel ports, probably Southampton. Need to know, gentlemen." He strolled off up the deck, hands clasped behind his back.

"Wonder how long we'll be in England," Anderson said once Taggerty was gone. "Any chance we'll ride out the war there?"

"Doubt it," Lartz said. "The whole reason they want doctors now more than ever is this big push somewhere in France. That's where I'm betting we go."

Frank knew that if he wanted to meet up with Helen—and he did—it would have to be soon. If he wrote *Pinkney* in code, would she know where that was? He wouldn't have. But he could at least let her know he was in England. "I'm going back to the barracks to write Helen."

Anderson groaned.

It took Frank twenty minutes to find his barracks and fifteen more to get back to his bunk. His gear had been moved—Lartz's too. He climbed up and fished an airmail from his pack.

Positioning code letters to spell *England* was easy, but he almost forgot the tip-off line. He had to squeeze it in above the code: *Helen, you know how I love to travel the rough seas, so you can imagine how much I am enjoying the rocking waves.*

Then he made a mad dash to the latrine.

Hours later, when his group received their first call to the hold, Frank stayed facedown on his bunk. Every muscle and tissue in his body teemed with nausea, as if somebody had scooped out his insides and filled him with sludge. He was already shirking his Army duties, and they hadn't even arrived overseas yet. What kind of a soldier was he going to be?

26

FRANK

GREAT BRITAIN

Frank had been off the tanker and onto firm, muddy land for forty-eight hours. In that time, he'd formed two conclusions. First, he would never again take land for granted—it had required a full twenty-four hours for his body to realize he wasn't still out on the ocean. Second, Great Britain was so named because of the great cold here. Missouri winters dipped below zero, but that dry cold was nothing compared to this drizzling, never-ending, icy rain.

He had been so eager to get off the boat that he hadn't realized they were in Scotland until a line of men in kilts passed in front of them. The instant they landed, they'd been herded and forced to walk for miles. His unit joined others in long lines that snaked past Loch Lomond, where fall trees shone bright and beautiful, despite the bitter cold and unending mud.

Finally, still on foot, they reached a bivouac area. But instead of resting there, they boarded trucks that were lined up as far as he could see. Frank and Lartz stuck together and climbed into a half-filled truck parked next to a Scottish regiment equipped with bagpipes, funny hats, and kilts. Frank wasn't the only American soldier to stare.

A Scottish officer called to his troops, "Steady, men! Hold your kilts down. The bloomin' Yanks want to see if it's true that you have lacies underneath."

They laughed, but the laughter cut out suddenly as a roar sounded overhead and a wave of planes became eerily visible in the dark, moonless night.

"Bombers," Lartz said.

Frank held his breath and watched as six planes passed high over their truck. "Ours or theirs?"

"Ours," Lartz answered.

"How do *you* know?" Anderson demanded.

"They didn't drop anything," Lartz said.

Frank had imagined battles being fought around him while he and the other doctors and nurses did their jobs in hospitals, close but not too close. What if the bombers hadn't been Allied?

And what about Helen? She'd already gone through so much. Frank missed that unborn baby as if the child had been born and now lived in another land somewhere. He could only imagine what Helen's grief looked like.

Now she would be entering the war without child or husband. If she were still pregnant, she could have stayed in the States. Safe. The thought flashed through his mind: What if he and Helen didn't make it through the war?

He shut out that thought and pictured his wife holding a baby, their baby. He put himself in that picture, husband and father hovering over the ones he loved most in the world. Helen would be fine, and so would he.

Lartz had been right when he said they were part of the biggest buildup and supply push in the history of the world. Convoy after convoy of American troops joined Scottish soldiers as they set off in the same direction. Of course, with his lousy internal compass, Frank had no idea which direction that was. He kept scanning the sky for more bombers. The truck hit a bump, knocking him into Lartz. But with soldiers packed like cigarettes in a case, there wasn't much room to roll.

"Stop it!" someone shouted from the other side of the truck. Frank could make out the wiry shape of Major Johnson, who generally kept to himself. "Quit touching me!"

"Is he kidding?" Andy asked. "It would be physically impossible not to be touched in this tin can."

Lartz whispered to Frank, "I thought something was off with Johnson on the ship."

Frank remembered seeing the man roaming the deck the last day of the voyage. He'd looked like a wide-eyed coyote in wrinkled fatigues.

"There! You did it again!" Johnson's voice, an octave too high, silenced their transport, and in the quiet, Frank thought he heard the staccato of distant guns.

"Major, are you all right?" Sergeant Miller moved into the vacated seat next to Johnson.

Johnson drew back from him. "What do *you* think?"

Apparently, Sergeant Miller knew better than to answer—Johnson was far from all right. The man was terrified. Until this moment, Frank had never stopped to wonder whether he'd be too scared to function. What was it that made one man buck up, another act heroically, and another give in to terror?

And which one was he?

When they finally pulled into camp, it was still dark. They might have been anywhere, if that "anywhere" rained all the time and won awards for the coldest and most miserable spot in the universe.

"All out, mates!" shouted a British officer. "Last stop, Camp Pinkney."

"Told you!" Taggerty bellowed.

"Be ready to bug out in twenty-four hours!" the officer added.

Groans shot up from every truck.

"Didn't say you'd be leaving in twenty-four, did I? Just be ready. Tents are over there. Get your assignments here. Don't forget your allies are sleeping, so quiet as you go, right?"

The Yanks thundered out of trucks, grabbed their gear, then raced through driving rain to find their assigned tents. "I'm thirty-four!" Anderson shouted above the ruckus.

"Twenty-nine," Lartz said.

Frank had to shine his flashlight on his work order to see the number. "Thirty-four."

"Over here!" Anderson took off down the row of identical, sopping-wet tents. A sheet of canvas covered the entrance but flapped in the chilling wet wind like a flag in a hurricane.

Frank ducked under the flap, then stood just inside, waiting for his eyes to adjust.

Hang on a minute. He shut his eyes. They must be playing tricks on him. But when he opened them, he saw the same thing—two men in each cot, sleeping side by side, as close as he and Helen on their honeymoon.

"Why would they do that?" Anderson whispered.

"Don't ask me," Frank whispered. Half the bunks were empty. The other half were doubled up. "And don't get any ideas, Anderson."

"I mean, I've heard jokes about the Brits," Andy began, "but I didn't think—"

Before Andy could finish, one of the men in the nearest cot shouted, "Shut up and get to bed, you Yanks!"

"No thanks," Andy said. "Wrong tent. Not our cup of tea."

"Ours neither, mates," he said, sounded miffed. "You lads just wait until you try a night in this leaky tent with only your one issued blanket and no body heat but your own. Then we'll see whose cup of tea you are."

Anderson raised his eyebrows at Frank. Frank shook his head. They shuffled to the far side of the tent. Andy threw his barracks bag onto the corner cot. It squished like a sponge. Frank fingered the cot he'd been about to sit on. Soaked. A drop of water plopped on his head. He eased closer to the Brits and felt three more cots until he found one that was damp, but not soaked. Exhausted, he spread out his blanket and lay down fast. The blanket smelled like wet goat. He lay there shivering, listening to raindrops thump the canvas roof. Patrols of MPs plodded past outside. He wanted to get out of here and find a better spot, in the woods maybe. But he reminded himself that he wasn't in Camp Ellis. They were under strict orders not to leave the tents for anything except the latrine.

An icy blast ripped through, ruffling the canvas and showering him with water droplets. He tried to cocoon himself in his tiny Army blanket, but he couldn't have it under him and over him at the same time.

Minutes later when Anderson crept up with his blanket and climbed onto Frank's cot, Frank played possum and didn't object. They lay back to back, lying on one blanket, covered by the other.

After a few minutes, Frank whispered, "If you ever tell anyone, Andy, I'll—"

"They could pull out my fingernails, mate."

Frank and Anderson woke up in the dark with the rest of their tent-mates. Frank had slept, but he felt stiff and damp, his knees creaking as he got to his feet.

"Nice sleep, mates?" asked one of the Brits. "Chummy, were we?"

Andy jumped up, scowling. "We're not the ones who—!"

Frank stepped between them. "You Brits had the right idea all along. Besides, I expect it's been years since Anderson got to climb into anybody's bed."

The soldier frowned, then burst into the heartiest laugh Frank had heard since his brother had caught him trying to dance the Charleston. Half a dozen eavesdropping limeys joined in, and finally, even Andy.

No sign of light peeked at the horizon as Frank and Andy followed their new mates to the latrine. Frank smelled it before he spotted the wooden shack, where fifty or sixty men jockeyed for position in two lines. Next to the latrine stood another shack with a corrugated tin roof. Frank opted for that one and found a couple dozen men crammed in front of three cracked mirrors above rusty sinks. He joined one group and managed to wet his face before trying to shave with ice water. He'd have to remember to ask Helen how she felt about beards.

Feeling scruffier than before, Frank trailed others to the mess tent, where apron-clad soldiers stood over charred trash barrels and plopped scoops of Spam next to suspicious strips of "American beef."

Once inside the mess, Frank took a seat on the nearest bench and struck up a conversation with a British major named Bradford. The man's deep-set eyes didn't miss a trick as they scanned the tent, the table, and Frank himself. After they'd exchanged names, ranks, and medical histories, including training and pre-war specialties, Bradford grinned over his mug of tea. "We're very glad you Yanks jumped in when you did, though we wouldn't have minded the company a bit earlier."

Frank returned the grin. He liked the guy already, in spite of his posh accent. "We might have made it here sooner if anyone had told us what lovely weather you Brits enjoy."

"Ah, that reminds me of a story," Bradford said. "It seems President Roosevelt and Churchill went to heaven, but St. Peter closed the gates in their faces, saying, 'You two fellows have caused too much trouble on earth. We don't want you up here.' Churchill said, 'What will we do?' 'I'll tell you,' said Roosevelt. 'You kick the gate down, and I'll pay for it.'"

They talked baseball and argued the merits of American and European football. Frank told him about the oil tanker that brought his unit across the Atlantic and nearly killed him before he'd made it to the war.

When they got up to leave, Bradford asked, "Where are you off to, Lieutenant?"

"Need to write my wife."

"The little woman you left back home worried about you, is she? Has she heard what you Yanks get up to over here?"

"She'd be crazy to worry, and she's definitely not crazy. Besides, she's not even back home." The second he said it, he wished he hadn't. Frank had been the one warning Helen not to broadcast the fact that they were married once they were overseas. It might not matter. But the wrong officer could make it tougher to get leaves if the higher-ups were afraid married couples would lose focus and forget why they'd signed up.

"If she hasn't remained in the colonies, where is Mrs. Daley?"

Frank stopped. They were standing in a mud puddle behind a row of tents. Ropes tied to wooden stakes stretched from the backsides of tent canvas. He glanced around to see who else might be listening. "My wife is in the Army too." They wandered aimlessly around Pinkney while Frank told Bradford all about his and Helen's lightning romance and marriage.

"I admit I've heard of a number of hasty marriages. But your Helen sounds lovely," Bradford said.

"She is." He glanced around. Everywhere, mud and tents. "Major?"

"Yes?"

"Which one of these tents is mine?"

By the time they reached his barracks, Frank was regretting his loose lips. "Major, I have to ask you not to tell anyone about Helen. The US Army's funny about married couples on the same continent."

Bradford laughed. "Your secret is safe with me. Now go write your letter. They'll be coming with assignments soon."

V-mail 18 October '44, Wednesday
Lt. Frank Daley, MD
The land of mud and rain

Dearest Helen,

I apologize for the letter I wrote while in the throes of nausea. My morale improved as soon as I got off that boat. How I hope you get a better one! And soon—before I move on!

Nearly all the picturesque villages we pass through show evidence of bombings, though these stone houses are built to stay. The weather is cold and wet, devoid of sunshine. But the ████ have won me over by their tenacity, spirit, and their honest belief that this, their fifth year of war, will be the last. I suppose, then, that we shouldn't lament our diet, which will mainly consist of K- and C-rations.

You and I must connect soon before we're sent to different countries.

With love, wherever you are,
Your Frankie

P.S. We are not playing at war here. Wear your helmet!

27

FRANK

Camp Pinkney, England

The weather served up an unbroken string of rainy days. Each morning Frank expected to move on, but the 11th General seemed stuck in the mud. He took advantage of the downtime and tried to track down Helen's unit. With the aid of Major Bradford, he got the name of the advance man and found out the 199th was still stateside waiting for transport.

For the time being, a combined American and British unit was established at Pinkney under the joint leadership of Major Bradford and Colonel Croane. Croane had been in a position of leadership for the 11th General since they left Camp Ellis, though Frank rarely saw him. Frank confided to Lartz that if Santa had a bald and beardless brother—a lazy, though not evil, twin—he would look just like Croane.

On the third day since their arrival at Pinkney, Colonel Croane took front and center after roll call. "At ease, men! I think you've all been told of our mission while we're here. But I'll leave it to Major Bradford to explain your assignments."

The colonel outranked Bradford, but nobody had any doubt which man they'd follow into battle. Bradford exuded a confidence Frank envied. As Bradford took his place in front of the unit, he seemed to eye each soldier conspiratorially. "You men have come here at a crucial time in our joint history, a time other men will look back upon when they assess the fate of the world." He sounded like Churchill did on the radio, only younger. "Until further notice, we shall be assisting in a nearby hospital. Your duties are to begin this morning."

Andy whispered to Frank, "I'll bet we'll stay at the hospital till the war ends."

Frank ignored him.

Bradford continued, "This is a purely unofficial arrangement, gentlemen, while we await more permanent orders. The general hospital is understaffed, yet overflowing with patients. I'm certain you will be of great help during your short time here. Unless there are further questions . . . ?" He turned to Colonel Croane, who shook his head. "Then you are to report to your transport immediately. You will be driven directly to the hospital. Be prepared to walk back to camp once your shift ends. But do not—I repeat, do not under any circumstances—walk alone."

Frank didn't like the sound of that. General hospitals were supposed to be safe havens.

Andy scrambled beside him as Frank headed for a truck, half-full already. "I'll tell you what, ol' man. I'll work in their hospital. But I draw the line at anything closer to the front. I'm a skilled physician. I'd be wasted in a mobile unit."

"You're wasted half the time anyway," Frank muttered.

"That's not funny!"

"I thought it was rather amusing," Bradford said, coming up behind them.

"And they say Brits have no sense of humor," Frank commented.

"Who says such a thing?" Bradford demanded in mock outrage. "Those are fighting words, gentlemen." He bounded into the waiting truck, and Frank climbed in after him.

Anderson hopped in last. "Is everybody crazy around here?"

Frank worked beside Bradford all day on the burn ward, feeling like an ignorant intern. In addition to soldiers wounded in battle, the hospital serviced a steady influx of civilians. Bradford explained that many of the sick and injured walked for miles with wounds suffered from exploding bombs or mines. Other patients were flown in, or driven in because they needed surgery. Each patient deserved the best, and Frank, next to Bradford, did not feel like the best. The man reminded him of his brother. Jack had always been the best at everything—from sports, to academics, to spying.

Over the next few days, the wounded poured into their war-weary hospital like molasses into a dirty, overflowing jar. Frank learned more than he wanted to about bombs, a subject Bradford seemed as well versed in as he was in treating burn patients. He could identify the type of bomb by the whistle it made, the mark in the earth . . . and the burns it left on its victims.

"These three men met up with an incendiary much like the kind dropped on London." As he talked, Bradford wrapped the soldier's arm with the light touch of a gentle lover. He'd seen Helen treat patients that way.

"It would have been a light incendiary," Bradford continued, "a magnesium body with a cast-iron nose filled with pellets that can burn for ten minutes, consuming anything in its path. I've seen them wave through the sky like a ribbon. Usually you hear the first two explosions and think that's the end of it. And when you believe it's safe, the third explosion can knock off a roof. Some of the nasty buggers have a delayed high-explosive version set to go off a few minutes after they land with the initial explosion. That's exactly the right time to kill any would-be rescue team."

"That's what happened," the soldier muttered, his mouth only opening enough for words to wrinkle on the way out. "I'm a medic." His face contorted as he tried to pull himself up and look around the ward. "The soldier I was working on?"

"If he's here, we've got him covered. Just be thankful you made it out." Bradford stood, one hand to his lower back. Frank had no trouble identifying the pain from bending over cots all day because he shared it.

That afternoon, Frank assisted in three major grafting surgeries, and then Bradford left him on his own to perform two more. He was terrified and caught himself holding his breath to steady his hands. The wounds were both large, and he'd never worked on that kind of surgery in training. There was no way to know if he'd done a great job or a lousy one, but he was pretty sure he'd done no harm.

It was dark out when Bradford found him again. "We need to get back and catch a couple of hours' sleep, Lieutenant. You did aces today."

"Yeah?" Frank didn't know Bradford well enough to tell if he meant it or was just being nice. Still, it felt good to hear. He started to tell the major to go ahead without him. Then he remembered they weren't supposed to walk alone, and he didn't see anyone from Pinkney still in the hospital. "In a minute." He wouldn't get any sleep if he didn't check on his surgical patients one more time.

Twenty minutes later, he found Bradford outside, leaning against the battered hospital facade and smoking a cigar. When he saw Frank, he ground out the cigar stub and started walking.

The night shivered, and stars blinked from a black-cold sky. The smells were the scents of autumn in Missouri. Frank had been thinking about his sister and her husband all day. He hadn't heard from Dot in weeks. He'd thumbed through every English newspaper he could get his hands on and never could find news of the Philippines. According to the armed services' broadcasts, the invasion was going well. Dotty had written that she was afraid the Japs would evacuate prisoners to Tokyo. Jack probably knew more about Boots's situation than Dotty did, but Frank hadn't heard from him, either.

"Any word from your Helen yet?" Bradford asked.

"No. But thanks for asking." It occurred to Frank that he didn't even know if Bradford had a wife. "Do you have a family back home?"

"I do, as it happens. Elaine and I have been married twelve wonderful years, and that's twelve out of twelve. We have two lads, Lance and Richard, ten and six—quite a match for Elaine, I'm afraid."

Frank thought about the child he and Helen had lost and how hard it would have been to be so far away from a son or daughter. "Do you worry about them?"

"I do. They're staying with Elaine's mother in the countryside, so that helps."

"Your wife must worry about you, too."

Bradford took so long to answer that Frank was afraid he'd overstepped his bounds. He didn't usually pry into other people's lives.

At last, Bradford said, "Elaine and I and the boys are in this war together. We're trusting God to see us through to peace."

Frank didn't know what to say.

Bradford stared at the path ahead of them as if he could see his family there. "When Lance was born with a weak heart, we didn't know how long he might live. I was a physician. I should have been able to rescue my son. And Elaine has always worked toward peace and enriching the lives of the poor and suffering at home and abroad. But we found ourselves helpless to help our own child."

Frank kept still. He understood that sense of helplessness. He hadn't been able to help Helen or their unborn child.

"Ah, we have nearly arrived," Bradford said as the camp came into view. "I fear I have taken a circuitous path to answer your question. Let me conclude by saying that my wife and I found peace in Christ, with a bit of help from the hospital chaplain. That faith, that peace, has served us well."

"Thank you, Major. I needed to hear that." Frank could have said more. He envied the man's strength, his faith, and the peace that showed itself whether he was performing skin grafts on a patient or walking into camp with a friend.

At supper, Frank made sure Lartz loaded up on everything. He was starting to look like the cadavers in med school. The pyramid mess tent, pitched over a concrete slab, wasn't much warmer than their barracks, and steam clouds rose from plates like fog on early Missouri morning cow dung. Frank took his time stepping over the long wooden bench and sitting down so he could scan the tent. "Anybody seen Anderson?" The last time he'd seen Anderson, Andy claimed he was headed out to find a drugstore since the Army PX wasn't set up yet. It had sounded fishy then, and it sounded fishy now.

Lartz whispered, "He didn't come back last night. He's probably sleeping it off in a bar somewhere . . . and not alone."

"I don't really care," Frank muttered, "as long as he made it to Western Union before he passed out. I gave him just about everything I had, and he promised to send my telegram to Helen."

"Saved me a spot, gents?"

"Speak of the devil," Lartz said.

Anderson, disheveled and bloodshot, wormed his way onto the bench across from Frank. A couple of Brits wrinkled their noses and slid farther down.

"Just tell me you sent my telegram." Frank could have sent it himself in three days, when he finished the burn rotation, but he didn't want his wife to have to worry seventy-two hours longer than necessary.

"What telegram?" Andy asked.

Frank wanted to reach across the table and strangle him. "You'd better have sent it, Anderson!"

"First thing I did, ol' man." He was already feigning a British accent. "Shame you couldn't have come along like the good ol' days, Daley."

"Wait a minute . . ." A nurse partway down the table broke into a big smile. "Daley. Are you Frank Daley? *The* Frank Daley?"

Anderson dropped his fork. "*The* Frank Daley? Doubt it."

"Fever therapy!" she exclaimed.

Frank laughed. "How did—?"

"That was you, mate?" one of the Brits said. "Well done, you!"

Frank couldn't believe it. In residency when he'd worked on the disease ward, medical personnel were always delaying diagnoses because they had to go to the library and look up the many possibilities for the patient's fever. So Frank had made up a poem about fever therapy to help remember how to handle various treatments. He'd really just wanted to save himself from all those library runs. But the poem spread like poison ivy. "Don't tell me that poem made it overseas before I did."

The nurse said, "On the field, we received a hundred patients with fevers and no manuals to look things up. We used your poem. And here you are in person!"

"Here he is," Andy muttered.

After supper Frank walked the nurse—Becky—back to her barracks. They chatted about everything from the new penicillin—"the best warrior in this man's Army"—to the never-ending British rain. Becky said she'd been sent to Pinkney from a field hospital for a full medical workup. "One of the patients fresh from the battlefield, in a fit of frenzy, knocked me out. I guess I was unconscious long enough to worry them. I tried to tell them it was nothing."

Frank wouldn't have thought her old enough, experienced enough, for a field hospital. "You are so brave," he said. "I don't know how I'd do in a field hospital."

She laughed and put her hand on his arm. "You? Now I know you're having me on. Anyone can see how brave you are." She didn't look away, and her tiny hand still rested on his arm. She made him feel like he really might be brave.

Was she flirting? Was *he*? "I'm married," he blurted out.

Without removing her hand, Becky said, "Oh-h-kay?"

Why did he feel he had to clarify his marital status? They were just talking. Since when couldn't a married man talk to a nurse? "Well, good night, Nurse." He took a step backward. "I have to write my wife." That wasn't what he meant at all. "I love writing my wife. I didn't mean I have to."

"Good night then, Dr. Frank Daley." She turned and ducked into her barracks.

Frank jogged back to his.

28

FRANK

CAMP PINKNEY, ENGLAND

Frank couldn't help smiling as he strolled to the PX before sunrise to mail Helen's letters. Maybe one of hers would have gotten through. He longed to know how she was, where she was.

While still a hundred yards from the PX, he heard arguing coming from inside—Mort was at it already. The fellow seemed daily to have gotten up on the wrong side of the cot. "Buy cigarettes, soldier!" Mort shouted. "They're good for what ails you, and you can't afford them candy bars."

Frank knew the Army sold cigarettes at a loss, believing they calmed men heading into battle. Candy, on the other hand, turned men into boys. Frank stepped through the flimsy screen door and let his eyes adjust to the single overhanging lightbulb. Boxes lined the walls of the ten-by-twelve, and shelves looked fully stocked.

"No mail yet! What do you want, Daley?" Mort barked.

"A spot of kindness and a drop of compassion?"

"Good luck with that," said the private who'd been angling for candy over cigarettes. He stormed past Frank empty-handed.

"Another satisfied customer?" Frank mused.

Mort glared up from the box he was cutting open. "You looking for Lartz?"

"Should I be?"

"He was in here last night, badgering one of the limeys about their German captives. He kept pressing for information about how the Germans were treating prisoners, whether they're letting the Red Cross in or not."

Frank had known something was weighing on his friend, but he hadn't asked. His mother's voice, still echoing in his head, insisted, *"We Daleys are private people. Don't be nosy."* He hadn't been nosy where Lartz was concerned, but maybe privacy wasn't what his friend needed now.

"There you are. Lieutenant Lartz said I might find you here." Major Bradford caught him outside the PX. "I thought we might walk to the hospital this morning, if you're up for it. It's stopped raining, and I'd like to show you a church you shouldn't miss."

"Sounds good." He fell in with Bradford, glad for the walk.

"Mind if I ask? Is your mate all right?"

Frank shrugged. Here was the second person to ask about Lartz today, and the sun wasn't even up yet. "What makes you ask?"

"He's been hounding the higher-ups, I hear. Something about where the Germans are holding prisoners. Your Colonel Croane seems quite irritated with the lad's persistence."

"Why would Lartz want to know about prisoners?"

Now it was Bradford's turn to shrug. "Just a guess, mind you. But does your man have family over here?"

"Nobody in service." At least he knew that much about his best friend.

"Then perhaps civilians he fears may have fallen to the enemy? If so, he has good cause to be concerned, especially if his relatives are Jews. We're aware of forced-labor prison camps that torture, starve, and kill their captives."

Frank had heard the rumors. He knew Lartz's mother was Jewish, but he didn't know much about the rest of his family.

God, take care of Lartz and his family. Frank surprised himself with the prayer, which came naturally. Maybe Major Bradford was rubbing off on him.

Bradford took a path into the woods, and they trudged through wet leaves and under canopies of orange and yellow until they came out onto a stone pathway.

"Good of you to take me along, Major. Helen loves old churches."

"She would indeed like this one. See that tower? The bell still rings for national moments."

Even from this distance, Frank could see how magnificent the stone face was, the tower massive, dominating the countryside. "How old is it?"

"Just over nine hundred years." After a minute he added, "I have something to confess. This isn't strictly a sightseeing venture. More like an exploratory mission. What do you know about aircraft?"

Frank stopped. "Not a thing."

"No worries." Bradford pulled a folded parchment from his inside pocket and handed it to Frank.

Frank unfolded the oversized paper. On it were sketches of fighter planes, bombers, helicopters. Under each were words or phrases identifying the aircraft: *Heinkel He 11, Heinkel He 177, Junkers Ju 188, Junkers Ju 88, Messerschmitt Bf, Focke-Wulf Ta*—

"I don't understand." He tried to hand the schematic back to Bradford, who refused to take it. "Are these German? What do you want me to do with this?" He tried to refold the thing, but he'd always been lousy with maps. He could never quite figure out how to follow one, and he had even more trouble trying to refold them.

"Memorize it for starters," Bradford said. "We'll be getting assignments tomorrow and moving out before long. Where we're going, we'll need someone who can identify what's flying above us. After you have these in hand, I'll see that you get a roster of our own planes—the RAF, that is. I assume you can recognize your own Yankee aircraft."

"Assume again." This time when Frank shoved the paper at Bradford, the major took it and folded it easily before handing it back. "Why me, Major? Don't get me wrong—I kind of like the idea of knowing who's flying over my head. I just don't know why you want *me* to do it." He'd felt the same way when he'd been put in charge of the disease ward in Battle Creek.

Bradford grinned. "I like you, Daley. Unfortunate for you, right? I did ask Colonel Croane why he hadn't seen to your promotion to captain before you left America, as all promotions have been frozen in this theater."

Frank sighed. This was not news to him or to any of the should-have-been captains in his outfit. "Our beloved Colonel Croane missed our promotion deadline by twenty-four hours, resulting in our persisting rank as lieutenants and a lower pay grade."

They walked through the old church, and Bradford served as guide, filling in bits of English history. But it was clear to Frank that the whole outing had been a ruse to get him alone and arm him with homework. It was also clear that Bradford had picked the wrong horse in this race. Frank would do his best to memorize all the aircraft on the chart, but he couldn't promise not to be found cowering in the nearest trench if he actually spotted one.

Lt. F. R. Daley
V-mail Oct 27, 1944

Dearest Helen,

Mail! Mail from you, my angel wife! There is no greater gift. You cannot imagine how desperately I needed to hear from you today. I think you might have been embarrassed if you'd seen your husband dance around the barracks when his name was called for mail and he saw three letters from you. The dancing might have made you laugh, especially if I told you how Anderson and I spent our first night in this camp. Perhaps more on that later. Perhaps not.

We are seeing close-up the many effects of war.

Something is troubling my friend Lartz, and now it's troubling me as well. So many worries. I believe you and I finding each other is one of the few good things to come out of this war.

With love, wherever you are,
Frank

29

Helen

Helen couldn't believe her luck. She was on her way to Europe—
more importantly, to Frank—in luxury unlike anything she'd ever
seen. As the 199th rushed out of their transport trucks and onto the
docks in New York, there sat "the Queens," the two greatest ships
in the world—the *Queen Elizabeth* and the *Queen Mary*. Even in
the murky light of dusk, Helen could make out the grandeur of the
giant tiered ship that would be their home for a few days—the *Queen
Mary*. "It looks a bit like a wedding cake, doesn't it?" she said, thinking of the sweet wedding cake she and Frankie had at the Blackhawk.

Naomi stuck her arm through Helen's, nearly tugging her off
her feet. "Can you believe it? We'll be on the fastest, most luxurious
troopship in the world!" She led their little parade across the wide
gangplank and onto the deck. Fresh ocean breezes wafted through,

bringing the smell of fish and something heavenly being cooked on board.

"I sure hope Frank caught a boat like this one," Helen said, remembering how nauseated he got in cars and trains.

"At least you know he's safe on the other side," Naomi said.

Victoria pushed her way between them. "Only because some other soldier's wife let you know."

Helen tried not to let on how much Victoria's words stung. Why hadn't Frank sent *her* a telegram? She'd had to get the news from Anderson's wife. It would be one of the first things she'd ask her husband when they finally got together again. Victoria, of course, had made much of the oversight. That gal stirred up trouble wherever she could. Days ago, poor Lydia had confided that her husband had been operated on for a foot injury, and she feared he flirted with the nurses. Now, Victoria seized every opportunity to launch into a tirade about unfaithful husbands on the home front.

"Let's get inside and explore!" Peggy elbowed Victoria out of the way and pulled Naomi and Helen through the mass of men and women eager to claim turf on the famous ship. Peggy was tall enough to see over most of the nurses and feisty enough to shove through. The gals—Lydia, Naomi, Peggy, and Helen—had managed to stick together this far and vowed to stay together as long as they could.

Helen felt tinier than ever as she stared around the giant cruise ship. As fantastic as it was, she could see how war had changed the *Queen*. The superstructure must have been white before, but the Army had painted everything gray. She wondered if a change in color would really make the monster ship harder for the Germans to see. She sure hoped so. Suddenly the war felt close. She'd worried so much about Frank on his voyage over. She'd worried about Eugene and the rest of her brothers. She'd hardly had time to worry about herself.

Peggy led them through crowds of gawkers, down narrow corridors, and on to what must have been a glorious stateroom. Elegance had been replaced by triple-tiered wooden bunks. Their shoes clanked on the metal floor as they lugged duffels, helmets, and boots across what had been miles of carpet.

"I've seen pictures of the *Queen Mary*," Peggy said. "Gee, I wish we could have ridden her in her heyday."

"You have no idea of the glamour and excellent service that were the hallmarks of the *Queen*." Victoria plopped onto a bunk in an ideal location, wedged into a corner. "I have always preferred the *Queen Mary* to the *Elizabeth*. I found the extra expense well worth it."

As if "Queen Victoria" hadn't spoken, Peggy continued her own narration. She pointed out a massive wall covered with bulletin boards and notices. "Right there used to be tapestries and paintings."

Helen could imagine the prewar opulence. Even the Army couldn't hide the finely carved woodwork, or the beams and panels now covered with leather for protection from the commoners. One day, maybe she and Frank could take a cruise on the fully restored *Queen Mary*.

"Say, how many of us are they loading onto this boat?" Lydia asked. Like Helen, she'd abandoned her cap, and her straight black hair swung in a fashionable ponytail.

"Ten thousand," Peggy answered. "Maybe more."

"Go on!" Naomi gave Peggy a little shove. "That's twenty times the population of my hometown."

"You're not in Kansas anymore, Naomi," Peggy teased.

"I wasn't in Kansas before. Iowa."

"Same difference," Lydia muttered.

Helen grinned. Not at Liddy's Midwest slam, but at the line about not being in Kansas anymore. *The Wizard of Oz* was one of the few movies Helen had seen. She'd taken her little sis when Vin had come for a visit.

"Hang on to your hats, gals!" Peggy shouted. "We'll be in England before you know it. They stoke this baby so the U-boats can't hit it."

U-boats? Helen didn't want to think about that possibility. Peggy had the news before the *Stars and Stripes* did. She was always asking patients about their battles. Helen, on the other hand, liked talking to her patients about their families, their plans, their dreams. "Let's get settled. I want to write Frank."

The gals groaned as expected, but they followed her and picked bunks close together.

"I don't know why you bother," Victoria said, without looking up from filing her fingernails. "He doesn't write you."

Helen had learned her lesson. She knew Frank hadn't stopped writing her. Nobody had received mail while they were waiting for a ship. But that telegram thing—that, she didn't understand. She started a letter on her last piece of stationery from the Palmer House. "My dear Frankie," she said aloud as she wrote. "How glad I am that I have you to write. Why, I know some pretty sad and lonely wolfesses who have nothing better to do than their nails."

The next day was their first mail call, and Helen got seven letters from Frank. As she curled up on her bunk and shuffled her love letters, she thought about a game she used to play with her little sister: "If your room were on fire, what one thing would you take with you?" Vin always gave the same answer: a doll their oldest sister, Anne, had given her on her fifth birthday. Helen never gave the same answer twice: "My blue dress." "My basketball." "My diary." Now, fingering the papers stretched across her bunk, she knew how she'd answer. "If the *Queen Mary* got torpedoed and you could only take one thing into the water with you, what would it be?" Helen smiled to herself as she silently answered, *These letters from Frank.*

30

Helen

ABOARD THE *QUEEN MARY*

First thing in the morning, Helen and the others reported for duty to the supply sergeant, a grizzled fellow who looked like he would have been at home bear hunting in the wilderness and would have preferred it to overseeing a flock of females.

"I want this whole place in shape by nightfall, or you ladies will be spending the night where you stand!" he barked. Helen assumed he meant the double-wide pantry and the crates scattered on the floor. "You're not just tidying up. I want a count on every item. Label each one. And double-check your numbers."

"Aye aye, Captain!" Peggy winked at the old geezer. That gal could get away with murder.

Victoria sat on a nearby crate and complained, "This isn't what I signed up for. I'm a nurse, not a janitor."

Helen ignored her and asked, "Does anyone know where this ship will dock?"

"Peggy?" Lydia pressed when nobody ventured a guess. "Don't tell me you're in the dark with the rest of us."

"'Fraid so. I do know that we'll soon be called the 199th *hôpital général*, if that's a clue."

"*Oui!*" Victoria cried. Peggy had made her put on box labels, though she couldn't keep up. "*J'adore Paris!*"

Helen had been certain they'd end up in France, but they'd have to take another boat across the Channel. So with any luck, she'd be in England long enough to see Frank before her unit moved on. "Frank and I want to see Paris together," she said, remembering planning and dreaming on their honeymoon.

"Well, if it isn't my favorite flock of nurses!" Bill Chitwood set down two large boxes. "Bandages for the one-nine-nine."

"Bill!" Helen really was glad to see him, although it made her feel weepy, like running into a cousin she hadn't seen in years and realizing how much she'd missed him. She hadn't seen Bill since Battle Creek. "I wondered what you'd gotten up to."

"Don't ask." He opened one of the boxes.

Helen reached in and pulled out rolls of fabric bandages. "Golly . . . do they really think we're going to need all of these where we're going?"

"Now, Nurse Eberhart. You know better than to speculate," Bill said.

Helen put her fists on her hips in mock outrage. "That's Nurse *Daley*, Private Chitwood."

"That's Private Chitwood, ward *master*!"

"I'm impressed," she said. Bill had lost weight, making him look a decade older than when they were in Battle Creek. What would he be like by the war's end? What would *she*? "How's Jennie?"

Bill's smile widened. "Jennie's swell. Writes me every day."

"I hope you write her every day too," Helen said, grateful that Frankie matched her two or three daily letters.

"Purt' near, ma'am. I'm looking forward to the day I can see her in person. I sent her a picture of me so's she wouldn't be too shocked when we finally meet up."

"Are you telling me you've never seen each other?" Victoria asked. "You don't even know what she looks like?"

"Don't care," Bill said.

"You will," Victoria said.

Lydia seemed to share Vic's incredulity. "What if she's nothing like her letters? She could be a kid."

"Or an old woman," Victoria added.

Helen jumped to Bill's defense. "Jennie's brother knew Bill in Texas, in boot camp. When she couldn't get hold of her brother, she got worried and wrote Bill. He wrote her back. They've been writing ever since."

"Sounds like true love to me," Peggy said.

Lydia opened her mouth, then must have thought better of it and went back to unpacking.

"What do you know about where we're going, Bill?" Naomi asked.

"Soon as we hit dirt, we'll be joined by an outfit arriving on the good ship USS *West Point*, the one they used to call *America*. We'll be rushed to a more permanent location with them."

Helen dropped her box and stared up at him. "Don't say rushed, Bill. I have to see Frank before we move on."

Peggy was checking numbers on the boxes against numbers on their clipboard. "Going by my previous experience with the Army, 'rushed' is an unreliable description for anything they do."

"Can't argue with that," Bill said, heading back the way he'd come.

"Frank will find you," Peggy said. "*And* I heard that the best hotels in Paris give servicemen one or two nights free until closer to Christmas."

"Sometimes I'm glad you're a know-it-all, Peggy," Helen mused.

They worked all day and had just finished the last box when Bill showed up with one more. Victoria had been gone for hours, and Lydia left when they were nearly finished with what they'd thought was the last box.

Peggy groaned. "Bill, couldn't you have waited until we were gone? Dinner starts in fifteen minutes, and I'm not going like this." She finger-combed her naturally curly, naturally unruly red hair.

"You go on, Peggy," Naomi said, wiping sweat from her brow. The poor gal might have been finishing the loading job at the canning factory where Helen had worked before nurse's training. That job turned men and women old before their time, a lifestyle Helen had recalled whenever she felt overwhelmed with student nursing.

"You go too, Naomi," she said.

"I'm fine, Helen." Naomi leaned over to pull the lid off the new box, and Helen could see her bite her lip and try to mask her back pain.

"Go! Bill and I have things to discuss. His Jennie, my Frankie. Right, Bill?"

"If you say so, Nurse."

Naomi and Peggy protested further, but Helen won, and she and Bill dug into the box, which was filled with small brown bottles. While they stuck on labels and recorded the inventory, they talked about Jennie and Frank. But Bill wasn't quite himself. Helen could tell something was bothering him. "You didn't let Victoria get to you, did you, Bill?"

"Nah. I'm not worried about Jennie." He sighed. "I'm more worried about how I'll look to her."

"Are you kidding? You're a catch! She'll have your picture, too, so no surprises."

"It's not that. I'm worried I might not come back . . . whole, if you want the truth of it. I've seen a lot of fellas go home in wheelchairs and worse. I'd never want Jennie to settle for half a man."

Helen searched for something to say. "Oh, Bill. Nothing's going to happen to you! You're going to be just fine."

He dropped the box he was working on. "You can't know that! How do you think all them boys on your ward in Battle Creek got sent there, minus some pretty important body parts?"

"How can you even say that? It won't happen to you." Helen realized she'd stuck the wrong label on two bottles. She ripped them off and wadded them up.

Bill wouldn't let it go. "You and I have both seen too much of this war already, and we're on our way to see a whole lot more. You can't control a world at war, you know."

"Fine. But even if the worst does happen to you—and it won't!— what you and Jennie have goes deeper than that. She'd love you no matter what, and you'd be all right. You'd get through it together."

Bill stopped handing her bottles and gave her a raised-eyebrow look that made her think of a cantankerous cowboy. "Is that what you'd do if Dr. Frank greeted you at the docks in a wheelchair, with no legs and nothing from the waist down?" He looked away.

Helen did not want to hear this. Or picture it. Her hand shook when she grabbed the bottle out of Bill's hands. "Yes, of course it's what I'd do. But it's not going to happen. We're all coming out of this in one piece. And I don't want to hear another word about it. Let's get this box finished."

～✦～

Lt. Helen E. Daley, 199th General Hospital
Aboard the Queen Mary

Darling,
Can't believe I'm sitting here in my cozy stateroom. My bunkmates are quiet and peaceful, with the exception of Victoria. Thankfully, she is a gadabout and seldom here.
Still no word from Eugene. Gosh, I'm worried about him. Pray for him, okay?

Sorry for the interruption—we were just visited by Nurse Simpson, chief nurse aboard, an odd soul, shorter than I am. Her nose twitches like a bunny's, and with her hair pulled into a bun, her ears, which are rather pointed, stick out, as do her buckteeth. Lydia whispered to me, "Offer her a carrot," which sent me into a fit of giggles that I could not, of course, explain or excuse.

But that wasn't the worst. Naomi and I had wrapped our raincoats and rubbers in our bedrolls, and Nurse Simpson was quite upset because we didn't follow packing orders. Naomi did so by mistake, and I by design. I've never worn ugly rubbers and don't know why I should start now.

I suppose I shall learn soon enough. If you see someone having lost their shoes in the mud (as forewarned by Nurse Simpson)—guess who?

With love,
Tiny

P.S. I know it's far-fetched, but I can't help picturing you standing open armed, waiting for me wherever the Queen Mary docks. I can see you there, that clever look on your face that says, "Aren't I something to have pulled this off?" And I say, "Amen!"

31

Helen

LIVERPOOL, ENGLAND

Frank wasn't waiting on the docks when they landed.

"Helen, you knew he couldn't have been here. *We* didn't even know where we'd dock," Naomi said.

"I know." But in spite of all that knowing, she'd hoped Frank would be here waiting for her.

Victoria made herself known by bumping into Helen. "Maybe he doesn't want to see you as badly as you want to see him."

"Go away, Vic." Helen took one last look back at the *Queen.* The whole world seemed encased in a fog mixed with black smoke from factory chimneys visible across the water. From the docks, she could see crumbled bricks and burned lumber, bombed-out buildings everywhere.

A hand clamped her shoulder. "Welcome to Liverpool, Nurses!"

Helen looked up into the smiling face of Bill Chitwood.

"What's in Liverpool?" Lydia asked.

"Fish," said Peggy Know-It-All. She sighed. "I could happily eat a dozen crabs about now. And two dozen lobsters."

Bill chuckled. "Now, you're onto something there, Nurse."

They huddled together, stamping their feet. It didn't help.

"Put your helmet on, Helen," Peggy urged.

"I hate hats." She'd slung her helmet over her arm. Thank heavens she'd worn her Army boots or she'd have frozen feet. "What are we waiting for?"

"Transport." Like a good soldier, Peggy was wearing the drab rubbers, her helmet, and Army-issued attire.

"There are trucks all over the place," Naomi said. "You can't tell me none of them has room for us."

Lydia's face had turned bright red from the cold. "I'm all for sneaking back to the *Queen* until the Army makes up its mind."

Finally, Simpson, the bunny nurse, rounded them up and pointed out their transport trucks. "Move along!" she shouted as they piled in. Once the truck filled, Simpson introduced them to Colonel Pugh. Helen could imagine him featured in the newsreels they ran before picture shows. He wasn't as good-looking as Frank, of course, but he exuded confidence. As she eyed him taking command, she decided the jury was still out on him.

Wedged between Lydia and Naomi, Helen said a silent prayer of thanks for her height, which proved short enough to have the wind blocked by other bodies. Colonel Pugh sat next to Peggy, who peppered him with questions.

"How long are we going to be here, Colonel?" Peggy asked.

"The Liverpool assignment is temporary," Pugh conceded. "You should be ready to depart on twenty-four-hour notice."

"Where are we going after Liverpool?" she pressed.

"You might as well know that we'll be moving south to the coast, where we'll board the SS *Léopoldville*. We'll sail to a town on the

French coast, Étretat. The major harbor, Le Havre, was, I'm afraid, completely destroyed, forcing us to take the long way around. Our ultimate destination is Rennes. It was the first city in France to be liberated, a happy event which transpired on August 4."

August 4 was Helen's wedding day. Surely this was a good sign.

"Still, nobody gets out of this truck until I give the word," Pugh said. "Understood? The Germans left undetonated mines for us, so you'd better watch your step."

"Wait. Mines, as in land mines?" Helen hadn't meant to say it out loud. But she'd seen what those mines could do to a person.

Pugh turned to face her, and Helen couldn't decipher his expression. Did he think it was a stupid question?

"Parachute mines, dropped from the air. They could be camouflaged by the rubble, hidden and waiting to explode." Pugh continued to stare at her.

She wanted to ask him what good it did to watch your step if you couldn't see the things anyway. But for once, she held her tongue. She didn't want to risk setting off Colonel Pugh's own undetonated bomb. For all she knew, this colonel could have a temper to match her dad's.

Finally, Pugh turned away from her and resumed his instructions. "Until we bug out, you'll have plenty of work at the hospital in Liverpool. Some of our fighting men from Normandy will be there in long-term care. We have wounded arriving daily, many flown directly from what's turning into a major battle, perhaps *the* major battle inside Germany at present. Troops from our infantry divisions attempting to clear the Germans from the Hürtgen Forest have met with appalling resistance. Be prepared to care for these brave soldiers suffering from explosions, mines, exhaustion, exposure, and perhaps worst of all, trench foot. Trench foot has accounted for more casualties than all other causes combined in this area."

Helen hadn't seen many cases of trench foot, but what she had seen had been horrifying. When troops were confined in foxholes for over forty-eight hours, their feet—cold, wet, and immobile—could contract the dreaded condition. If left untreated, feet and legs might have to be amputated.

Pugh's voice droned on: "You'll be sleeping in a warehouse. It was a broom factory before the war. Do not, under any circumstances, leave your barracks by yourself. Go in groups to the latrine. Trucks will take you to and from the hospital. I can't reiterate strongly enough that nothing is safe to touch."

Their truck went silent, except for the thumping and sloshing of tires plowing through mud and potholes.

"Can you see over there? Beyond the wall?" Pugh pointed to what might have been a town square before bombs leveled it. But *leveled* was the wrong word because nothing about the scene was level. Mounds of rubble and debris dotted the ground.

It reminded Helen of a rough model she'd helped Eugene build for a school project the night before it was due. They'd used gravel and cardboard, the only materials at hand. It hadn't been enough to make a replica of the Rocky Mountains. Eugene had brought home an F and taken a belt-beating from Dad. Helen couldn't have been more than seven or eight, but she remembered jumping in front of Dad and screaming, "Stop hitting Genie! You'll have to come through me to get him!" Dad had dropped the belt.

She pictured Eugene as he might be now—trembling, his feet buried in a cold, wet foxhole.

"Once we get to France, undetonated bombs might also be waiting for us in alleys or in town squares. And you will be forbidden to pick up souvenirs, so better get into that habit now," Pugh was saying. "The Germans have rigged hundreds of vicious booby traps with you in mind."

The man grew quiet then, and Helen wondered if he was picturing every evil he'd seen in this war.

She was, and she hadn't even seen it. Yet.

Helen

LIVERPOOL, ENGLAND

Helen didn't know how much time had passed in the truck. Possibly only an hour or two, but they were the coldest hours she'd ever lived through. She could no longer feel her toes or fingers. She'd be of no use to patients if she lost her fingers to frostbite.

"We're here!" Peggy shouted.

Helen tried to peer between the bodies of surrounding nurses. Wind sliced through her coat and felt like ripples of ice water poured over her skin. She caught sight of a mass of rubble piled higher than the truck. The only building that could have been a hospital was bombed out. Their truck motored past a long line of open flatbeds, each carrying dozens of casualties. Nurses stilled at the sight of so many wounded. Helen stared into each truck they passed as if she expected to see Frank. Or Eugene, or Bud, Ed, Clarence, or Wilbur, even though she knew Bud and Clarence were in the Pacific.

235

Pugh stood up, balancing himself against the cab. Helen had to admit that he'd told them more than most officers would have, warning them without talking down to them. Maybe he'd turn out to be an okay joe.

"Nurses!" Pugh shouted the second the truck came to a halt. "You have an hour to get settled in your barracks. Trucks will pick you up at 0800 sharp. Any questions?"

Gals were already climbing out of the truck, landing on tiptoes, obviously spooked by Pugh's warnings of unexploded mines and bombs. Helen had a hundred questions to ask the colonel, but she went to the top of her list. "Colonel Pugh, what about mail?"

He shook his head. "No outgoing mail for another week. You won't receive mail from overseas for three weeks since your APOs weren't released."

Overseas mail, yes. But what about in-country mail? Helen was afraid to ask. As soon as he discovered she had a husband in England, he'd probably put her in chains until Frank left the country. But she wouldn't know where to meet Frank unless she got a letter. She had to ask. Besides, he'd find out she was married sooner or later. Helen raised her hand, feeling like a schoolgirl.

Before Pugh could call on her, he answered her unasked question. "If you've gotten mail from soldiers on this side, check with the duty officer in your barracks."

Yes! Helen lowered her hand. A few yards away, what was left of a cement building leaned low to the ground. Smokestacks stuck up from the roof like periscopes on a submarine. A faded sign read, "Barrington's Broom Factory."

Helen dashed to the broom barracks and was first in line to sign in. "Helen Eberhart." She signed where the burly woman pointed. "Any mail for me?"

The woman thumbed through a box of letters. "Eber—?"

"Eberhart." Helen spelled it for her.

"Sorry, luv."

"Wait!" How could she be so dense? "Daley. Helen Daley?"

The woman frowned.

"I just got married. I'm sorry. I'm not sorry I got married. I'm happy about that. It's just, well, the Army doesn't seem to want to change my name and—"

"Here you go." The woman handed Helen a pack of letters. "Seven. Looks like you're not the only one happy to be married."

Helen thanked her, then ran to the nearest bunk, where she started in on the letters. She savored every word, imagining Frank saying them. It sounded like he missed her as much as she missed him, and he was doing everything he could to get them together.

She resented every lost word, sliced or blacked out by the censors. As Frank put it, *Speaking of the weather is one of the few freedoms left to us. Incidentally, it's cold.* Reading between the lines of letter number four, Helen thought Frank had taken on the job of identifying aircraft. It was frightening to think the enemy could turn up anywhere, thanks to airplanes.

She'd just finished the last letter when the duty officer who had signed Helen in brought her a V-mail. "Not like you need another one, but here you go. It was at the bottom. Almost missed it."

Helen grabbed it from her and managed a quick "Thanks!" as she tore it open.

The woman turned back. "Your transport's waiting, and they don't wait long."

Helen glanced up. The place was empty, except for two nurses hustling out. She vaguely remembered Peggy and Naomi trying to get her to leave with them, but she'd been anchored in Frank's world. "Gee, thanks!" She pulled on her coat, grabbed the letter, and ran.

Trucks were already driving off. "Helen! Over here!" Naomi shouted.

"Hurry!" Peggy stood up as their truck blew noxious fumes from the tailpipe. Helen ran to catch up. Peggy grabbed her wrist and pulled. Naomi and Lydia helped hoist her into the truck.

"You didn't even hear us, did you?" Naomi said.

She shook her head and thanked them. The sun wasn't shining, but it was light enough to read. She pulled out Frank's last letter.

Lt. F. R. Daley 0440863
11th Gen. Disp. APO #63
12 Nov 1944

Darling Tiny wife,

You must hurry and get here so we can share a big bowl of sweet potatoes!

Balfour, my old buddy, is with Admiral Halsey, though I haven't heard from him in months. Pray for his safety.

I told you about pompous Colonel Croane, who spent a fortune on fancy combat boots. So I commented, "Why, Colonel, those look nearly new," and he's now furious with me.

Rosey landed his fourth term of office the same day you landed. Of the two, your landing is bigger news! My hope is that you didn't catch my 5,000-ton tanker. They say the Queen Mary, for example, is 65,000 tons! I forgot to tell you we had a visit from the actual queen. She wore a powder-blue dress and matching hat (since you like details). No joke! She toured our hospital and was having tea when I left her, but I don't much care for the stuff, so I went on my way.

Guess you know that Lartz has become a good friend. He is a closed-off fellow, and I worry about him. Helen, I am waiting for a convoy of patients coming in from the field. There has been fierce bombing nearby, and sounds of war keep us on our toes. All doctors must work through the night here. Pretty sure I spotted a Messerschmitt Bf. Messerschmitt or no Messerschmitt, I've learned to pray while I work.

With love, wherever you are,
Frankie

P.S. I was looking at a map of the United States tonight and thinking what a wonderful place it is. It's too bad it's not large enough for everyone to live there. At least there is a spot somewhere for us.

Helen

The Liverpool train platforms teemed with British soldiers and civilians. Dozens of US privates milled around, laughing too loudly, ignoring the frowns shot at them by old people sitting on the only bench in sight. Helen took out the slip of paper that gave her a legal right to travel from Liverpool to Birmingham. Frank's letter had contained the code. When she'd read "sweet potatoes," which he hated, she'd circled the first letter in every other sentence and come up with Birmingham. It hadn't been easy to wrench a leave so soon after their arrival in England. Colonel Pugh was no pushover, but apparently he did have a heart. With prayer and persistence, she'd pulled it off, an official two-day leave. Nobody had asked to see it yet, but she'd be ready if they did.

Steam billowed and puffed as two trains pulled out of the station, and still her track stood empty. Staring at the cold, blackened concrete walls that felt more like the walls of a cave than part of a train depot, she kept wiggling her toes, but her feet felt tingly. She should have worn those horrible boots instead of heels. Regulations stated that she had to be in uniform, but they didn't specify which uniform. She'd chosen the lightweight seersucker because it looked better than the wool, and maybe that had been another mistake since the wind rippled through the thin dress that was intended for spring and summer. But she wanted to look her best for her husband, to make his eyes light up and his heart pound the way hers did every time she saw him.

Someone bumped her shoulder, hard, and her pack slipped off and fell to the platform. Yellow silk pajamas peeked out from the jarred zipper as she squatted to retrieve the pack. Knees knocked her from all sides, and she thought she might get trampled. "Hey! I'm down here!"

Somebody laughed. A couple of people backed off, but a train was chugging into the station, and the crowd moved like a bowling ball down the alley, straight toward the tracks. Helen stood on tiptoes. This was her train. Judging from the size of the crowd, not everyone was going to make it.

But *she* was.

With the skill of Eugene on his home basketball court, Helen faked left, spun right, slipped between a couple of giants in British uniform, and worked her way almost to the front as the ugly black snake of a train screeched to a stop. Inside the lit cars, faces pressed against little windows. Heads jerked every time the train coughed. Finally, with a sigh like a dying breath, it came to a stop.

A porter appeared on the metal train steps, and the train vomited out its contents—French, English, and American soldiers, civilian women and children and old men. Wave after wave of weary human flesh emptied into Helen's crowd as the mass of bodies shoved back.

She grabbed the steps' rail, but three young boys shoved past her. *No you don't!* Helen recalled the countless times she'd summoned superhuman strength to keep from getting pushed around by her brothers. Head down and elbows out, she sprang ahead, hoisting herself between the towheaded boy and the one with red hair.

"Too right," said Towhead. "Go get 'em, Yank!"

The others laughed. Helen managed a half salute and kept shoving. When she reached the narrow train car, she found it already clogged with soldiers, some waving to families or girlfriends, others simply stuck, like she was. The corridor ran the length of the train, past a series of boxed-in compartments, containing bench seats facing each other.

She passed six compartments, all filled with passengers sitting as close as the Eberharts on their church pew. Helen yearned for a seat so she could take off her shoes and set down her pack. It was going to be a long trip if she couldn't get off her feet. She ducked under one soldier's arm and was about to shove between a couple of Brit officers when a well-dressed woman coming from the opposite direction shook her head and gave her a sad smile. "It's no use, luv. There's not a seat to be had. Have to wait for a debark."

Helen returned the smile, added a shrug, and planted herself at the door to one of the glassed-in compartments. First passenger out, Helen would have that seat, no matter what.

It was a dozen stops before anyone left the car, but Helen got to the empty seat first, replacing a woman in a handkerchief scarf and a thin gray coat. Her wide, liquid eyes had seen too much war, Helen thought. Thankfully, the old woman's bum was twice the size of Helen's, so the bench felt roomy.

Across from her, two women Helen guessed to be in their forties were locked in an argument, both on the same side, ranting against an invisible debater.

"I haven't heard from the boys since we sent them away." The woman reminded Helen of Anne, her oldest sister—big-boned, brown hair in two braids that wrapped her head, the kind of woman you could count on to bring food to a funeral and not leave until every last dish was clean and dry. "Sometimes I wonder if Henry and me made a mistake sending them out. Tommy's only seven, poor lad."

The other woman put her hand on her friend's arm. She was pretty, with auburn hair fringed around a perfectly round face. "Don't you think such a thing, Madge. You did right by your boys. We all done. Nobody's got more bombs dropped on 'em than Liverpool, 'cept London."

A British officer turned from his spot by the window. "She's right, ma'am. My parents hail from Liverpool, and they say that city's had over five thousand tons dropped in the blitz. Over four thousand dead, and more injured. Birmingham's right up there as well. You did right sending your children to the country."

"But I've had no word from Charley, my oldest, for nearly a year," Madge said, desperation raw in her throat. "He's not with his brother, and that's all I know of it."

Helen half listened to the lieutenant's attempt to comfort the women. Her mind drifted to the child she'd lost. Would she have had the courage to send her child away if it meant saving his—or her—life? She felt a burning behind her eyes and wondered if she'd ever get over her loss. How many women—British, English, Scottish, American . . . German, Italian, Japanese—had lost their children in this war?

Conversations broke off. She closed her eyes, hoping no one would talk to her. She wanted to think, to pray. It had been three months since she'd been with Frank. Sometimes her marriage felt like something she'd seen in a movie. On the voyage over, she'd woken early one morning, disoriented. For a second she hadn't known where she was. Was she really on a ship headed to Europe? And in the next second she'd thought, *Am I actually married?*

Who is this man I'm going to see in Birmingham? What do I really know about Frank R. Daley? I haven't met his family. Maybe they're mobsters, Irish gunrunners. Maybe he has another wife. Or a dozen of us.

She opened her eyes and was surprised to see her compartment half-empty. Gazing out at the corridor, she only spotted two smokers.

"I wish I had your dream," said the woman who looked like Anne. The other woman had called her Madge.

"Was I sleeping?"

Madge smiled, making her look even more like Anne. "And dreaming about some lucky bloke named Frankie, if I'm not mistaken."

Helen grinned, embarrassed. "Did I say anything awful?" She joined the other women in a good-natured laugh at herself. Then they grew quiet again, looking out the window at row after row of rubble, piles of stone that must once have been homes.

Helen couldn't shake the feelings of guilt, as if she'd bombed the country herself and forced children from their homes. It was ridiculous. True, German blood ran through her veins, and Helen had often overhead her parents arguing in German. But they were American citizens. She had come to this country to help. Still, she couldn't quite look the women in the eyes.

When the train stopped and the two women stood to leave, Helen said, "I'm so sorry for everything, everyone you've lost. I'll pray that your children make it home safely."

"Pray?" demanded the younger woman. "Ha! Look out that window. Where is God? *I* haven't seen him around here!"

"He's here," Helen said softly.

"She's right. God didn't do this. But He can help us through it." Madge put an arm around her friend, then told Helen, "You be safe now."

"You too." She felt like crying, as if her sisters were leaving without her. *Pull yourself together, Helen.*

At the next stop, the last two riders in Helen's compartment left, turning the whole room over to her. She put her feet up and watched the train pull out of the little depot. They didn't pick up speed. Instead, the train stopped five minutes later. Helen watched the trickle of passengers getting off. She wished the Brits had grids on train walls, like Chicago's elevated rapid transit system, so she'd have an idea where they were.

When the train pulled into a huge station, she wondered if it could be Birmingham. Not wanting to be trapped in the wrong station, she stayed in her compartment. Sure enough, a few minutes later they pulled into another busy station. This time the porter ran through the corridor, making a heavily accented announcement in what might as well have been a foreign language. She wondered if she'd ever get used to British English, especially Liverpool's version.

She was on the train that ran between Liverpool and Birmingham, so she couldn't go wrong if she waited for the last stop. Then Frank would be there, and everything would be all right. More than all right.

She lost count of how many stations they pulled in and out of. Four? Five? How many towns lay between Liverpool and Birmingham? They'd turned off the heat inside the compartment, so maybe they were almost there.

The train stopped again. People got off, but she didn't see anyone waiting to get on. With a whoosh, the connecting car door opened, and the porter stormed up the corridor. "End of the line!"

He was about to pass her. Helen jumped in front of him. "Is this Birmingham?"

He gave her a look like she was a fly on top of his wedding cake. "Right. Birmingham. England."

The train jolted, as if rammed by an oncoming train.

"What was that?"

The man sighed. "We reverse the train now. Off with you, unless you're going back to Liverpool."

Helen grabbed her bag and dashed off the train. The platform was filling again. On the other side of the tracks were a dozen platforms. She surveyed the area, hoping to spot Frank.

Panic growing inside her, she ran from one platform to the next. Once, she thought she saw him. But when she ran up and tapped his shoulder, the GI who turned and smiled at her wasn't Frank.

Where was he? He had to be here . . . unless she'd gotten the code wrong. It was getting dark. They only had two days together, and she was wasting time looking for him. Frank had spoken to her advance man, so he would have known where she was coming from and when she'd get there. He would have taken a train to get him to the station before she arrived. Cold sweat sprang to her forehead, while soldiers left in friendly groups as if off to a party.

Methodically, she checked each platform four more times. He had to be here. But he wasn't.

"Pardon me, ma'am. Lieutenant."

Helen glanced up into the most handsome face she'd ever seen—a cross between Errol Flynn and William Powell. His accent wasn't Liverpool, and she doubted it was Birmingham.

"You're lost, are you not?" His voice was kind, mellow, charming even.

"I must be." She felt tears trying to break out, so she started walking away.

He took a step after her, then stopped when she glanced back. "I beg your pardon. You looked as though you might need assistance. And we are allies, are we not? Could I assist you in some way?"

Could he? Or was he putting the make on her? Did it matter? She was abandoned. She needed help.

The man must have known what she was thinking. "I'm really not trying to have my way with you." He smiled. "Are you meeting someone?"

"I thought I was meeting my husband in the Birmingham station today, but—"

"Ah. But *which* Birmingham station?"

"There's more than one?" She felt like an idiot. Of course there was more than one. Didn't Chicago have stops all along the lakeshore, from the South Side up to Evanston and Northwestern? Why hadn't Frank thought of that?

"Six stations, I'm afraid." He studied her face, but if he thought she'd let him see her cry, he had another think coming. He put his arm around her shoulders to guide her. "Come along. Let's see what we can do about this."

34

FRANK

BIRMINGHAM, ENGLAND

Frank ran the length of the tracks, shouting Helen's name. He knew it wouldn't do any good, but he'd go crazy if he didn't do something. What if she hadn't received his letter? Or she'd forgotten the code?

A civilian with two children called after him, "You again, Yank?"

He nodded and kept running. This was Frank's second trip through Birmingham's east station. He'd been to the others, all five of them. His arteries constricted as his heart pounded, nerves and synapses sparking. His dad hadn't been much older than Frank when he had his first heart attack. Had it felt like this?

He dropped his pack and forced air into his lungs. In seconds, he was off again, asthma or no asthma. He rechecked every platform. Maybe she was racing from station to station looking for him. They could spend her entire leave circling each other.

How could he have messed up like this? He'd caught a lift to Bristol station and arrived in Birmingham an hour before Helen's train was scheduled to pull in.

What if something had happened to her? He'd never forgive himself.

That thought made it harder than ever to breathe. He hated his asthma. He hated train stations. And Brits. And soldiers. And war. Most of all, he hated himself. Why hadn't he found out about Birmingham stations before sending the code to Helen? Of course there would be more than one station in the second-largest city in England.

An announcement squealed and scratched over the loudspeaker— probably for arrivals or departures. He couldn't understand it. He turned to a young woman who was staring at the boards. "Excuse me. Did you hear the announcement?"

She frowned at him, then took a step back.

"Never mind."

"'Hoy there!" An old man in the olive uniform of the Great War hobbled toward him, waving something in his hand. His mouth moved, but Frank couldn't hear as a train pulled beside them.

Something in Frank chilled. He thought about the telegrams he'd seen delivered. A boy he'd gone through residency with got a telegram saying his brother had been killed in the Pacific. Frank had been there when the messenger walked up, waving the telegram . . . like this man.

"Are you Lieutenant Daley?" The old man pronounced it "Dally." "Yes."

"You're to stay where you are, Yank." He didn't hand Frank the paper, which looked like a note, not a telegram.

"What?" A million thoughts raced through his mind. Maybe Anderson hadn't answered for him at roll call. Frank hadn't been able to secure a leave, so he'd just left. And why not? At first, the men could get a leave every four days, then every seven. Frank hadn't taken a single day. He'd saved his days for Helen. But now, all leaves were being denied, so Frank had taken his own leave.

"I knew 'twas you, didn't I just?" said the old soldier. "Running around like we're all on fire. I says to Clive, 'It's that bloody chap calling out for Helen.' And isn't it just?"

Frank's head was swimming. His stomach felt as nauseated as it had on the oil tanker. "What was me? I mean, you have a message? For me?"

"Said I did, didn't I? You're to stay right where you're put, you are."

"Who gave you the message? Was it a woman? Helen?"

"Don't know about no Helen, do I?" He waved the note as if he were holding the British victory flag. "Come straight from the major general, that did."

Stunned, Frank watched the man turn and walk back to the depot. Major general? Was some officer commanding him to stay put? No, Helen had to be behind it. On the other hand, maybe somebody had complained about the crazed American, and this major general was on the way to lock him up.

He couldn't just sit around waiting for—

"Frank! Frankie!"

He could have picked out that voice in a bomb raid. "Helen!"

She was standing beside a British officer, who towered over her with a proprietary look on his too-perfect face.

"Frankie!" Helen strutted toward him. She was gorgeous. Amazing. She was his Helen.

Frank took off for her, clouds of steam parting between them. A whistle blew. People shouted. But all he saw was Helen. His wife. He scooped her into his arms and spun her until he was dizzy—dizzy from the sight of her, the feel of her.

Helen pressed her hands to his chest, laughing. "Frank, set me down, darling."

Darling. Everything else melted away—the last three hours, the war, everything.

"Frank—Lieutenant Daley—I'd like you to meet Major General Wallace Butler. He rescued me at the end of the line. I don't think I would have found you without his help." Helen smiled meaningfully at Frank, obviously expecting him to say something.

"Thanks for helping my wife." He pulled Helen closer to him.

"My pleasure." His smile revealed straight teeth Frank would have enjoyed knocking out. "Could I give you a lift somewhere?"

Helen returned his smile. "That would be—"

"Unnecessary," Frank said. "Thanks all the same."

Helen started to object, but Frank stepped in front of her and shook the Brit's hand. "Well, thanks again!" she called over her shoulder as Frank dragged her away.

The fellow tipped his hat. "Anytime."

And at last, Frank was alone with Helen. He had pictured this moment for weeks and imagined all the things he would say to his wife. But he didn't know where to begin. And apparently, neither did she. He wanted to let her know, face-to-face, how happy he'd been when he'd learned she was pregnant, but that she should never think the miscarriage was her fault. He wanted to tell her that he knew God would give them children when the time was right. But he didn't want to start their time together in sadness.

They kept walking out of the station. "I'm . . . I'm sorry about the mix-up." He didn't dare look at her. The last thing he wanted was for her to think of him as a dummy. But that's what he was. "I should have checked which station. Now we'll have to take a cab, I guess."

"I have a little extra money," she said.

An awkward silence passed between them, something Frank, in all his imaginings, had never pictured.

"At least we've found each other now." She shifted her bag and took hold of his hand.

"Here! Give me that." He took the bag from her. He should have taken it the minute he saw her.

In the cab they chatted about little things. She told him about Liverpool and bunking in a broom factory, and he tried to describe Camp Pinkney to her. "I like most of the soldiers there, even the

Brits. I hope you get to meet Major Bradford. You'd like him. I think he's headed for a field hospital, though."

"That doesn't sound good."

"I know. Becky, this nurse on leave from a field hospital, was knocked unconscious by one of our injured Yanks. They sent her to Pinkney to check her over, and she's already working at the hospital there."

Helen cocked her head to look up at him. "Becky, huh? I hope she's old and ugly."

An inexplicable guilt surged through him, throwing him even more off balance. "What? No. I mean, everyone's ugly compared to you."

She studied him for another uncomfortable minute. "You really are adorable when you blush."

For the rest of the ride, Frank let Helen do the talking.

Hours later, Frank sat on the tiny bed in their tiny room in St. Gilbert Hotel, 95 Hagley Road, and wondered if anyone, anywhere, had ever felt this much happiness. Even though he doubted the ancient gas heater warmed the room a single degree, he'd kept dropping in another sixpence because it made the room cozy as it blew nonstop. He and Helen had talked and made love, slowly, listening to the rain on the window. Then his angel had drifted to sleep, and he'd unpacked his provisions and used the old heater to make toasted cheese sandwiches, his specialty—the only thing he knew how to cook.

Helen coughed in her sleep. He pulled up the quilt, tucking it over her shoulders.

"What?" Helen sprang up in bed. "Frank?" She wrapped her arms around his neck. "I was afraid I was dreaming again." She took in the room with the look of a soldier who feared the enemy closing in. "How long was I asleep?"

"Maybe an hour." Frank stroked her soft hair. His fingers slid through the curls. "I've gotten to watch you the whole time."

"But I don't want to waste a minute of our time sleeping!" She scooted to her knees and faced him. "We have to squeeze every second out of this day."

"Mind if we eat first?" He slid both sandwiches onto a hand towel and presented her with one.

"You did this? How wonderful! So you shall be our official chef?"

"I wouldn't go that far." He watched her take a big bite, then sputter. When she swallowed, her smile looked fake. "Too hot?" he asked.

"It's perfect," she said. "I guess I'm not so hungry. You go ahead."

"What's wrong? You don't like cheese?" Frank had been elated when he'd found his favorite cheese in the market. "I should have asked. I thought everybody liked cheese."

"I'm sorry, Frankie. I do like cheese, just not sharp cheddar."

Frank had wanted to wow her with the grilled cheese trick he'd learned from Jack in college. He felt slighted somehow, until he saw the look on Helen's face. "It's my fault for not finding out my wife's likes and dislikes. So, no cheddar, but . . . ?"

"Okay. I like Swiss and American and Muenster. And I might have been able to pretend I like cheddar if it weren't so sharp."

Frank stood up. "We'd better borrow an umbrella and go out to eat then." He would have been content to stay inside this room the whole time, but he wanted whatever Helen wanted. He only hoped it wouldn't be too expensive. "Name it, Mrs. Daley. Where do you want to go?"

"Dancing!"

"Dancing?" Where was he going to find a place to take her dancing? But he was not about to be accused of making her "kowtow" again. "Great idea."

She bounced out of bed, shivering when her bare feet slapped the cold floor. "Brrrrr! Well, come on." She held out her arms. "I'm not dancing by myself."

He lifted her off her feet and swung her around, grateful that she didn't want to go out. They danced to whatever tune she sang in her thin, high voice that reminded him of tinkling bells, so much like her laughter. He dropped another sixpence into the heater, and they danced some more, his arms wrapped around her to keep her from shivering. She taught him the fox-trot, or tried to. Later, he paid the desk clerk to run out and get them potpies and biscuits.

They were playing cards when Helen said, "I wasn't going to bring it up, but about that telegram . . ."

"I thought you'd want to know your husband was safe." He put down his hand, two jacks, and asked for three cards, still amazed that Helen knew as much about poker as he did.

She glanced at him, then back at her hand. "It might have been better coming directly from you, though."

"I couldn't leave camp. Anderson was going into town."

"Oh."

"It wasn't cheap." He'd had to go without chocolate and toiletries for a month.

"Right." She dealt herself one card. "So Anderson could afford to send his wife a telegram? And you couldn't? I'm just asking, darling."

"Wait a minute. Are you saying Andy used the money I gave him for your telegram and sent one to his wife instead?"

Helen put down her cards. "Yes! She's the one who told me you boys were on the other side."

When Frank could gain control of himself and his language, he explained everything to Helen. "Andy will pay for this."

Helen scooted onto his lap and kissed his cheek. "I'm sorry. I should have known you wouldn't send me secondhand information that way."

"You should have, Helen."

"Should have what?"

"Should have known. Why do you always jump to the wrong conclusions about me?"

"Always? I said I was sorry about the telegram." She moved off his lap.

"What about the letters you wrote before and after your miscarriage? You sounded like you were ready to leave me and carry on alone."

"But I explained that. You know I didn't get a single letter from you that whole, horrible time."

"So you jumped to the conclusion that I was such a scoundrel I'd stopped writing my pregnant wife?"

She didn't answer. Frank knew he should stop talking. But he couldn't. "How could you *not* have known how happy I'd be to be a father? And then how desperately sad I'd be when I wasn't?"

Her eyes swam with tears. "I was sad too! And alone."

Frank had never seen his wife cry, but she was crying now. "That's just it, Helen. You weren't alone. You never have to feel alone again." He put his arm around her, and she leaned into him, sharing her tears. She didn't say anything for so long Frank wished he'd never brought it up. He couldn't stand the fact that on their short rendezvous, he had made the woman he loved cry.

Finally, she seemed to run out of tears. She slid back onto his lap and put her arms around his neck. "I should have trusted you, Frankie."

An awkward silence followed Helen's words, and Frank didn't know what he could say to fill it. "So . . . ," he said in as light a tone as he could. "You should have trusted me. And I never should have trusted Anderson."

In the morning they braved the cold rain and strolled the streets of Birmingham. They took it all in, as if bombed-out buildings were no more than beautiful mountains, and fully armed military police trained performers for their enjoyment alone. It was as if when they were together like this, the world couldn't possibly be at war with itself.

35

Helen

EN ROUTE TO THE ENGLISH CHANNEL

Helen had given up trying to sleep as the cramped truck bounced over frozen dirt roads. Colonel Pugh had shown up at the hospital and warned them to be ready to leave on twenty-four hours' notice, something he'd said every day since their arrival in Liverpool. But this time, he hadn't been kidding.

The truck stopped, and they piled out onto a dock. The moon peeked through thick, gray clouds and shone on limestone cliffs eroded by monstrous waves into weird, hollow shapes. A biting wind tore at her coat, and she had to hold it closed.

Bill elbowed her. "Not scared to cross the Channel, are you, Nurse?"

She punched his shoulder the way she did with her brothers. "Nope. I know a ward master who would save me if anything went wrong."

His laugh rattled his six-foot frame down to his boots. "You know I got to keep an eye on you nurses. So, where's that fella of yours?" He gazed around, as if searching for him.

"I know where Frank was, but not where he is now. Pretty sure he's not in England, though." After their wonderful rendezvous in Birmingham, neither of them had been able to get away for another reunion. When her period was three days late, she'd tried not to hope she was pregnant again. After all, her pregnancy would complicate everything. But when she found out she wasn't pregnant, she'd burst into tears. "And how's your gal?"

Bill's weathered face softened. "Jennie's swell."

"And you still write her every day, right?"

"Yep. I know you'll ask me that every time I see you."

Helen laughed. "Count on it!" She angled her back to the wind. "How long do you think they'll keep us waiting out here?"

Bill nodded toward the only ship at the dock. "Not long. That one's ours, the SS *Léopoldville*. She'll take us across the English Channel to Étretat, on the French coast. Sooner or later, probably later, we'll catch a train to Rennes."

Peggy waved, then shoved her way over. "Bill, darlin'!" She looped one arm through Helen's and the other through Bill's. "All aboard!"

The trip across the Channel took longer than Helen anticipated. Right away, waves rocked the *Leo*, and the passage got even rougher once they lost sight of land. Bill kept them entertained with stories that sounded like Texas tall tales. Unless he was making things up, the guy knew something about everything. Yet he never came off as a know-it-all.

"Didn't anybody think to add seats to this ship?" Victoria asked.

Helen had to agree. It wasn't good for her to stay on her feet so long. Already, she imagined she could feel the veins in her legs trying to poke through. She hoped she'd never have her mother's varicose veins.

"Don't be talking down the *Léopoldville*," Bill warned. "She's a good ol' gal. Used to travel between Belgium and the Congo. Since she's been a troopship, the *Leo*'s made two dozen voyages, not always this route. Have to keep the Jerries off balance."

"Don't tell me German subs are lurking in the English Channel," Lydia demanded.

He shrugged. "You'd be surprised."

"We all would," Peggy said.

No transports were waiting at the French docks when the *Léopoldville* arrived. Helen had never seen so many seasick soldiers and nurses. The deck sounded like a torture chamber, and the fish in the sea would have plenty to eat for days. But she'd never forget the sight of that Normandy coast, the high cliffs as white as the cliffs of Dover. Low gray clouds met the tips of jagged rock, and the scent of fresh sea air scrubbed out her hospital lungs.

They were herded like cattle off the ship, and whatever louse was in charge issued the order to march into Étretat. Positioning herself in the middle of the herd, Helen let them carry her along, but she refused to march. Her legs already felt wrapped in barbed wire.

"Helen! Over here!" Peggy waved like she was flagging in bombers.

Helen shook her head.

Peggy gave in and pushed through to Helen. "You can't see anything from here!"

"And I can't be seen."

Peggy started out marching but eventually dropped to a walk beside Helen. "I wonder how far it is from Étretat to Rennes. You think we'll get time off? I'm going to Paris if I have to go AWOL."

Helen knew Peggy, unlike Frank, was kidding. If Helen ever got a leave, she'd go wherever Frank was. But if he got a longer leave, maybe they could see Paris together.

After an hour or so, they stopped. Helen had no feeling left in any part of her body—only a frozen fatigue. "Please tell me we're here."

The crowd broke apart, and Helen could make out what had

likely been an attractive town square once upon a time, a time before war. In the center of the dirt square stood a pile of red-tinted wooden shapes that looked like children's toys—sticks and disks with holes in them. She thought about Eugene trying to build his forts with pencils, spools, and balls. He'd begged Dad to buy him a set of Tinkertoys, but the answer was always no.

She'd finally gotten a letter from Eugene. He'd addressed it to Helen Eberhart, so it was a wonder she'd received it at all. The letter was short, and some of it didn't make sense. His handwriting looked like somebody had bumped his arm while he tried to write.

And she couldn't do a thing to help him.

A French officer strode from the shadows and commanded attention. "Go no farther! Observe. These innocent-looking bits of wood are triggers from German booby traps found in the area." His accent was heavy, but his English good. "Our engineers disabled the explosives this day and will hunt for more. Welcome to the war zone!"

Colonel Pugh asserted himself, making it clear who was in charge. "Don't wander outside the yellow stripes you see there and there." Pugh pointed at a crooked, narrow trail, made even narrower by yellow tape. "Those strips mark the only paths cleared of mines and booby traps. This area around Étretat hasn't been liberated all that long, and the enemy had a lot of time to leave their mark. Nothing is safe to touch. Since we shouldn't be here long, you've been given sleeping quarters in the factory just there." He turned and pointed to a building that had obviously been bombed to bits. Yet the yellow-taped road led directly to it.

Helen didn't care. All she wanted was to get off her feet. Colonel Pugh kept talking, but she tuned him out and gazed at the stars. Ma used to say stars were heaven's light peeking through pinholes in the velvet sky. Helen hoped they were peeking in on Frank for her.

Suddenly everybody started moving, treading lightly down the yellow-taped path to the ruins of the blackened factory. The north wall stood intact. They entered by the bombed-out side and unrolled their sleeping bags on the cement floor. Helen thought she'd never get to sleep, but in seconds, she was out.

Peggy had to shake her to wake her up. "Come on, dream girl! Ten minutes to fight for well water and the best seats on the outdoor toilet."

"Are we moving on already?" Helen rolled up her bedding, then grabbed her toothbrush.

Peggy glanced back at her. "Where were you when they told us we'd work at the hospital until transport arrived?"

The "hospital" was in the remains of a bombed school gymnasium. Tents covered the roof, where red tiles had been blown off. Nurses were dispersed to various areas but given no instructions. A dozen nurses in Helen's unit milled around, waiting for assignments.

Not Helen. She eyed the ten or twelve closest patients and started with a boy who reminded her of Hudy. Gauze bandages covered his upper torso, his head, and one eye. "Hey, soldier! I'm new in town. What's new with you?" She said this while reading his chart. Burns, infection, and trench foot.

The boy—he couldn't have been eighteen—tried to sit up but couldn't move without pain. "I'm Johnny from Kansas City, Missouri." His voice had surprising depth, a natural baritone.

"No kidding? My husband is from Missouri!"

"You're married? And your husband let you come over here by yourself?"

She laughed. "Did he *let* me come? You don't know me very well, soldier."

"Sorry, ma'am. I didn't mean nothing by it."

She gave him her best smile so he'd know she'd been kidding him. "As it happens, he's here too. In the war, I mean. I'm not sure where exactly."

"What's his name, if you don't mind me asking?"

"Frank." She leaned in and whispered, "Don't tell anyone, but when I write him, I write, 'Dear Frankie.'" It might have been her imagination, but she thought she felt heat coming from the boy. She caught Bill's attention and asked him to get a thermometer.

"'Dear Frankie,'" Johnny repeated. "Guess *he* won't get a Dear John letter."

"Somebody back home write you a Dear John letter, Johnny?"

"My gal." He shut his eyes. "We was supposed to get hitched soon as the war ended. She says she found herself another guy. I reckon she'd have ditched me soon as she got a look at the new me anyways."

"Well, it's her loss, Johnny." She took his temperature and didn't like it. "I know a dozen gals who'd go gaga over you. Want me to fix you up with some? We're all suckers for a Missouri accent."

"Don't suppose you'd like to marry me yourself."

"I would love to marry you." She tied his arm bandage, ripping off the tape with her teeth, a habit she should break. "I just have to ask my husband first."

The next day when Helen got to the hospital, she went straight to Johnny's cot. It was empty. She stopped a nurse rushing by with a tray full of meds. "Where's this patient?"

But she knew, even before the French nurse frowned at the bed and said, *"Mort."* Helen struggled to hold back tears at the thought of Johnny's sweet, deep voice. She should have done something, stayed the night. Worked harder to bring his fever down. She thought of Frank and tried not to picture him as a patient in a hospital close to the front. She thought of Eugene and all of her brothers. And she hoped that if they needed a nurse, they'd get a better nurse than she'd been to this poor Missouri boy.

Helen lost count of the number of patients she treated that day and the days following. Although their standing orders were to be ready to bug out in twenty-four hours, they didn't. Work was nonstop as the hospital received a steady stream of casualties from the Allied troops' attempt to clear the Germans from the Hürtgen Forest. She dressed wounds that carried the stench of death, and she replaced shoddy dressings applied by civilians in the field. Her patients were a mix of GI, English, French, and civilian. She would never get over how young they all were. She was twenty-four and felt like an old lady around them.

On Christmas Eve, Helen was administering insulin to patients when cheers rose from the hallway.

"Mail call!" said an amputee who'd been in the hospital since the 199th arrived in Étretat. He was a former high school quarterback from Michigan. Nobody had warned him about Hitler's Tinkertoys.

Helen's mind filled with the promise of a letter from Frank. It would be the best gift she could hope for since there had been no way for them to spend their first Christmas together. She told herself it was okay—they'd spend every future Christmas together. But she'd wanted them to establish their own Christmas traditions. She didn't even know if her husband opened presents on Christmas Eve, as her family had always done, or on Christmas Day. Did he want a star on top of their tree, or an angel?

"Don't you want to see if you got a letter?" asked Michigan Quarterback.

Helen set down the syringes she was about to load. She hadn't put the needles in yet. "Well, if you insist!" She ran to collect what she guessed would be a pile of letters.

One lone V-mail was waiting for her, and half of it had been blacked out.

My darling Helen,

Thanksgiving was lonely. I can't imagine Christmas without you. But I feel blessed to be able to miss someone as wonderful as you. I can't write about my present assignment, so I'll just say that when I have time to eat, the food is much akin to the nasty weather. I ran across a new phrase the other day: parochial xenophobe, one who hates every country not his own. Seems a dangerous disease, if you ask me, as we are seeing the gruesome results of such a mindset.

With love, wherever you are,
Frank

P.S. Good night. Hope you keep warm in your sleeping bag. Is there room for two?

Peggy and Naomi came running up. "Just the gal we've been looking for!"

Helen tucked her letter into her pocket and forced a smile. "What's up?"

"In case you haven't noticed, it's Christmas Eve, you ninny!" Peggy locked arms with both Helen and Naomi. "What we need is a Christmas party!"

Somehow, Naomi, Peggy, and Helen worked out party details while finishing their shift. They pulled in Lydia and Bill, who declared that having a party was the best idea he'd heard since fried possum. Bill put himself in charge of "finagling treats and eats," and within an hour he'd produced a boxful of candy bars and two bottles of Scotch. Naomi would lead the singing—hymns and Christmas carols. And Peggy was in charge of the games. Helen volunteered to read the passage in the Bible about the birth of Christ. Every soldier had been given a leather Bible, Army-issued like their weapons, and she hadn't used either—gun nor Bible. High time she did delve into that Bible.

Helen and Naomi had nearly finished delivering the nightly round of meds when Bill ran into the hospital, wheezing from the effort. Helen expected him to yell, "Merry Christmas!" or to let them know the party was starting without them. Instead, he stood in the hospital entryway and shouted, "Incoming!"

Naomi sighed. "How many?"

"Too many! Truckloads."

Bill wouldn't say more, but Helen knew he had details—he always did. She pulled him aside. "What's going on, Bill?"

"Look, the general himself gave the order. It's top secret."

Helen had experience penetrating layers of secrets, thanks to her siblings. "Okay. Just nod yes or no. Are the injured coming from a major battlefield?" He shook his head. "From another hospital?" No. "Was it a bomb?"

Again, Bill shook his head.

"Bill, you think we won't ask our patients? You think they won't tell us?"

"Aw, okay. But you didn't hear it from me. It's the *Léopoldville*—she went down. Sank like a stone."

Helen felt a wave of nausea pass over her. "Our *Léopoldville*?"

He nodded. "We were her last voyage, before this one."

"But how? How did it happen?"

"German U-boat. A torpedo sank her, stern first. There were over two thousand GIs aboard, plus Brits and Belgians. I heard maybe half of them drowned. Tweak of fate and we'd be at the bottom of the Channel 'stead of them."

For an instant, Helen was back in the Cissna Park cistern, struggling against the putrid waters closing over her head. She could almost smell that dank, slimy water. Then another picture flashed through her brain—Battle Creek. The lake. Going down and down.

In her mind, drowning was the worst way to die.

A roar of engines sounded outside as trucks and ambulances pulled in. Nurses ran to the long line of trucks filled with the injured. Helen worked triage, sending the hypothermia patients inside first. Some of the soldiers had two broken legs from jumping onto smaller rescue boats. Others suffered third-degree burns, shock, and frostbite.

They worked through the night, treating wounded, fighting infection, fighting sleep. Christmas sneaked in while no one was looking.

36

FRANK

NORTHERN FRANCENORTHERN FRANCE

Frank greeted Christmas in a field tent hospital not far from the Normandy coast. He and Lartz worked as a team, while the bombing grew louder, more insistent. When it started to get dark, they lit lanterns and hung them on tent posts.

Frank was headed back to his tent for a couple hours of sleep when he spotted someone in a jeep. The horn beeped the old two-long, three-short code.

"Jack!" Frank jogged up and saw that his brother sported a leather cargo jacket with *Airbourne* written on it. "So now you're part of a British flying unit?"

"Like it, little brother?" Jack asked without answering Frank's question. "Guess I should stop calling you that, you old married man." He leaned across and shoved the jeep's door open. "Hop in!"

Frank obeyed, and just like that, he was once again under his brother's spell. "Where to?"

"Just a Christmas joyride." Jack floored the accelerator so hard it made Frank's head jerk back. "Merry Christmas, Frank!"

As they rode, they exchanged news, though Jack remained vague about his antics.

"I can't believe you could show up for Christmas, Jack. Remember that Christmas when you got a bike and I didn't?"

Jack laughed. "Ah, what fond memories! So it really was all about the presents."

"No." For a while now, Frank had wanted to break through the Daley privacy barrier and talk to Jack about things that really mattered. Who knew when they'd get another chance? He cleared his throat. "Jack, there's something I've been wanting to talk to you about."

Jack frowned over at him. "A bit late for the birds-and-bees honeymoon talk. Didn't they teach you anything in med school?"

"Funny. And not what I meant. Since I've been over here, I've been thinking about a lot of things."

Jack interrupted. "Here we go with another lovely memory of gifts not received."

"I'm serious, Jack."

"Oh no! Tell me the war hasn't sapped the fun out of you."

Why was it easier to talk to Major Bradford than to his own brother? He tried again. "Okay. It's just that since I've been here, I've been thinking more about God and Jesus and faith and everything."

Jack narrowed his eyes at Frank. "Don't tell me you've had a fox-hole conversion. Bombs overhead, bullets flying, prayers shooting up from trenches?"

Frank had to work to keep in his frustration. "Don't you ever think about God, Jack? Honestly, if I do end up in a foxhole, with bombs and bullets flying, I'd like to believe God was in there with me."

"Like that psalm about shepherds!" Jack exclaimed, as if he'd come up with the right answer on a radio quiz show. "And the valley of the shadow of death?" he added, in a dramatic radio voice.

Frank nodded. "And fearing no evil." The words were coming back to him. They'd had to memorize that psalm to be confirmed in the church.

Jack's grin widened. "Remember that alley behind the old shoe factory? I'd talk you into running through it with me after dark. And we'd race, shouting out, 'Though I walk through the valley of the shadow of death!'"

Frank joined in. "'I will fear no evil: for thou art with me.'"

"Don't forget the bit about a rod and staff comforting me, although I think I'd rather have a gun."

Frank shook his head. "I can't believe that alley scared you like it did me. I would have bet you'd never been afraid in your whole life."

"And you would have won that bet, little brother. I knew that alley scared you. You were just a kid." Jack fixed his gaze on Frank. "But you're not a kid anymore."

Frank turned away and saw flashes of lightning, or artillery fire, in the distance. He wasn't a kid anymore. But unlike his brother, he wasn't fearless. Not by a long shot.

Jack dropped him off in front of the tent hospital. They shook hands, and Frank got out. "Don't be a stranger, Jack." He watched his brother disappear into the darkness, hand raised in a victory wave.

Frank was still waving when he heard someone shout, "Doctor! We need help here!"

He turned to see a British soldier and a GI escorting three captured soldiers. The GI explained, "These three came running out of the forest with their hands up, yelling, 'Me Polish!' We don't know what to do with them, but they don't look so good."

He was right about that. Before Frank could say anything, Lartz took command. "We'll take them," he said with an authority that surprised Frank. They freed up three cots and directed the captives there.

"Should we leave a guard?" the GI asked.

"That's not necessary," Lartz answered.

Frank wasn't convinced. "You sure about that, ol' buddy?"

Lartz was already inspecting a head wound on the frailest captive. "I talked to two soldiers last week who told me that the Germans force Polish boys between the ages of sixteen and nineteen into battle, then position them on the front lines as shields. These boys won't hurt us."

As if he understood, one of the boys nodded vigorously.

They treated the Polish patients, who had bruises and cuts over their entire torsos. The youngest had been blinded in one eye, and the oldest could barely hear, a condition Lartz diagnosed as rifle trauma. "I think he's been beaten, pounded in both ears with the end of a rifle. Maybe two rifles."

That night, Frank dug out his Army Bible and read the inscription from the president of the United States encouraging every soldier to read the Bible and pray. A week ago in triage a GI had asked for a Bible. He'd been so desperate for one that when a nurse brought him a New Testament, he'd hugged it to his chest and wept. And it wasn't just the Allies who prayed. Frank had seen more crosses than swastikas on his German POW patients.

He dug out his flashlight and read the Twenty-Third Psalm over and over until he fell asleep.

Frank woke to the thunder of combat boots. His first thought was that they were being overrun by storm troopers. Instead, British infantry soldiers had entered the camp. "Everybody out! All medical personnel are hereby ordered to evacuate!"

From what little Frank could gather while pulling on his uniform and packing up, the Germans were pushing back in an all-out offensive against the western front. Lartz said somebody had dubbed it the Battle of the Bulge because the Jerries had taken the American front line and bowed it backward. And Lartz ought to know. He quizzed every soldier and every patient about battles and captives.

The ground shook as Frank joined in the dash to the transports. Bombs had never sounded so close. He hoped he was hearing Allied bombs, but a bomb was a bomb no matter who dropped it. Their tent hospital was now part of the battlefield.

"Where are we going?" Anderson directed his question to anyone who might have an answer.

One of the GIs called back, "Trains. Sending you south, I think."

They didn't have time to ask more because two minutes later, the trucks ground to a halt. A big open sedan drove alongside, and Colonel Croane stood up in the back to make the announcement: "This is war, soldiers!"

"Say it isn't so," Frank muttered.

"News to me," Andy said.

"All medical personnel vital to the war effort will now be required to join mobile units farther south," Croane continued.

"Mobile units?" Anderson repeated, several decibels louder than Croane.

Colonel Croane ignored him. "You've no doubt heard of the direct hit from a German bombing on Verviers and the aircraft strike on medical installations in Liège. We believe the Jerries are sensing defeat and doing their all to deliver their best blows now."

"Over by New Year's," Frank whispered to Anderson.

"Not a good bet," Lartz chimed in.

Frank knew Lartz was right, but he could still hope, couldn't he?

Thirty minutes later, he was squeezing into a boxcar with Lartz, Mort, and Andy. The cattle car had never been meant for humans. It smelled like rotten sheep dung . . . and blood. They were in the next-to-last car, a good move by Mort. Although they had to share it with seven other guys, most of the other cars were standing room only. The train jerked forward before they managed to slide the door shut.

Mort moved to a pile of hay at one end of the car. Frank and Andy joined him, along with a doctor from San Francisco, to speculate on where they were really heading. They sat close together in the dark, the only light two glowing circles from the smokers' cigarettes.

"I heard that the push into Germany is costing the western Allies heavy casualties," Mort said. Frank had heard that too. "A guy I know," Mort continued, "he said doctors and nurses in those units have to work under gunfire that never quits."

The San Francisco doctor, Greg, was the only one who had first-hand information. "I left my last evac hospital two days ago. Talk about under the gun. We admitted thirteen hundred casualties during a fifty-six-hour period. Nobody could go back and sleep. We were all on duty nonstop."

Frank kept an eye on Lartz, who seemed more withdrawn than ever. He moved to the boxcar door and pushed it open a crack, breathing in as if he had to get fresh air or drown.

"Lartz! It's already freezing in here!" Andy complained.

Lartz pressed his head to the doorframe, then banged his forehead against it—once, twice, three times.

"Hey, buddy! You okay?" one of the doctors from another unit shouted.

Frank started for Lartz and almost toppled over when the car jerked. Moonlight seeped through the cracks and illuminated Lartz's face—the stubble at his chin, the bags under his eyes. "Tell me what's wrong, Lartz."

When Lartz finally turned to him, Frank felt sure he had never seen more sorrow. "It's this place," Lartz said, his voice as rough as his unshaven face.

"This ain't so bad," one of the other doctors said.

Anderson chimed in. "Don't tell me you're going to let a little ol' cattle car get you down."

Lartz turned his back to them. Then in words only Frank could hear, he said, "This isn't a cattle car." He touched a stain on the doorframe. "And this isn't cow blood."

"What do you mean? We don't even know if it's blood."

"*I* know. We're on a German train. What do you think this boxcar carried before the Allies took it over?"

"I don't know," Frank admitted.

"Jews."

Frank didn't know what to say.

"They herd the 'impure' races onto trains, crush them in until nobody can breathe. And if some are unlucky enough to live, they're taken to camps and forced into slavery."

"Lartz . . . do you know what's happened to your mother? Maybe there's something we can—"

"I want to be alone, Frank." Lartz stuck his head so far out of the boxcar that Frank feared he might fall. Or jump.

Frank waited a few minutes, but Lartz was done talking.

"Is he giving you the spiel about Jewish slaves?" Anderson asked.

Frank sat down again. "He says this boxcar carried Jews to labor camps."

"He's probably not wrong," Greg said. He twisted what was left of his cigarette into the floorboard.

Nobody spoke for a long time. Frank was too busy watching his friend and preparing to leap to his rescue, if necessary. For as much as Frank didn't want to believe everything Lartz said, he did.

37

Helen

ÉTRETAT, FRANCE

"We're bugging out." Bill whispered this news flash to Helen as she dug into the flesh of a squirmy private who'd gotten too close to a land mine. Every inch of his tall, skinny body was layered in shrapnel.

"When?" She dropped a chunk of metal into the basin. It clanked against a pile of shrapnel that could have been melted into a good-sized statue.

Bill shrugged. "Tonight? Today?"

"Why the rush?"

"Top secret, I guess. Just count your lucky stars we're not farther east. That crazy general Gerd von Rundstedt doesn't know when to quit. He's launched an all-out offensive against the western front and bowed the American line almost to the Meuse River. I know a fella in a medical unit on the Belgian border. They had to evacuate under fire."

Gunfire had kept Helen awake all night, though she didn't know who was doing the shooting. "What about our patients?"

"If we can't take them with us, the Army will move them to safety. They'll be all right, Nurse." Bill always sounded so sure.

Helen knew it was egotistical to think her patients couldn't get along without her, but without a buffer of nurses, these boys would be shipped back to the war before they were ready, if anybody ever was ready. *Patch 'em up; ship 'em out.* That was the Army's motto. She shot up a quick prayer for Frank, for Eugene, for all of her brothers, and for the rest of her boys in this place.

Bill had been right, and that night the 199th boarded a cold train that smelled like sweat and cigarettes. They traveled deeper into the French countryside, and Helen imagined rolling hills and quaint, red-roofed buildings, though she couldn't see a thing out of the frosted window. She had no idea how far it was from Étretat to Rennes. How was Frank going to find her now?

"These are officially the slowest trains in the world." Bill plunked himself down between Helen and Peggy. He had to curl his legs to fit. "I could walk faster than this."

Only Lydia laughed. Helen was glad to see her doing something other than crying about her unfaithful husband. Two "friends" from home had written Liddy that they'd spotted her husband out on the town with a "gorgeous blonde."

Peggy sighed. "Well, I for one am glad we're finally on our way to Rennes."

"Me too," Naomi said.

"I didn't say I'm not happy to leave Étretat," Bill said. "That old Frenchie nurse had me pulling guard duty on top of my regular duties. I had to walk the perimeter most nights. I didn't mind that so much, except nobody would give us guards firearms. I suppose if I'd met up with a Nazi, I'd just talk him to death before he could shoot me."

"You should have complained to Colonel Pugh." Helen had developed a respect for Pugh as a leader and as a doctor in Étretat. She'd assisted him in several tricky surgeries, and he'd remained calm and confident, even when he'd opened up a sergeant and found two bullets they hadn't anticipated, both close to the heart. She appreciated his bedside manner, the respect he accorded his patients and his nurses. He had a full head of hair, and Helen detected the start of graying temples. It made him look distinguished, but friendlier too, as if he'd almost been a rogue but something had changed his mind. Pugh had gone on ahead of them to Rennes, and Helen was glad he'd remain in their unit.

"I complained to Duty Nurse Simpson," Bill continued, "who pointed out that, although I hadn't been issued a gun, I'd received an identity card like the rest of y'all." Bill pulled his personnel card from his wallet. "You suppose she thought my picture would scare off the enemy?" He fingered his description: *6'3", 170 pounds*. Then he pointed to the statement in large letters, the same line that appeared on nurses' cards, explaining that the holder was protected personnel under the Geneva Convention. "I ain't so sure the Jerries would check my card before shooting me. And even if they did, they'd have to be able to read English. And if they did, they'd have to care about that Geneva Convention."

Helen squirmed in her seat. "How can they make a train with no bathroom?"

"There's one at most every station and stopover," Bill said.

"Yeah," Peggy said. "But the last one was hours ago."

Victoria turned around from the seat in front. "I have to go too."

Helen gave her a sympathetic smile. Victoria was such an odd duck. Even bundled up, she was pretty as a starlet.

"I think the train's slowing down," Peggy said.

"How could you tell?" Bill quipped.

Helen peered out the smudged window, hoping to see a station. She saw nothing but wide-open spaces and barren ground, with a few tufts of weeds. "Where are we?"

"The middle of nowhere," Bill answered. "Probably a French out-post. Maybe just for mail passing through." He pointed to a tiny, worn-out shack with half its shingles missing.

"Think I'll wait here," Naomi said, frowning at the shack.

Lydia pressed her tiny nose to the glass, making Helen think of a kid at Christmas. "I'm fine here too."

Peggy stood up. "Well, *I'm* skipping to the loo, whether there is one or not."

"Same here!" Helen scooted out, followed by Victoria and Bill.

They weren't the only ones who needed to skip to the loo. Several GIs beat them to the tiny station, where a long metal arm hung over the tracks, ready to catch a bag of mail. Nobody manned the shack, but there was a bathroom inside, and soldiers were lining up inside and out. Luck of the draw that Helen was at the wrong end of the train, putting her little group last in line. And gents were no gents when it came to lining up in this man's Army.

After standing outside forever, Helen's group made it inside, where it was marginally warmer.

"Shut the door, will ya?" Victoria shouted. She'd managed to weave her way in front of them. She'd be the next one in.

Bill shut the door behind Helen, and she had to admit it was an improvement. Then he went back to chatting with the GI ahead of them, a private on his way to Rennes to report in.

"What's taking Victoria so long?" Peggy whispered.

Helen was too stressed to be polite. Victoria had been in the bathroom for at least five minutes. "Follow me and we'll find out." They moved up, and Helen banged on the door. "Hurry up, Vic!"

"Almost out!" came the reply.

More minutes passed. The GI chatting with Bill turned back to join in shouting at Victoria to hurry. "You sure she's all right in there?"

"Her?" Peggy replied. "That gal ain't been all right since George Washington died."

"Hold your horses!" Victoria opened the door, sporting a new hairdo and red lipstick.

"You little—!" Peggy started.

"Ladies first," said the GI with an eastern accent. "But please, don't take so long."

They didn't. They took turns, all in less time than it had taken Victoria.

Helen, Peggy, and Victoria waited for the guys in the relative warmth of the outpost. Then Bill led the way out of the station and back onto the platform.

The first thing that struck Helen was how cold it was. And the second thing . . . their train was gone.

Helen

38

BETWEEN ÉTRETAT AND RENNES, FRANCE

"I can't believe they just left us here to die!" Victoria whined for the umpteenth time.

"It's going to be fine." Helen felt more like throwing a punch than throwing a fit. At least Victoria had her boots and helmet. Helen had left both on the train.

"Can trains back up?" Victoria asked.

"Not a chance, sweetheart." Peggy, too, had her boots and helmet.

Helen stepped ahead, not knowing if anyone would follow her. "We can't get lost if we keep to the railroad tracks. They went that-away, and so will we."

"Aw, we'll probably catch up and pass those slowpokes before they know we're missing," Bill offered, joining Helen.

The rest fell in. The GI shuffled a few paces ahead, then turned to walk backward as he talked. "Private First Class Nelson, fresh out of Albany. So, what are nice girls like you doing in a place like this?"

That, at least, gave them something to talk about. Nelson came from a long line of military men, so there'd been no question about his enlisting. Victoria, through tears, admitted that she'd signed up on a whim because her then-boyfriend enlisted. But when they broke up, the stupid Army still expected her to keep her commitment.

Bill took a turn. "I've been a farmer, a cowboy, a short-order cook, and a coal miner. I liked every job but never settled. I became a ward boy because I liked helping out at the Red Cross in my town. And now, here I am, ward master of the 199th." Then he told them all about his gal, Jennie, waiting for him across the sea.

Helen and Peggy already knew each other's story, but they gave the highlights. Peggy had gotten fired up reading the war news every day, until she couldn't stand it. One day, she tossed the paper and ran—literally—to the nearest enlistment center and signed up.

"How can you walk in them shoes?" Bill stared at Helen's low, square-toed heels. "What happened to your boots?"

"I thought I hated those boots because they're so ugly," Helen admitted. "But if my boots walked up to me right now, I'd kiss them on their soles."

Suddenly Nelson wheeled back around and drew his gun. He signaled them to shut up. Helen heard it too—a shuffle, and something else. Why had they talked so loudly? Most cities in France had declared themselves liberated, but that wasn't how the Germans saw it. Pockets of soldiers could be hiding out anywhere, doing whatever damage they could. Waiting . . .

And here they were, three nurses, one private, and an unarmed ward master. Helen felt her A-fib kick in, making her short of breath. It was her fault that they were all out in the open. She was the one who made everyone follow her on the train tracks. She should have kept her big mouth shut.

Victoria began wailing. "We're all going to die! I don't want to be captured. I want to go ho—!" The last word was muffled by Peggy's gloved hand across Vic's mouth.

"Down on the ground!" Nelson ordered.

Everybody except Helen obeyed. She strained to see where the noise was coming from.

"Nurse!" Bill took her wrist and tried to pull her down with the rest of them.

She shook him off. She could see someone stand up from behind a bush. One person, tall and lean. He had a rifle, but she recognized the uniform. An Aussie—she'd patched up a couple of them in Liverpool. "Over here!" she shouted.

"Helen!" Peggy cried.

The lone soldier jogged toward them. "G'day, mates!"

"See?" Helen pulled Peggy to her feet. "He's one of us."

Harold, a downed pilot from the Royal Australian Air Force, talked nonstop as he joined their troop. "I was in the first wave in June. Bounced those Jerries at Normandy with your American lads. Ah, you should have been there!" He described the battle from his perspective in the air, where soldiers swimming and fighting and dying looked like ants, hundreds and hundreds of ants. Helen didn't even know if any of her brothers had been part of the invasion. She glanced into the black night behind them and felt watched, targeted. They really were sitting ducks.

"So I told me mates I'd be back," Harold explained. "And there I was, doing an overfly, when me engine stopped, and down we went. My best mate died on impact—rightest bloke you'd ever meet. . . . And here I am, not a scratch on me."

He did have a scratch on him. Helen could see that his left forearm was wrapped in what looked like the sleeve to his uniform, or his mate's. He'd started out jolly, like the Aussie patients in Liverpool.

But as they walked and he related his losses, the strain crept onto his face until he lapsed into silence.

"What say we take a break, gents?" Helen suggested. "I don't know about you, but I could use a breather." What she really wanted was to get a better look at the Aussie's wound.

Nelson frowned, his gaze taking in the dark forest on both sides. "I don't know how safe it is out here, Nurse. The Germans gave up most of this area, but not all of it. And not all of *them*."

Trying to hide how scared she was, Helen answered, "Well, if they're going to capture us, we might as well go on a full stomach. I've got sandwiches." She dug in her pocket, where she'd stashed two peanut butter sandwiches before they boarded. Her pack had candy bars, but it was still on the stupid train. She divided the sandwiches, giving Harold the biggest piece and herself the smallest.

"I'm a lot hungrier than this," Victoria complained.

"You're lucky Helen's sharing," Peggy snapped. She took one of the smaller pieces and walked to a fallen log a few feet away. "Anybody care to join me?"

The others headed for the log, but Helen touched the Aussie's shoulder. "Mind if I take a Captain Hook at that arm?" She'd learned the art of rhyming phrases from a patient who hailed from Sydney.

When he hesitated, she added, "We nurses have to keep in practice. Don't want to lose my touch." He let her remove the soiled bandage, which stuck to the wound. When she pulled it away, a mixture of pus and blood oozed.

"It's no grand thing," Harold said.

"We need to clean it, or it will be a very grand thing, soldier." She turned to the others, seated on the felled log like children at a church picnic. "Anybody have clean water? I could use ointment, too—whatever you've got."

Bill handed over a roll of sterile bandages. "Like I tell Jennie, you'll never be sorry for carrying bandages, especially during wartime." He squinted at Harold's forehead. "That's a nasty bump. Is that from the crash?"

"It is."

"You didn't pass out, did you?" Helen asked as she began to wrap his wound. He was so tall she hadn't noticed the bump on his forehead.

"I did pass out, I think, though I can't tell you for how long, as I don't know myself."

"Dizziness? Headache?"

He shook his head, then winced.

"You should get a good checkup when you're back with your mates."

He nodded, then joined Nelson, probably to get away from her nursing.

"Give me that!" Peggy was pulling on Victoria's purse.

"Let go!" Victoria shouted. "It's just my makeup."

Peggy stood up and yanked the large purse, nearly pulling Victoria off the log. A strap snapped, and the contents of the bag spilled onto the muddy ground. "I knew it!" Peggy cried. "Candy bars!" She looked at Victoria as if seeing her for the first time. "You've been hoarding a dozen candy bars and half a dozen sandwiches, all the while complaining about your too-small piece of Helen's peanut butter? What is wrong with you?"

Victoria put on her pouty face. "You broke my purse!"

"That does it! I'm appointing myself head of food service." Peggy and Bill gathered the goods and stuffed them into Peggy's pack.

"You can't do that! Just because you didn't bring any food doesn't mean you can take mine," Victoria whined. "If anybody is head of food service, it should be *me*."

"You? No." Peggy loaded the last chocolate into her pack and closed it. "You, Victoria, are as of this moment head of latrine service."

They walked as fast as the slowest soldier, which was usually Victoria. Helen tried hard not to slow the group herself—if only she'd worn her boots! It might have helped to have a longer stride. Every extra minute in this wilderness put them in greater danger. A few times, they stopped and listened to a flurry of gunfire—Allied or enemy, or both. She wondered if her husband had learned to identify gunfire as he had planes.

It had been dark and freezing for quite a while when Victoria announced, "I quit! I quit the Army. I quit this stupid walk. If you want me to go on, you'll have to carry me." She sat down in the middle of the railroad tracks.

"Look up there." Bill, ignoring Victoria's antics, pointed off to the right. "See that speck of light?"

Helen wasn't sure she saw it. "What is it, Bill?"

"Why don't I go find out?" He jogged off, his long legs taking him into the darkness and out of sight.

"Shouldn't you go with him?" Helen asked Nelson. "He doesn't have a weapon."

Out of the pure black night came a yelp worthy of a cowboy stampede: *"Yeee-haw! Yanks!"*

Helen ran toward the sound and was soon passed up by Peggy and Nelson. Harold hung back with her. A barn came into view, and as she got closer, Helen saw something else—a tiny American flag.

They passed a surreal night in the barn with two GIs separated—"not lost"—from their unit after a fierce battle near the coast. When the haggard members of Helen's little troop limped into Rennes, they were minus the Aussie, who'd veered off on foot to Paris after Bill convinced him he'd have a better chance of finding his mates there. The kindly farmer who had sheltered them in his barn had been forced to turn around when one of the horses picked up a stone and a painful limp. But he'd gotten them close enough to Rennes that they'd finished the journey on foot.

Cold, hungry, and suffering from blisters on her blisters, Helen staggered into the Allied base. She glanced around her, happier than she'd ever been to see so many US soldiers.

Naomi and Lydia came running up to her, nearly knocking her over. Naomi couldn't stop crying. "We were so frightened for you! At first, I thought you must have gotten on the wrong car. But when you didn't come back to your seat, I walked the length of that train over and over. I nearly lost it when I finally accepted the fact that you weren't on board. That's when Liddy and I started screaming at them to stop the train."

"We almost got ourselves arrested," Liddy said, sounding proud of herself.

Naomi continued, "But the Army brass refused to stop. They had orders not to. I've been trying to get them to send out searching parties ever since we got here."

"Me too!" Lydia chimed in.

By this time, they'd attracted quite a crowd of soldiers and nurses. Helen introduced her traveling companions to Lydia and Naomi.

"Is my major upset?" Private Nelson asked.

"Everybody's upset," a baby-faced GI answered. He was chewing on something that might have been a candy bar, and it was all Helen could do not to grab it from him.

"Step aside!" A middle-aged captain shoved into the circle. "General McNeal wants you in his office this minute."

"Can we get something to eat first?" Victoria asked.

"Now!" The captain turned on his heels, expecting them to follow.

"He's nice," Helen whispered to Peggy. She turned to Naomi. "Where's Colonel Pugh?" She'd kind of thought he'd be the one to send out a searching party.

"He got sent out before we arrived. Pugh doesn't know about any of this yet," Naomi answered.

Peggy looked as worried as Victoria. "Do you think they'll throw us in the brig, or whatever they call prison in the Army?"

Before Helen could answer, Nelson did. "They could court-martial us. I've seen it happen."

Peggy wheeled on him. "But it wasn't our fault! That's not fair."

Bill shook his head. "In my experience, the Army isn't known for its fairness."

39

Helen

RENNES, FRANCE

Helen and the others were ushered into a surprisingly warm building. It might have been considered a shack back home, but here, it was palatial. She stomped her feet to get the feeling back in her toes. At the far side of the room an aging general sat behind a small desk. With his head bent over his work, he presented an odd-shaped skull, hairless except for a grayish ring, not unlike a bald eagle. His bulbous nose was pink at the tip, and what she could see of his face looked like he'd had a rough time with acne when young.

Since there were plenty of chairs to go around, Helen took one and began prying off her shoes.

"Attention!" the captain barked.

Nelson straightened. Bill leaned against the wall and raised his hand in what might have been a head scratch or a salute.

The general stood up so fast his chair scraped the concrete floor. "Stand at attention! You *soldiers* have caused me and the entire United States Army more trouble than you're worth! Your orders were to stay with your unit."

Victoria's sniveling turned into sobs.

"We're sorry, General," Peggy said, saluting as if an afterthought.

"Did I ask you to speak, Nurse? Your negligence not only endangered your lives, but your capture would have put the Army in an untenable position. I don't care if you're medical personnel or frontline soldiers. When I give an order, I expect it to be followed. Do I make myself clear?" He glared around at them until his fiery gaze rested on Helen.

Helen was still seated. She had her shoes off and couldn't imagine standing up on her blisters. She glanced around at the others. Even Peggy had tears in her eyes. Bill and Nelson looked ready to bolt. She forced herself to stand, shoes dangling from one hand. "Unbelievable," she muttered. She must have been louder than she thought. Peggy's eyes got big, a signal for Helen to shut up.

"Did you say something, Nurse?" the general roared.

Peggy was probably right. Helen should keep her mouth shut. On the other hand, she needed to think of some way to get them out of this mess. "Sir, permission to speak?" Helen had never used those words before, but she'd heard them often enough.

The general seemed to be thinking it over. "Make it brief."

"Thanks. It's just that this whole thing isn't what I'd expected. When we volunteered, everybody told us how desperately the Army needed nurses, how happy they'd be to see us."

"That's not untrue. If you had remained on the train, none of this would have transpired." Helen thought she detected a slight softening in the general's tone.

"The train left without us! Sir. How could they desert us like that? You're right. We could have been captured or killed. We were so scared!"

Victoria's sobbing grew louder.

Helen set her shoes down and brushed her hands together. "This would never happen in Chicago, a gentleman abandoning a lady to the worst that city might have to offer. I thought the Army was here to protect and defend, but nobody came to *our* rescue."

Behind her was pure silence, except for a muffled laugh she'd have bet belonged to Bill. An idea was forming in her head, and against her better judgment, Helen decided to give it a shot. "I can't even imagine what my uncle will say when he hears about this."

The general definitely looked like a candidate for a heart attack. "I couldn't give a rat's backside what your uncle—"

"Not to mention what all the *Trib*'s readers will think," Helen continued, as if merely reflecting.

"*Trib*?" Peggy repeated. "As in the *Chicago Tribune*?"

"Uncle Jim writes for the *Trib*." Helen turned back to the general. "I wonder what people back home will think once they hear how the Army treats nurses who volunteer."

The general swallowed so hard his Adam's apple looked in danger of bursting through his neck. Helen couldn't tell whether he believed her or not. "Let's all calm down. We value our medical personnel. Of course we do." He eyed the three nurses in the room. "I suppose I may have been a bit hasty."

"Hasty?" Bill said. "No, sir. I don't think I felt a bit of haste when we were dodging bullets, running through forests and open fields to get here."

General McNeal propped his elbows on his desk and tented his fingertips. "For now, we'll consider that what you nurses went through may have been ample punishment. *For now.* The captain here can show you to the mess tent, and to your quarters."

Helen felt the flush of victory but tried not to show it as they followed the captain out. Bill fell in behind her.

She was still in the doorway when McNeal shouted, "As you were, men!"

Helen turned around. "But, General, they shouldn't have to—"

"Dismissed, Nurses!"

Helen tried again. "Sir, Bill is medical personnel. He's—"

"Get out while the getting's good, Nurse," Bill whispered before lining up with Nelson and the others.

Peggy reached back and nearly dragged Helen through the doorway as the captain shut the door. Even in the hallway, Helen could still hear General McNeal reading them the riot act.

Victoria hugged Helen. "That was wonderful! Why didn't you tell us you have an uncle writing for the *Chicago Tribune*?"

Helen felt like crying. "Peggy, what have I done?"

"You don't really have an uncle at the *Trib*, do you!" Peggy's question wasn't really a question.

Victoria gasped.

"Do you think General McNeal figured that out too?" Helen asked.

Peggy shrugged. "Probably."

"Do you think it would help if I went back in there and apologized for making it all up?" She'd do it, too. She didn't care what he'd do to her.

Victoria grabbed Helen by the shoulders and shook her. "Helen! Don't you dare go back there! He'll throw us all in jail."

Peggy lifted Victoria's hands from Helen's shoulders, then put her arm around Helen. "Come on. We need to get something to eat."

"Bill and the others," Helen said as they walked faster to catch up with the captain, "will they be getting something to eat?" But she knew the answer to that one. They'd be starving wherever they were.

And it was all her fault.

40

FRANK

Spending the night in a boxcar was nothing like riding in a real train. The car swayed and jerked. A guy from Indiana said hobos called boxcar trains "rattlers," and it wasn't hard to figure out why. When they pulled into the yards, Frank jumped out before the train came to a stop, then breathed in the frigid air and waited for the nausea to fade. He eyed Lartz, who had to lean into the wind to make his way over.

Anderson angled himself between Lartz and Frank, turning them into windbreaks. "Where are we?"

"Marseille?" Lartz ventured.

Frank surveyed the yards and wondered if they could really be close to any city—no lights, no buildings in sight. They'd been dumped in what looked like a parking lot for rusty trains. Scores of soldiers poured from boxcars, and Frank's company fell in with a unit comprised of GIs who looked like they'd seen too much action already. Together they set out in the dark, marching for miles before seeing any proof of human existence, and then only a farmhouse, abandoned. Although the night didn't seem to get warmer, the ground thawed, leaving ankle-deep mud. Each step felt like tugging a plunger out of the muck.

Anderson dropped back to chat with the men in the beleaguered unit. When he returned, he was overflowing with information. "We should reach Marseille in an hour. No snow in the forecast, but lots of rain." He lowered his voice. "They lost over half of their unit in some godforsaken French or Belgian forest. Now they're headed into battle again. Makes me glad I finished med school. I just want to settle into one place for the rest of the war. Marseille is as good a place as any. They must have a decent hospital. I shouldn't mind waiting out the end of the war with the charming women of Marseille."

"Want me to send your wife a telegram to that effect?" Frank offered.

It was morning when they finally stumbled into their assigned barracks, a dilapidated gymnasium filled with bunks. Frank tossed in his duffel, then headed for the post office. It would be too much to hope for mail from Helen here, but he could at least mail his letters to her.

The small Army post office wasn't far from the barracks. A light shone through the window, so he went in. A boy, who looked about twelve years old, manned the counter. Frank handed him eight letters, all to Helen. "These are important," he warned.

"Sure, Joe! V-mail super!" the boy answered in a thick French accent. He grinned, revealing a missing tooth. "I look for mail, Joe?"

"For me? Why not?" He pointed to his name on one of the letters. "Lt. Frank Daley, MD."

"Doctor!" The boy sounded impressed.

Frank waited so long that he suspected the kid had left by a back door. "You still there?"

"Ah, *oui*!" A moment later, the boy returned waving two letters. *"Voilà!* You big shot?"

"What? 'Fraid not."

"You . . . letter from president United States of America?"

Frank took the letters—one was from Helen, thank goodness and hallelujah. The other came from the US Senate Committee on Military Affairs in Washington. Truman had answered. About time. "Thanks. I'll be back."

Frank wanted privacy to read the letters, and he had to walk the length of the camp through puddles to get it. Andy's travelogue said Marseille was a port, so maybe the Mediterranean had flooded.

He settled onto a damp stone bench at the top of a hill. From his vantage point, he could see what must have been downtown Marseille. The sun shone dimly through the gray sky, and a civilian couple strolled past him without a glance as he unfolded the first letter.

Truman or Helen? No contest.

My dear Frankie,

Have I told you lately how much I miss you and love you? I'm looking forward to a more permanent location (though, of course, I can't tell you where that will be).

Silly me! You know how I love to swim, but I forgot my swimsuit!

Right now, we're too busy to swim. Our patients suffer from bullet wounds, shrapnel, and burns, as well as diseases. Every time I meet a soldier, he reminds me of one of my brothers. I hope you've heard from Dotty and she's heard from Boots by now.

Never have I wished I spoke French, but I do now. Civilians seem lovely, and I wish I could get to know them better. Nonetheless, we are too busy.

I am so sorry we are missing our first holidays together.
Even now, I imagine us with Schnapps and Junior and perhaps
Junior the Second and Third, cozy in front of a fireplace in our
own home. Great picture!

So, my love, shall it be.

I pray that this New Year will bring peace to the world and
us to each other.

With love, wherever you are,
Mrs. Daley

Frank pictured tiny Helen curled onto her bunk, thinking of him, writing to him. He hadn't thought it possible to miss his wife even more, but he had been wrong.

Rennes. Clever Helen. He wasn't sure where Rennes was in relation to Marseille, but he'd find out. He had to see her—soon.

After rereading Helen's letter, he opened Truman's, which turned out to be a disappointment. Frank had written his old Missouri senator three times, lobbying for equal pay for married couples in the Army. Twice, Truman had written back, first agreeing that it seemed unfair, then promising to look into it. This letter didn't even go that far. Senator Truman was regrettably tied up with war concerns in Washington, DC.

Frank had trouble thinking of Truman as vice president instead of the stubborn Missouri senator he'd been for a decade. Truman would be sworn in on January 20. Well, Harry S. better watch out, or he might not get Frank's vote again.

Frank returned to the barracks only to discover that there was no bed for him. All top bunks were occupied. All bottom bunks . . . were underwater. He was still gazing at the absurd scene when the boy from the post office ran up.

"Monsieur!" He removed his beret and twisted it in his hands. *"Je vous en prie. Ma petite soeur?"*

Frank had no idea what he was saying. "English?"

"Er . . . sick. Very sick. Marie, my sister." He lowered his hand, and Frank thought he might be signaling that he was talking about a child.

"A child, Marie, is sick?"

"*Oui!* You come?"

"Now?"

"*Oui! Merci!*"

Frank glanced back at his sleeping comrades and sighed. What the heck? He wouldn't get any sleep anyway. He pulled his small doctor's kit from his pack and left.

He followed the boy out of the city and down a country path, now pure mud. In broken English, the kid, whose name was Michel LeBlanc, said his sister had something wrong with her legs and Michel considered it a tragedy because the family needed money from her work in the laundry. That, or something was on fire.

By the time they reached Michel's home, a tiny farmhouse that might have been quaint a hundred years earlier, the sky was a slab of slate. Frank tried to clean the mud from his boots as they stepped inside, but Michel took off his boots, so Frank did the same.

A kerosene lantern gave the only light. The smell of wet wood and mold permeated the air. The house had little or no heat and no electricity. A gray-haired woman appeared in an arched doorway. She regarded Frank with suspicion while firing questions at her son, or maybe grandson. Frank couldn't understand a word of the heated conversation. Under other circumstances, he might have appreciated the beauty of the French language. But right then, it sounded like gunfire.

Michel gave Frank a crooked smile. "My mother." He turned to her, and Frank was pretty sure he was being introduced as a doctor and a hero. If the kid only knew . . .

Frank smiled. "Madame." Then he said to Michel, "Where's your sister?"

The woman nodded for him to follow, then shuffled into a small kitchen with a cast-iron stove. Michel disappeared, and Frank warmed his hands over the stove. When Michel returned, he was accompanied by a pretty girl with braided hair and huge brown eyes. Thinner than her mother, the girl wore a long skirt, the color and pattern faded to a dull lavender gray. Two little boys peeked from behind her.

Frank pointed to the empty chair at the wooden table, and Michel helped his sister sit. "You . . . Marie?" He'd been expecting a child, not this petite young woman.

She nodded, and the hint of a smile passed over her face like a shadow, replaced by a wince of pain. When he knelt beside her, he understood. Her legs were covered in blisters, some red, others yellow with pus. The sores probably covered her torso as well, but the girl seemed so shy, Frank didn't have the heart for a full examination. He'd have to get her to come in for a proper exam.

The door flew open, and in walked a giant. That's what he looked like, backed by pale light and ducking under the archway. He charged as if discovering his wife with a strange man, a man who now held his daughter's leg, her skirt shoved to her thigh.

Frank dropped the leg with a thump and stood to face the man, who was a head taller than he. "Me—Dr. Daley," he stammered, sounding like a bad Tarzan movie.

"You come to help Marie?" His accent was thick, but Frank had no trouble understanding him.

"Yes!"

"We try everything," said Monsieur LeBlanc. "Our doctor, she give oil—no, lotion, yes?—for the *peau*, the skin, yes?"

"May I see the lotion?" Frank had ointments in his bag, but ointments and lotions wouldn't cure this, not if his hunch was right.

LeBlanc shook his head. "Gone. Lotion no good. Marie still suffer. Three doctors, one American, they try. She no get better."

"You help her?" Michel asked, his eyes pleading.

Frank grinned at the barefoot little boys, brave enough to stand beside their mother now. "I think so."

"You too have lotion?" Her father frowned, his skepticism evident.

Frank searched his bag for vitamins and found the small bottle he had for his own use. He set the bottle on the table. "One in the morning and one at night. I'll bring more tomorrow if I can."

For the next hour, he did his best to clean the wounds. He applied ointment to help with the pain. The cure wouldn't be easy, and he hoped they'd give it time. Malnutrition didn't happen overnight, and neither did its cure.

Michel's mother urged him to eat with them, but he lied and said he'd already eaten. He didn't want to take their food. This was a farm, but he hadn't seen any animals. Marie needed protein. And fruit and vegetables. If the Army had any, he vowed to get some for them. At any rate, he could scare up more vitamins. He closed his bag and smiled at Marie, then her mother. He turned to the father. "I'll come back with more vitamins."

He started to leave, but Madame shouted, *"Non! Arretez!"* She crossed the room and rattled French to her husband. Frank didn't want to be around for another argument. He nodded again, then opened the door. The wind blew so strong it nearly forced him back inside. With the wind came sheets of rain. He'd never get back to camp in one piece.

Monsieur LeBlanc shut the door. "You come." He put on a jacket that wouldn't have kept out a spring shower, much less this storm. Then he opened the door.

Confused, Frank followed him. Maybe good manners dictated that Monsieur LeBlanc walk him back to base. The thought occurred to him that they might be headed to a sick neighbor's. He'd be happy to try to help all their neighbors. Only he could barely keep his eyes open.

"Vite!" LeBlanc led him around the back of the house to a stone barn that had seen better days. "You sleep!"

Frank would love to sleep here. He didn't have to report in until tomorrow. He knew there would have been no room in the house. But a barn?

He trudged through the mud, hoping there would be a dry place for him to curl up in the barn. Monsieur LeBlanc swung open the barn door. No animals, and it seemed dry enough, though very dark. They walked the length of the barn. Then LeBlanc kicked aside a smattering of hay, leaned down, and opened a trapdoor. He held it up and nodded for Frank to climb down. Frank stepped onto the wooden ladder.

"*Résistance.*" Monsieur LeBlanc handed him the lantern and left.

Frank watched the man until his form disappeared into the black of the barn. There was a musty smell of old hay and even older manure. He climbed down the ladder and held up the lantern.

Frank could hardly believe his eyes. He might have been entering a Paris hotel room. Okay, maybe not Paris. Maybe not a hotel. But the bed had clean sheets and two blankets. There was a table with a loaf of bread and two bottles of ale.

Résistance. This family hid members of the French Resistance . . . and now, one American doctor.

As he drifted to sleep in the best bed he'd had since his second honeymoon, Frank began to plot his next honeymoon. Helen would love it here.

~⚓~

Lt. F. R. Daley, MD
Cold, cold December

My darling wife,

I can't wait to see you swim again, though I much prefer an oil tanker on the wild waves.

My, but it's great news that Danny has his prosthetics. He'll get used to them, though it won't be easy. And Hudy and Jimmy will help. They must all come for a visit when you and I are in our own home.

Remember our starlight strolls at Battle Creek? How I wish we could walk together this evening! Schnapps could come along. Our little pet must miss us, as we do him.

Everyone here understands my one goal is to see you again. But I no longer simply mark time as I did in Battle Creek. I cringe when I remember how content I was to get by with the least effort possible. Now I believe our contentment comes when we're doing what God intends us to do.

Lartz worries me more each day. I pray for him almost as much as I pray for my beautiful wife. Lartz knows so much about this war, and he's an excellent doctor. Did you know his specialty will be delivering babies?

Every letter from Dotty sounds more determined than ever to find Boots, in war or in peace. Remember Bradford, the major I've been wanting you to meet? He talks about peace more than he talks about war. Quite a unique fellow. I'm hoping I'll run into him again.

I miss you so. All New Year's Resolutions point to us.

With love,
Your Frankie

41

Helen

RENNES, FRANCE

Marseille? As soon as Helen read Frank's coded message, she'd searched for a map of France. Bill was the one who came through with one. Helen took it as a peace offering. She'd apologized a hundred times for getting him in trouble with the general, but he hadn't seemed like the real Bill with her . . . until now.

"That battered ol' map looks like it survived the Blitz," Bill said, "but there's enough of it to figure out that Rennes is over a thousand kilometers from Marseille. I reckon you and your husband couldn't be farther apart and still be in France."

"And he wants me there on New Year's Day! I don't know how I can pull it off, but I will."

They were on a rare break. Jeeps filled with GIs drove past, waving at her and at the Frenchwomen, who returned the greeting. Life may have started going back to normal for the civilians in Rennes, but their city had been reduced to rubble, first from three German bombs that blew up an ammunition train, killing over a thousand people, then from constant Allied bombing. Nearly every civilian had suffered from German occupation. Now, nearly as many German prisoners were crowded into POW camps as civilians living outside them. Bill said there were three or four camps scattered around the city. Yet Rennes had a medieval charm that Helen couldn't wait to show her husband. She hoped he'd make the trip to Rennes one day.

The hospital was a school transformed to meet the needs of patients, doctors, and nurses. Nurses slept in the dormitory, so Helen woke up on third, ate on second, and cared for patients on first. German prisoners had their own ward in the basement, where X-ray machines abandoned by German doctors had been commandeered by US troops.

"I'd better get back to work," Bill said. Helen still had time, though. She'd woken up well before dawn, thinking about being with Frank to start the New Year right. Since she hadn't been able to fall back to sleep, she'd already checked on her patients. What she wanted to do now was walk and think. They'd been warned to go out in pairs, but nobody else was awake. Victoria was snoring, though the gal swore she'd never snored a night in her life. Peggy, Liddy, and Naomi had stayed on the ward with Helen until after midnight because a truckload of wounded GIs rolled in just as they'd been about to leave.

Helen figured she'd walked through the toughest neighborhoods in Chicago alone. She could handle Rennes. Besides, she wouldn't go far, and she'd turn back at the first sign of trouble. Bill had shown her on the map how two rivers—the Vilaine and the Ille—converged in Rennes, and that's where she wanted to walk. She followed the scent of water and fish. Everywhere she walked, she stepped on broken glass and debris. Barren trees stretched to a gray sky that looked smoky, as if bombs had just done the damage that lay everywhere. Rennes had been the first town in France to be liberated, on the same day as Étretat, her wedding day. She imagined walking with Frank, her arm looped in his, her head on his broad shoulder.

A deafening roar jarred her from her reverie. She looked up in time to see a tank turn onto the street and head straight for her. She didn't move, couldn't move. The tank kept rolling toward her, its firing arm swaying as if looking for a target. Finally, her brain got through to her legs, and she backed out of the way. The tank rolled beside her, and she saw the big white star painted on its side, along with the name *Hitler's Hearse*. The lid popped up, and an Allied soldier stood from the belly of the tank, then two more behind him. They laughed as if out for a joyride. The guy in front reminded Helen of Eugene as he lit his cigarette and leaned against the open lid. Helen felt a pang in her heart for Genie. She'd give anything to know where he was right now.

A tall GI, his hair so short he might have been bald, stopped talking to the others in the tank and turned to stare down at Helen. He let out a wolf whistle. That was Helen's cue to hightail it back to the hospital.

Halfway there, Helen spotted Bill running toward her as if escaping a firestorm. "Oh, Nurse! I need help. The screaming! I don't know what to do!"

Helen ran past him, calling over her shoulder, "Let's go!"

The minute she stepped inside the hospital, she heard him. Helen thought she'd heard every scream of pain imaginable, but this didn't sound human. And it wasn't coming from the hospital ward. It emanated from the basement, the German POW ward. She glanced back at Bill, then headed down. Bill overtook her, taking the stairs two at a time.

At the bottom, two MPs stood guard at the closed ward doors. One stepped to block Bill from entering. "Only medical personnel allowed in there."

"What do you think we are?" Bill demanded. "Turnips? Didn't you see me run out of here a minute ago?"

The MP squinted at Bill's name tag. "You're not cleared."

The unearthly shriek sounded again. Helen couldn't stand it. "Are you deaf?" She pushed in front of Bill and tried to get past the MP. The other officer closed ranks to block her. She shoved them, but they didn't budge. She forced a professionalism she didn't feel. Her big brother was an MP, after all. Ed would be as immovable as these men. "There's a man in extreme pain on the other side of these doors. Do you know if there's a doctor in there?"

"There's no doctor," Bill said.

The howl grew worse. It reached deep inside of Helen until she couldn't take it. "I'm going in." She faked right and twirled left.

"I'm with her!" Bill pushed in after her.

One of the MPs started to follow them, but the other one, who looked a decade older, took his arm. "I don't care whose side he's on. Nobody should be in that much pain."

Once inside with the doors shut, Helen's wave of relief quickly changed into panic. She was staring at perhaps a hundred German soldiers, their beds only inches apart, and every bed full. Weeks—maybe days—ago, they'd been shooting Americans. And now, here they lay in the same beds as the Americans upstairs, under the same blankets and clean linen.

A heavyset nurse Helen didn't recognize ran up to her. "I tried to help him." She glanced at one of the French nurses, who held her position at the opposite end of the room.

A fresh outburst of the unearthly cry jarred Helen into action. She had no trouble locating the patient. Sweat dripped from his forehead as he writhed, clutching his mattress. One hand cuffed to the sidebar was bleeding, not from the handcuffs, but from his fingernails digging into his palm. He kicked. Every vein in his face looked ready to pop.

Helen reached for his free wrist to take his pulse, but he jerked his hand away so fast it caught her on the chin. She reeled backward but kept on her feet.

"Nurse?" Bill was by her side. "Did he hurt you? Want me to get the MP?"

"He is crazy Nazi!" shouted the French nurse.

Helen ignored her and the ache in her jaw. "I'm okay."

The patient moaned so pitifully. She had to get through to him. Helen racked her brain for the dormant German that should still be there. *"Sich beruhigen. Was ist los?"* She hoped she'd asked him what was wrong and told him to calm down.

The startled soldier drew his knees up to his chest, but regarded her as if in a dream. Then he poured out his heart in rapid-fire German.

Helen didn't understand everything, but enough. "I think it's his catheter."

Bill barely touched the man's abdomen and sent him into more horrific howls. "His bladder's gonna bust."

Helen looked around for help. The heavyset nurse had disappeared, and the other nurse, also French, huddled over a patient forty beds away. "Nurse, can you help with this patient?"

"Mais non. I cannot leave this one!"

Great. She checked the man's chest, dodging his hands as best she could. Bill helped, taking a few punches while she searched for the root of the problem. Then she saw it. A piece of limp tubing had pulled out of the catheter incision. The bladder couldn't empty. No wonder he was wailing. "We need more tubing, Bill. This one will never go back in. It's not stiff enough."

Bill scratched his head.

"He'll die if we don't do something fast." She hollered to the nurse on the other end of the ward, "Nurse! Where's the surgical tubing down here?"

"No more. Try the closet upstairs."

"Bill, I need you to run upstairs and—" Bill wasn't there. "Bill!" Then she saw him leave through the basement door. Tears burned her throat. She couldn't believe he'd leave her.

Seconds passed that felt like hours as Helen tried to reposition the catheter. But it was no use. She couldn't make it work.

"Step aside! Comin' through!" Bill burst onto the ward carrying some big brass's uniform on a hanger. "Got me an idea!" He was trying to unbutton the jacket, but he gave up and yanked it off the hanger and threw it down.

"But what—?"

"How long you reckon it would take to sterilize this hanger?" Bill was already untwisting and cutting the hanger with clippers.

"You're a genius, Bill!" Helen grabbed the straightened hanger and ran it over to the sterilization center, where she did the best she could the fastest she could.

The patient screamed in pain, and maybe in fear that his only hope had left his bedside.

Minutes later, Bill was shoving the sterile metal into the catheter. Together, they pushed in the reinforced tubing, using the original incision and guiding it into the bladder. The second the catheter hit its mark, urine shot out. Helen jumped back just in time. But Bill was soaked. Soaked, but grinning.

The patient's face softened, his eyes transforming from pain to relief. *"Danke, danke."*

"I'll do cleanup." Bill looked nearly as relieved as their patient.

"You're not doing anything until you shower, Bill. Go!"

It took Helen nearly an hour to clean everything and restore order in the basement. By noon, she felt too tired to eat, but she needed the energy. She barely looked at whatever they plopped on her plate before collapsing at her usual table. "What a morning!"

The second Helen sat down, Victoria popped up, her tray still full.

"Was it something I said?" Helen joked.

"More like something you do," Victoria muttered.

"I told you I'd smack you silly if you said another word!" Peggy gripped the table as if ready to bound over it and down Vic's throat.

"I didn't say a thing!" Victoria protested. Then in a whisper: "At least I didn't say it in German."

Peggy started up, but Victoria was already out of range. She rammed into Lydia, who was headed for the table with her tray.

"What's with her?" Liddy took the vacated seat next to Helen. Seats had opened up all around her.

Helen's mind had been so fuzzy that she only now understood. "Was that about this morning? And that German prisoner?"

"I thought she made it up," Peggy said.

"She probably did, at least most of it," Helen guessed.

Peggy leaned across the table, for once *not* knowing all. "Start from the beginning and don't leave anything out."

Helen related the whole thing, from the minute Bill had come running, to the end, when she'd rushed upstairs for her assigned rounds. Peggy didn't interrupt, and Liddy only stopped her once, to scold her for walking alone in Rennes.

"I guess we're supposed to hate the enemy." Helen forced down a couple bites of cold toast. "But nurses aren't supposed to hate their patients, are they?"

Peggy sat back and stretched her arms above her head. "It's a conundrum, all right. I guess you better be prepared for some flak."

"Me? What about that nurse who wouldn't go near the patient?"

"The *German* patient," Liddy put in. "Don't get me wrong, Helen. It's a bum rap, and Victoria's a rotten egg. Still, some of the guys around here lost buddies to Nazis just like that one. Maybe even that very one."

Helen knew that. She also knew she could never let a patient suffer, or die, no matter who he was.

It was late afternoon when Colonel Pugh found her on the ward. "I have been hearing quite a bit about you, Nurse."

Great. She kept counting out pills into tiny cups and waited for the ax to fall. "Can't imagine why." It made her angry that gossip would have traveled all the way to the top already. Didn't people have better things to do than listen to rumors? "I'm flattered to be the topic of so much conversation."

"General McNeal himself said—how did he put it? 'That nurse has spunk.' He suggested I keep my eye on you. I get the feeling he doesn't appreciate spunk and harbors a deep skepticism about your uncle the newspaperman."

She stopped what she was doing and turned to face him. "So, this is you keeping an eye on me?" She loaded the pill cups onto her tray, wishing they had more generous doses of drugs like penicillin and pain meds—everything was rationed. "If you'll excuse me, Colonel Doctor, I have work to do."

"One moment, if you please. I also heard that your German is pretty good."

That did it. "So what's that make me? A spy? Did you know my maiden name is Eberhart? Very suspicious, don't you think?"

He laughed, actually laughed. "I see I haven't been misinformed—about the spunk. No, Nurse, I don't think you're a spy. And I'm thrilled that you understand German. We have a ward full of German soldiers, most of whom cannot speak English. That makes them difficult to treat. I simply wanted to ask if you would mind helping us on the German ward. We still need your services here, but we have had a devil of a time getting nurses to work in the basement."

All the steam went out of her. "Oh. All right. Sure."

"*Danke* very much."

As Helen delivered the meds, she couldn't help thinking that it was no accident she'd ended up right where she was. She liked what Frank had said in his last letter about doing what God planned for him to do. For now, it looked like the plan for Helen Eberhart Daley included taking care of the enemy in the basement, and very likely making new enemies above.

42

Helen

RENNES, FRANCE

Helen watched giant snowflakes strike the glass and lace their bar-racks window like a belated Christmas card. A quick look was all she could afford. They had received a new batch of wounded, and nurses were already shorthanded, thanks to a mean virus going around. Naomi joined her at the window. "You have the day off, you know."

"I can pitch in until I need to leave." Helen was catching the night train to Marseille. She'd be with her husband on New Year's Day. Everything had fallen in place so fast. Colonel Pugh had gone to bat for her, convincing the general that they needed a healthy Nurse Daley, and that she needed a three-day leave.

"You're a good egg, Helen," Naomi said.

"Nice to hear somebody thinks so." Helen wasn't exactly surprised that half the nurses had been ostracizing her. Even the hint of German sympathy raised suspicions. What did surprise her was that she cared.

She locked arms with Naomi. "We better get going. Lots to do, especially in the basement. I can't count on the French nurses down there."

"Maybe the French nurses know who the enemy is." Victoria said it loud enough for the whole dorm to hear, though most were still asleep.

"We all know who the enemy is," Naomi said. Helen could always count on her friend to stick up for her, even though deep down Naomi probably agreed with Victoria.

"Go back to sleep, Vic!" Helen shouted. How Victoria could sleep so much in the midst of all there was to do boggled the mind.

"Who can sleep with German soldiers in the same building? All you're doing is making them stronger, Helen. I'm not the only one who thinks this way either. A lot of us have been wondering why you'd be so eager to help the enemy."

Helen had felt the glares, heard the whispers. She tried not to let it get to her.

"Where did you learn to speak German anyway?" Victoria demanded.

Helen stopped and turned to face her. "Same place I learned to speak English—in the United States of America."

"Well, you better watch yourself," Victoria warned.

"And you'd better watch *your*self, Victoria!" She stormed out with Naomi and told herself it didn't matter. Soon she'd be with Frank. So what if everybody else was against her?

Already, Victoria had formed her own little troop of nurses to snub Helen. Even Liddy kept her distance when Victoria's clan was around. If it hadn't been for Peggy and Naomi, Helen wasn't sure she could have kept that stiff upper lip.

Finally, it was time to go to the station. Helen was dashing back to barracks for her pack when Victoria stopped her. "There's a French farmer asking for you outside."

"I don't know any French farmers," Helen said. "Though I'd be happy to meet one if he actually did present himself. I'd love to know how to grow French fries and French green beans."

"Fine. I don't care if you see him or not," Victoria said.

Bill would be by to pick her up in fifteen minutes. She might as well wait outside.

She could use some fresh air to get rid of the stench of ammonia and urine and rotting flesh.

She was buttoning her coat as she stepped outside. When she looked up, she saw a giant coming toward her. If she'd had to guess his occupation, she would have guessed farmer. And when he said, *"Pardon, Madame?"* she knew he was Victoria's French farmer. Whoever he was, if Vic had sent him, Helen didn't want anything to do with him.

"I'm sorry." She turned to go back in.

"Madame Daley?"

She wheeled around. *Please, God, don't let it be Frank.*

The man shuffled closer. "Hélène Daley?"

Fear knocked the wind out of her. "Is it Frank? Is he all right?"

"Frank? Oh yes. Lieutenant Doctor? Friend of my brother in Marseille."

Frank was all right. This man said he was. *Thank You, God.* She stared up at the giant. "I don't understand why you wanted to speak to me."

He handed her a folded sheet of paper. "No Marseille."

She opened it and saw right away it wasn't Frank's handwriting: *Don't come to Marseille. I love you, Tiny.*

"How did you get this?" Helen looked up from the scrawled note, but the man was gone, along with all hope of seeing her husband.

Unless . . . "Victoria!"

43

Helen

RENNES, FRANCE

Helen stormed back to the barracks and found Victoria lounging on her bunk. "Tell me the truth! Did you just try to pull off the cruelest practical joke in the history of cruel?"

Naomi the peacemaker intervened. "Helen, what happened?"

She spilled the whole story about Vic's French farmer and his mysterious message canceling her trip to Marseille.

Peggy was first to render a verdict. "Helen, honey, we both know Vic is rotten to the core."

"Hey!" Victoria cried. "I'm right here, you know!"

"Exactly!" Helen said.

"But I don't think even Victoria would do a thing like this. And if she did—which, I concede, is not out of the question—I don't think she'd use a giant Frenchman."

Naomi read the message out loud. "Does it sound like Frank? Does he ever call you Tiny?"

Reluctantly, Helen nodded.

Naomi continued with a logic that had eluded Helen. "Victoria wouldn't have known that."

"See?" Victoria sounded like a five-year-old.

"I'm so sorry, honey." Peggy put her arm around Helen.

"I told you I didn't do it!" Victoria shouted. Then she launched into a fresh tirade of denial so vehement Helen had to believe her. If Victoria had done it, she'd have been bragging about it. By the time Vic ended her harangue, they had quite an audience, with nearly every nurse looking on. As Helen walked away, she heard Victoria's self-satisfied conclusion: "See, I told you we couldn't trust her. She's dangerous!"

Helen couldn't stay in the barracks another minute. No one wanted her here anyway. Fine. She'd go where she *was* needed and wanted.

She headed back to the ward, Frank's curt message running through her brain. *Don't come?* What kind of a message was that? Why wouldn't he want her with him in Marseille? Didn't he need to see her as desperately as she needed to see him?

The second she stepped onto the ward, someone shouted, "Nurse Daley, did you forget it's New Year's Eve?" The question came from Private First Class Gerald Landis, a boy who might never have a life out of bed again. He reminded Helen of Eugene, something about the way Genie talked, like he needed to dodge somebody's fist after every word.

She walked to Gerald's bed and saw that it needed clean sheets. "Honestly, Private, I did forget. Thanks for the reminder, and hold that thought, will you?" She hurried to the cabinet for sheets and glanced at the duty roster to see who was supposed to be on. Peggy, Lydia . . . and Victoria. *Great.*

"Sorry we're late!" Peggy called from the doorway. Liddy was right behind her.

"Glad you made it. I don't think the last shift changed bedding. Is Victoria coming?"

"On her way," Liddy said. Helen wondered if Lydia had switched allegiance. But she didn't want to think that way, to have sides in their own unit—especially since Helen's side kept getting smaller and smaller.

Helen returned to Private Landis. "Okey-dokey, sir. You know the routine, right?"

"I'm sorry about this, Nurse. I didn't even know I was doing it. And you have to—"

Helen cut him off. "Nothing to be sorry about. It's as natural as belching. Why, Nurse O'Hare over there—" she pointed to Peggy—"does this all the time. Don't tell her I told you, though."

"I heard that," Peggy said. She was stripping the sheets of an ambulatory patient one row over. "Accidents will be accidents, I always say."

Helen rolled her patient to his side so she could remove the wet sheet, make sure it hadn't penetrated the plastic guard, then slip in the folded fresh sheet. The private had lost the use of one arm, and it dangled as if it didn't belong to him. Helen had to drape it over the boy's thin waist. His left leg hadn't fared much better than his arm when he'd gotten too close to an exploding grenade. She tried not to picture Frank like this. Right on this ward, they had a patient who'd had a practice as a GP in South Carolina. And in Liverpool, she'd treated two nurses who had been part of a battalion aid station on the Belgian border. One nurse, blinded in one eye, had second- and third-degree burns on her legs. They'd done what they could before sending her back to the States. The other nurse suffered disfiguring burns to her breast, but she'd been returned to duty. Helen had so many lives at stake in this war. She prayed they'd all come back in one piece.

"Thanks, Nurse," Private Landis said.

She gave him the best smile she could muster. "It's nothing, Private. And I'm sorry I forgot it's New Year's Eve."

"Well, *I* haven't forgotten!" Victoria made her grand entrance in a snazzy black V-neck dress that dipped low enough to show too much. It earned a few wolf whistles from the patients.

"Nice uniform," Sally said. Helen loved Sally, the plump nurses' aide who had a lovely smile for every patient and wasn't afraid of hard work.

Victoria brushed an invisible something from the bottom of the dress, which was too close to the top of the dress. "Don't envy this dress, Sally. It does look *nice* on me, but it wouldn't on you, dear."

"Sally knows enough about nursing to never wear a dress like that," Helen said. "She's not afraid to get her hands, or her uniform, dirty in the line of duty. And speaking of duty, you'd better get to it. We're changing all the beds, something your earlier shift neglected." Peggy had told Helen about Colonel Pugh's visit to the ward that morning. He'd caught Victoria stretched out on an empty bed reading magazines, and he'd written her name on the night roster himself. Helen wished she could have been there to see it.

"I can't do everything," Victoria whined. "In case you haven't noticed because you spend so much time in the basement, Nurse *Eberhart*, half of our *Allied* nurses are out sick."

"Knock it off, Vic. Get to work!"

"Catfight!" shouted a patient. Others seconded the notion.

Helen hated herself for taking Victoria's bait in front of patients. "Maybe later, fellas. Right now, we're too busy. Time for your night-time meds."

Groans sounded from all over the ward.

"Just so you know," Victoria said, "I have a big date tonight, and nobody's going to make me miss a New Year's Eve celebration. Liddy's coming with me. Major Grayson is meeting me by the river for fireworks."

"Haven't you seen enough fireworks to last a lifetime?" Helen had always loved the national anthem, but she wasn't sure she could ever again join in on the line about bombs bursting in air.

"Some New Year's Eve," muttered a soldier a few beds down.

Across the ward, mumblings agreed with him.

Helen gazed around the ward at the patients, mostly boys who hadn't had the chance to celebrate many New Years. Tears pressed against her eyeballs and threatened to make her head explode. Had she ever felt this melancholy?

Stop it! She commanded the gypsy in her to do something about it. She headed out, calling back, "Peggy, can you cover for me for a bit?"

"Where do you think you're going?" Victoria yelled after her. "To the basement?"

It took only twenty minutes to shame four bottles of Scotch out of the officers in the officers' club. Each of them had received two bottles for personal use, and they hadn't parted with their treasures easily. Thankfully, Colonel Pugh had stepped in to help persuade a couple of reluctant majors. "Happy New Year, Nurse Daley!" He handed over the fourth bottle.

"Happy New Year to you, too, Colonel." And for the first time, she saluted him.

Helen burst onto the hospital ward, her secret hidden in two brown bags.

"It's about time," Victoria muttered.

Helen let it pass. She set out the four bottles on a gurney.

"Helen, you're amazing!" Victoria read the labels. "Want me to take them to our barracks before the patients see?"

Helen faced the ward, then whistled through her teeth the way Eugene had taught her. Once she had their attention, she shouted, "I've brought a little something from the officers' club, a New Year's gift from the big brass. Peggy, see if you can't scrounge up more pill cups, will you? Sally, can you help me open these things?"

Victoria stared at her as if this waste was beyond her comprehension.

Sally had no trouble opening the bottles. Then she and Peggy set the little cups onto trays while Helen searched the cabinets for more pill cups.

"Weren't there four bottles here, Helen?" Sally asked.

"Right." She glanced at the gurney. One bottle was missing.

A private by the door, recovering from typhoid fever, said, "That foxy nurse took it. Her and the tall one with a ponytail."

Liddy? Helen's melancholy returned like an enemy waiting for the right moment to drag her down. She refused to let it.

"Okay, gents! If it's New Year's Eve you want, it's New Year's Eve you'll get!" Carefully, she poured just a touch of Scotch into each cup. "Now, don't make a habit of this, gentlemen! And don't drink it until everyone's been served. I want you to think of this as New Year's medicine for our heroes. To you, men!"

They passed one dose of Scotch to every soldier on the ward who could hold a cup. Then Helen and Peggy made a special tray for the patients who needed help—the armless boys, the young soldiers with the shakes so bad they couldn't steady their drinks. Outside, fireworks boomed and banged.

"Peggy," Helen said. "You're loud. You do the countdown."

"I'd love to!" The ward hushed for a full minute until Peggy began her count, loud enough to be heard upstairs . . . and down. "Ten, nine, eight, seven, six . . ." Helen joined the count, and so did the other nurses, along with most of the soldier-patients: "Five . . . four . . . three . . . two . . . one! Happy New Year!"

They toasted one another at the stroke of midnight and brought in a New Year Helen thought none of them would forget.

When the laughter and tears and cheers died down, the nurses returned to work.

An hour later, Colonel Pugh stepped in to wish everyone a happy New Year. Since most of the patients were asleep, the nurses had divided the shift, and Helen and Sally were the only ones on duty. Peggy would take the last half of the night shift.

"Lieutenant Daley, a word?" Helen joined him. "I thought you should know that I've had a complaint on your behavior."

Helen sighed. "And the New Year isn't yet one day old."

Pugh gave her a conspiratorial grin. "True. One of the nurses—"

"Let me guess. Might her first name be Victoria?"

He grinned wider. "She reports that you encouraged underage drinking in our hospital."

"Guilty as charged. Mind if I ask what you said to her, Colonel?"

"I believe I told her that any *man* old enough to fight for his country must be old enough to drink a thimbleful of Scotch for medicinal purposes on New Year's Eve." Then he broke into laughter so contagious that Helen found herself laughing with him.

A door banged and shouts filled the hallway. Victoria ran in, her hair a mess, her face covered with mud, and what looked like blood on her dress. "Help! It's Liddy! I think she's dead!"

44

Helen

RENNES, FRANCE

Pugh took off at a dead run, Helen close on his heels. He slowed to let Victoria catch up. "Where is she?" he demanded.

Victoria's words came in fits and starts. She smelled of Scotch . . . and blood. "Down there!" She pointed to the darkness across the road from the hospital. "She drank too much. She's not used to alcohol. We were just walking back, and she wandered off, and I saw her stop at that pile of debris. I thought she was going to throw up on the booby-trap pile, but she was saying something about a wooden soldier, that her husband collects them. She picked one up—it was in that ditch beside the pile, and—" Vic broke off in tears. She said something else, but her words were too slurred to make out.

Helen and Pugh raced down the hill.

"There she is!" Pugh slid the rest of the way down and crouched beside the still body.

In seconds, Helen was there. Liddy lay on her back, with Pugh listening for a heartbeat. "Is she . . . ?"

"She's alive," Pugh said.

Helen wanted to see for herself. She reached to take Liddy's pulse. That's when she saw the source of the blood. "Doctor!" Blood gushed from Lydia's hand. A sliver of wood stuck out where a finger should have been.

"It exploded," Victoria said. Helen hadn't realized she was there. "I hate that husband of hers! Liddy was only trying to get that soldier to give to him."

Helen unbuckled her belt and tied it around Liddy's hand. "We need to stop the bleeding."

Pugh took off his jacket and placed it over Liddy, then picked her up and started climbing the hill back to the hospital.

Liddy opened her eyes, and Helen burst into tears of relief. The poor girl was shaking, trembling all over. But she was alive and conscious.

"You're going to be okay, Liddy." Helen touched her cheek as Pugh carried her like a baby in his arms.

Pugh whispered, "I'm taking her to surgery."

"I'll assist." Helen ran ahead to the ward. Why had she brought that Scotch? If she hadn't, Liddy would still have her fingers. If Liddy didn't make it, Helen didn't think she could live with herself.

Victoria followed her. "What should I do, Helen?"

"See to the ward. Wake up a couple of nurses to help you, but don't treat any of the patients until you sober up."

Vic started to protest, then gave up. "All right."

By the time Helen gathered instruments and prepped for surgery, Colonel Pugh had Liddy sedated. They didn't speak as Helen started an IV and cleaned the wound. Two fingers were gone, and Liddy's hand looked like a wrinkled black leather glove.

"Helen, we need a specialist. I've never performed this kind of surgery."

Helen looked up. He'd never called her by her first name. "You can do what she needs right now, Doctor."

"John."

She looked him in the eye and saw doubt there, and maybe a little fear. "You're an excellent doctor. I've watched you work, and you're the best we have."

"I might disfigure this girl even more than—"

"You can't think about that now. Do what you can. Stop her bleeding. Close the wound to infection. And pray. This isn't going to be Lydia's only surgery."

He nodded. Then together they stopped the bleeding, and John stitched the wound so tenderly that Helen was reminded of her mother mending school clothes at the kitchen table, a single light shining on her.

When they were finished and the hand wrapped and bandaged, Pugh pulled up a chair and sat inches from his patient. "You should get some sleep, Helen."

She was already pulling a chair to the other side of Liddy's make-shift bed. "What about you?"

"I'm fine. I think she'll be out for hours. But I want to be here when she wakes up. She needs to get on a hospital ship back to the States. If I can get her to Paris, I can get her transport out of there and onto a ship, but I'll need to make some calls."

"Do it," Helen said. "I'll stay with her. I'm not going anywhere."

He shook his head. "I don't want her to wake up and not see a doctor here."

Peggy cleared her throat from the entryway. She must have been eavesdropping. "Is she going to be all right? Vic told me what happened."

"Come on in, Peggy." Helen filled her in on the medical details.

"How can I help?" she asked. "Naomi's covering the ward."

Pugh smiled wearily. "I have a feeling you're just the nurse who can pull this off. I'm going to give you some names to call, and I'll tell you what to say. We need to arrange transport on the next hospital ship sailing to America." He jotted names and numbers onto a prescription pad. "Tell them you're calling with my authority. Don't take no for an answer." He tore off the sheet and handed it to her.

"I'll get it done," she said, and Helen knew she would. "How do I get in the general's office to use the phone?"

"You'll have to wake him up," Pugh said.

"I have a better idea." Helen knew that at least twice Victoria had managed to call her latest boyfriend on the general's personal phone. "Ask Vic."

For the next three hours, Helen and John—though it took some work for her to call him by his given name—sat vigil over Liddy. They talked about everything, starting with the 199th, but veering off into their childhoods and their medical training. John was an only child of older parents and confessed he'd felt lonely until joining the Army. "I always wanted to have brothers and sisters."

"Wish I'd known you then," Helen said. "I would gladly have given you a few of mine."

"How's the war treating your brothers?" he asked.

"I wish I knew. The two boys in the Pacific never write. Neither does my older brother the MP. I hear from Wilbur from time to time. He's in Europe somewhere."

"Your poor mother has four sons in this war?"

"Five." She wasn't sure she wanted to tell him about Eugene. But he was waiting. "I'm the most worried about Eugene. I think he may have been in Normandy, but of course, he can't tell me. He's not answering my letters."

That was enough. Helen didn't want to share her worst fears about Eugene. "Oh, and I have a brother-in-law gallivanting and quite possibly spying all over Europe. Plus a sister-in-law who served in the Philippines until the island got overrun by the Japanese. And her husband—which makes him my brother-in-law, I suppose—was captured and hopefully still in prison, we think, in Tokyo."

"You and your husband have very colorful families."

"This is true."

"Tell me about your husband." He said it with what might have been a melancholy smile.

For some reason she couldn't explain, Helen felt uncomfortable talking about Frank with him, especially now, after her husband decided not to have her meet him in Marseille as planned.

She was saved by the footsteps in the hall. Peggy was back, and she'd dragged a disheveled and obviously hungover Victoria with her. "All set!" Peggy handed John a slip of paper. "That's the contact and the authorization number to board the hospital ship. If she can make it to Paris in time, they can send her in an ambulance to catch the first ship out. Can't get out through Brest or Le Havre, so it'll be the long way around. Do you have somebody to take her? I'll bet Bill would do it."

John shook his head. "No, I'll do it. She might need medical attention on the way. She'll definitely need to be sedated."

"How are you going to sedate her if you're driving?" Peggy asked.

It was the right question. Helen had been hanging on until the minute she could collapse in bed herself. But Liddy needed her. And why not? She wasn't going to Marseille. "I'm going too."

Pugh turned to her. "You don't need to do that. Wait—I forgot about your leave, Helen. You're going to miss your train."

"My plans have changed," she said. "I'm going to Paris."

Victoria jerked to attention. "Peggy, did you lock the office?"

"What? No. You're the locksmith. That was your job."

"We can't leave it unlocked!" Vic looked from Peggy to Helen. "Oh, all right. I'll do it."

Helen couldn't have said how long the trip to Paris and back took. She fought to stay awake so she could keep John awake. They talked about almost everything and everyone . . . except Frank.

FRANK

45

MARSEILLE, FRANCE

"Hello?" Frank couldn't believe someone finally answered the phone. He'd tried calling Helen's base in Rennes all day, mostly at odd hours since he had to sneak to the only phone, jealously guarded by Colonel Croane. "Is someone there?"

"Whozziz?" The women's words slurred.

Frank hoped she wasn't too drunk to take a message. Thanks to Croane, he'd barely had time to track down Michel at the post office and arrange to get word to Helen before she boarded the train to Marseille. Michel had sent a message to his uncle, who promised to take it to Helen. But Frank didn't know if the plan had worked or not. He'd nearly panicked imagining his wife traveling all that way for nothing. "I need to talk to Helen Daley."

"Too bad," said the voice at the other end.

"No, please! You have to go get her. It's important."

"Then you'll have to go to Paris."

"Did you say Paris?" The connection wasn't great, and the woman's shaky voice even worse.

"Yep. That's where she is, all righty. Paris—with Colonel Pugh."

Whoever it was hung up, leaving Frank staring into space, wondering what on earth his wife was doing in Paris. With Colonel Pugh.

Frank and Lartz made their way to roll call. "Why would she go to Paris with that colonel, Lartz?" Lartz had no answer. Sullen, Frank joined the ranks of soldiers and doctors to stand before Colonel Croane, good ol' Chrome Dome, who hadn't a kind word for anyone and who never offered explanations, probably because he didn't know what he was doing. It was Croane's fault that he and Helen weren't together right now. The man had canceled all leaves without warning.

"Anderson, wipe that smirk off your face!" Croane snapped.

"Yessir, sir." Andy saluted, but even the colonel had to see how hungover he was.

Now it was Frank's turn apparently. Croane stood directly in front of him, sunlight gleaming from his bald pate. "That hair, Lieutenant Daley."

"All mine, sir!"

"You will cut it this morning. We are soldiers, and we will look like soldiers and win this war like soldiers!"

"How will cutting my hair help us win the war, sir? Remember Samson in the Bible? Didn't he win his battles *until* they cut his hair?" Frank didn't want to cut his hair. Helen loved his curls, and he loved feeling her run her fingers through them.

Croane's face reddened. So did his head. "Off with it, Daley!"

"I guess it's true, then." Under his breath, Frank muttered, "Chrome Dome."

"What?" Croane asked.

"Misery really does love company."

That afternoon, Anderson, Lartz, and Frank, hair uncut, found themselves on a slow-moving train bound for Alsace-Lorraine. "This is all your fault, Daley," Anderson said. They had to stand in the smoke-filled corridor outside one of the train compartments. Andy was on his second pack.

"Take it easy, Andy," Lartz said. "Who knows why Croane does anything? He's probably had our orders for days and wanted to spring it on us last-minute."

"Who do you think you're kidding?" Anderson shot back. "If Daley hadn't made that crack about misery loving company, we wouldn't be here now. In case you haven't noticed, we're the only Yanks aboard."

"Not my fault if Chrome Dome can't take a joke. He's lost his sense of humor—one more casualty of war." But the truth was, Frank would have given anything to take back those words and return to Marseille. Andy was right. Except for a few British soldiers, the other passengers appeared to belong—women carrying shopping bags, one with a chicken under her arm, and men beaten down by hard labor from the looks of them. "Quit griping, Andy. It's better than a box-car." Soon as the words were out, Frank wished again that he'd kept his mouth shut. Lartz winced as if hit in the gut.

Oblivious, Andy said, "At least we could sit in that boxcar. And it didn't smell like chickens." He lit up again.

"Give it a rest," Frank begged, feeling the smoke in his lungs. He coughed to make his point, then couldn't stop hacking.

Lartz moved away from them, and Frank suspected it wasn't only the smoke that drove him. Frank stared out the window at barren fields frosted by the cold night. How was he going to pull off a rendezvous with Helen now? He'd planned three perfect days in the farmhouse barn. The LeBlanc family seemed as excited as he was.

And now, every minute on this blasted train was taking him farther away.

And closer to Germany. Alsace-Lorraine formed an eastern border with Germany. Croane had gleefully informed them that more people spoke German than French there. He'd added that the Germans had occupied Alsace-Lorraine in 1940 and continued to occupy major portions of the area.

Someone cracked open a window—probably so they wouldn't die of smoke inhalation, a fate worse than freezing in the unheated train corridor. Through the open window, the sounds of war grew louder. Bouts of gunfire punctuated the night, followed by occasional whistle-bursts of bombs. He'd finally memorized the aircraft chart Major Bradford had given him, so he might have identified the planes if they hadn't been invisible beyond thick clouds.

Frank joined Lartz away from the smokers, and they found an empty compartment. Frank wondered if this could be the right time for Lartz to open up about whatever was troubling him. "Lartz . . . I know you've been asking around about Germany's treatment of Jewish POWs."

Lartz sucked in a long breath but didn't look at Frank.

"I hope you know I consider you my best friend. I'd never want to pry. But I'm here if you want to talk."

"Thank you, Frank." Lartz studied his hands. He had the hands of a surgeon, fine-boned for a man, but with unexpected strength. "I don't know much. My parents separated when I was in grade school. I stayed in Illinois with my father, and my older brother moved with my mother . . . to Frankfurt." He grew silent, but Frank waited him out. He hadn't even known Lartz had a brother. "Mother's a Jew in Germany—not a safe thing to be these days. I haven't heard from her in four years."

"What about your brother?"

"He might be in a labor camp. Or he might be a Nazi soldier. I haven't heard from him since they left America."

The train passed through mountains and over bridges that had seen better days. Frank wanted to comfort his friend, but he was out of his depth. Which would be worse—to discover your brother was a slave, or to find out he was a Nazi?

When the train came to a final stop in Strasbourg, which, Lartz informed them, was the former capital of the region, they fell in with the British soldiers, who seemed to know where they were going. The three American doctors were definitely in the minority. In crowded, cobblestone-paved streets, Frank gazed in wonder at the spectacle of workhorses pulling hay wagons next to fully armed tanks. Gunfire, no longer distant like thunder, sounded so close that Andy ducked twice before they got out of the city limits.

They reported to a small British outfit, where Major Bradford greeted them like long-lost cousins.

"Good to see you again, Major." Frank meant it, too.

"Shall we repair to my office?" Bradford led the way to a tent with three wooden folding chairs and a small desk. Lartz, Andy, and Frank took the chairs as directed, and Bradford settled onto the corner of his desk. Frank decided that Bradford couldn't have looked more like a British officer if they'd hired an actor to play him. "I'm glad you're here, Yanks" he began. "For now, you're needed at the local hospital. Our boys have suffered heavy losses in the Ardennes. The worst of the injured are being sent here. You'll have your hands full, lads. Still, don't get too comfortable. We're pressing into Germany even as we speak, and the enemy doesn't like it one bit. They've still got too many weapons, including some of ours, and they believe they can win this thing. So we'll be setting up a joint battalion aid station deeper inside Germany, which is where you come in."

Anderson looked ready to implode. "Shouldn't we stay on here? Wouldn't our skills be better used in the hospital? In the US Army, it's the medics who patch up soldiers on the field, then hand them over to us for skilled medical treatment."

Frank wanted Andy to shut up. He wasn't thrilled about a battalion aid either, but why should they get special treatment?

"That's the way we've done it too, Lieutenant," Major Bradford said. "But we're finding our losses on the field are too high. Not acceptable. Giving better care to the wounded on the field *before* they reach the hospital—that's our goal. We've set up battalion aid stations at crucial junctures inside enemy lines. Lines, I might add, which we are steadily pushing back. Our greatest need now is for trained doctors to man the stations. We can have sterile instruments on hand in the tent, cots and water mere yards from the battle. Your immediate care will make all the difference in this push into Germany."

Frank nodded as he listened. He had to admit it made sense. He couldn't count the number of times he'd cursed, thinking that he might have saved a patient, or a limb, if only they'd gotten to him sooner.

Bradford gave a crooked grin that made Frank think of Jack. "I don't know what you did to get sent this way—and I won't ask. I'll just say I'm glad you're here . . . and I hope whatever you blokes did to incite your commanding officer was worth it."

January 11, 1945
Lt. Helen E. Daley

Dear Frank,
    As I said in my last letters, I was disappointed not meeting you in Marseille. Now I admit that I was also hurt, even though I'm trusting that you didn't break our reunion lightly, and I pray that all is well with you now, as it's been so long since I've received a letter. Surely soon it will be raining letters from my husband.

Yesterday we received a patient who thinks he may know a Lt. Daley who is a doctor on the move with the 6th regiment, but I assured him my Lt. Daley is with the 11th General and not the fighting 6th.

I told you about Liddy's harrowing injury. We've received word that she is on her way back to the States on a hospital ship. I only hope her lousy, cheating husband turns over a new leaf and will care for her as she deserves.

With love, wherever you are,
Tiny

46

Helen

RENNES, FRANCE

"Can you believe they're giving us pineapple again?" Victoria complained. "That's the sixth meal in a row they've passed off pineapple as dessert."

"No wonder there's a shortage back home," Peggy said.

"Did anybody get mail?" Helen asked. Not since the staging theater had Helen gone so long without a letter from Frank. She knew she should trust God and trust her husband, but there had been moments when she couldn't call up Frank's face, his laugh, the sound of his voice. Although she'd kept writing him, she hadn't written about Paris. He might not understand. Neither of them had seen Paris, and they'd promised to see it together. And anyway, she hadn't actually seen the city, just the hospital.

337

"I got a letter from Liddy's sister," Naomi said.

Helen felt a pang of guilt for not writing Liddy yet.

Naomi sighed. "Poor Liddy arrived home just in time to learn that her husband got another woman in trouble."

"The cad!" Helen exclaimed.

"It gets worse," Naomi said. "His girlfriend is five months pregnant and demanding he divorce Liddy and marry her."

Helen felt like crying—for Liddy and for herself. "I'm off. I'm going to try the showers again." There'd been no hot water for a week, but maintenance promised today would be the day.

Maintenance lied. Helen endured an ice-cold shower. Still shivering and towel-drying her hair, she raced back to the ward and rammed into Colonel Blalock. Nurses rated him the most handsome male in Rennes, but Helen couldn't see it. He had patrician good looks, a broad forehead and prominent nose, and a cleft in his chin that Victoria couldn't stop talking about. Helen suspected him of dyeing his hair black. He stood six feet tall and looked the right weight. But as Helen said whenever the subject of Colonel Blalock came up, "Handsome is as handsome does."

"Excuse me, Colonel." She said it not as an apology for bumping into him, but as a request that he let her pass.

"Thought I'd find you here." He sidestepped to block her way, then laughed, like they were playing a game. "Some of us have arranged a private party off base in a lovely tavern in Rennes. I would like it very much if you would be my guest."

"No, thank you." Again she tried to edge past him, but failed.

"Why not?" His question carried one part incredulity and two parts shock.

"I'm married, Colonel Blalock."

He laughed. "So?"

She had to grit her teeth to keep herself from saying what she was thinking. "So, I only go to parties with my husband."

"Come on. I know better."

"Colonel Blalock, do you also know what *no* means?" She tried again to get past him.

"I see. You only accompany colonels if they take you to Paris."

This time, she shoved past him hard and kicked the door shut behind her.

Victoria was standing just inside. "He's right, you know. It's all over the hospital that you and Colonel Pugh had a fling in Paris."

"What? We did no such thing!"

Victoria tilted her head and raised her eyebrows. "You didn't go to Paris with Colonel Pugh?"

"No! I mean, yes. But not for a fling, for crying out loud. You know that! We took Liddy there."

"And then what? You see, it's the then-what that spreads the rumor."

Helen couldn't believe it. So now everybody not only labeled her a German spy, but they thought she was an adulteress, a wolfess? That explained why Pugh had kept his distance from her since the Paris trip. He was probably fighting the same rumors.

Vic wasn't done yet. "Frankly, Helen, I don't know what you see in Pugh. Not when Colonel Blalock is knocking at your door. I always thought you were a little batty. Now I know for sure. Blalock is a catch!"

"You can have him!"

"I wish. But I'm with Major Grayson now."

"You know he's married, right?"

"But he's planning to leave his wife. I love Bob. I just don't know if I should tell him. Or wait? I know he loves me. I just wish he'd come out and say it." Her whine would peel the hide off a skunk. "Don't you think Bob is the biggest catch in the unit?"

"Do you want an answer, an honest answer?"

"Of course I do!"

"Your Major Grayson is a two-timing cad, and everybody but you knows it."

"You're lying!" Victoria drew herself up to her full five-foot-seven and glared down at Helen with a fierceness that brought to mind lions and gladiators. "You're just jealous because you've had to settle for Colonel Pugh!"

"Stop saying that!" Helen liked Pugh as a friend. She respected him. But that was all.

So why did she feel *caught*?

Colonel Pugh found her in the afternoon. "Helen, I have to go to Paris for a few days." He paused, and she hoped he wasn't about to ask her to go with him. She couldn't look him in the eyes. "I'm hoping you'll agree to take over for a couple of days as supervisor of the German ward."

Helen swung from relief about Paris to angst about supervising the whole German POW ward. She didn't want to do it, but she couldn't say no. With a quick plea to God in Heaven, she said, "I can do that, Colonel."

"Good. The patient in bed eight is Colonel Blalock's. He concerns me. I don't believe the colonel understands German, so perhaps you can clarify for him."

Helen figured Blalock was one of those doctors who didn't think their Hippocratic oath applied to Germans. "I'll check on him, Doctor." Victoria was going to love this—Helen in charge of the Germans.

Helen found Bill, and they descended the concrete stairs to the POW ward. "How you holding up, Nurse?"

"Not the best day to ask, Bill."

They began with the first row, skimming charts. When she got to the first trench foot patient, she lifted the covers to check his feet. His toes felt like ice. "Bill, this patient needs stockings. Where do they keep them?" Stockings weren't a convenience or comfort. A good pair of socks had been known to stave off amputation.

"None of the German patients have stockings," Bill said.

"Since when?"

Bill shrugged.

"Do I have to do everything?" she muttered. "Who's the supply sergeant?"

"Sergeant Orrick's in charge of medical supplies."

"Terrific." Orrick looked like a Chicago gangster and acted like one too. Helen thought the man's hair might have been painted on, parted in the middle to accent his crooked nose. "I don't think General McNeal will mind if I use his phone to call the good sergeant."

"Be my guest!" Bill shouted over the groans and cries of the patient he was wrestling, a young man who suffered from violent nightmares.

Helen hurried to the general's office, only to find he wasn't in. But his secretary, a friend of Sally's, let her call for supplies.

Orrick answered on the ninth ring. "What is it?"

"Sergeant Orrick?"

"Who wants to know?"

Helen wished it had been the general calling and getting such rude responses. "Lieutenant Daley. I'm temporary supervisor of the POW ward."

"Yeah. I know who you are."

"We're in dire need of stockings for my patients." This was followed by silence. "We can use four dozen pair of medical stockings. When can you deliver them?" She thought again. "Never mind. I'll come pick them up."

"No."

"Really, Sergeant, it's no trouble."

"I meant no, you can't have four dozen stockings."

"I see. Well, how many do you have?"

"None. Not for that Nazi ward. And not for you, lady."

"You weasel! I'm your superior. I'll report you for insubordination. You better get me those stockings right—!"

"Auf Wiedersehen." Click.

Helen stared at the receiver. That jerk, that gangster! He was probably selling the supplies on the black market. She stormed back to the basement, enraged at yet another proof that she had absolutely no control over anything.

"Didn't go well?" Bill ventured when she stomped past him.

Helen filled him in. "He is such a scoundrel, Bill! He doesn't care if all our patients lose their feet or legs."

Bill's countenance never changed during her tirade. "I got this." He strolled off, leaving Helen more wound up than ever.

Fifteen minutes later, Bill returned with five dozen pair of surgical socks. Elated, Helen tried to get him to tell her how he'd done it, but he gave her his crooked cowboy grin and politely refused.

She took a pair of socks and laid them over Bill's shoulder. "Bill Chitwood, I dub you Knight of the Ward Masters."

Bill bowed. Then they began the tiresome task of putting socks on every patient in the basement.

As soon as she finished the tedious sock duty, Helen found Blalock's patient in bed eight, the one Colonel Pugh had asked her to check on. Even handcuffed, the man thrashed so violently his gown was soaked with sweat. He was babbling in German, something about needing to get to work at the factory or they'd fire him and his children would starve.

She checked the man's chart for Blalock's diagnosis and treatment. All he'd scribbled on the clipboard was *Patient appears to have had a concussion, but is recovering nicely.*

Below it, Helen wrote, *Patient is* not *recovering nicely. He is incoherent and out of touch with reality, not unlike certain doctors around here.*

~✤~

Lt. Frank R. Daley, MD
Jan. 23, 1945

WANTED!
Blonde
Height: 5'3"
Weight: 123 when last seen
Waist: 26" when last seen
Shoe size: 8AA—no kidding
Stocking size: 9 1/2
Glove size: 7
General size: 13
Elsewhere: 34"

Dearest Helen,

If you see anyone answering the above description, please bring her to me at once, personally.

I was desperately counting on our rendezvous. We shall have it yet, darling. I'm already trying to figure out how to get us back to the rendezvous place. Until then, I wait eagerly for your letters to lessen the physical pain of your absence.

It's good to be with Major Bradford again. He is such an interesting fellow.

Just stopped writing to listen via radio to Hitler in German, ranting to cheering crowds. But Stotle, my German prisoner patient, says the voice doesn't belong to Hitler. Who knows?

The Russian offensive is going well. Everyone agrees it's making us look as bad as it is the Germans, though.

I have 26 patients here, including one former prisoner from Italy, one from Puerto Rico, and one from St. Louis. All are intriguing and intelligent fellows.

Cold and snow! Last night I had to disregard my sheet and sleep on my blanket—sheet too cold to get into bed. If you were here, I would jump in first and warm the bed for both of us.

With love, wherever you are,
Your Frankie

Capt. Frank R. Daley, MD

Dearest Helen,

I'm now convinced that war IS hell. I am sitting on a pile of rocks, writing with numb fingers. Suffice it to say that last night Anderson and I slept on mud-soaked ground in a pup tent, and our standard of living was higher than anyone else's. Where I'm going, I don't expect to receive mail, as I may be dodging bullets and tanks. But I'll continue writing and hope you get the letters. Sorry I can't say more, but the censors would only cut it out. (Say, fellas, cut it out, will ya?)

Looks like I will have to stop now and get to work. There is so much to do here. War gets into every corner.

With love, wherever you are,
Your Frank

47

FRANK

Frank had never seen so many wounded. Most of the patients suffered severe injuries, compounded by mud, the cold, and infection. Some were too far gone when they arrived. This week alone, he'd had two patients die on the operating table. The only upside was that after three days at the battalion aid station, he and Lartz and Anderson had been called back to the Strasbourg hospital to perform surgeries.

Helen's letters had finally caught up with him—nine in one day, with a January 5 and a February 1 letter in the same batch. He'd arranged to meet Bradford for supper, but no way could he leave his cot until he finished reading. He smiled at a letter that began with Helen's hearty congratulations on his new rank of captain. Frank hadn't mentioned it—except to write *Capt. Frank R. Daley* on his V-mail. It had been all his clever wife needed. He had to admit he liked the new rank. And although Bradford refused to confirm it, Frank suspected he'd played a part in the promotion.

Helen could make him laugh out loud, as with the limerick she sent from the *Stars and Stripes*:

I once had a girl—her name was Nellie.
She fell in the ocean—right up to her . . .
Knees. *

*The poet apologizes for the fact that this poem does not rhyme because the water wasn't deep enough.

Frank knew how strong his wife was, but he still worried about her. In one letter, she fed his spirit as if she could read his mind:

Naomi says I must stop this fruitless, but draining, activity called worry because worrying is a bit like telling God He can't handle things. Mom used to say that worry is always borrowed, usually from a future that won't even happen. I never thought of myself as a worrier, but I do worry about you, and I worry about Eugene, and I worry about everyone. More and more, I get the feeling that I have control over less and less. Do you know what I mean?

Frank read the news of her brothers as if they were his own. Eugene was home. Safe. Helen had no details, but between the lines, he suspected her brother had been discharged, possibly for shell shock.

In no letter, however, was there mention of Paris or Colonel Pugh. Frank tried not to let his imagination run wild.

Bradford had finished eating by the time Frank got there. "Sorry I'm late."

"No problem, mate. I saw you leave the post with a handful of letters and surmised I should go ahead and dine without you."

Frank downed his dinner as fast as he could without making himself sick. He had a favor he wanted to ask, but he was waiting for the right time. They chatted about patients and other doctors.

"How is your friend, Lieutenant Lartz?" Bradford asked.

Now or never. "Major, I wonder if I could ask you for a favor. I don't even know if it's something you could do."

"I am intrigued. In our brief acquaintance, I've not taken you as a favor-asking man. Ask away."

"It's not for me. It's for Lartz. Only I'm not going to say anything to him in case nothing comes of it. Lartz is tearing himself up over his mother and his brother." Frank filled Bradford in on what he knew about Lartz's family. "If you could do anything to help find them, to let Lartz know where they are . . . Well, that's the favor. And I know it's a big one."

Bradford didn't speak for a long minute. Frank could almost hear the wheels spinning. "I'd be happy to give it a go for your friend."

Frank felt some of the weight lift off his shoulders. "Thanks so much, Major."

"Don't look now," Major Bradford said, "but I think it's stopped raining. Care for a stroll?"

Two days of rain had erased every trace of snow. Now, as they took the high road, the air smelled clean, cleansed. Both moon and sun were visible at polar ends of a gray sky. Bradford was the first to speak. "How are you and Helen? It's been a while since you've seen her, I take it."

"I miss my wife as if she were a physical part of me that's been poorly amputated."

"I understand. I miss my wife and boys in much the same fashion."

"Once I return to the battalion aid unit, who knows when I can get a leave? I need to see my wife, Major. I'm not above going AWOL."

"I see." Bradford kept eyes front, his face betraying no emotion.

Frank was already second-guessing himself for confiding to his commanding officer that he'd go AWOL if necessary. Bradford had become a good friend, but he was a lifer in the military. He played by the rules. Frank should have kept his mouth shut because he was going to see Helen, even if the entire British and American military tried to stop him.

"Let me think on this, will you?" Bradford said. "I believe I'll have a little talk with our friend Fritz."

Fritz, one of the German prisoners, had made himself indispensable. Frank didn't know the man's real name or how he'd been captured or even how he'd won the trust of the whole camp, but the German POW had more freedom than the American and British soldiers. Fritz was one of the drivers who carted around officers, delivered food, and repaired weapons. He carried the mail to and from the main post office in Strasbourg and manned the post office in camp. That made him the number one person Frank wanted to see every day.

Three days later, rendezvous plans were set. Bradford had come through with a three-day leave for Marseille. Frank had written a coded letter to Helen and a fairly cryptic letter to his Marseille friends. Fritz promised the letters would be delivered on time, but Frank stopped by the post office to double-check.

"*Ja*. I mailed your letters to your sweetheart," Fritz said.

"She's not just my sweetheart. She's my wife."

For the first time, Fritz looked directly into Frank's face. The man had big bones, no fat, and outweighed Frank by forty pounds. Fritz's eyes, normally the size of shooter marbles, had shrunk to peewees or slags. It was unnerving to be stared at by someone who may have killed Allied soldiers. "A good wife is hard to find and to keep, *ja*?"

Frank had never thought of it in that way. Helen would always be his. And yet, she hadn't written him about Paris. Or Pugh. Finally, he answered Fritz's question. "*Ja.*"

All was going according to plan. In less than twenty-four hours, Frank and his wife would be in the barn paradise. He hated making her travel so far, but she could take a direct train, and he wanted her to meet his Marseille family. He stuffed a few essentials—including the four candy bars he'd been saving—into his pack and waited inside the tent for Fritz. When Frank had admitted how bad he was with directions, Bradford had arranged for Fritz to drive him all the way to Marseille and back. Anderson and Lartz would cover for him while he was gone, but he'd have to be back by Wednesday night.

"Are you sure you can trust Fritz?" Andy asked. He was stretched on his cot, reading a girlie magazine he'd "confiscated" in town.

"Of course." Frank did feel a bit uneasy about traveling with Fritz. But the guy would be saving him about five hours over public transportation, hours he could spend with Helen. German or not, Fritz was his new hero.

"He can trust Fritz," Lartz said. "That guy's been in camp over a year and has the trust of all the higher-ups. They let him drive to Paris to pick up ammo."

"Besides," Frank added, "he's the best driver in Alsace-Lorraine. And his English is better than Andy's."

"Hey!" Andy complained.

"His sense of humor is better than Andy's too," Lartz added.

"So what's not to trust, right?" Still, a feeling of unease threatened to bring him down.

A jeep pulled up outside and honked.

"Too late to back out now," Anderson muttered, not glancing up from his magazine. "Nice knowing you, Daley."

Frank left the relative warmth of the tent and stepped into the windy, cold night. The jeep was running, and Fritz sat behind the wheel, a wool cap pulled over his ears. Frank tossed his duffel in the back and started to hop in front.

"Sorry. Supplies and map. And mess. Ride in back, please?" Fritz said.

Some officers preferred riding in back, but Frank liked the front because he got less carsick, something he wasn't about to admit to Fritz. Anyway, he didn't want to start their trip with Fritz assuming leadership. "Feels too much like you're a chauffeur." He reached for the door latch.

Fritz revved the engine. "I *am* chauffeur." He put his hand flat on the opened map. He wasn't kidding about the mess. An extra gas tank sat on the floor, with an assortment of tools. "I deliver supplies for Major Bradford in Marseille." He motioned to a box that filled the seat under the map. "No room."

"Okay, Fritz. You win. But you're a driver, not a chauffeur." He hoped Fritz wouldn't ask him to define the difference because he wasn't sure he could. He climbed in and pulled down the seat, which put him head and shoulders above his driver. Up that high, the wind would be murder.

The jeep jerked its way out of town, bouncing on cobblestones. Frank felt the familiar wave of nausea before they'd left the city. At least he'd known enough to skip supper and carry rations in his pack for when his stomach settled. He kept swallowing and making himself focus on the road, tricks that had helped him in the past.

In no time, they were climbing the rugged terrain above Strasbourg. The jeep took a sharp turn onto a dirt road Frank hadn't known existed, although he'd been down the main road several times to the marketplace.

"Really appreciate this." Frank leaned forward to be heard over the rumble of the tires on an increasingly bumpy road. It had to be a shortcut. He was glad not to be driving. He never would have found this road in a million years. Plus, there were no guardrails. He didn't know what would happen if they met another jeep.

"I like to drive," Fritz said.

"I hope I don't get you in trouble, Fritz. Have you thought about what you'd say if you're stopped on the way back?"

"I say hello. Can they arrest me? I am a prisoner already. And chauffeur."

"Still, you didn't have to do this. The major told me he gave you the option because of the risk."

"You are the one taking a risk, *ja*? And I believe you consider your wife worth this risk?"

"She's worth every risk." He wasn't sure what risk Fritz was referring to, though. This time, he had an official leave.

"Please to tell me how you met her?"

Once Frank started talking about Helen, he couldn't stop. Fritz listened, but Frank knew he was mainly talking to himself.

They'd been on the road a while when Frank caught a glimpse of a sign. He hadn't been paying attention, and he didn't get a good look, but it hadn't looked like French, or English. "What did that sign say?"

"What sign?"

"I think it was the name of a village, but it wasn't in French. I think it was in German."

"Alsace-Lorraine, both German and French." This was true enough. Most of the signs in the city were in French and German, some in English, too.

"But we should be out of the province by now, shouldn't we? All France now, right?" And most of the liberated French towns had torn down everything German that reminded them of the occupation.

Fritz didn't respond.

Frank may have had the worst sense of direction in Missouri, and the language skills of a post, but something felt wrong. He squinted into the cold, silent night. A fingernail moon didn't help.

"Wait a minute." A river ran alongside the road, about a football field down a valley, through thick woods. Frank hadn't noticed it before because his thoughts had been on Helen, but this was no little river, no stream. "What river is that?" It had to be the Rhine. Too big for anything else. Only it shouldn't have been there, not if they'd been traveling west and south, like they should have been. *The*

Rhine runs left. That's how Lartz had tried to help him with directions around Strasbourg. He made up sayings like that so Frank wouldn't get lost. *The Rhine runs left leaving town.* Even if they were still in the province, the river should have been on their left.

"Fritz?" Frank leaned forward, craning his neck to see his driver's face. "We're going the wrong way, buddy."

"Do not worry."

"Don't worry? What's that mean? I want to know exactly where we are!" Frank reached over the seat for the map, but Fritz covered it with his hand.

"We will be in Marseille before your wife arrives. I give you my word."

"That's not what I asked. Fritz, are we in Germany?"

Silence.

"Fritz! Turn this jeep around now!"

But he didn't.

"Stop! Halt!" His nausea had turned into a knot. If he'd been diagnosing himself, he would have called it an ulcer. "I have my revolver. Stop the jeep!"

Fritz still didn't answer. The jeep continued at the same pace, in the same direction. Frank drew his weapon and pointed it at Fritz's head. But now what? What was he supposed to do? He couldn't shoot Fritz. And even if he could, then what? The car would spin out of control, careen down the valley into the Rhine. And if he survived, *he* was the enemy here, not Fritz.

He was the prisoner of war.

Frank felt the dark forest closing in on their jeep as Fritz killed the headlights and drove them deeper into enemy territory. The man maintained his silence. No matter what threats Frank threw at him, they fell like confetti. There was nothing for him to do but holster his weapon and let himself be hauled deeper inside Germany. He hadn't a clue where they were, but his imagination took him to terrible places.

Just when Frank didn't think the road could get worse, Fritz swerved onto a path with barely room for one vehicle. It occurred to Frank that they hadn't passed a single car coming or going. They bounced as the path grew rockier. Frank had to hold on to keep from being thrown out of the jeep. On the other hand, would he stand a better chance out of the jeep? On foot? Without a hint of how to get back?

The jeep slowed, and Fritz turned in at a solitary stone cottage, vine covered, with a thatched roof. Frank felt like Hansel without Gretel.

Fritz killed the engine, pocketed the key, then turned to Frank with a face that revealed nothing. "Ten minutes. All will be well. Please."

Frank gripped the gun so tightly it might have gone off by accident. He wanted to ask a million questions—Where were they? *Why* were they? Was Fritz escaping? Taking him hostage? Only before he could get out a word, his captor hopped out of the jeep and strode to the back of the cottage and out of sight.

Frank checked his watch, his hand never leaving his gun. What if he never saw Helen again? He pictured her at the train station, looking around for him. He could try to escape. But on foot? There was no key in the ignition, and he'd never learned how to hot-wire a car. Frank rued the day he'd refused to let Jack teach him.

In the valley of death, I fear no evil because You're with me. The words weren't exactly right, but he said them over and over in his head.

Fritz had been gone five minutes. Seven. Nine. If Frank planned to make his move, he needed to make it now. He could at least investigate. He was climbing out of the jeep when Fritz emerged from the bushes next to the cottage. He jogged to the jeep and got in. "Thank you," he said, as if he'd made an innocent stop and only regretted wasting Frank's time.

Frank looked at the dimly lit cottage. A curtain was drawn back, allowing a strip of light to fall on the unruly yard. The face of a brown-haired woman appeared in the window, her eyes huge, sad. Frank settled back in his seat.

Fritz started the jeep and headed back the way they'd come. He drove carefully, but in complete silence. Frank was fairly certain he was taking the rocky path in reverse.

"Fritz, are you a spy?"

Fritz's laugh was devoid of humor. "I am not spy."

When Frank finally spotted the Rhine, he was sure Fritz was headed back to Strasbourg. They crossed a different bridge into the region, and no one stopped them. He'd lost precious time. If they did go back to camp, he'd have to report Fritz, then find another driver or try driving himself. Again, he pictured Helen standing in the station, wondering where he was.

Then he saw a signpost, a wooden arrow pointing in the direction they were heading: *Marseille*. They weren't headed back to base. Fritz was taking him to Marseille!

Neither of them spoke until hours later when they reached the Marseille train depot, with forty minutes to spare. Probably more, since French trains were notoriously late.

Frank didn't know whether to arrest Fritz or thank him. He got out and started to grab his pack.

"You can leave it. I will drive you both to your farm."

"No. We can find a taxi." No way he'd trust this German with his Helen, or with his Resistance family. As soon as he had his wife safely in his arms, Frank planned to get to a phone and call Bradford to tell him about their little foray into Germany. "You should go back to camp."

"I will. But first, I wait for your wife," Fritz said. "You waited for mine."

48

Helen

MARSEILLE, FRANCE

Helen reread Frank's coded letter for the umpteenth time as she sat in her train compartment, wedged between two men who smelled like oil and cigar smoke. She smiled at the line asking her if she ever regretted being an only child.

The train jerked to a stop at the third Marseille station. She and Frank had learned their lesson about multiple stations. This time, Frank had repeated the number three fourteen times in one letter. She stood, and her heart raced from a mixture of excitement, nerves, and maybe fear. Would she and Frank feel like strangers after all this time apart? Or what if he canceled on her like last time but she hadn't received word from the French farmer?

She stepped off the train, her foot touching ground as the engine heaved its last sigh.

"Helen!"

She heard him before she saw him. And when she did glimpse her tall, handsome husband, she couldn't run fast enough into his arms. He lifted her up and spun her around. She hoped he couldn't feel how much weight she'd lost. He kissed her, soft but so intense. *God in Heaven, thank You for this man, my husband.* He was no stranger. He was the love of her life.

Frank chattered as they weaved through the crowded station, asking about her trip, her fellow nurses, Rennes. She answered all his questions, but none of it seemed important now. She asked him about Dotty and Jack and Lartz. He asked about Eugene.

"I've written Genie several letters," she explained. "He's staying in Cissna with my parents. Mom wrote that he isn't helping with the farm. She doesn't say more, but he must be in awful shape if Dad's not making him pitch in. It makes me crazy that I can't do anything for him."

"At least he's safe and at home. If he's shell-shocked, it might be a long recovery. Maybe we'll be able to help when the war's over and we're all home."

She hooked her arm though his, just as they'd done back in Battle Creek. "Want to tell me where we're going, husband of mine?"

"We're staying with the LeBlancs, the family I wrote you about. Well, not exactly staying with them. More like in their barn."

She laughed. "Their barn? Well, that should be one to tell the grandkids." A silence fell between them, their personal UXB, the reminder of the child they'd lost, the grandchildren that might never follow.

Frank looked flustered. Then he dropped her bags and scooped her into his arms again. "It's okay. We'll have those grandkids soon enough, Granny." He kissed her. "Have I told you how beautiful you are, Mrs. Daley?"

"Take me to the barn and tell me again." They left the station, hand in hand, at a run.

At the exit, Frank stopped and glanced around.

"Aren't taxis over there?" Helen pointed to a long line at the front of the station.

"Right." He continued looking in all directions.

A horn beeped, and Frank waved at a jeep. "We have a chauffeur. He's a decent driver and got me here right on schedule—with one minor detour."

The jeep inched into the line of taxis and military vehicles. Helen studied the driver. He was dressed in the blue denim shirt of Army fatigues, but something about him didn't look Army. She climbed into the backseat with Frank and had to sit on his lap, which she found rather a good idea.

"You are crowded?" Their driver had an accent Helen identified as high German, like her mother's. "You want to ride here?" He patted the seat beside him.

"We're fine where we are." Frank wrapped his arms around her. "Helen, this is Fritz, POW trustee from camp. Fritz, this is my wonderful wife, Helen Eberhart Daley."

Helen shot her husband her best *are you out of your mind?* look.

Fritz pulled the jeep out of line, to the honks and complaints of other drivers. "Good name is Eberhart."

"True," Helen said. "But better name is Daley."

Instead of having Fritz take them to the barn, Frank had him drop them off at the Palais Longchamp, a fantastic palace that curved inside the Parc Longchamp. Any other time, Helen would have wanted to explore the park, dotted with pavilions, flower gardens, and waterfalls. But now, all she wanted to explore was her husband and squeeze every minute out of their time together.

They thanked Fritz, and he promised to pick them up at the same spot in two days. Helen tried not to think about that, the moment when she'd have to leave Frank. "Why didn't he take us to where we're staying?"

"Long story," Frank answered. "He's a good guy, but I don't feel right taking a German POW to the doorstep of a Resistance fighter."

Helen didn't say so, but she didn't see anything wrong with that. Marseille was liberated. She watched Fritz drive off.

Frank looked around. "Pretty sure it's this way."

Several miles later, Frank shouted, "There! I knew it was around here somewhere."

"Are you sure?" Helen fought the irritation that had seeped in like British drizzle. They'd started out in the wrong direction, circled the city, and wandered the countryside, traveling three times as far on foot as they would have in Fritz's jeep.

"Sorry, Helen."

She forced a smile. "I love you."

"Even though you now know you married a man who will never be able to take a direct route anywhere?"

"Maybe partly because I've married such a man. It's all part of the wonderful package of you." She did believe it . . . even if she didn't quite feel it at the moment. All she felt were sore feet.

Frank put his arm around her and guided her up to the cottage door.

Before he could knock, the wooden door cracked open, then was thrown wide. The woman standing there had been beautiful once. Helen could tell by her high, classical forehead and the slope of her jaw. Wrinkles had turned what might have been alabaster skin into old leather.

"Madame LeBlanc, I'd like you to meet my wife."

"Bonjour. Merci beaucoup, madame." Helen's French, in spite of the hours with French patients, was limited. But her patients claimed that her accent was excellent and what she lacked in vocabulary, she made up for in style.

Madame launched into animated French until Helen apologized

for not understanding. Still, she was fairly certain the woman had been singing Frank's praises.

Frank took two bottles of vitamins from his pack, his own Army-issued vitamins. She wished he'd told her before. She would gladly have donated her bottles, which was probably why he hadn't told her.

Madame clutched the bottles to her apron. Tears trickled down deep wrinkles. *"Merci."* She waved them inside and shut the door.

A young woman tiptoed up to Frank, her eyes shining, her gaze never leaving his face.

"This is Marie," Frank said, "the best patient I ever had."

"*This* is Marie?" From her husband's letters, Helen had expected a little girl, not this beautiful woman, who might have been Vin's age. Her long hair flowed over a sleeveless flowered dress that exposed just enough to prove her womanhood.

Marie gazed at Frank with undisguised idol worship, then turned to Helen with raw hatred.

A boy emerged, all smiles and yellow teeth. Frank introduced him as Michel, and he shook Helen's hand with both of his. "Yes! You are beautiful American lady! We welcome you!"

She returned the handshake and thanked them all in a mixture of French and English as two little boys peeked around the corner.

"You will eat dinner with us, yes?" Michel said.

Helen turned to Frank, hoping he'd read her mind that she needed to be alone with him. Besides, she didn't want to take food from them.

Frank smiled down at the boy. *"Merci beaucoup.* But no, thank you. Another time?"

Michel nodded, though Helen could tell he didn't understand. The last thing she wanted was for them to think these Americans were too good to join them. Michel started to translate to his mother, but Frank put a hand on his shoulder and whispered something.

Michel glanced at Helen, his cheeks reddening. *"Oui.* Of course." He rattled something in French to his family. Madame grinned, and the boys giggled. Marie, however, turned on her heel and stomped out of the room.

Michel led them out back to an old barn. Apparently Frank hadn't been kidding about their sleeping quarters. The boy shoved open the door, then grinned sheepishly before waving them in. He shut the door and disappeared.

Slits of light through wooden slats revealed a barn smaller than her father's. No bins for corn or coal. No chickens or cows or horses. Stray bits of straw and dirt littered the floor, and even the absence of cows couldn't take away their lingering odor. "I love what you've done with the place," she teased. At the far end she spotted a haystack. She turned her best smile on her husband. "I think a little roll in the hay might be in order."

He took her hand and nearly dragged her there, both of them laughing. "You ain't seen nothin' yet, schveetheart!" he shouted in a terrible Cagney or maybe Bogie accent that echoed. He brushed aside hay, then opened a trapdoor. "After me." He climbed down first and waited on the wooden ladder.

Helen sensed the shimmery glow before Frank lifted her from the ladder and set her down. It was as unexpected as it was fantastic, a fairyland oasis in the middle of war-torn France. A small table held fresh flowers and a kerosene lantern, with two candles, a bottle of wine, and a loaf of bread. Beyond the table was the most inviting bed Helen had ever seen, covered in handmade quilts, with a cylindrical pillow that stretched the width of the bed. "How did you do this?"

"I didn't." Frank looked as awestruck as she felt. "They can't afford the wine, or the kerosene. I doubt if they can afford the bread."

"We'll pay them back."

"They won't accept it. I've tried."

"Then we'll give them gifts." Maybe she could buy them something in Marseille and—

But that's where speculation ended. Frank swooped her into his arms and carried her, as if over an invisible threshold, to their bed beneath the barn.

The next day, reluctant to leave their hideaway, they stayed in bed, snuggling and talking. Frank told her about the men in his unit, and she could see how much her husband cared about them, especially about Major Bradford.

"Bradford isn't just a war hero, Helen. He cares more for peace than for war. When the Nazis finally surrender, he's committed himself to moving on to the Pacific and working for peace there."

"He sounds like a good man."

"He believes he and his unit could make a difference in the occupation after the war ends," Frank continued. "It's all about a lasting peace and leaving the world a safer place."

"It's a wonderful goal, darling. He isn't married, is he?" She couldn't remember if Frank had told her already.

"What? Oh, yeah. Married for ten or twelve years. They have two sons."

"How awful for *them*." She couldn't imagine what Mrs. Bradford had been going through since England's war began. She remembered the woman on the train, the one who'd had to send her children away to keep them safe.

Helen didn't want to think sad thoughts, not now. She scooted closer to her husband and again took in the romance and wonder of their Resistance hideaway. "Frankie, let's talk about us."

He wrapped his arms around her. "What a good idea. As it happens, you've landed on my favorite topic—us." He gazed around their little room. "I can't think of a better place for us, can you?"

"Not at the moment," she answered.

"You can see why I hated canceling our rendezvous here," Frank said.

Helen thought of that horrible night when she'd believed Victoria had made up the story about the French farmer and the canceled reunion. And just like that, the old anger sparked, and before she could shove it down, she snapped, "I can see why you hated canceling. What I don't know is *why* you canceled."

Frank sat up. His arm slid out from under her. "Excuse me?"

"I was all packed and couldn't wait to see you. And your note came as such a . . . well, a surprise. It didn't even give me a hint why you canceled."

"Not this again. Tell me you didn't assume I didn't want you to come. That would be too . . . I can't even think of a word."

"No, Frank. Of course not. I'm sure you must have been busy, with side trips out here after hospital work." She thought her voice sounded light and chatty. "You probably worried you wouldn't have enough time with me. But, darling, I wouldn't have minded."

He looked at her as if only this minute recognizing her . . . and not liking what he recognized. "Is that what you thought, Helen?" She started to answer, but he didn't give her a chance. "I *was* busy when I was in Marseille before. Still, I made time to arrange everything."

"Well, I'm sorry I caused you so much trouble."

"That's not what I'm saying. Colonel Croane didn't give us any warning before canceling our leaves, then shipping us out. It wasn't easy getting a message to you before we left."

"Wait. You left? You weren't in Marseille?" She touched his arm, but he pulled it away.

"How could you think I'd cancel our rendezvous just because I was busy?" She'd never seen him this angry. His lower lip curled . . . just like her dad's. "Don't you know me at all, Helen?"

Right now, she wasn't all that sure. "Maybe I don't."

"Don't you know I'd move heaven and earth to be with you?"

Helen could see he meant it. Her pent-up fury fizzled, and an awful guilt replaced it. What was wrong with her? "I'm sorry, Frank. I was just so hurt. I felt abandoned. And alone."

He stared at her now, and it was not a look of love. "Is that why you went to Paris with Colonel Pugh?"

The words landed like a punch to the gut. "How did you—?"

"How did I find out? I called you New Year's Eve, late. I tried all night to get hold of you, and it wasn't easy sneaking to the phone. So you can imagine my surprise when a drunk nurse answered the general's office phone and told me my wife was in Paris with another man."

Helen's mind was racing faster than her heart. Who would have—? Then she remembered. *Victoria.* She'd been the one in the general's office when they left to take Liddy to Paris. "You don't understand, Frank."

"Clearly."

"You're not being fair!" she protested. "You've got it all wrong."

He raised his eyebrows at her. "You didn't go to Paris?"

"Well, yes, but—"

"Colonel Pugh didn't go with you?"

"Will you let me explain?" She tried to think. She wasn't hiding anything. There was nothing to hide. "I didn't tell you because I was afraid you'd misunderstand. And you have."

"Have I?" He wouldn't even look at her. "You should have told me, Helen."

"You're right. Just like you should have told me about Marie."

"I told you about Marie!"

"You didn't tell me she was beautiful. And not a child."

"Fine. I apologize." But he didn't sound like he meant it.

"Fine. So do I!"

At a sudden pounding above, they both stared up at the trapdoor as if expecting the Nazis to storm in and capture them.

"Who is it?" Frank said, which wasn't how Helen would have handled the interruption.

"Michel," came the answer.

Frank bolted out of bed. "Just a moment!" He pulled on his pants, tried to button his shirt. "Helen, get dressed."

"No." She scooted deeper under the covers.

He shook his head at her and started up the ladder.

"Frank?" she whispered. "What do you think you're doing?"

He didn't bother answering her, but climbed the ladder and shoved the trapdoor. It clattered against the barn floor. "Michel? Is anything wrong?"

Helen peeked from her covers and saw the boy's smiling face overhead.

"My *maman* invites you to eat with us."

"That's so kind of you," Frank said. "When?"

"Now."

Helen was glad she hadn't gotten dressed and climbed the ladder instead of Frank. Let him be the one to disappoint.

Without a glance her way, Frank said, "Thanks, Michel. We'd love to. Tell your mother we'll be right along."

Helen heard Michel's footsteps overhead as Frank climbed back down.

"I don't want to go," Helen said.

"We're going." Frank sat in one of the two chairs and pulled on his socks and shoes.

"You go! I'm staying right here."

"I'm going," Frank said. "And I'm not going without you. So you can either get dressed and walk or have me carry you there in your nightgown."

"You can't talk to me like that!" Who did Frank think he was, giving her ultimatums?

Frank turned to look at her. He might have been counting to ten. "I'm sorry, Helen. But we need to accept their invitation. These people have been more than hospitable to us. They've gone out of their way to be kind. The least we can do is have a meal with them."

She knew he was right, even though she wasn't about to say so. She didn't want to hurt this family's feelings any more than he did. Without another word, she hauled herself out of bed and got dressed.

Frank fell in behind her as she started up the ladder. "Do you want me to go first so I can give you a hand when you climb out?"

"No, thank you." She could hear winter in her voice.

Michel was waiting for them outside the barn. Helen squinted at a sun that barely peeked from behind gray clouds. They followed Michel inside, to a small room beyond the kitchen, and were directed to sit on the couch. Helen scooted as far away as she could from Frank, but it was a short couch. That's when she spotted Marie frowning at them from a wooden chair off in the corner of the room. If this were a cartoon, the kind Eugene loved, smoke would have been coming out of her ears. Helen thought the girl looked even more beautiful than yesterday. Wisps of her long, dark hair framed a classic face, then continued to her bare shoulders. She'd obviously dressed for Frank instead of for the season.

Helen got up and walked to the kitchen. "*Madame, je vous aider? Help you?*"

Madame LeBlanc turned wide eyes on her. "*Non, non!*" She flipped her apron at Helen, shooing her out of the kitchen.

Forcing herself to smile, Helen returned to the couch without so much as a glance at her husband. Michel had pulled his chair up and was pumping Frank for information about America. Helen endured the glares from Marie as Michel turned to her. "You come from Missouri also?"

"Illinois."

Michel frowned. "Ellen Oye? I don't know Ellen Oye."

"You'd love it there—well, parts of it. Many farmers and lots of room, except for Chicago."

Now his eyes doubled in size. He had his mother's beautiful brown eyes. And Marie's. "Chicago! I know Chicago!"

"Helen was a nurse in a big hospital there," Frank said. "She's a wonderful nurse."

Helen glanced at him to see if he was mocking her. His eyes and his mouth had lost their edge.

"Almost as wonderful a nurse as she is a wife."

With that, something inside of her softened. She read love in his eyes. And longing. He reached for her hand, and she met it with her own. When he moved his thumb to stroke her palm so gently, she shivered.

Marie cleared her throat, making her presence known. She stood so quickly, her chair squealed. Michel turned to watch her storm to the kitchen. He shrugged. "Women, *oui*?"

Frank broke into his dimpled smile. "Women, *oui*." He tightened his grip on Helen's hand. "Pretty amazing, aren't they?"

Michel's eyes narrowed. Helen didn't know if the word *amazing* baffled him, or the thought that women were.

Finally, Madame LeBlanc ushered them into the kitchen. Michel's two little brothers hid behind their mother and made faces at the Americans, giggling when Helen returned the favor. Marie said something to the boys, and they shuffled out of the kitchen and out of sight. There were only four chairs at the kitchen table, and Michel directed them to sit on one side, while he and Marie sat across from them.

Helen assumed Michel's father wasn't home and his mother wouldn't be eating with them. Helen's mother would have been the same way, keeping her apron on and choosing to serve her meal rather than eat it.

Madame bowed her head, and they all followed suit while Michel said a French blessing.

"Something smells good," Helen said, repeating it in French, though maybe not since whatever she'd said made Michel laugh and Marie scoff.

When Madame stepped away from the old black stove, she was carrying two plates, fine china, the rims bearing hand-painted flowers and circled in gold. Helen tried to tell her they were the finest china she'd ever eaten from.

"*Bon appétit!*" said Madame.

The plate in front of her held two thick stalks of asparagus, the stems so long they extended over both sides of the plate. Helen had eaten asparagus before, but only the heads, the part missing from this picture. A trickle of white sauce marked the center of the stalks—definitely the origin of the lovely smell. *"C'est si bon."* She inhaled the savory aroma, fearing it had cost this family several months' worth of butter.

Frank had already taken his first bite, and so had Marie and Michel. Frank continued to smile, but she could tell all was not well. He chewed and smiled, chewed and chewed.

When she took her first bite, she understood. Chewing did little to dissolve the stalk in her mouth. She kept chewing, smiling idiotically, like Frank. They were still struggling with their first mouthfuls when Michel and Marie finished.

Helen refused to quit. When Frank tried, she kicked him under the table. She asked Michel questions about Marseille to give them more time to chew. It took over an hour, but they cleaned their plates.

Madame refused to let Helen help with the dishes, so they thanked her profusely and left the house. The wind had picked up, but the sun shone with patches of blue sky. Frank took Helen's hand in his.

"I feel like I've gone ten rounds in a boxing match," Frank said. "And lost. Are you okay, Helen? Are *we*?"

"I'm okay if you are, Frankie." She leaned into him and felt the real Helen and Frank had replaced those other two.

With what remained of the day, she and Frank strolled the streets and docks of Marseille. They stopped on the Cours Julien and listened to beautiful violin music coming from an open window. They bought trinkets and postcards in the square. And they took off their shoes and dipped their toes into the Mediterranean, the bluest water Helen had ever seen. That night, they made love in a way they hadn't before, with their eyes as open as their hearts.

When it came time to leave, they walked to their drop-off point, where they found Fritz waiting.

On the short ride to the station, Helen sat on Frank's lap and rested her head on his shoulder. Neither of them said much. Helen couldn't talk around the lump in her throat.

Fritz waited in the jeep while Frank walked her into the station. Her train was already in. "Of all times for the stupid train to be on time!" she said.

"I know." Frank looked as close to tears as Helen had ever seen him. "I hate the time we wasted in petty arguments and misunderstandings."

Guilt sprang to life in her. "You know nothing went on in Paris, right? You know I could never love anyone but you."

Frank took her in his arms. "I know. And you trust me too, don't you, darling?"

"I do." She smiled, remembering another *I do*.

"I like the way you say those words, Mrs. Daley," he said, still holding her like he'd never let go.

The whistle blew. The conductor called in French, urging passengers to board.

Frank walked her to the train steps, his arm around her waist. Then he lifted her up so they were nearly eye to eye when they kissed.

"I hate saying good-bye to you, Frankie!"

"One day soon we won't need to," he said. "Until then, just remember that I'll always love you, wherever you are."

Helen tried not to cry as she asked him, "When will we see each other again?" But what she was thinking was, *Will we see each other again?*

The train jerked, and Helen climbed aboard while Frank jogged to keep up with her. "Don't worry, darling!" he shouted. "We'll see each other soon!"

Helen ran to a window where she could watch Frank on the platform until the train pulled out of the station. She closed her eyes and tried to pray, to believe that they really would see each other again. Soon. But they both knew firsthand that anything could happen in war.

March 12, 1945, 8:45 am
Rennes, France
H. E. Daley

Dearest darling,

I know you're swamped with an entire unit with ptomaine poisoning, on top of the wounded you already had. Wish I were there to help.

No more news about the Russian–Japanese deal, so it was probably a false rumor.

Guess MacArthur is doing fairly well in the Pacific. Hope Balfour is OK with Halsey. Wish Dotty's husband would be released. Gosh, won't it be wonderful when we're all home! Could we have Dotty and Boots as our first guests? And Eugene. I haven't been able to get through to him in letters. I wish he'd write me back. Naomi says I need to turn it over to God. She's such a good gal. She doesn't say much about God or about her stateside husband. So when she does talk about either, I pay attention.

With love, wherever you are,
Tiny

P.S. As you've no doubt figured out by now, my clever captain, I have enclosed the letter I received from Dotty.

Dorothea Daley Engel
Feb. 18, 1945

Dear Helen,

It's hard to realize that we haven't met because I feel I know
you well. I can tell Frank did the right thing. He sounds very
happy in his letters to me.

I haven't heard from Boots since the card sent from his prison
camp. You know that before his camp was liberated, 2,000
prisoners were sent to other camps. His parents have thought
him to be in Japan the whole time, but perhaps now they are
right. I know it won't be much longer until he is free to come
home. I'm praying for him day and night. Keeps me out of
trouble!

Finally heard from Jack. He says he likes Belgium, though it
happens he was there for the Bulge, when the Germans pushed
back with great force. He lost friends and called it a "rough
trip," which for our brother is quite an admission. Glad we
didn't know at the time.

Thank you for sending the picture taken in Chicago. It's very
good, and for a time I was fooled, thinking Schnapps was a real
dog. I do so enjoy your letters.

Love,
Dotty

FRANK

BATTALION AID STATION INSIDE GERMANY

Frank tucked Helen's letter back into his pocket. He'd started carry-ing one letter with him wherever he went, which had been all over the place. How did Dotty do it? It was like she never doubted Boots, never doubted God.

Frank had to admit that he had his share of doubts. He knew Helen had told him the truth about Paris. But what about her relationship with her colonel friend? He knew nothing had happened between them, but he couldn't deny his feelings of jealousy. Colonel Pugh saw a lot more of Helen than he did. Frank wanted to be back in the barn hideout with his wife. He could still smell her cologne on his sleeve, or at least he imagined he could. Weeks had passed, and still he hadn't been able to arrange another rendezvous. It wouldn't be easy now that he'd been assigned to battalion aid. It was all he could do just to stay alive. Acting purely on adrenaline, he'd pulled a dozen soldiers, kicking and screaming, from the edge of a live battlefield. It made him think of Nurse Becky. It felt like years since she'd told him about being knocked unconscious by a patient in a field hospital.

Their aid station was not much more than a three-sided tent—slushy-mud floor, sagging canvas roof—with room for seven cots. They could have used three times that many. Frank thought about Anderson and Lartz, still assigned to Strasbourg, where battalion aid evacuated patients stable enough to be moved. Why Major Bradford had chosen him to advance into Germany with the British outfit was still a mystery.

Frank would never admit it to Anderson, but he was right: this was not what they'd signed up for—carrying a medical bag onto the battlefield only seconds after the cross fire that had turned dozens of soldiers into wounded, crying boys. Or worse yet, corpses. Anderson had sent word from Strasbourg that he'd been granted a seven-day leave to see his brother, who was wounded in Holland. From Lartz, Frank had received no word at all. And as far as he knew, Major Bradford hadn't found out anything about Lartz's mother or his brother.

The stray snowflakes that had floated over the battlefield earlier turned back into rain as he crouched over a GI so young, so thin, his helmet made him look like he was playing soldier. Blood gushed from his left thigh, and Frank had to fight with the kid to get close enough to tie a tourniquet.

"I won't let you cut it off!" The kid landed a fist squarely on Frank's jaw.

Frank struggled to recover, throwing his shoulder up for defense while wrestling with the tourniquet. "Nobody's going to cut off your leg, soldier." Nobody would cut it off here, in this mud. Back in a real hospital, though . . . Frank placed the boy's arm around his shoulders. "Let's get out of here before the Jerries decide to come back and invite their friends."

He half carried, half dragged the kid back to the aid station. Cots in the battalion aid tent were so low to the ground, he had to kneel in mud beside the bed to treat his patient. In the next cot over, a British enlisted man groaned and tucked himself into the fetal position. Frank glanced at him, but there was nothing more he could do.

"What's the matter with him?" the kid asked, sinking into the cot so that it nearly touched ground.

"Too much chocolate." The soldier had reported eating a gold-wrapped chocolate bar he'd "confiscated" from a German pack. Frank knew the Jerries left behind poisoned candy for unsuspecting GIs.

"Are you a real doctor?" the kid asked.

"That's what my medical license says."

"So what did you do wrong?"

Frank laughed. The boy wasn't stupid. "Long story, the moral of which is, 'Never tease a bald colonel.'"

That night, Frank was about to try for a couple hours' sleep when he spotted a lone soldier standing by a barren tree a few yards out. The tip of his cigarette glowed in the dark night, and not a single star broke through the clouds. But Frank knew he was looking at Bradford.

He walked out to join him. After a minute of silence—if you didn't count the sporadic gunfire—Frank said, "Mind if I ask you something, Will?"

"If it's about your mate, Lartz, I haven't forgotten about him, nor his mother and brother. I am working on it."

"That's great. Thanks. But that wasn't what I was going to ask."

Bradford tossed his cigarette to the ground and crushed it with his boot. "Ask away."

"Why me? Why did you choose me to come along with your unit? Not saying I mind. I just wonder."

"You're a good chap, Daley."

"Thanks. But now that you have four British doctors assigned to Strasbourg, isn't one of them a good chap?"

Major Bradford made the nasal sounds that served as laughter for many Brits Frank had met. "You're American."

"True."

"That's why I chose you, Yank. Don't get me wrong. I've watched you work, and you'd have been my choice, no matter what nationality you were. You're an ace at identifying aircraft and patching up patients."

The compliment took Frank by surprise. Bradford had seen him at his worst, treating burn patients back at the hospital near Pinkney, when he'd been afraid to do grafts on his own. Plus, the man wasn't known for his praise. "Thanks. I think."

"Look. You've seen the number of Germans surrendering this week. You know how shorthanded we are since this push into Germany. I need more than your medical skills, Captain."

Frank hoped Will wasn't counting on his soldier skills just because he'd been promoted. "I should warn you I'm no hero, Major."

"So you've said on numerous occasions. I believe you've ceded that role to your sister and brother. But there are many kinds of heroes. Not all are John Wayne."

"My five-foot-tall sister would make a better John Wayne than I would."

"Don't sell yourself short. I'll bet the lovely Mrs. Daley considers you heroic."

Frank thought about one of the last letters he'd received from Helen—which had also been one of her saddest. She'd just lost a patient. "My wife says we just have to do the right thing, the next thing in front of us, the thing we can do."

"A wise woman. As it happens, I hope to be placing a 'right thing' in front of you starting tomorrow."

Frank braced himself.

"We're expecting more German soldiers to try to escape through battalion aid stations. Infiltration is at an all-time high. Some of the German officers, especially the SS, have been caught wearing dead men's uniforms, mostly British and American. We believe some of those masquerading as Brits and Yanks have already made it through, perhaps through our own station."

Frank couldn't fathom it. Could any of the wounded he'd treated have been Germans? "So what are we supposed to do? If they're like Fritz, they can speak better English, or American, than half our troops."

"True. And that's why we need more filters at the battlefield level. I was going to go over this in briefing tomorrow, but you might as well hear it now. We need to police every soldier that passes through here. We Brits are well represented, so we should be able to weed out Jerries trying to pass as members of the queen's regiment. But you're our only Yank, Captain Daley."

"If they speak English, how am I supposed to know they're German?"

"You'll quiz them."

"You mean like, what's the capital of North Dakota?" Frank wasn't sure he knew the answer. Bismarck, maybe?

"If they're SS, which the smart ones are, they've been trained as spies, mate. They'll know more about your American history and geography than you do. They may have gone to your universities."

"Then how am I supposed to—?"

"Talk with them. Don't grill them, though. Remember, they may all be Yanks. You don't want them to think you're suspecting them of being traitors, not after what they've been through. I'll give you a heads-up if we suspect one. Then you try your Yankee wiles, eh?"

For the next few days, Frank suspected every soldier who came into the battalion aid station. Most were British, but Bradford sent each American to Frank. He talked to them about high school, if they went to college, what cars their dads drove, where they went through training. He got so tired of the same questions that he had trouble focusing on the answers. It didn't help that he worked through the night two nights in a row.

He was treating burns on the torso of a boy from Ashland, Ohio, who said he planned on going back to Ohio State when he got home.

"And where did you go to college?" Frank asked.

"Huh? I just told you Ohio State."

"Right. Sorry." Frank could not ask one more question. If this kid were a Nazi, Frank would eat his helmet.

"I want to play football," the boy said.

"Yeah? I played in high school. But I didn't get my growth spurt until college, so I wasn't much good. I like baseball better anyway. You're not a Reds fan, I hope?"

"Nah. The Indians. My dad grew up in Cleveland."

"So you're a Bob Feller fan." Suddenly Frank was wide awake. Baseball! Why hadn't he thought of it before? Now there was something he could talk about all night. He knew trivia no German would ever know.

It worked. For the next few days, Frank talked baseball. It seemed every American soldier loved America's pastime. Talking about ERAs and no-hitters brought home a little closer.

He was pulling another all-nighter when Bradford took him aside and handed him a cup of joe, black. "I think we're the busiest we've ever been. I had to send Rafferty and Jones on stretcher duty. You holding up?"

"Coffee helps." Frank wondered if he'd ever go back to sugar and cream.

"Good. I'm sending you a bloke with a tricky broken leg. I think we need to go ahead and set it here. Run your talk on the fellow, will you? He's American. One of the men had a funny feeling about him. No reason. And the chap's been wrong before. I think he suspects all Yanks."

Frank knew exactly who the "chap" was—Sergeant Whigham. Even Frank felt like he was under suspicion of the good sergeant. "Send him over."

The soldier hobbled into the surgical unit—a too-fancy name for the small area at the back of the tent equipped with only a table, a stand for surgical instruments, and a cot. Frank ripped his pant leg to get at the wound. He was already 90 percent sure his patient, named Leonard Fry, was American because he was so tall, basketball height, with broad shoulders and big-boned hands. If he was a Jerry, he was a lucky son of a gun to have run across an Allied uniform that fit him.

After running through the usual questions and getting the usual answers, Frank said, "I'll bet you played basketball before the war, Leonard."

"Only with my brothers. And please call me Lenny."

A quick intake of breath was the only reaction to Frank's manipulation of Lenny's leg, which must have been hurting like the devil. The femur was broken in three places and the fibula shattered. "Guess this ends my basketball career. Ah well, I like baseball better anyway. Used to dream about playing for St. Louis."

Frank nearly dropped the guy's foot. "You're a St. Louis fan? Browns or Cardinals?" At home, Frank never missed listening to either team on the radio. He loved the Browns and the Cards. His job had just gotten a lot easier. "Who'd you root for in the World Series?"

"I love Stan the Man Musial," Lenny began. "But you had to go with the Browns. They were a ragtag, patched-together group of misfits, alcoholics, and retreads, who somehow pulled it together to win games."

"And they had to win ten out of their last twelve to get there," Frank said, testing his new friend.

The guy shook his head. "Eleven out of twelve, including whipping the Yankees four in a row."

They settled into a steady stream of St. Louis baseball talk, from Dizzy and Daffy Dean to the Gashouse Gang. It was the best conversation Frank had enjoyed with any soldier, except Helen, of course. Local anesthetic made it possible for them to keep talking all night.

When Frank went over to get each of them a cup of coffee, Bradford was pouring himself a cup. "Is the bloke one of you lot, then?"

Frank grinned. "He's American. One hundred percent."

A commotion behind them made Frank drop his coffee. He turned in time to see his patient holding a gun to the throat of another patient.

Bradford charged toward them.

"Stop right there, Major." Lenny spoke in English, but the American accent was gone now. He looked over at Frank. "It was great talking with you, Doctor. My brother went to school in St. Louie."

Frank couldn't move, couldn't breathe. How could he have been so wrong?

Bradford stood his ground. "Nobody has to get hurt here. Let the patient go. You keep his gun and be on your way. We're medical here, and—"

A gun went off, so close it was deafening. Frank couldn't hear anything except the ringing inside his head. He waited for the patient to drop.

Instead, it was the SS officer. His eyes registered surprise, then resignation as his legs gave out and he tumbled to the ground. The gun dropped, and the British soldier behind him, Sergeant Whigham, his own gun still smoking, stepped up and recovered the weapon.

Four Brits took hold of Lenny, or whoever he was, while two more helped the British patient back onto his cot. Sergeant Whigham checked Lenny's leg, where the bullet hit. "I guess we need a doctor."

Frank took charge, ordering them to lift the captive to the operating table. For the next several hours, guarded by two British soldiers, Frank removed the bullet and reset the leg.

Afterward, he apologized to the patient taken hostage. Then he searched out Major Bradford and found him pouring hot water over a tea bag. "I don't know what to say, Will. I'm really sorry. That man knew more about St. Louis than I did. I would have staked my life on his American citizenship. I guess I did—and not just my life. All of ours. I did warn you I'm no hero."

"Stop apologizing, Doctor," Bradford said. "That's an order. It's probably happened to the rest of us, and we haven't found out yet. The SS are the most highly trained agents in the world. Yours just happened to see a way out. I believe he thought you were onto him. When he saw you coming over to me, he got worried."

Maybe. Frank didn't quite believe it, though.

"Let's get you that coffee." Bradford poured, which was a good thing because Frank's hands were shaking.

Frank took a sip. It tasted more like tea than coffee. "Guess I've turned out to be your weak link, Major." Jack never would have fallen for that Nazi's deception. "I was genuinely scared back there."

"As was I, Captain."

Frank didn't know whether to believe him or not. Bradford hadn't looked, or acted, scared. "Do you know Psalm 23? Is that one as famous on this side of the ocean as it is on ours?"

"It is indeed. And even more so since Great Britain entered the war, I'd venture."

"I've been saying the part about fearing no evil every night before I fall asleep. Not sure it's done the trick, though." He stared down at his full cup, thinking that tonight was the closest he'd come to a genuine valley of the shadow of death.

Bradford's eyes smiled as he took a large sip to empty his cup, then stood. "Well, I could use some sleep about now. I suggest you do the same."

Frank gave up trying to sleep just as the sun topped the horizon. The camp stirred with soldiers heading for the mess tent. His mind filled with what-ifs. What if the Nazi had shot that patient? What if the SS sent more officers disguised as Americans? What if he failed to stop them? What if they stopped *him*? So many things he had no answers to.

He took a deep breath and repeated to himself for the thousandth time, *"I will fear no evil: for thou art with me."*

March ██, 1945
████████

My darling husband,

I was over the moon to receive 3 letters from you today. When I think of the ridiculous and time-wasting spats I initiated in ████, when we had so little time together, I am still ashamed, though confident that you've forgiven me and that we are now closer than ever. Our love, I believe, is more real—and God smiles on our marriage, don't you think?

Thank you for agreeing with me about Eugene. You're right—he wasn't made for war, but he's courageous to do what must be done to get better. Mom's brief letter said that Genie is now helping out around the house and even farming a bit. My dad is a hard man to help, so Eugene must be gaining strength.

Shall I tell you of my harrowing case with twins, two German POWs brought in yesterday? They were guards in a slave labor camp, where there was an uprising. Both were stabbed near the heart. One died shortly after arrival. This sent his brother into a fury that required Bill and three MPs to restrain him. We have him in restraints and would like to treat him—but he spits viciously whenever a nurse or doctor approaches. So goes another day in the war.

I have been told that I must take a sick leave as my cough distresses patients. I don't know if I'll do it—so much work on the wards. Peggy says we should give my cold to all German and Japanese soldiers and declare the war at an end. I cannot wait until that day.

With all my love, wherever you are,
Your loving Tiny

⌖

Captain Frank R. Daley, MD
20 March 1945 9 pm Tuesday

Oh, darling,

I'm so worried about your coughing fits. Get a chest X-ray. Atypical pneumonia, practically symptomless at times, can, if untreated, leave bronchiectasis in its wake. Do you have circles under your eyes, and how do you feel?

I have been giving more thought to the Lithuanian patient you wrote about some time ago. As a worker in a German prison for so long, he may have picked up a number of things. The prisoners we've seen here had the worst atrocities performed on them. One fellow's skin had been systematically cut from his arms, legs, and sides. They are all hollow-eyed and skeletal. How can one human do these things to another?

More and more, I find it hard to live in the present. I replay the past, the moments when you and I were together. And I dream of our future.

Darling, we must both make every effort to get together the instant this war in Europe ends, as one of us may well be sent far away. All here are expecting to serve another two years in Japan or the Philippines, and many in the CBI (China, Burma, India). Major Bradford intends to bring his message of peace to the war zone. He expects to be part of the occupation, even if Japan is defeated the same time Germany is.

Know that wherever we are, we will always be together.

With love,
Your Frankie

50

Helen

RENNES, FRANCE

If the war really was winding down, Helen couldn't see it. The Rennes hospital was overcrowded, with more patients arriving every day. She longed for another rendezvous. She'd gone so far as to wrangle a three-day leave, then had to admit she had no idea where to look for her husband. She'd ended up working all three days right here, where rumors grew like tumors: Nurses would go to Belgium when Germany surrendered. Then no, nurses would go to Germany. Nurses would go to the CBI. Or to Japan. Then, all nurses would head for Russia, where atrocities were rumored to occur daily.

She called out, "Good morning!" to the packed ward and received a few weak greetings in return.

Peggy rushed over, her green eyes dots on her haggard face. "I thought you'd never get here!" She handed Helen a clipboard.

"I'm ten minutes early, you know."

"I still thought you'd never get here. How's the cough?"

"About the same. I'm okay. Anything I need to know?"

Peggy yawned. "I need sleep."

"I can see that." Helen lowered her voice. "How's Phil?" Phil was a nineteen-year-old from Arkansas who had lied about his age and enlisted months before his eighteenth birthday. He came to them on a stretcher. Helen gathered that he'd been holed up in a muddy trench for days during the Battle of the Bulge. He'd been wounded, returned to battle, then wounded again while stuck in the trenches. They'd removed the shrapnel with no problems, no infection. But Helen had been first to notice the boy's rotting fingernails. For a week, she'd stayed past her shift to shave his nails with a razor to let them drain. She'd convinced Captain Sutherland—the new doctor, Pugh's recruit—to try antibiotics, but Phil hadn't responded to treatment, and his fingernails fell off like autumn leaves. Then his fingers blackened and had to be removed.

"He's not so good," Peggy said. "Sutherland says they'll have to amputate his arms to the elbows."

As Helen prepared morning meds, she thought about all the strange diseases soldiers were picking up here and in Japan and the Philippines, so many odd strains of fungi and bacteria. Frank wrote that Lartz had been having trouble with his hands for some unknown reason. Lartz had sent her an amazing sketch of Frank, and he'd done one of Helen from a snapshot. She prayed he wouldn't lose the use of his hands. Frank was pushing to get his friend shipped to the States for better care.

"I don't like that cough, Nurse," Phil said, as she wrapped what was left of his hands.

Helen muffled a cough that threatened to rattle. "I'm not crazy about it either, Phil." She used her teeth to bite off the stubborn tape, then checked Phil's bandage.

Bill Chitwood leaned down to smile right into Phil's face. Helen loved him for that. Most of the nurses shied away from Phil, as if they feared catching his bad luck. "How's it going, Phil? I saw you got you a bunch of letters last mail call."

"I reckon my ma's forcing everyone in Arkansas to write me."

"Good for her!" Helen said.

Bill frowned at Helen. "Shouldn't you be in bed yourself, Nurse? If you don't mind me saying so, you look like death warmed over."

"How could any gal mind such a lovely description of herself, Bill?"

"Nurse!" Sutherland shouted at her. He was only a couple of inches taller than Helen and so skinny his uniform hung like a bag around a coat hanger. But next to Pugh, he was the best doctor they had.

"Doctor?" She followed him outside to a flatbed truck full of patients. When he turned to her, his eyes swam in tears. "Nurse Daley, I'm putting you in charge of these men." His voice broke.

"What's wrong with them? Do we need to quarantine them?"

Sutherland looked horrified by the suggestion. "No! They're liberated. The last thing they need is quarantine. They were prisoners in one of the worst of the forced-labor camps inside Germany. They're going to need special care, Nurse, and constant attention."

Not for the first time, Helen felt guilty for having German blood flowing through her veins. She felt guilty for not having believed the reports about torture the first time she heard them over a year ago. She believed them now. She'd seen the horror with her own eyes. Sometimes, like now, she wanted to run away, to get as far from the hospital, from the war, as she could.

A quick prayer was all she could afford as she climbed into the back of the truck. She might have been entering a graveyard, a boneyard filled with skeletons. Two of the bald heads and crooked bodies belonged to women. Some of the men were naked. Others wore parts of uniforms, coats and shirts soldiers had taken off their backs to give to these victims of inhumanity. "You're safe now." She forced herself to stay calm. "We have you now, and we'll take good care of you. Nobody's going to hurt you anymore."

Bill was beside her before she could call for him. "Nurse, what can I do?"

"Get some guys to help carry our patients onto the ward."

"I can help you get them to the ward." He lowered his voice, though Helen doubted any of the patients could understand what he was saying. "But once they're inside, I don't know what we'll do."

Helen frowned at him. How could he not know what to do? Then she remembered they only had one empty bed, and that one only because its occupant died overnight. There was more room in the basement, but she refused to put these poor souls with German soldiers.

"Give me a minute." She hopped from the truck and ran back to the ward. About two dozen American soldiers were recovering from injuries sustained en route to a battalion aid station yards from the front. Their unit had repulsed the Germans, extending newly conquered territory deeper into hostile country, when SS troops firing machine guns burst out of the forest. Surviving GIs had been patched up by medics and sent to the hospital, where doctors and nurses, including Helen, had worked all night to remove bullets and shrapnel.

Helen believed her patients were good guys. She really hoped so. She pulled a folding chair in the middle of the beds, then stood on the seat. It was pretty wobbly. So was she, to tell the truth. "Could somebody give me a hand?"

Five soldiers rushed to help, although *rushed* wasn't the right word. Two had to grab crutches and hobble. Two more had their arms in slings and their feet wrapped.

"We've got company on the ward, gentlemen." She explained about the patients and the lack of beds. "It's a lot to ask. I know you guys are hurting yourselves."

Phil spoke up first. "You can have my bed, Nurse." He struggled to swing his feet over the edge of the bed. "I don't mind the floor. I slept on worse."

"Thanks, soldier!"

"All right. Count me in," said a guy who didn't sound happy about it.

"I'll get blankets from the nurses' quarters!" Naomi shouted.

All of a sudden, the hollering and shuffling stopped. Silence fell over the ward as emaciated survivors were carried in, held like babes in arms by nurses and soldiers. Beds and cots emptied, freeing far more than needed, and still no one spoke. Naomi returned with Peggy, Sally, and others, all carrying their own bedding. Helen directed traffic, assigning each nurse from one to three patients, who clung to the women as if they were saviors. She pulled Sally aside. "Can you get help and bring them broth or soup?"

Sally didn't move, and for a minute, Helen thought she hadn't heard. Then she sprang into action. "I can do that."

The last patient in the truck was a man whose cracked skull looked blackened from burns that left marks of varying shapes. He'd refused to leave the truck until everyone else was out. Bill helped Helen lift him out of the truck. The man had no visible muscles in his legs, only broken bones. One eye had been cut out, and the other receded so deeply into the socket that at first, she thought it was gone too.

"I'm Nurse Helen." She put his arm around her neck and felt nothing but bone. Every movement had to be torture for him, but he refused to be carried.

Bill helped her get the patient onto a bed close to the others. But when she started to pull the sheet over him, he panicked and tried to get out of bed. "Okay. You don't have to have it. You're the boss here." She handed sheet and blanket to Bill and smiled at the man until he lay back down.

"Maybe he doesn't understand English," Bill whispered.

Helen tried comforting the man in German, but he didn't respond to that either. She'd stick to English. No way did she want to align herself with his captors.

Bill fetched supplies, and Helen managed to superficially clean wounds and breaks that must have been left to heal on their own, only to have been rebroken. Everything they tried brought agony to both patient and nurse.

Captain Sutherland called in Colonel Pugh, and the two doctors worked feverishly. Pugh asked Helen to join him on rounds, but when he saw the terror that would bring to her patient, he changed his mind. "This is worse than anything I've ever seen," he said. "I hardly know where to start. They've all been systematically tortured and starved. They suffer from typhus, frozen feet, gangrene. I suspect eight out of ten of these patients have tuberculosis."

As if in sympathy, Helen had one of her coughing fits.

"Nurse?" Pugh said. "Helen? You should get off your feet. Go on. Get some rest. We'll be all right here."

Helen glanced at her patient, whose gaze never left her. "Maybe later, if he falls asleep." But she knew she couldn't leave the ward, not with so many others who needed her help.

Peggy and Sally brought in broth for the survivors, but most of them couldn't keep it down. All across the ward, nurses were starting IVs, some assisted by other patients. Pugh and Sutherland were setting up blood transfusions for some of the feeblest patients.

Sally walked up so quietly that Helen didn't see her until she was placing something beside the bed—a small bouquet of tiny purple flowers. "I picked them today." She smiled down at Helen's patient. "I'll bet it's been a long time since they've seen flowers . . . or purple."

For the next few hours Helen talked to her patient, in English. She doubted he understood a single word, but she kept it up. Story after story. "So I made it to Marseille," she continued. "And this time my husband showed up in the right station." She skipped the part about their German driver. "I admit Frank did get us lost on our way to the barn." She remembered how tired and cranky she'd felt as they wandered around lost and cold. And at the same time, all of these people were suffering under unimaginable terror.

Several times when her patient appeared to have fallen asleep,

Helen tried to break free from him to help with other patients, but his skeletal arms found strength enough to cling to her. She could have gotten away, but she didn't have the heart.

Bill stopped by, sweat drenching his uniform. "Might as well give up, Nurse. Lem's not gonna let you go."

"Lem?"

"Reminds me of a feller I knew back in Texas. Used to date my little sister."

Helen sat back down and held "Lem's" hand. As far as she could tell, none of the nurses had left after coming onto the ward. Some held hands with their patients. Others dozed off in chairs beside beds long after their shifts ended. Even Victoria pitched in, working an extra shift to put up meds for their regular patients.

Helen jerked awake to a dimly lit ward. She couldn't stop coughing. Bill was kneeling beside her, and for a second she couldn't remember where she was and why she was there.

Bill frowned at her. "Nurse, you need to get some sleep. We can handle things."

Then it hit her. The ward. The camp survivors. "I can't sleep!" But had she? The last thing she remembered was struggling to stay in the chair and keep her head from falling on her patient.

Her patient. Helen stared at the empty bed, stripped of bedding. "No. Bill, no!"

Helen burst into tears that led into a coughing fit. She couldn't believe she'd fallen asleep. She hadn't been there for her patient when he needed her most. She hadn't helped him one bit, and he'd died on her watch.

"Bill, will you please take this nurse back to the barracks?" Colonel Pugh said. He and Bill were talking behind her. Was she the nurse they were talking about?

Bill took her arm and lifted her out of the chair. "Come on, Nurse. I'll help you to your bunk."

She tried to jerk her arm away. "I'm not going anywhere! I have patients here!"

Pugh stepped in. "Nurse, I order you off this ward right now. And you're not to return until Captain Sutherland or I determine that you're well enough."

Bill put his arm around her waist and moved her toward the door. "It'll be all right."

"It won't! I have to—"

"You've done enough, Helen," Pugh said.

But she hadn't done enough. That poor man had survived his slave labor camp, only to die here. Helen stopped struggling. Her arms and legs felt as though they'd been filled with gelatin. She was no match for Bill. She was no match for anybody.

FRANK

51

Somewhere in Germany

Frank's British unit moved deeper into Germany, one day in thick woods, the next in open, muddy fields. Everyone said the war would end any day now, but it was getting hard to believe. So far, Frank had pegged two German soldiers trying to impersonate GIs as they limped into the battalion aid station. Not much of a challenge since neither could speak a word of English beyond "I am American GI." Still, he wondered how many infiltrators had slipped past him.

Tomorrow would be Good Friday, but it didn't feel like Easter without Helen. This year Easter fell on April Fool's Day. Had it really been only one year since he'd been awestruck in the chapel at Battle Creek?

"Captain Daley?"

"Here!" Frank answered without turning around. He was changing his last bandage and hoped this didn't mean they'd found something else for him to do. He'd been on his feet for ten hours.

"You're wanted outside." Sergeant Whigham put a hand on his shoulder—a hand that nearly swallowed up Frank's shoulder. They'd arrived at an unusual and unexpected friendship since the day Whigham shot "Daley's Nazi," as the company referred to him, though always in good humor. "Bring your kit, mate. I think you're going off somewhere."

"Great," Frank muttered. He scrubbed his hands, grabbed his kit, and followed Whigham. "So where am I supposed to—?" He looked up the hill and spotted a jeep. Standing in the driver's seat was his brother.

"Jack?" Frank jogged up to him. "How did you find me?"

Jack jumped from the jeep and slapped Frank on the back. "Look at you! They told me you were in a battalion aid. What did you do to deserve this?"

Frank was used to the question. "Nothing to get me here. But quite a lot since."

"You mean that stuff about the St. Louis fan who happened to be SS?"

"You heard about that, huh? Not my finest hour, I'll admit. But things turned out okay." He hadn't planned on telling Jack, but now that it was out in the open, he didn't really mind. "So what about you, Jack? Dotty wrote that you were in Belgium at the right time. Mother and Daddy wrote that they haven't heard from you in weeks. They're worried sick."

"Okay. I'll get in touch. But I can never tell them the really fun parts of the war."

Apart from his time with Helen, Frank couldn't recall any "fun parts of the war." He studied his brother. Jack's uniform, a crisp lieutenant colonel's, complete with the proper silver oak leaf, suited him. Frank wondered if the rank was really his, but knew it would do no good to ask. The jacket hung loose, as if he'd borrowed it from a bigger man. It was the kind of thing that would have put Frank on his guard if a soldier breezed into the aid station wearing it.

Jack slid back behind the wheel. "What are you waiting for?"

Frank hesitated. He glanced around for Whigham.

"Your papers are in order, if that's what you're worrying about." Jack patted his front pocket. "Two-day pass, right here. You're wasting time, little brother!"

What the heck? Frank had always given in to Jack. He tossed in his kit and jumped in.

Jack punched his shoulder. "I like the double bars, Captain." Frank grinned. He kind of liked those silver bars too. "Hang on to your hat, Frank! I'm going to show you Germany."

"This *is* Germany."

The wind whipped so hard that they had to shout. "Ah, you haven't seen Germany until you've smoked a cigar in Heidelberg!" Jack said.

"Heidelberg? But it hasn't fallen yet, Jack!"

"It has."

"We haven't heard about it."

"You will. We've taken Mannheim and Ludwigshafen, after bombing both to pieces. Heidelberg's not an industrial or transport hub. Nothing worth bombing, but a lot worth seeing. The Nazis will gladly declare it an open city and hang on to all that lovely history. It's been their pet stronghold, which may be why Patton plans to make it his post. Allied occupation begins at sunset today." Jack glanced at his watch. "In twenty-seven minutes."

Even the sun cooperated as their jeep tore through the countryside. They crossed the Rhine as the sun set, making the water sparkle like the diamonds Frank wanted to give Helen one day. From high cliffs, castles gazed down at them with spirals and towers as extravagant as in a fairy tale. If Heidelberg turned out to be everything Jack claimed, Frank would bring Helen here.

It was pitch dark by the time they sped by the crooked signpost: *Heidelberg*. The first living thing to greet them was a giraffe. "Look at that!" Frank exclaimed.

Jack seemed unimpressed, as if giraffes always roamed the hills of Germany. "Yeah, that's a problem. Zoos haven't been much of a priority." He swerved to avoid a crater in the middle of the road.

"Was that—?" Frank began.

"Bomb. Probably one of ours." Jack slowed, then stopped, idling the engine as they looked down on the city that lay before them in near-total darkness.

"Guess we haven't restored electricity yet?" Frank ventured. He'd imagined people dancing in the streets like the French after liberation. But that was crazy. The Germans weren't liberated; they were defeated. Maybe this was what defeat looked like.

Jack, uncharacteristic in his silence, eased the jeep onto a side road that wound around to a tiny bridge. Without warning, he steered off the road and parked under the stone bridge. "Let's walk from here. I have a little job to finish before we celebrate." He grabbed a leather satchel from under the seat.

"What job?"

"Papers. A certain German officer will have left papers for me. Not a big deal."

Surrendered or not, it sounded like a big deal to Frank. He wished Jack had told him about it. He might not have come so readily. When they were kids, Frank had followed his big brother anywhere, no questions asked. But as Jack had said on his last visit, they weren't kids anymore.

"Jack, tell me why we're really here."

"Not getting cold feet, are you? This'll be fun."

He followed Jack down a thistle-covered hill to the back of a two-story, fairly modern building. Jack handed the satchel to Frank, then dug around in the window box until he came up with a key.

He pressed his ear to the door, then unlocked it. They went inside, shutting the door behind them.

"Jack?"

"Shhh." Jack pulled a flashlight out of his pocket and shone the light down a short hallway. He motioned for Frank to follow, and they walked straight down the hall to a big office. The door was open, and the flashlight revealed a giant desk littered with papers. Papers crunched under their boots.

Jack began riffling through the stacks on the desk's surface. Then he moved to the drawers, taking a paper here, a paper there. "Give me the satchel, Frank."

Frank held the bag open while Jack stuck in files. "Can I ask what all this stuff is? And why, when the city's already fallen, you have to—?"

Jack cut him off. "See if you find a calendar."

"Tomorrow is Good Friday. March 30, 1945."

"Find a calendar, Frank." There was no teasing in his voice.

Something inside of Frank fluttered, as if his heart were a bird and wanted out. Jack wasn't kidding around. That meant something serious must be going on. Frank's thoughts went to Helen. He squinted at the far wall until he remembered the penlight Bradford gave him his first night in the aid station. He turned it on.

"Keep the beam low," Jack said.

He wanted to ask why, but he lowered the flashlight. Frank's eyes were already adjusting to the dark, and with the help of his flashlight aimed low on the near wall, he made out a dozen framed certificates. "This guy must have been a big deal, huh?"

"A German general," Jack whispered. "Calendar?"

"I'm looking." But there was nothing else on the walls. He joined Jack at the desk. That's when he spotted a desk calendar. "Jack, will this work?"

Jack took it and flipped pages. "Hmmm."

"Is that a good *hmmm* or a bad *hmmm*?"

"Both. Right calendar. Unfortunately, that surrender I was telling you about, the fall of Heidelberg? It hasn't happened yet."

"What?" Frank grabbed the calendar. There was nothing written for today or tomorrow, except a tiny squiggle. Then he got it. Jack was kidding. Even here, his brother would be king of practical jokes. "Sure. So the German general has it marked on his calendar for tomorrow?"

"*He* didn't mark the calendar, and I can't tell you who did or why. But it's real." Jack looked over at him. "I got it wrong, Frank. Heidelberg is still a German stronghold. They haven't surrendered the city, and they're not going to for another thirteen hours."

52

FRANK

Heidelberg, Germany

Jack wheeled around to the only window in the office. The glass was cracked, and the window had an iron grate over it. "Tank! Down! Get down, Frank!"

Jack didn't have to tell him twice. Frank was flat on his stomach, scrambling under the desk before the German tank passed outside the window. On top of the monster tank, German soldiers were laughing as if in a victory parade.

Once Frank no longer heard the roar of the tank's wheels, he reached across the desk and slugged Jack as hard as he could, catching him on the shoulder.

"I guess I had that coming."

"How are we going to get out of here without getting captured? Or worse? There's no way I'm spending the rest of the war as a German POW. I've seen what they do to their prisoners, Jack!"

"Hmmm. Now that's a good idea."

"What idea?"

As usual, Jack didn't explain. "Come on!" He hopped up in boxing stance, then shuffled around, shadowboxing the stale air. "Admit it—don't you feel your juices flowing? I always thought it was selfish of me not to share my best wartime adventures with you."

"Are you being serious? Because you should be." Frank had never really thought about why his brother hadn't married. He'd had lots of opportunities. Maybe this was why. Being married was serious business. Frank wasn't just scared for himself. He was even more worried about Helen, their marriage, their future family.

"Good thing I stole that jeep. It's a Nazi jeep, in case you hadn't noticed."

"Yeah, that's great, Jack. That ought to make them go easier on us." What would Helen do if he didn't make it out? He couldn't stand the thought of her receiving the telegram. They'd promised each other they'd be okay, they'd get out of the war and . . . so many promises.

Jack moved to a closet he'd already searched.

"Are you thinking we could hide in the closet until Heidelberg surrenders?" Frank asked, slim hope trying to find a way in. "I mean, if it's really going to happen when you say it is, I guess we could. But what if the general comes to work in the morning? Don't you think—?"

"We're not sticking around for the Allies to ride in." With a flourish, Jack produced a black leather trench coat and a German military lid. "Sorry, Frank. Unless your German is better than I think it is, you're my prisoner of war. So, no uniform for you. We'll have to rough up the one you're wearing." He tried on the coat and frowned. "Generals can get so fat." He took it off and turned it inside out before putting it back on. It didn't help. He pulled the belt tight and turned up the collar. "Perfect. Now, ready to get down and dirty?"

"Down and dirty" wasn't just an expression. Frank followed his brother through a maze of city sewers as they crept beneath the still-German stronghold. He had to bend in half, and still his hat got knocked off twice. Above them, dank, wet cement dripped thick drops, making him smell worse than his unit's latrine. The tunnels grew so convoluted that he was sure Jack was lost and afraid to admit it. For all Frank knew, Jack may have led them straight to a German outpost by mistake.

Jack exited first, then waved for Frank to follow. "Jeep's over there."

Frank emerged and looked around until he spotted the jeep, a football field away, right where they'd stashed it. "Never doubted you, Jack," he lied.

Jack took off the trench coat, turned it right-side out, and put it on, clean as a whistle. He wrinkled his nose at Frank. "Good. The way you stink, nobody would doubt that you've been a POW for years." He ripped the shoulder of Frank's uniform, leaving the sleeve to hang down.

"I had to pay for this uniform." He and Helen had put themselves on a strict budget, and there was no room in it for a new uniform.

"That's what you're worried about?" Jack asked.

"One of many things." Frank was scared. Scared, but not alone. . . . *Thou art with me.*

"Here you go." Jack handed him a gun, too small to be Army-issued. "Wear the sleeve like that, over your hand, and keep the gun in that hand."

Frank started to protest, but took the gun and kept his mouth shut.

"I heard you were a good shot at Camp Ellis." Was there anything his brother didn't know about him? Jack took hold of Frank's wrists and crossed them. "Keep your head down. I don't have handcuffs, so hold your wrists together."

They walked like that to the jeep in the light of a full moon, and nothing happened, not even the heart attack Frank feared he might be experiencing. Jack settled behind the wheel, and Frank slumped beside him.

"Tilt your head to the side." Jack shoved Frank's hair over his eyes. "Let me do the talking if we get stopped."

"Don't worry."

Instead of trying to sneak out of Heidelberg, Frank's costumed brother drove straight up the same street the tank had taken when it roared past the general's office. After that, Frank kept his eyes shut, as if that could keep the enemy from seeing him. He flashed back to games of hide-and-seek when he'd closed his eyes and hoped Jack or Dot wouldn't find him.

Suddenly he felt Jack stiffen. He heard the quick intake of breath.

"Heil Hitler!" Boot steps closed in on them from the road ahead.

"Keep still, no matter what," Jack whispered. The jeep jerked to a halt.

Jack stood up behind the wheel, and Frank could see him extend his arm in the hateful salute. *"Heil Hitler!"*

It made him shudder, hearing Jack mouth those odious words. But he hoped the words sounded as convincing to the Nazis as they did to him.

A chorus of return heils sounded from an approaching jeep, only a few feet away. Frank didn't dare look up to see how many of them there were. He'd lost all feeling in his hand from squeezing the gun so tight. *Your rod and Your staff, they comfort me.* He prayed until he could sense God with him as never before.

Jack spouted a string of angry German words. Frank wished he'd taken his high school German classes more seriously.

Someone's hand smacked the side of the jeep, and more German followed. A lively exchange ensued, with Jack growing louder, and the other voices weaker.

Finally, Jack put the jeep in gear, and Frank couldn't stop himself from peeking.

The slap came so fast, Frank never saw it coming. Blood trickled down his face, and it felt like his nose might be broken. Confused, he waited for whatever else was coming.

Jack shouted something in German. Then he laughed, and the

jeep jerked forward and sped away. After an agonizing minute, Frank risked a glance behind him. The Germans were driving away.

"Sorry about that sucker punch," Jack said.

Frank wheeled around, confused. "Wait. That was you?" Automatically, he lunged toward his brother.

"Easy, sport. Not yet. Never know who's watching."

Right. Frank settled back to POW position but kept a lookout for more trouble. He didn't release his grip on the gun until they were well out of the city. "Here. You better take this back before I shoot you." He wiped his bloody nose with the sleeve of his uniform, which was already ruined.

Jack took back the pistol and tucked it into his boot. "You all right?"

He felt the bones in his nose. It was going to hurt and leave him a couple of shiners, but it wasn't broken. "What went on back there?"

"Just a little territorial squabbling with my fellow SS officers. They wanted to take charge of you since you were caught in their city. We're pretty sure they're going to try to kill all prisoners of war."

"How did you convince them to let you keep me?"

"Threats and promises," Jack answered, cryptic as ever.

Finally, Frank felt free to stretch. His arms and neck ached, and his nose, which had stopped bleeding, was starting up again. "I owe you."

"Aw, I know. It's nothin'."

Frank started to tell him that wasn't what he meant. He'd meant he owed Jack for the slap. That was how he and his brother had always operated. Frank would have repaid with one of his own slaps, delivered when least expected. But things were different now. They weren't kids anymore.

It was morning when they drove into the battalion aid station. Major Bradford listened to Jack's condensed version of their adventures.

When he stopped laughing, he urged Jack to stay for a few days until he could rest up.

Jack didn't even stay the night. Frank suspected he might have been headed back into Heidelberg, but this time he was on his own. The war would be over before long. The bigwigs were already meeting, dividing countries like pieces of pie, Jack had said. Frank and Jack said their good-byes with their customary handshake and arm punches. Then Frank hugged his brother.

Frank fell into his cot, exhausted. But sleep wouldn't come until he could write Helen and tell her how much he loved her. He fell asleep with the pen in his hand, gripped tight as a gun.

～❧～

My darling Helen,

    Jack just paid me a visit, one I'll save to relate to you when we're together again. About this time a year ago, you came into my life and changed my world. Life is better, richer, deeper because of you. Easter means so much more now. I want you to know that no matter what, I will always love you, wherever you are, wherever I am, wherever we are.

                                Love,

                            Your Frankie

P.S. Thanks for the April Fool's card—same day as Easter this year, I think. (If I'm wrong, April Fool's!)

53

Helen

RENNES, FRANCE

It was Helen's second day back on the ward after nearly a week flat on her back as a patient instead of a nurse. She still felt weak, and her cough lingered a bit. The only reason Colonel Pugh had okayed her return to duty was their need for every able-bodied nurse to help handle the truckloads of German POWs that arrived next to truck-loads of wounded GIs.

A week had passed since they'd learned of President Roosevelt's death, and every doctor and nurse still hashed over medical details of his cerebral hemorrhage and how so much about his medical condition had been kept secret. Yet to Helen, Roosevelt's death didn't seem real. Neither did her life.

Physically, she was almost back to health. She'd done triage all day, then worked long hours in the basement. But even as she forced herself to smile at patients, there were things she couldn't get out of her mind. Liddy's accident, Lem's death, along with so many others she'd tried to save. Everything was spinning out of control, even— maybe especially—her own thoughts.

At the end of the day, all she wanted to do was curl up on her bunk and try to shut out the conversations all around her.

Naomi came and sat on her bunk. "You okay, gal? Lookin' mighty glum."

Helen didn't have the energy to deny it. "I was just thinking. Dad used to tell us, 'God helps those who help themselves.' Well, I've tried—and failed—to help myself. To help my patients. But my patients die. And I couldn't even keep myself well."

Naomi smiled. "You do know that line about God helping those who help themselves isn't in the Bible, don't you?"

"Are you sure?"

Naomi nodded. "It's more like, 'God helps most when you admit you can't do it on your own.'"

"Huh."

"What are you gals whispering about?" Peggy joined them on Helen's bunk. "Are you two keeping secrets?"

"Of course not," Helen said. But she didn't want their conversation broadcast either.

As always, Naomi came to the rescue. "Helen was wondering if she and Frank might end up in the same unit if Germany ever gives up."

Naomi wasn't lying. Helen did ask herself that a hundred times a day. "Peggy, do you think there's a chance?" she asked.

"Germany will never give up," Victoria said. She'd taken the bed next to Helen's, and Helen was convinced she'd done it to drive her crazy. It was working. "I heard that if German soldiers lose a battle, they run to the woods. They're getting ready for years of guerrilla warfare."

"Well, I won't be around to see it," Naomi said. "Soon as I get my marriage certificate, I'm putting my name at the head of the go-home-to-hubby list."

"What's the holdup on the certificate, Naomi?" Helen asked, glad her Frankie had seen to it that they both had a copy of their marriage license overseas.

"I'm not sure. Ralph has to find it and mail it to me."

"So your husband is the holdup?" Victoria made it sound like a taunt. "Wonder what that means."

Helen was the only one Naomi had confided in about her husband troubles. She rarely talked about lazy Ralph. Helen suspected that half the gals didn't even know Naomi was married. "Mail has been so slow from the States," Helen said. "Bet you get that certificate before Hitler says, 'I quit.'"

Naomi yawned, signaling the end of this conversation. "I need sleep. I'll never get used to the DBST." Double British Summer Time may have saved the armies daylight, but it sure did rob everyone of sleep.

Naomi returned to her bunk, and Helen stretched out on her own. She wanted to sleep too, but it was no use trying, not with Victoria's radio blaring. Vic turned it up. The music, which hadn't been bad, faded, and somebody began pontificating: *"Attention, GIs and all Allied servicemen and women!"*

Victoria shushed everyone, adding, "Helen, are you listening?"

It was the usual diatribe about fraternization with the enemy. Victoria glared at Helen during each warning, as if she knew the words were meant for the German in the room, and friendship with her equaled fraternization with the enemy.

Helen didn't move her gaze from Frank's photo, the one of him standing in an open boxcar, a three-day beard making her husband look virile and wonderful.

"Be vigilant as our victory comes to completion! Do not be taken in by the enemy out of uniform. Do not sympathize with German civilians."

"Hear that, Helen? You really do need this," Victoria said.

"And you don't, Victoria, since you never sympathize with anyone anyway."

"... these people, whose goal it is to conquer and subjugate Americans and our allies."

Finally, the music resumed—a lovely, sad song, "My Buddy."

But of course, Victoria couldn't let the music reign. "I just think you need to be careful with those Germans in the basement. Who knows what they might be plotting the minute the war's over?"

"*You* certainly wouldn't know, since you only nurse the easy patients," Helen said evenly.

"At least *I* will never be accused of sympathizing with those ... Germans!" Victoria glanced around as if waiting for applause.

"Most of them are just kids," Naomi said. Helen felt a surge of affection for her friend. An only child, Naomi had grown up hating conflict and avoiding arguments, a luxury never afforded in Helen's family.

"Don't tell me we have another sympathizer in our midst," Victoria muttered.

Peggy hopped from her bunk and charged Victoria. "The last I heard, *Nurse*, good nurses are supposed to sympathize with their patients!"

Victoria opened her mouth to argue, but Peggy wouldn't let her. "That's the last I want to hear about it! Do you hear *me*?" Peggy eyed their fellow nurses, daring anyone to object.

"I think we all hear you," Naomi put in, shutting off the radio and returning to her own bunk.

Instead of trying to sleep, Helen took out her last blank V-mail.

H. E. D.

Dear Frankie,
  I want you to know that I'm back on my feet again and feeling fine. You mustn't worry about me. I can almost feel the war grinding to an end, can't you?

You must let me know if you hear so much as a whisper about the Pacific. Promise? Remember we said we'd never keep secrets from each other. Everyone here says Army doctors still in Europe when the war ends will be shipped off to the Pacific. They're the ones who'll get first pick of transport, leaving us nurses stranded. If you and I don't find each other the minute the war ends, it could be months, or even years, before we're together again. But I know that my loving husband will move heaven and earth for another rendezvous. Soon!

With love, wherever you are,
Your loving wife

54

FRANK

STRASBOURG, ALSACE-LORRAINE

Major Bradford, Frank had discovered, could pull some powerful strings when he wanted to. He'd managed to arrange passes to attend a memorial service for Roosevelt in Strasbourg. And he suggested they pay a visit to Lartz, who had undergone two surgeries on his hands. Plans were in motion to get him shipped back to the States for a major operation that could improve finger mobility.

Since they'd arrived in Strasbourg hours before the memorial, they made the hospital their first stop. Lartz wasn't the only doctor-turned-patient. Anderson had been admitted with stomach pains and liver distress. Frank heard Andy's booming laughter before they found the room. "Andy, how did you arrange bed and breakfast during wartime?"

"If it isn't *Captain* Daley!" Andy hadn't forgiven the Army for promoting Frank and leaving him a lieutenant. "How's the war going,

Captain?" He turned to Bradford. "Major! I am honored! Ladies—" this he addressed to the two French nurses—"we are in the presence of real soldiers, fresh from the battlefield. To what do I owe the honor?"

"Major Bradford and I are attending Roosevelt's memorial service," Frank explained. "Thought we'd drop in on you and Lartz first."

For the next hour, Anderson did most of the talking. He pumped Bradford for information that might help him get a good assignment when the war ended. Andy was dead set on returning to the States and skipping the Pacific.

Frank checked his watch. "We need to go see Lartz now. But tell me the truth, Andy. Have they convinced you to give your liver a rest and quit drinking?"

"Nothing of the kind! You've mixed up the cart and the horse, sport. I drink purely for medicinal purposes."

"And on that note," Frank said, "we're off."

Lartz's ward was so quiet Frank felt guilty for the squeak of his dress boots. Lartz was trying to turn the page of the book he was reading, but his bandaged hands might as well have been sporting mittens.

"Read any good books lately?" Frank asked.

"Frank!" Lartz looked genuinely pleased to see him. He closed the book and set it aside. "You look good. Hey! Congratulations on that promotion, Captain Daley! Well deserved and high time."

"Thanks, buddy."

"And you, Major Bradford—thanks for coming. Are you going to the memorial service?"

Bradford nodded. "So, Lieutenant, are they treating you well?"

"No complaints."

Frank didn't know what to say. His friend did *not* look well. An awkward silence passed. Then he picked up the book Lartz had been reading. "*The Robe*? Helen really liked it."

"How is Helen? Have you two been able to work out another meet?"

"Helen is wonderful. Still in Rennes. The Army's doing its best to keep us apart, but we're determined to see each other the minute the war's over. What about you? When are you scheduled to go home?"

Lartz sighed. "It's day-to-day. I don't think I'm at the top of the list any longer. They think I must have handled some kind of chemical-warfare gas residue. They're not sure surgery is the way to go." He turned to Bradford. "Major, what are your postwar plans?"

"I'll move on to the CBI," Bradford said.

Lartz nodded. "You've been fighting a lot longer than we have. Doesn't quite seem fair that they'd make you go so far away and keep fighting."

"Actually, I volunteered to go. I've had enough of warfare and fighting. I want to go to the Pacific and work as hard at peace as we have at war. I don't just want to occupy territory. I want to help build peace in the region."

"Good for you," Lartz said. "I'd join you if I could. Which is it, Major? China, Burma, or India?"

"Or Japan." Bradford took off his hat and set it on the foot of the bed. "Probably China. I'd like to keep my unit together." He shot Frank a grin. "Except I suppose we could do without a Yank or two."

Lartz turned back to Frank. "Do you think they'll send you to the Pacific?"

"Not if I can help it. But I probably can't help it." He glanced at Bradford. "Right now, all I can think of is starting a new life with Helen in the USA."

Frank listened as Lartz, sick as he was, drew out Bradford on why he was doing what he was doing.

Bradford surprised Frank by sitting on the edge of Lartz's bed and lowering his voice. "Lartz, your friend here asked me for a favor. He requested that I do what I could to locate relatives you suspect might be in Germany, and in peril." He glanced back at Frank. "I chose to wait until I could tell you face-to-face what I've found out."

"Did you find them?" Frank asked, afraid to look at Lartz.

"No. Or, rather, not exactly. I wish I had better news, Lieutenant. Of your brother, I have no news at all, except that I believe he succeeded in denying the presence of Jewish blood in his veins."

Lartz nodded, as if he already expected this. "And my mother?"

"I am very sorry, Lieutenant. Your mother was arrested and sent to a slave camp inside Germany. Ravensbrück."

Lartz didn't look away, but his eyes filled with silent tears.

"She died there," Bradford said. "We believe she died three years ago, soon after her arrival."

Lartz stared down at his hands. A tear escaped and landed on the bandaged fist. For a full minute, he said nothing. Then he looked to Bradford. "Major, thank you. I don't know how you did it. I've been trying to get news of them ever since I got here. Now that I know, I . . . well, it helps."

It was time to go, and not just because of the memorial service. Frank could tell that his friend needed to be alone. There were so many things Frank wanted to say to him. He still considered Lartz the best doctor, best artist, best friend a guy could have. "Take care, my friend," he said, reaching for a handshake, but turning it into a shoulder pat at the last minute. Lartz's hands didn't need shaking. "We'll visit you again soon. Or better yet, get well and come help us out." Then he leaned down and gave Lartz as firm a hug as he felt the man could handle.

Once they were outside, Frank thanked Bradford. "Do you think Lartz will ever get back to obstetrics?"

Bradford shook his head. "Not with those hands."

"It doesn't seem fair, does it?"

"He could, however, acquire a specialty which doesn't require precision hands—psychiatry, dermatology, X-ray."

Knowing Lartz, Frank believed he'd do just that. But he also knew his friend would miss bringing babies into the world.

Frank wasn't sure what he'd expected, but the memorial service for President Franklin Delano Roosevelt, although simple, was impressive. Crowds of soldiers and civilians, French, English, and American, overflowed into the streets for blocks and filled the square. Most spectators couldn't have heard a word of the tribute, and even fewer could understand. But they remained reverent and attentive. Frank would have given anything to have Helen with him. And now, Harry S. Truman, a fellow Missourian, sat in the president's chair, making decisions that would affect the world.

As for Frank, he had one goal: Get himself and his wife home to the USA. Maybe it was time to write another letter to Harry.

～≺❦≻～

Captain F. R. Daley 0440863

17 April 1945, 11 p.m.

My dearest Helen,

Surely this war must end soon. I have written Truman and requested to be assigned with my wife in the USA. I feel it is the least one Missourian can do for another.

According to the Stars and Stripes, we bombed Bordeaux with over 100 planes, which is a good start. All the French armies there are attached to the 6th Army Group, which joined my former 11th General.

Though I can't tell you where I am, I can say that we (I, Major Bradford, and one medic) performed 80 operations in the last 24 hours. We are well equipped with German supplies and equipment left behind. I can barely hold my pen to write you. Tried to sleep. Woke because it was cold and I was too lazy to get under a blanket after having just flopped onto the cot. I lay there for a while thinking of my wife and how wonderful it would be if you were to walk in with a "Don't you have a clever wife, Frankie" look on your face.

The evenings are long. We are the prisoners after we leave our makeshift hospital. There is a strict curfew, and our orders are not to go out again. An order has been issued that we should not say hello, not even to well-intentioned civilians. Will, Major Bradford, believes we must work at peace after this war . . . or we shall simply find ourselves in another.

I've received 12 more patients since I began this letter. Some poor GI scalded his face and hands, thanks to the enemy's grenade. On the other hand, a German prisoner burned his feet severely in a similar manner, though he insists he is a civilian and stepped in lye.

I miss you. Be happy, Tiny.

With love, wherever you are,
Frankie

~❧~

H. E. D.
1 May 1945

My dear Frankie,

How I miss you! I wonder if you ever get tired of me saying the same things in my letters: Naomi is sweet. Victoria is nasty. Peggy O is crafty. Bill is funny. And so on.

Patients confirm Mussolini is dead, and hopefully Hitler too. I have also heard that the Seventh Army is in Munich, the birthplace of my mother.

Mom wrote that the cost of marriage licenses in Illinois is going up from $1 to $3, and aren't we lucky we cashed in on that one. Her letter said nothing about Eugene or the letters I've written him.

*And now for the best news: Danny, my amputee patient
in Battle Creek, is getting married! His fiancée, Betty Lou, is
a nurse's aide at Percy Jones, but I never met her. Hudy will
be best man. Jimmy sulked at that, but now he's proud to be a
groomsman. Isn't that wonderful? It's as if a normal life is still
going on back home.*

> *With love forever and always, wherever you are,*
> *Tiny*

~~~

3 May 1945
Capt. F. R. Daley, MD

Dearest Helen,

*I had to stop this letter when barely started so that I could
dive for cover like a real soldier. As it happens, your husband
may be awarded two more combat stars, making a total of three
unearned—like a baseball game with no hits, three runs all
unearned and three errors. I always thought I'd be proud and
overjoyed if I received a medal, like Dotty and, no doubt, Jack
have accumulated. Turns out I'd much rather receive a letter
from my lovely wife. Today, in spite of gunfire and tragedy, I
experienced true joy from receiving the greatest gift—12 letters
from the best and most beautiful wife in the world.*

*I have a lot of medical equipment here (almost as much as
for the entire 11th General before), much of it purloined from
the Germans. I should have good use for it. I expect patients to
arrive in great numbers. We do have mosquitoes here, but they
are supposed to be the non-malaria-bearing type. I hope they
know that.*

> *With love, wherever you are,*
> *Your Frankie*

FRANK

GERMANY

Planes buzzed overhead. Frank could identify most of them, and they weren't friendly. His stomach growled, and he couldn't blame it—nothing but C-rations for dinner, K-rations for lunch. And no breakfast.

Frank and Bradford had relocated six times in nine days, searching for the perfect location for their new medical mobile unit, consisting of ninety enlisted men. So far, they'd found a dozen perfect spots . . . for mosquitoes. Frank wanted to get them closer to the airfield. Besides patching up soldiers who could be sent back to their units, he and Bradford would be responsible for the more severely injured. They would treat then evacuate them to safer hospitals. Orders were to form a pup tent city with cots for five hundred patients, and they were told that five hundred liberated American POWs would pass through daily. Each soldier would need to be deloused, reclothed, and rated whether or not he was "physically whole and able," which would put him at risk for being returned to battle duty.

That afternoon, Frank and Bradford needed to make a foray through enemy territory to secure a better, more permanent location. They set out on bikes they'd rebuilt from parts found in a junkyard. All around them, shades of green peeked from tree limbs and clearings. Birds called from the woods, where the sweet scent of pine permeated the air.

"Right this minute, it's hard to believe there's a war going on," Bradford said.

"I know what you mean." Frank followed him out of the woods and onto barren ground marred with unnatural holes, craters left by bombs. Abandoned campfires, debris, and detritus showed signs of Germans who'd retreated to the woods when their homes were destroyed.

Bradford pulled away on his bike as they climbed a steep hill. Exhausted, Frank lagged behind, amazed at the ease of Bradford's uphill ride.

Suddenly a boy darted from behind a broken tree trunk. He raced swift as a hawk, or a vulture, then stopped in the road. Bradford slammed his brakes and skidded to a halt. The barefoot boy, dressed in oversized shorts and no shirt, stared at them in defiance, his scabbed rib cage puffed out, his dark eyes cold. Frank couldn't tell if he was five or fifteen. He held something in his fist, which he shook at them as he screamed, *"Ich habe keine Angst vor dir!"* The boy spit out the words, which Frank thought meant, "I'm not afraid of you."

Without warning, he raised a skinny arm, and Frank saw what looked like a small pineapple. The boy pulled something from the pineapple and threw it at Bradford.

"No!" Bradford dropped his bicycle and turned away.

Frank heard a sound like gunshots and felt a sweep of air lift him from his bike and drop him, hard, to the ground. His ears filled with the sound of rushing water and muffled drums. He lay on his back. His eyes burned. Smoke floated above him. But the sky had never looked so blue. And the clouds . . .

"Hey, buddy."

Frank opened his eyes. His head felt like a tank was sitting on it. He tried to remember where he was, what had happened. It was like being trapped inside a nightmare and not knowing the source of fear.

Somebody was talking to him, but the words were rustling paper, blowing sand. He squinted up at the smudged face of a soldier, a Yank. The soldier's lips moved, but Frank couldn't make out what he was saying. He struggled to sit up. Pain knifed the back of his head. He fell back down. Something was wrong with his leg. He looked down and saw a belt tourniquet tied around his calf.

The Yank tried to lift him, but Frank pulled away. He couldn't think. Couldn't remember.

And then he did. The bikes. The boy. "Will." Frank tried to shout, but his throat was raw. "Will! Bradford?"

The bike lay beside the trail, a tangle of metal in a pool of blood. An ambulance was parked on the trail, its motor running.

Frank looked to the soldier, who hovered above him.

The guy shook his head and mouthed the word *sorry*.

Two soldiers lifted Frank, while the Yank kept talking to him. Frank couldn't understand them over the roaring in his ears. But he didn't need their words. He knew.

Major Will Bradford was dead.

In the following days, Frank went over and over those last few minutes. If he'd been in better shape, he might have been the one in front. Or he and Bradford could have ridden side by side, and the boy wouldn't have . . .

Physically, he recovered fast. He went through the motions of life, but his mind was numb. All he'd suffered was a slight concussion and a wound on his calf where he'd caught a piece of shrapnel. But his friend was gone. He wrote Helen about Bradford, playing down his own injuries.

Routine gradually turned into duty, and Frank threw himself into his work in a way he'd never done before, as if everything he did served to end the war. As he worked on each patient, he prayed for them as he'd suspected Bradford of doing, silently, fervently.

What remained of the new unit—about sixty enlisted men, three medics, and one doctor—formed a pup tent village so close to the airfield that Frank could hear and feel the rush of planes coming and going at all hours. Most were American, piloted by Frenchmen. Stretchers continued to arrive with wounded of all nationalities. He worked under blackout conditions, and even the ambulance vans drove with lights off, the cause of no small number of accidents. Medics hauled battlefield wounded in buses captured from the Germans.

And everyone waited for Germany to surrender.

~⌇~

France
May 7, 1945, 10 p.m.
V-E Day!

My dearest darling,

This is it, Frankie! Hard to believe, but it's really here.

While I administered meds on the general ward, everyone kept running in with more news, confirming what we've been hearing. It is official! The war in Europe is over. I wish you could call me, darling. You can tell me where you are now, don't you think so?

I think it is wonderful, for besides meaning so much to everyone, V-E Day means you and I can be together. It won't really feel like a victory until Japan gives up, until Dotty has

*Boots, until we are done with the Army occupation, and until
I am with you forever. But it does feel like a beginning.*

*I don't mean to be selfish by only thinking of us. I realize
what V-E Day must mean to soldiers and civilians over here.
I assure you that in France, there is great joy tonight. The
French are yelling and screaming outside, and the world sounds
boisterous and rather glorious. People are singing, "Let the Rest
of the World Go By" in French. I know the words in English,
and they are my feelings as well.*

*I think everyone should go to church tomorrow to express
our thankfulness. This peace is almost unbelievable. I wish you
were here to talk with me. Our orders are to march in full dress
behind the infantry in some sort of parade all over town. I shall
have blisters as my souvenirs if I don't find a way out of it.*

*But for now, I will sit back, thank our God in Heaven, and
try to grasp how much all this means to us and to everyone.*

I don't see how Japan can last with the world against her.

*With love always and forever, wherever we are,
Your Tiny Wife who adores you*

Later—

*Oh, my darling. Naomi just delivered your letter containing
such sad news. I know how you felt about Major Bradford. He
must have been a remarkable man to have earned your respect
and your friendship. I hardly know what to say, my love. I wish
I could be with you to comfort you. You didn't say that you were
injured seriously, but I would like to know for certain that you
are all right. Once again it seems I can do nothing to help. So
I will ask God to help you through this.*

FRANK

ENTZHEIM, FRANCE

Frank was working alone in the OR tent, removing shrapnel from the leg of an eighteen-year-old kid from Kansas who had played football in high school and baled hay in summers, and would never walk again. His sergeant had taken seven recovering soldiers to the airfield for transport to the US, leaving a couple dozen patients for another flight. He wanted to keep busy. Otherwise, his thoughts turned to Bradford, and he relived those tragic moments over and over.

Behind him, Frank sensed somebody entering the tent, but he couldn't turn around to see because he was tying off stitches. "Hello?"

"Why, if it isn't the famous Captain Daley!"

"Lartz?" Frank pulled off his rubber gloves and bloody coat, then turned around. "Aren't you supposed to be in the States?"

"On my way. I heard about Major Bradford, and I thought I'd

stop and see how you're holding up. I'm sorry, Frank. He was a good man."

"Thanks, Lartz." Frank hugged his friend. "You look good." It wasn't a total lie. Though still bone-thin, he had a bit of his spark back.

Lartz held up his hands, showing simple bandages, with fingers free. "I can use these again. I'd like to help out while I'm here. I was in the supply plane when we heard the news."

"What news?"

"You're kidding, right?"

Frank's patient groaned, and Frank ran over and checked to make sure the morphine drip hadn't clogged.

"You don't have a radio in here, do you?" Lartz asked.

"Have one. It doesn't work."

Gunfire exploded in the distance, and Frank suspected the news involved a new offensive, a last-ditch attack of some kind.

"The war's over in Europe," Lartz said. When Frank didn't respond, he added, "Not in Japan. Not yet. But it's V-E Day, Frank."

Frank looked up from the mangled leg that probably couldn't be saved, then to the comatose boy brought in that morning on a stretcher after a UXB exploded. From where he stood, Frank could see down the rows of beds, lines of patients converging like train tracks in the distance.

Was this what the end of war looked like? Was this victory?

Lartz moved to the nearest patient. "Let me give you a hand."

More relief arrived in the form of two young medics who had traveled from Strasbourg with Lartz. "We can handle things here for a few hours," Lartz said. "Why don't you take a break, Frank?"

Against standing orders, Frank walked to town in darkness to the sounds of sporadic gunfire, soldiers celebrating their victory. He needed to think. He ambled past buildings that were still devastated. Rubble was everywhere, lying in his path, ready to trip him. Just because the war was declared over by a few men behind closed doors, these buildings wouldn't suddenly go back to being churches and homes. The land wouldn't un-scorch. Will Bradford would not come back to life.

And no one who had survived this war would ever be the same.

Inside, Frank felt a tug so hard he couldn't ignore it. And he'd tried. He longed to return to the States and build a new life with Helen. He wanted a family.

But what about a peace like Bradford had talked about? Most likely, Frank would be sent to wherever he was needed in the CBI for two years. Volunteering to stay with his unit, perhaps to lead a unit to China, would mean committing to more than simply occupying territories for a couple of years.

Frank walked purposefully back toward the hospital tents, praying for Helen, for Lartz, for Dotty and Boots, for Bradford's family, for every soldier, every civilian who had suffered loss in this war . . . no matter which side they were on. He watched the sun rise over the tents, outlining the big red crosses on their sides. And as the new day dawned with pink and purple promise, he thanked God, prayed for peace, asked for guidance.

And got it. Frank knew what he had to do.

Only how on earth was he going to explain it to Helen?

～✹～

8 May 45 0800
Captain F. R. Daley
Entzheim, France

Dearest Tiny,

It is such a beautiful morning. The war is over in Europe, though it's hard to believe. Around here last night, it was pretty dangerous. The exuberant French were shooting into the air and sending up flares everywhere, as if the flames could do no harm. More than a few shots kicked up dust on the path behind my tent.

Lartz came to see me on his way to the coast, where he will catch a ship to the US. He seems much improved and was a great help with my patients. I shall miss him.

How I wish you were here with me to process what all of it means! People continue to be sick and wounded, despite the declaration of the war's end. We are expecting a flood of ex-prisoners from both sides. Most soldiers who come into camp— though not the truly abused patients, you understand—are so happy to be free, they're like little kids, and some of their elation is contagious. You should see how happy they are to get a shower, even though it's icy cold.

Helen, I am working on getting us together. I have been planning a V-E Day rendezvous for months, in fact. You have no doubt heard that most doctors in the European theater will be shipped to the CBI as soon as transport is available. You and I have big things to discuss. I have made certain plans—perhaps they have been made for me—and I need to talk with you face-to-face.

It's more urgent than ever that I see you. I believe I have secured the where. Now we must determine the when and how. Once you are here, we can get around on my new old motorcycle, which one of the men in my outfit rescued from the junkyard and helped me restore. What a wonderful time we will have, my darling! All will be well.

With all my love, wherever you are,

Your loving husband,
Frankie

P.S. I have figured the Army's point system, and the only points counted are as follows:

1 point for each month of service
1 additional point for each month overseas service
5 points for each combat star or decoration
12 points for each child under 18 years
The critical point is 85, the number a soldier needs for a furlough stateside. I figure to be around 30. All I lack are 5 children. What do you think?

Helen

RENNES, FRANCE

Helen didn't even like watching parades, much less participating, even though this one was mandatory for the off-duty hospital personnel. She marched exactly one block before ducking behind a bombed-out building, then making her way back to the hospital, where she was needed.

She was changing sheets on the ward when Naomi ran in. "I knew you'd be here! You better hustle. Colonel Pugh wants all married nurses in his office. Now! I think it may be assignments."

Helen's heart did the skip as she followed Naomi. Everybody, including Frank, seemed sure that doctors would be sent to China, Burma, India, or even Japan. But nurses had no idea what the Army had planned for them. Helen had been hoping against hope that she and Frank could talk things through *before* she got her assignment.

Pugh's office was standing room only as he rose from his desk. "I apologize for the lateness of the hour, but I have a deadline. And so do you, nurses. Before sending in your assignments, I want to know if you wish to stay with the unit here or opt out of the unit and eventually return to the States when transport is available. If you stay in the unit, you will be choosing to go to the CBI."

"Yahoo!" someone exclaimed.

"Bye-bye, unit! Don't think it hasn't been swell."

The others laughed. Someone shouted, "I am out of here!"

Someone else said, "Line forms behind me, gals!"

"And me!"

Even Naomi agreed. "I'm already on the list to go home."

Of the seven married nurses in the room, only Helen hadn't spoken, a fact that had not gone unnoticed by their commanding officer. "Nurse Daley?" Pugh said. "I assume you, too, prefer the USA?"

"Well . . ." Had there been a single day of the war when she hadn't dreamed of returning to the States with Frank? But that was just it. It wasn't just returning. It was *with Frank*. "Colonel, I want to go where my husband goes."

Colonel Pugh frowned. "Nurse, your husband is headed for the CBI."

"I know." She thought Pugh was about to say more, but he was drowned out by the other nurses:

"Take the States, gal!"

"Are you crazy, Helen?"

"You probably won't be able to be with Frank anyway!"

Blah, blah, blah. Their voices splashed around her like ocean waves.

"Helen, you know Frank would never want you to put yourself in danger," Naomi said. "Even if you'd be away from a battlefield—and you may not be—you know all the diseases coming out of there."

Helen hugged her friend. "Don't worry about me, Naomi. Just

go home and be happy." When they stepped apart, they were both fighting tears.

Colonel Pugh took over. "Nurses, report to your barracks. Someone there will work up paperwork for your assignments." Helen turned to go, but he stopped her. "Nurse Daley, a moment, please." He waited until they were alone in his office. "Thank you for staying, Helen."

Since the Paris trip for Liddy, they'd both kept their distance. Yet they'd managed to maintain a friendship built on mutual respect. Helen recalled how they'd sat vigil over Liddy and talked about everything. She wondered if he was thinking the same thing as he focused all his attention on her.

"Helen, I want you to reconsider." She started to protest, but he wouldn't let her. "You've done your duty—to your country, to your patients, and to your husband. It's time to think of yourself now."

In her mind, Helen pictured two scenarios. In one, she was singing around the house, her house in the United States of America. Everything in the house was familiar, comfortable. In the second image, all she could make out of the background was a scorching-hot jungle. In the foreground stood Helen in worn-out Army fatigues. And Frank.

"Colonel," she said, "I *am* thinking of myself. I'm going to the CBI."

Helen

ENTZHEIM, FRANCE

If Helen had been terrified of her first airplane ride, let alone flying with thirteen Frenchmen on a bullet-ridden service airplane, that fear was nothing compared to the full-fledged, all-out terror of her first motorcycle ride. She knew Frank believed her screams were exultations at speeding through utter darkness around curves. They were not.

Frank had arranged the miracle rendezvous at the eleventh hour, and she'd barely had time to get to the airfield for the flight to Entzheim. She'd been right about the Army sending him to the CBI. That much, he'd told her in his letter, while hinting that there was more. She hadn't told him yet about her decision to go to the CBI, so they both had more to tell. She'd wait for the right time and pray for the right words.

433

At last, they arrived at a tiny stone cottage in the middle of a fallow field. "Welcome home, Mrs. Daley!" Frank helped her off the back of the monstrous motorcycle. Her knees buckled, and he swept her into his arms. "Looks like I need to carry you across the threshold."

She threw her arms around his neck and kissed him. When she looked into those amazing brown eyes, she felt her own eyes blur with tears.

"Helen?" Frank sounded alarmed, confused. "Are you okay? Don't you like our temporary home?"

"Silly, I love it! And I love you. And I love us." She kissed him again as they stood on the threshold. "The only thing I don't love is that motorcycle."

"Now I know you're teasing." He carried her into the cottage that smelled like lavender. Sweet white curtains covered every window in this one-room fairy tale. Sergeant Whigham had gotten permission from the owners to use it while they were away.

"It's perfect, like my husband."

He set her down. "I know it's tiny, Tiny. The bed pulls from the wall, and the kitchen is just a big hot plate. I wanted to have the fire going, but I was afraid to leave it burning." He made a move for the logs stacked beside the blackened stone fireplace.

"I have a better idea for getting warm."

He dropped the logs and came to her.

The next morning, Frank apologized a hundred times for leaving Helen on her own, but he had over two hundred injections that had to be given to clear a unit for travel, plus a dozen patients with serious-enough complications that he couldn't leave them to the medics.

Neither of them had said a word about assignments. She suspected Frank didn't want to spoil this present paradise by talking about their separation, since he probably thought she'd be going to

America with the other married nurses. In the airplane, she'd had time to think. And by now, she knew her husband well enough to anticipate his initial reaction to her news. He wouldn't like it. But eventually, he'd see she'd done the right thing. This way they'd have a chance for more reunions. They might not end up in the same location, but at least she wouldn't be an ocean away from him.

Frank had stocked the small icebox, and she started simmering vegetables and stock to make chicken noodle soup. Lunch for her husband. This was what she'd believed could never make her happy. Helen had grown up cooking and cleaning, and she'd vowed that she would never get trapped into domesticity. Yet she couldn't stop smiling as she cooked, and she kept catching herself humming while she dusted. Helen had never felt so "wifely," and she wanted always to feel this way.

"Darling, I'm home!" Frank shouted as his noisy motorcycle groaned to silence.

Helen had heard him coming, rushed to the tiny bathroom mirror to check her hair, then dashed to the doorway and waved to her home-coming husband. "I love those words!"

"And I love you!"

They ate a quick lunch, and then both of them jumped on the cycle to do house calls. "First stop is to a family and their big-headed baby," Frank explained.

"What does the baby have?" Helen had seen babies with various syndromes that presented in larger-than-normal heads.

"Nothing like that. The baby's fine. It's their other eight children. Had your tetanus shot?"

He knew she had. "And typhoid, and everything else." She stopped herself just short of adding, "I am on my way to the Pacific, you know." But she didn't want to ruin the magic of enjoying now. The CBI was the elephant in the otherwise-perfect room. She didn't want it unleashed until it had to be.

The following day at the airfield, Frank introduced Helen by saying, "Men, this is my wife, Lieutenant Helen Daley, the most wonderful woman in the world."

"That's what he says even when you're not here, Lieutenant," said a man whose eyes reminded her of their old family doctor in Cissna Park.

"Helen, I'd like you to meet Sergeant Whigham, my right-hand man."

Helen liked him immediately. "Sergeant, thank you! We love the cottage you found for us."

"My pleasure." He nodded to Frank, and something she couldn't identify passed between them.

Only after Frank finished work in the dispensary did she learn the secret. When they went out to the motorcycle, a picnic basket was sitting on the patched seat.

Frank drove slowly to the woods, where spring flourished, with trees leafing and birds singing. They watched the sun set while picnicking on an Army blanket and eating fried chicken that tasted better than caviar. They talked until the sun left the woods dark with little warning. Then they rode "home" under stars that shone like they had in Battle Creek such a long time ago.

That night, Helen's last night in Entzheim, neither of them slept, though both pretended to. Finally, Helen sat up. "Should we talk about the elephant in the room?"

Frank sat up beside her. "The Chinese elephant? Right. I know you saw in my letter that I'll be going to the CBI."

"I did. And—"

"Hang on, darling. Let me get this out. I've rehearsed it in my head a thousand times. I am going to the CBI. And I've volunteered to lead what's left of Major Bradford's unit, which boils down to Sergeant Whigham and me. But I want to help work at peace for the world, like Will talked about, even though it will mean I'll stay there longer. I know I should have talked to you first. If I could have, Helen, I would have. Please try to understand."

"I think it's wonderful, Frankie!"

"You do?" He looked so relieved she laughed. "I'm not positive how it's going to work out," he said. "But it won't be quick, transitioning from war to peace. We'll have to finish this war first, with Japan. And our unit will be part of the occupation. It means I'll be gone for a long time. I know we planned on going back to the States together, darling, but I think we both knew that was unrealistic."

"Frank?" She didn't know whether to laugh or to cry out of frustration. He wasn't letting her get a word in edgewise.

"I was thinking that once you're in the States, you could stay with your mother in Cissna Park. Wouldn't it be good to be with Eugene for a while? Or with my parents and Dot—she'd love that. Or maybe you'd be happier in Evanston. You could work at the hospital until—"

"Frank! I'm not doing any of that!"

He stared at her as if she'd slapped his face. "Okay. Of course. It's your decision where you want to be once you get the transport back to the States."

"Silly, I'm not going to the States."

"What are you talking about? Everyone says married nurses get to go back home as soon as transport is freed up."

"Not me. *You're* my home. I'm going to the CBI with you."

Frank got out of bed so fast, Helen nearly toppled out too. "Tell me you're kidding!"

"I told Colonel Pugh I didn't want to go to the States without my husband. This way, with both of us in the CBI, we'll have a chance to get together. Don't you see?"

"Helen! I can't believe you did that! What were you thinking? We're not playing house! It's still war. People die! Japan may not surrender for months, years! And even then, my unit will be part of the occupation."

"So will I." Her anger was beginning to match his.

"No."

"Excuse me?"

"I said no. You're not going."

Helen tried to control her temper, but it wasn't easy. "Look. I'm a big girl. I can take care of myself and—"

"You can't! That's just it."

"What are you talking about?"

"If you tag along—"

"Tag along?" Who did he think he was? She was a soldier. She'd volunteered for overseas duty before she ever met him. He had no idea the things she'd done, the patients she'd saved. And lost.

Frank paced beside the bed. "If you follow me, Helen, I'll have to take care of you. And that's not what I want."

Something inside of her snapped, stopped.

He went on, filling the void between them with words as sharp as daggers. "I'm sorry, Helen. But I forbid it. I can't handle having you there, having to worry about you, trying to find ways to get us together. It would be too distracting. I just can't do it. I don't want to do it."

"I forbid it"? "Too distracting"?

Helen's heart hurt from pounding in her chest. She would not cry. He could not hurt her. And he couldn't tell her what to do.

She lay down, turning her back on him. Fine. She'd never really wanted to go anywhere but the US when the war ended. "I'll talk to John—Colonel Pugh—tomorrow as soon as I get back."

She felt him ease back into bed and could hear his heavy breathing. "Good night, Helen," he said, not touching her.

She didn't answer. If she knew anything, she knew this was not a good night.

59

Helen

RENNES, FRANCE

Helen didn't remember much about her return flight in the service plane. She and Frank had barely said two words to each other before she crammed in with an entire unit of French soldiers. Her mind kept replaying Frank's words. Hurtful, horrible words that seemed to come from someone she didn't know. Was that the real Frank? How would she know? Maybe *her* Frankie was a product of her imagination, a wartime fantasy. The war—and the fantasy—were over. And this was marriage, her marriage, over which she had no control.

She expected to be flooded with questions when she returned to the nurses' barracks in the late afternoon. She'd made it in time for the next shift, but she wanted to wash up before she faced everyone. She'd have to find Colonel Pugh and get him to put in her request to change assignments.

She turned into the barracks and nearly collided with Peggy. "Sorry," Helen said. She'd have to tell Peggy she wouldn't be staying with the unit now.

"Helen? Are you just getting back?"

"Yes. Why? What's up?" Helen had never seen the gal so flustered.

"Oh, honey, while you were gone, something happened."

Helen felt a tightness in her chest. "Tell me."

"Honey, it's Bill."

Tears sprang without warning. She felt dizzy. "Bill? Is he—?"

"No. He's not dead."

Relief came and went as Helen fixed on Peggy's unchanging expression. "What is he then? Is he okay?"

Peggy put a hand on her shoulder. "Come and sit down."

"No!" She drew back. "Where's Bill?"

Peggy took a deep breath and nodded. "Okay. It wasn't long after you left. We ran out of needles. Can you imagine that? No needles? Bill said he'd take care of it . . . like he always does." She swallowed. Helen was afraid she wouldn't go on. "He was gone too long. A couple of us went looking for him when we finished our shift. Colonel Pugh was the one who found him."

Helen thought of a million questions. None of them would come out.

"He was by the river. Unconscious, probably left for dead. We don't know what happened. Or who did it. Or why." Peggy was crying now. "He had the needles in his fist."

Helen couldn't stop her tears. She didn't even try. "I want to see him." He had to be on the ward. She turned and headed that way. Peggy called to her, but Helen didn't listen. All she could think about was Bill. It wasn't right. Or fair. The war was over. How could this happen? And to Bill! Wonderful Bill, who had been her right-hand man, her go-to guy, her buddy. She'd known Bill longer than she'd known her own husband. She'd spent more time with him.

Once on the ward, she blocked out everything and everyone and looked for Bill. He wasn't hard to find. His lanky frame hung over a bed shoved to the back corner. She ran past patients and didn't stop until she was at Bill's side. His head was bandaged, the white gauze wrapped around his forehead like a turban. The one eye she could see was shut. She studied his face. Except for the bandage, he looked perfectly fine. Her heart stopped pounding as she took his big hand in hers. "Bill, what did you do?"

He stirred, his hand slipping from hers. "Nurse? Nurse Daley?" His voice sounded like an old man's. Not Bill's. Not teasing, fun-loving Bill's.

"I'm here, Bill." She took his hand again and held on. "I go away for a couple of days, and look what happens." She was aware that her own voice sounded as old as his. All the teasing had gone out of her, too. "Are you okay? Are you in any pain?" She wanted to ask him if he knew who did it. She would take care of them herself. "Bill?"

"Not now." He rolled over to face the wall, turning his back on Helen.

Naomi walked up to them and put her hands on Helen's shoulders. "Why don't you both get some rest? You can talk tomorrow."

"I want to talk now!" Helen insisted.

"I don't want to talk to her," Bill said.

Helen felt cut to the core. Again. First Frank, and now Bill? "Come on. How many patients have we treated who were a lot worse off than you are? Honestly. I can't even see a scratch on you."

Naomi took Helen's hand and tried to pull her away.

Helen yanked her hand back. "Bill, this is ridiculous! Talk to me. Look at me, will you?" Her voice was too loud, but she couldn't help it. "*Look* at me!"

"I can't." His voice was muffled.

"Don't be stupid. Of course you can."

And still he wouldn't look at her. "Didn't they tell you? I'm blind."

Lt. Helen E. Daley
Rennes, France
23 May 1945

Dear Frank,
*I hardly know what to write, which makes sense, as I hardly
knew what to say to you when I left you at the airstrip in
Entzheim. Of all the seasons of this war, this recent one may
be the hardest. And yet they claim the war is over here. I feel as
if a bubble has burst and I no longer know what was real, or
what is real now.*
*I am sad that you chose not to be with me, or at least to have
the chance of our being together. I don't understand, but I do
want you to know that I'll be all right until you finish doing
what you feel you must. Colonel Pugh was able to rescind my
previous assignment. The gals and I will work in a hospital on
the coast of France while we await transport.*
*Bill Chitwood, the ward master from Battle Creek and one
of my best friends over here, was struck on the head and left
for dead. He did not die, but he is totally blind. I thought you
would like to know.*
*Frank, I will continue to write and let you know my plans.
I hope you will do the same.*
Be safe.

> *With love, wherever you are,*
> *Helen*

Helen had written Frank more out of duty than desire. She couldn't
seem to shake the hurtful words he'd shouted at her the last time
they were together. She had been so sure that her husband loved her
as much as she loved him, wanted her as much as she wanted him.
Now she wasn't sure about anything. It had taken all she had to sign
her letter *With love* . . . as they had done so many times.

As she descended the steps to the hospital ward, Helen prayed, *Father God, I have never felt this inadequate in my entire life. And I can't think of a thing to do about it . . . except to come to You empty-handed and ask You to take care of all of us.*

Bill was sitting up as if waiting for her. His glassy eyes, uncovered now, stared straight ahead without seeing.

She cleared her throat as she neared the bed. "Morning, Bill. I—"

"Nurse, I need to ask you a favor."

Helen shot up a quick *Thank You* to God. This was the most Bill had willingly said to her since her return from Entzheim. "Anything, Bill. You know that."

"I want you to write a letter for me."

"That's a good—"

"I'll dictate it. And you have to promise me you'll write it just like I tell you."

"Of course. I can do it now, if you like. It's not my shift yet, so I have time." When he didn't answer, she said, "I'll get some stationery and be right back."

It was a good sign that Bill wanted to send a letter. She guessed he'd want to tell Jennie about his injury. She fished a V-mail from her pack and hurried back before Bill could change his mind.

Bill hadn't moved an inch.

"I'm back." She removed his chart from the end of the bed so she could use it to write on. Then she settled on the edge of the bed and spread open the V-mail. "Okay. Is this to Jennie?"

"Yeah." He gave the address, and she filled in the lines.

"If you're going to be very wordy, I should warn you that I've only got a V-mail. I could go back for a piece of stationery if—"

"This won't take long."

"Okay. Shoot."

"'Dear Jennie'—she spells it *i-e*."

"Got it."

"'Well, this war is finally over. I thank you for your letters. They helped me pass the time and—'"

"Hold it a minute." Helen was writing as fast as she could, but it wasn't quite fast enough. "Okay. Go on."

"'I liked having a pen pal. But now, I just don't need that anymore. That's why I'm writing.'"

"Bill?" Helen didn't like where this was going. "Don't say that. Jennie wasn't just a pen pal to you."

"You promised you'd write what I asked you to. It's my letter."

They were silent for a minute. Then Helen gave in. "Go ahead."

"'I doubt either one of us expected whatever we had going to last once the war ended. And anyways, I've decided I'm staying here, in Europe.'"

"What? Bill, what are you saying?"

"I ain't saying nothing to you, Nurse. Either write or don't. I'll find somebody who will."

"You don't have to do this, Bill. Wait until you feel better."

He turned to her now, his eyes like blue marbles, glassy and unseeing. "Should I wait until I'm not blind? Because I'd be waiting forever." He turned away. "Are you going to write or not?"

She didn't have a choice. "Go on."

"'I found me the sweetest little French gal, Jennie. Hope you understand. And I hope you find a fella of your own.'"

Helen was crying as she penned the words. "I don't know why you're doing this. You're hurting her, Bill. I thought you loved Jennie."

"I'm hurting Jennie *because* I love her!" Bill cried.

Helen stopped writing. It was as if God had been poking her gently all along, and she hadn't paid attention. Now she felt that poke all the way to her heart and soul. Frank was just like Bill. They would both choose to hurt the ones they loved if they believed hurting them would give them a better life. Bill said those hurtful things because he loved Jennie.

And Frank had hurt her because he loved her.

Helen stood up from the bed. She folded the V-mail. "I'll mail this when I get back."

"Get back from where?" Naomi called from two beds over.

"I have to see Frank!"

Seventeen hours later, exhausted and frustrated and all cried out, Helen limped into the barracks and collapsed onto her bed. She'd forced her way onto a service plane to Entzheim, only to find the base nearly deserted. Frank could have been anywhere, as long as that anywhere ended up in the Pacific.

Peggy and Naomi did their best to console her. "It will all work out," Naomi said.

"She's right," Peggy insisted. "Helen, you and Frank were meant for each other. It was love at first sight."

Maybe. She'd certainly loved the way he looked at first sight. But what she felt now was so much more—admiration, caring, delight. She loved him for wanting to be a daddy, and she loved him for trying to comfort her when they both felt the loss of Junior. She loved that he'd written her every day of the war, often two or three times a day. She even loved him for hurting her because he'd done it to keep her safe. They both had a lot to learn about love and about marriage.

Helen sat cross-legged on her bunk. "How could I have been such a dumb Dora? I should have known Frank was just trying to get me to go back to the States for my own good."

"I could have told you that," Peggy said.

"I was just so hurt," she admitted. "And mad. And now he's gone. And it's too late for me to tell him I understand why he said those things. I don't know what to do."

"Do what you've been doing since day one," Naomi said. "Write the man."

Lt. Helen E. Daley
Rennes
2 June 1945

Dearest Frankie,

Please forgive me, my darling. Your wife can be a dumb
Dora, and you have to love her just the same. I understand now.
That's what I want you to know. I realize you said the things
you did to make me change my assignment. You wanted me
back in the States, but not because you didn't want to have to
deal with me. You were taking care of your thickheaded wife.
And I love you for it.

I have Bill to thank for this realization, though my
understanding was not his intent. He dictated a Dear John
letter to Jennie, the woman he's loved and written throughout
the war. It was only when I confronted Bill about his hurtful
words that I discerned his motive of love.

And yours.

Frankie, you may have been notified that a crazy woman
stormed your old Entzheim airfield in search of you. I had
quite a time demanding the French pilot let me stow away on
his service plane a second time. I did so want to give you a real
kiss good-bye, instead of the weak one at our cold parting. But
I shall save that warm kiss for you, along with many more—a
lifetime of them.

It's official. Until the Army can free up transport for me to
the USA, I will be stationed at the hospital in Marseille. Naomi
will be with me. Peggy and Victoria will be there too until their
CBI ship comes for them.

As of yet, I have no plans as to where I'll live in the States, or what I'll do once I get there. I only know that I'll be thinking of you every minute and praying for you.

I love you more than I ever thought possible, my darling Frankie. And I need you to know that I know you love me.

With love, wherever you are,
Your Tiny Wife

P.S. After I wrote Bill's "Dear Jennie" letter, I wrote her one of my own, telling her the truth. I'm confident that she will come through and be waiting for Bill when the hospital ship pulls into harbor. I pray that they live as happily ever after as you and I will.

P.P.S. I realize that you may be out in the ocean, where no mail will get through, but I have to write you just the same.

60

FRANK

COASTAL FRANCE

For weeks, Frank and Sergeant Whigham had been waiting with thousands of soldiers for a ship out. Frank worked a regular shift in a civilian hospital, but he still had plenty of time to write his wife, which he continued to do, even though he hadn't received a single letter from Helen since she'd stormed away from their rendezvous in Entzheim.

Hurting Helen, forcing her to safety in the US, had been the hardest thing he'd ever had to do. He just hoped it hadn't cost him his marriage. He'd wished he could take her in his arms and do whatever it would take to be together now and forever.

In the beginning of their terrible separation, he must have written Helen a dozen letters apologizing for the way he spoke to her and explaining why. When he got no response, he decided to write her the way he always had, filling her in on his life, his longing, and his love.

Frank Daley, MD
18 July 1945

Dearest Tiny,

It is sweaty hot here, but I am drinking tea at the Red Cross, where I think of you, as I do every minute. Although we may leave for the CBI at any moment, some say we may not get out until Christmas. In the meantime, I am treating civilians and former prisoners of war, including many of the slave laborers. So at least I am put to good use while I wait.

I ran into Anderson awaiting a ship as I am. In spite of his threats (promises?) to quit the Army, he is aimed squarely at the CBI. His parting shot at me was that I shouldn't expect to get a ship out before him since he still has friends in high places. Andy claims that leaving here first means he will reach Japan or the CBI first and return to the States before me.

His comment did not upset me because I know that when I do return to the US, I will have the most wonderful wife in the world waiting for me.

I win.

With love, wherever you are,
Your loving husband, Frankie

P.S. Darling, I read in the Stars and Stripes that European cattle are 75% tuberculosis. Now they tell us?

It was almost unbearable not hearing from Helen, though no one seemed to be receiving mail. He could imagine her already in the States, but he knew better. Soldiers heading to the CBI were priority for transports.

It was August when Frank walked with Anderson and one of Andy's fellow partyers to see him off at the docks. "The day before yesterday was Helen's and my anniversary," Frank complained, "and we spent the day in opposite ends of France, waiting for ships to take us to opposite ends of the world."

"I sympathize," said Andy's buddy. Frank couldn't remember the man's name, but he already liked him better than Anderson. "Perhaps we should all keep in mind that thus far, we have survived the war with two arms, two legs, sound mind and body."

Frank raised his eyebrows in Andy's direction. "True, except for the sound mind part."

"That's us!" Anderson said. "They're calling our unit!" He turned to Frank and stuck out his hand. "Frank, ol' man, always a pleasure. See you on the other side."

Frank shook Andy's hand. "Right. Save me a spot!"

It was another hour before they began loading the ship. Even by the sea, where a breeze swept up from the waters, Frank was so hot that sweat pooled under his arms and dripped from his forehead. When Anderson and his buddy finally shoved their way up the gangplank, Frank wanted to dive into the water and cool off. He watched the battleship swallow hundreds of soldiers without rocking, not even when waves pounded the sides. He hoped his ship would be that big. In the meantime, he'd go back to his barracks and dream about Helen.

Frank had fallen asleep when Sergeant Whigham raced into the barracks and skidded to a stop. "Sir! Our ship is in!"

Captain F. R. Daley, MD
Aboard the Marine Panther
6 August 1945

My dearest darling Tiny,
    I'm off to the Pacific! I am pleased because this puts me one step nearer to joining my wonderful wife in the US. I only hope that soon you will be settled and waiting for me so that we can begin our new life TOGETHER.

Sergeant Whigham tells us that the war news looks pretty good, but the typhoons are supposed to be too dangerous to permit invasion before September.

I have heard from Dotty, and her news is not good, unless you believe in the myth that "no news is good news." Prisoners are being exchanged and released, but nobody is talking about Boots. And yet, her love, his love, their love endures.

I must stop writing, for even though I was able to take something to prevent nausea, I find that it is not foolproof. Since I have no way to mail this letter now, I will save it and continue to write later, when I have my sea legs.

Later—Just heard a rumor that we have dropped the atom bomb on Japan. And it may be more than a rumor. Sergeant Whigham says the bomb hit Hiroshima, and there's a chance Japan will surrender, though the two colonels and one general present at the time of Whigham's account strongly disagree. They say the emperor would lose face and would rather kill himself than surrender. I say either scenario works for me.

Your loving Frankie

Three days later, Frank stood on the deck of the *Marine Panther*, watching soldiers dance, hug, scream, and shout. The smell of salty brine mixed with the odor of Scotch and brandy spilled and splashed as the celebration spread. Murmurs, then rumblings, had begun even before the ship's loudspeakers broadcast the news: A second atomic bomb had been dropped on Nagasaki. Frank felt as if he were inside an opaque cocoon—there but not there, still waiting, still alone.

Sergeant Whigham put a hand on Frank's arm, and Frank realized Whigham had been saying something to him. "Sorry, Sergeant. What was that?"

"I said, you look like you lost your best friend. You heard the news, didn't you?" Whigham looked older, but tougher than ever. Bradford had once confided to Frank that Whigham had signed up in order to dodge the law. But he'd given his all for the war effort. The man who had shot "Daley's Nazi" was the closest thing Frank had to a friend on this voyage.

Frank forced a smile. "Sorry, Sergeant. I'm trusting that I haven't lost my best friend . . . but I sure do miss her."

The next few days, their ship wasn't the only one tossed about by waves, as bad news followed good news. Celebrations stopped cold when word spread that an American battleship, a ten-thousand-ton cruiser, had been sunk with a loss of nearly a thousand men. Reports of overwhelming war losses were coming in from all sides: millions of deaths worldwide. And the devastation of those two atomic bombs was unfathomable. Word of a Japanese surrender came from Guam and the Swiss delegation, only to be denied by sources in Washington, claiming it was all a mistake and misunderstanding.

Then it came. Frank listened on the ship's radio as President Truman made the official announcement of the Japanese full sur-render and acceptance of all terms.

The war was officially over.

15 August 1945, 1:20 pm

Darling Helen,

 The war is over. Even Japan says so. My first thought as I listened to President Truman's announcement was to wonder how you took the news and when you would get to the States to celebrate. Our outfit doesn't know what our fate will be, but there will be a full-scale occupation, and we will be part of it.

 I'm assuming that censorship terminates with the end of war, so I am enclosing the announcement of V-J Day in our ship's bulletin, a special extra.

*Word from the well-informed Sergeant Whigham is that our
ship, the Marine Panther, is nearing the Panama Canal. My
father has always said that the canal is a sight worth seeing, so
I think I might as well go on deck to try to catch a glimpse of it.
As always, I shall pretend that you are by my side, seeing what
I am seeing.*

*I would imagine that Anderson and his crewmates must
have made their passage through the canal in the middle of
the night. Your Victoria as well, since she no doubt worked the
same deception as Anderson to find herself on an early ship. At
least I should be able to see the canal in daylight. I would be
willing to bet that Andy slept through the whole experience,
passed out from the free-flowing rum supplied since the victory
announcement.*

*I'll go up on deck, see what I can see, and come back with
a report for my beautiful wife.*

With love, wherever you are,
Your Frankie

Frank had barely left his bunk when shouts rang out above him.
He picked up his pace and was joined by others as the cheers grew
louder, rivaling the end-of-the-war announcement. The deck overflowed with officers and technical personnel, soldiers and nurses.
Most of them looked as confused as Frank felt. He spotted Sergeant
Whigham at the railing near the bow, leaning so far over that he
looked drenched from sea spray. Frank made his way through the
crowd to reach him. "What's going on, Sergeant?"

"Looks like we're turning around!" Whigham shouted.

Frank stared at Whigham for some sign of teasing. "Sergeant, I
can't take another rumor."

"Captain, our ship received orders to turn around. Don't you feel
it? Every ship that's already passed through the canal has orders to
proceed to destination. They'll be in the CBI or Japan for two to four

more years. Every ship this side of the Panama Canal—and we're the first—turns around. Our peace mission will be run from the United States of America!"

It was true. Even now, Frank sensed the ship veering left, whatever direction that was. They were turning. Thank God in Heaven, they were turning around.

Frank felt Sergeant Whigham's hand on his shoulder. "Captain Daley, we're going home."

61

Helen and Frank

Helen had waited all afternoon for a chance to get outside and think. Dutifully, she delivered insulin shots, passed out pills, changed dressings, and assisted in OR. When she managed to escape for a few minutes, she walked down by the breakwater, just yards from the hospital. Tilting her face to the sun, she wrapped her sweater tighter around her shoulders. A cool Mediterranean breeze offset the August heat as she settled onto her perfect spot along a stone wall.

Once there, all thoughts turned to Frankie. He'd written her several letters after he left Entzheim, and she could tell he hadn't received hers explaining and apologizing. Now she'd had no word from him in days, which probably meant he was still crossing the Pacific. She wondered how much longer she'd be stuck in Marseille.

Bill had gone home on a hospital ship. Hopefully Jennie could do for him what Helen hadn't been able to do. Peggy should have been on a ship headed for the CBI. But when the trucks showed up for the single nurses, Victoria, thinking she'd get home sooner if she got on

the first truck, shoved past Peggy and took the last seat on the transport. Pugh simply changed Peggy's orders and kept her with Helen
and Naomi. Sometimes life really did work out.

"Helen!" Peggy came running up to her.

Helen groaned. No doubt Peggy had been sent to fetch her.
The doctors at this hospital conspired to make her life miserable.
Impossible to please, they were as whiny as babies and as crotchety
as old men. She closed her eyes. "Peggy, can't you see? I'm not here."

"I can see you won't be here long."

"Oh, all right." Helen slid off the stone wall. "You're no fun."

"You might have to change your tune. If you don't want to go
back to the hospital, where *would* you like to go?"

Helen didn't have to think twice. "I want to go home."

Peggy waved some papers. "You ready to stop feeling sorry for
yourself?"

"If you insist."

"Lieutenant Daley, you have twenty minutes to get your gear.
You're going to the United States of America!"

Fifteen minutes later, Helen said a tearful good-bye to Peggy and
Naomi, then boarded a ship already overflowing with soldiers. As far
as Helen could tell, she was the only nurse aboard. She didn't care.
This voyage would bring her another step closer to being home with
Frankie.

The tanker might have made a good barge, but it was a lousy
speedboat. As the days wore on, Helen missed Frank more and more.
Although she tried to focus on the fact that at least one of them
would be in the States now, she kept coming back to the other fact—
her husband was on a different ship sailing to the end of the world. It
might be two years before he could come home, and they didn't have
the money for her to visit him there. And what about mail? Would
he ever receive her letters? When would she get a letter from him?
Frank's letters were what had gotten her through this war.

When the ship finally reached the United States and Boston Harbor came into view, Helen felt like a foreigner in her own country. They docked to cheers and screams and cries of celebration on deck and from below, where a band played and people shouted and waved banners of welcome and victory. Helen waited on deck, allowing everyone else to scurry down the ramp and into the arms of people who loved them.

Nobody was waiting for her.

Helen was the last passenger to leave the ship. She struggled to carry her bags as she stumbled down the wooden ramp.

"Mrs. Daley!"

Helen peered around the dock, thinking she'd misheard. But there it was again. "Mrs. Daley!" She spotted a soldier striding toward her, calling her name.

The man stopped and broke into a grin that reminded her of Frank. "Helen!" He hugged her and lifted her off her feet, then spun her in a circle before releasing her. She didn't know whether to laugh or slap him. "Frank was right. You're a looker! Much too good for my little brother. But we don't have time for small talk." He took her bags and started off with them.

"Hey! Where do you think you're going?" Everything she owned was in those bags.

He didn't slow down, didn't even turn around. "Same place you're going. New York!"

Frank stood on deck of the *Marine Panther* and watched the Statue of Liberty come closer and closer. Every soldier on deck was doing the same, staring in awe and reverence at the symbol of the freedom they'd been fighting for. Some even saluted Lady Liberty. So did Frank. This was home, his country, the place where he and his wife would build their lives together. Maybe they would set up a practice in Missouri or Illinois, Florida or DC. He didn't care, as long as Helen was there.

And that was what robbed him of the joy he heard going on around him. He could never be really happy until Helen was home too. And that might not come for months.

As soon as the ship pulled into harbor, soldiers mobbed the deck, yelling down to loved ones waiting at the dock. Frank eased to the back of the crowd, bracing himself for the greetings and embraces that wouldn't be there for him.

By the time the ship lowered its gangplank, the sun had risen with an orange-red glow reflected in the shimmering sea. He waited as long as he could, then started down the wooden ramp, surrounded by other straggling soldiers.

"Frankie!"

It was his imagination. Of course it was. Helen's voice, sweeter than music. He heard it in his dreams and in nearly every waking moment.

"Frankie! Here! I'm here!"

This time, he turned toward the shout. There she was. Helen. His Helen, waving from the shore.

"Move it, buster!" Someone shoved him from behind.

Then he was moving. Running. Racing toward Helen, toward home.

This was the end of the war. Not for Boots and Dotty, not yet. Maybe never for Lartz and whatever was left of his family. Not even for Anderson and the other ships sailing on.

But as he reached his wife and she threw herself into his arms, he knew that for Helen and Frank Daley, the war was finally over.

The Story behind the Story

In a way, I began this book decades ago, growing up listening to the colorful stories of my parents. My favorites were their war stories—Lt. Helen Eberhart Daley, registered nurse, and Capt. Frank R. Daley, MD, served overseas in the Army during WWII, in 1944 and 1945.

When Dad was diagnosed with car-cinoma in 1996, I got him to tape his stories on a dozen cassettes. I flew back to Missouri each time Mom had to rush him to the hospital. The last trip there, he waited until we were alone in his hospital room. Then he said, "Dandi, I want you to drive back to Hamilton (their home, which was mine, too, growing up—an hour away from the hospital) now, while your mother isn't there. Go up into the attic and find an Army trunk. Put it in your car, but don't open it." I did as he asked. But when I returned to the hospital, I begged him to tell me what was in that trunk. "Letters," he said. My parents had written two to three letters every day they were apart during those war years. They'd saved each letter, tying stacks with Army boot laces. "I want you to have them because your mother will burn them after I die. She wouldn't want anyone reading about our love and mushy melodramas. So don't read those letters until we're both gone."

That was one of the hardest things I've ever had to do. I admit I found wiggle room and peeked into the trunk to discover over 600 letters untouched since 1945. But there were other treasures, too—Christmas and Easter cards in French, English, and German; medals; Bibles signed by FDR with a note to all servicemen encouraging prayer and the reading of Scripture. I began reading about the war, but I didn't open a letter.

My mother lived on until 2010 and came to live in Ohio with my family for her final five years on earth. She changed, becoming more sentimental and reflective, never melancholy, but full of the Spirit. She began telling me war stories I'd never heard before. She came from a family of thirteen that sent five sons and one daughter overseas in WWII. I wanted to pump her for every detail, and she remembered each hospital, patient, and rendezvous with Dad, including one in Marseille in a hideout beneath the barn of a Resistance family. We never mentioned the trunk—in my attic now—but she had to know I'd taken it since she helped my sister and me clean out her home for sale. Then came the day when I was trying to nail down a certain date in their war history. Mom

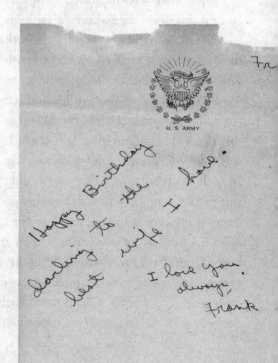

grew frustrated with my persistence and finally said, "Oh, Dandi, just check the dates on the letters!" We were both silent, suddenly acknowledging the treasure I possessed. Then she said sweetly, "Anything else?" We never mentioned the letters again, but I began reading.

When Mom went to be with the Lord (and Dad), I set to work in earnest. It was not an easy task in the beginning because I missed my parents. But gradually, they became young Helen and Frank, and I got to know them in a different way, to appreciate their sacrifice and their love. I arranged the letters chronologically and took copious notes in the early years, coordinating their personal insights with what history reported. Through the Internet, I tracked down Bill Chitwood, a ward boy from Mom's unit who became a friend. His memory proved fantastic, especially about the inner workings of wartime hospitals.

This novel is a work of fiction, based on the stories and letters of Helen and Frank. I've written a good deal of fiction over the past three decades, and most of my books contain kernels of reality. But I'd never attempted to shape a real story into a work of fiction. The

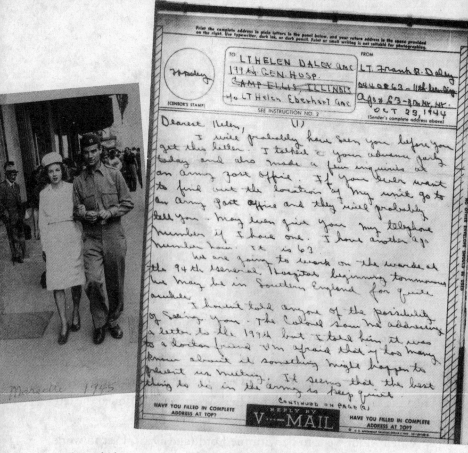

process led me to a number of false starts and delays. Even though I had letters and stories, it was tricky imagining thoughts and emotions, adding the conflict and opposition that a novel needs, building character arcs. But I kept writing, wrestling over which letters to include, how to turn stories I knew by heart into a narrative that would touch a reader's heart.

Helen's brothers all made it home safely from the war and lived to give me a bunch of cousins. Since my uncles were such good soldiers and sailors, I had to invent Eugene. But even though I never had an Uncle Eugene, his character is based on soldier patients my mom described, calling them "her boys." Bill Chitwood married his Jennie. Thankfully, he was not blinded, as was the fictional Bill. He joined Jennie in heaven before THE BOOK, as he always referred to the novel, was published. I'm so glad I got to meet him, and I hope a piece of Bill lives on in this novel. Lartz and Anderson, Frank's war buddies, had faded away by the time I was born, though they existed in a plethora of war stories. I invented Major Bradford. But the Nazi Cardinal fan ("Daley's Nazi") and "Fritz" were very real.

Frank's brother, Jack, did spy in the war as a member of the Office of Strategic Services (OSS), a wartime intelligence agency, which was the predecessor to the Central Intelligence Agency (CIA). Uncle Jack eventually settled in California, where he married and raised a daughter.

Dotty—Dorothea Daley Engel—was just like Dotty in the novel. With a life like that, she didn't need to be fictionalized. Aunt Dot never saw her husband again. For over twenty years, she refused

to believe that Boots was dead. She waited for him while working as Frank's nurse in private practice. Then one day a man came to her door and said he had been with Boots on the Bataan Death March and in prison afterward until very near the end of the war. Their Japanese captors put the prisoners on a clearly marked Japanese war vessel and put themselves on a clearly marked Red Cross vessel. The Allies bombed the war boat, and survivors had to swim to safety. Dotty's visitor made it, but Boots did not. The movie *So Proudly We Hail!* with Claudette Colbert and Veronica Lake tells Aunt Dot's story, but with a happier ending.

Dr. and Mrs. F. R. Daley ended up practicing in Hamilton, Missouri, where they raised two daughters, Maureen and Dandi. Helen and Frank were very happily married for fifty-one years.

Discussion Questions

1. A pivotal experience in her childhood made Helen resolve she'd grow up to be a nurse, while Frank followed his father's footsteps into medicine. When you were a child, what did you want to be when you grew up? What experiences or family influences shaped your vocation?

2. When do you think Frank actually fell in love with Helen? When did Helen admit that she'd fallen in love with Frank? Faced with the prospect of being separated by the war, Frank and Helen made a swift decision to marry. Would you have been among the friends who cheered them on or those who asked if they'd lost their minds? Why?

3. Both before and after their wedding, Helen and Frank had moments of doubt about their marriage, especially about how well they truly knew each other. What things would you list as essential to know about another person before marrying? What kinds of things can be learned over time?

4. Having only letters to connect them for weeks and even months left Helen and Frank vulnerable to misunderstandings. Once, as she endured long days with no word from Frank,

Helen filled in her own assumptions about what he was thinking and feeling, only to learn that he hadn't received her letters at all. In Helen's place, would you have jumped to the same conclusions? Can you think of a time when you constructed your own story about another person during a gap in communication? How much of what you believed was the truth?

5. Frank showed his jealousy a couple of times, most notably over Colonel Pugh and the trip to Paris. Helen also admitted her jealousy over Nurse Becky and Marie, the young French patient in Marseille. How did they handle moments of jealousy? Have you ever been jealous—of a spouse, a friend, a family member? How did you handle it?

6. What characteristics would you say are necessary for an enduring marriage? Which of these did you see Frank and Helen exhibiting, or learning, throughout the story? Where did they still need to grow?

7. Faced with the prospects of battles and bombings, Frank wondered, "What was it that made one man buck up, another act heroically, and another give in to terror?" How would you answer his question? Frank came to find comfort and courage from a verse of Psalm 23: "I will fear no evil: for thou art with me." How do you respond to fear?

8. Frank was quick to tell others that Dotty and Jack were the heroes in his family—not him. Why do you think he was reluctant to take on a "hero" label? How would you define a hero, and who has been one in your life?

9. For much of the story, Helen lived by the motto "God helps those who help themselves." But when she's forced to acknowledge how much is out of her control, Naomi advises

her that a better motto might be "God helps most when you admit you can't do it on your own." Which motto do you believe and live by?

10. This novel is fiction, but based on the experiences and letters of the real-life Frank and Helen Daley. How much do you know about your parents' or grandparents' histories? Can you think of any family stories that would make good fiction? If you were to write those stories, where might you have to use your imagination to fill in gaps or flesh out the details?

11. In her note to readers, the author makes a distinction between some true and invented pieces of this story—for example, Dotty's story adheres to the facts, but in real life, Bill Chitwood wasn't blinded, and Major Bradford didn't exist. As a reader, did it matter to you to learn that some of the characters were invented or their stories changed? Why or why not?

12. During World War II, Japanese and German citizens living in the US fell under cruel suspicion, and overseas, Helen faces some of the same prejudice because of her ability to speak to wounded German soldiers. In her place, how would you have responded to such suspicion? Would you have had difficulty caring for enemy soldiers?

13. Helen and Frank were part of what's been called "the Greatest Generation." What qualities have earned them this title? What names have you heard for your generation? Do you think the perception of your generation is justified?

14. Helen and Frank wrote to each other as many as three times a day, but slow and waylaid mail often meant long gaps in communication. Censorship made it hard to freely say all they might have wanted to. How different might their story have been if they'd had access to today's instant communication?

What difficulties due to their separation would have remained the same? With our new technology and the ability to stay in touch virtually all over the globe, do you think we've lost anything?

Acknowledgments

More than a decade ago, I sat across the table from Karen Watson, now associate publisher of Tyndale House. I'd given her the first chapter of this book and shared a few of the war stories. After that, whenever I ran into Karen, she'd ask me how that book was coming along. My father-in-law asked the same question, and I saw him more often than I did Karen. (Thanks for caring so much. I love you, Pap.) When Stephanie Rische, senior editor at Tyndale and a born encourager, paid me a visit, she read the dozen or so chapters I'd been working on, and she joined the voices urging me to finish.

I started working on the book in every spare minute until I had a draft of the whole thing—849 pages! Karen, who believed in this book when I only dared to dream about it, read every page and suggested there was a skinnier book inside this one and I needed to cut, cut, cut to find it. I got the novel down to 567 pages, and, most fortunately, I acquired the insight and wisdom of acquisition editor Jan Stob. Editor Sarah Rische skillfully and gently applied her sweet blessed tyranny to help me see past my parents to discover young Helen and Frank as characters in a novel based on my parents. Thanks, everybody, for all your help.

I'm so grateful to have been part of the Tyndale House family for over three decades. When I thought about placing my parents and their story into the arms of publishing, I knew they'd be safe in Tyndale hands. Ron Beers, thank you for believing in me (and in my books). Besides the talented Tyndale editors I've already mentioned, I have so many to thank for bringing this story to life: Shaina Turner (acquisitions editor), Danika King and Caleb Sjogren (copy editors), Midge Choate (product manager), Dean Renninger (designer), Jen Rockwell (marketer), Alyssa Anderson (publicist), and the entire sales team.

As always, my wonderful husband, Joe, a fantastic writer mainly of nonfiction narrative, helped me immensely all along the way. Thanks, honey! I'm grateful to our kids, Jen, Katy, and Dan, who listen to our stories over and over again but ignore the old adage: *Stop me if you've heard this one.* And finally, thank you to my generous big sis, Maureen Pento, who was and is my cheerleader from start to finish. I just want our mom and dad to be honored here, in our book.

About the Author

Dandi Daley Mackall is the award-winning author of nearly five hundred books for children and adults. She visits countless schools and presents keynote addresses at conferences across the United States. She is also a frequent guest on radio talk shows and has made dozens of appearances on TV. Her awards include the Edgar Award, ALA Best Book, NY Public Library Top Pick, the Geoffrey Bocca Memorial Award, Dean Arts and Achievement Award, and Outstanding Alumna Award from the University of Missouri; she is also the 2016 Hall of Fame recipient of the Council of International Reading Association's Award. Her novel *My Boyfriends' Dogs* is now a Hallmark movie. Dandi writes from rural Ohio, where she lives with her family.